Published by arrangement with Crown Publishers, Inc.

THE DECEPTION

Copyright © 1997 by Barry Reed.

SBN: 0-312-96494-3

inted in the United States of America

own Publishers, Inc. hardcover edition published 1997
Martin's Paperbacks edition / April 1998

Martin's Paperbacks are published by St. Martin's Press, 175 Fifth nue, New York, NY 10010.

9 8 7 6 5 4 3 2 1

BARRY REED

REED

THE

DECEPTION

St. Martin's Paperbacks

To my lovely wife, Marie,
who waited patiently
while I was off chasing the Muse

Deepest Appreciation to:

Carolyn Blakemore of New York City, for her editorial professionalism, her dedication, and her friendship

Frances M. Dyro, M.D., of Portland, Maine, for her neurological expertise

Catherine McDonald, my secretary, for her superb help and suggestions

Peter Matson, my agent, for his professional assistance and encouragement

Betty A. Prashker, my longtime editor and friend, who stuck with me during this literary journey

From righteous deception God standeth not aloof.

—AESCHYLUS

1

Karen Assad fidgeted in the pocket of her white smock for her pack of Carletons. She was dying for a cigarette and had about three left. Perhaps she could sneak a few puffs in the pantry later. In twenty minutes, she'd give the evening meds to Dr. Sexton's most promising patient.

Sitting at the desk in the nursing station, she perused the computer EKGs of three patients, watching the luminous squiggles track across the violet screen as a pilot would scan an instrument panel. All systems were go. At ten after midnight, the floor was quiet—at least for now. In the psych ward, this was as good as it could possibly get. The other nurses were off making midnight rounds and the young resident, Dr. Broderick, was engrossed in someone's chart.

St. Anne's was a showcase of medical technology, offering the latest in laser surgery, computerized radiographic techniques, and fiber optics, and a surgical staff without equal in the medical fraternity. Cutting into a patient at St. Anne's, with its cadre of medical specialists, world-renowned experts, and with the cardinal's peer-review override, was like operating in a fish-bowl. No one made a mistake—at least not for the record.

Karen had opted out of Surgery; at age thirty-six, with two young children and no husband, it was too demanding. She had dated a few surgical residents, but they were too intense, boring her with case histories, detailed diagnoses, medical terminology, patient prognoses. And they were too young, if not out of her class: Duke, Harvard, Columbia, Eastern establishment—WASP, mainly. An occasional Oriental with a 240 IQ. Yet it was always the same—differential diagnoses, treatments, prognoses. No one seemed to want to go to bed anymore. But the psychiatric ward at St. Anne's, apart from its maze of computers, sumptuous game rooms, and homey patients' quarters, was only a step ahead of the days of Freud and Adler; it lagged behind private sanatoriums in both staff and technology. Cardinal Minehan had tried to spruce up the department: Dr. Pierre Lafollette was enlisted from the Menninger Foundation in Topeka, Dr. Consuela Concepción Puzon came from the Academy Santo Cristobal in the Philippines, and Dr. Robert Sexton had risen through the ranks and was now chief of the department. Of course, it helped that Sexton was the cardinal's nephew.

Karen thought about it. For a while, she had been on days. But on that shift, she was going as batty as the patients. They wandered the halls, screeched, and threw rolls during lunch. When a plastic spoon came spiraling her way and hit her just above the left eye, she had had enough. She called in a few chits and landed her present assignment, supervisor of nurses from eleven to seven. Karen thanked God for this shift.

"Dr. Broderick"—she looked over at the resident—"I have to administer five milligrams of that new drug Capricet to Donna DiTullio, Dr. Sexton's patient. Would you take over the watch for a few minutes? Nurses Collins and Rinaldi are due back momentarily."

"Sure." Broderick looked up from his notes and pushed his owlish glasses up into his curly red hair. "The DiTullio girl's coming along quite well. Sexton's done a helluva job. Remember when she came here three weeks ago?—a real basket case."

"And she's such a nice person," Karen Assad added. "The doctor wants her to attend a group therapy session tomorrow morning at the Atrium. He'll have her back on the tennis courts come October."

"The Atrium?" Broderick pursed his lips.

"That's where the therapy sessions are held. It's like a leafy arboretum down there—ficus, bamboo, waterfalls. Even I could forget my troubles in that fantasyland."

Broderick shook his head. "I don't know. I walked over there last week. The sessions are held on the fifth floor. The whole thing's too open. Only has a four-foot railing. It's like treating psychiatric patients on the edge of a cliff."

"Sexton knows what he's doing." Karen checked Donna DiTullio's chart. "I'll never forget when they wheeled her in— completely wasted, her wrists slashed. Severe manic depression with suicidal ideation, under constant surveillance. I didn't think she'd last the week."

"That's just my point," Broderick said. "On the improvement scale, she went from one to eight-plus in three weeks. No one recovers that fast."

"Hey"—Karen Assad put a little edge in her voice—"we've got to take this psycho business out of the Dark Ages. Only a few years back, we'd have locked these people up in padded cells and thrown away the key. I've watched DiTullio's progress, administered her evening meds. Trouble with most tricyclic drugs is that they take too long to kick in. Prozac might take six to eight weeks, sometimes three months. Same with Halcion and Zoloft. But with Capricet, the effects take hold almost immediately. It's the best drug we've got."

Broderick wiggled his hand. "Oh, it's still a little early to tell. Sure, some patients respond pretty well, but others don't. And in DiTullio, it could have created a sense of euphoria, masking the deep underlying problem."

"Well, before she arrived here, Sexton treated her periodically for several months, and believe me, she seems like the old Donna DiTullio who won the New England tennis championship at Longwood last year.

"You know, I was there the other day when Dr. Puzon was giving her the Rorschach test. She asked her what one illustration depicted, and Donna looked at it, squinted, turned it upside down, then said it looked like an inkblot. Not a gargoyle or a man running down a staircase while playing a violin, mind you, but an inkblot."

Broderick grinned and nodded. "That's a new one. I gave that test to Mrs. Wheeler down in three-oh-six and she described it as two stingrays having intercourse, and uh . . . her phraseology was a bit more graphic."

Karen again fingered the pack of Carletons. If she didn't leave now, it would be another hour before she could light up.

"Sexton only allows outpatients and those who are ready for discharge to attend group therapy," she said. "The Atrium gives them a sense of the outdoors, well-being. It's the threshold to reality.

"Hey"—she glanced at her watch—"I've got to shoot the Capricet."

Broderick nodded again, readjusted his horn-rims, and returned to the patient's chart.

—

"Hello." Karen Assad rapped lightly on the open door. "Time for the little stab in the backside." She poked her head in.

Donna DiTullio was still awake. A small overhead light illuminated *Tennis* magazine, which she was reading.

Donna smiled. She liked Nurse Assad. During the initial confinement, she had resented the nursing staff, doctors, and assistants, but at night, when the hectic bustle seemed to calm down, Assad would spend some time with her, and just before her injection, they'd chat about little things—like growing up in Donna's world, high school, hiking up Mount Monadnock, summer camp on Martha's Vineyard, and tennis. Karen Assad had never gone to summer camp, never played tennis or climbed Mount Monadnock. Her world was tough inner city, the local school of nursing, a dead-end marriage, and constant work. But Karen was a good listener and a good cheerleader, and she had the ability to withstand the anxiety generated by working with psychiatric patients, many of them suicidal. Most of all, she felt a certain inner satisfaction in being on the team that brought patients back from the brink of hopelessness. Donna DiTullio, a few weeks shy of her twenty-second birthday, was one of those patients.

"Have you got a cigarette, Karen? Or maybe a joint?" A puckish smile tugged at the corners of Donna's eyes.

"I could use a cigarette myself," Karen Assad replied, "but I promised my aging grandmother I'd quit smoking if she'd quit drinking."

"What was the result?" Donna propped herself up on her elbows, her dark brown eyes now alert.

"A Mexican standoff," Karen said as she flipped off the overhead light. "We still drink and smoke, but we renew our promises every Ash Wednesday."

Karen was now all business. Capricet had to be injected just right—in the upper-right quadrant of the buttocks—to avoid hitting the sciatic nerve. She held the needle up to the light, squeezing the syringe slightly.

Almost reflexively, Donna DiTullio rolled over and pulled down her pajama bottom. A rub with an alcohol swab, a slight stinging sensation, and it was over. Donna welcomed the evening shot. It started to kick in within minutes, relieving any lingering anxiety, replacing it with a sense of well-being and slight euphoria.

"You're going to be discharged day after tomorrow," Karen said as she straightened the bedsheets.

"Do you think I'm ready?"

"That's what Dr. Sexton thinks. Everything points in that direction—your attitude, your outlook on the future. . . ." Karen noticed her patient glowed at the mention of Dr. Sexton, even before the Capricet had had a chance to take effect. She knew that Donna had been his patient even before slashing her wrists. He had been treating her for depression ever since she lost in the second round of the U.S. Open. And that was almost a year ago.

"I get along with my mom." Donna's lips tightened as she shook her head. "But Papa Gino . . ."

"We had a team meeting last week. I think you'll find a more understanding father from now on in. And maybe you should give up tennis as a competitive sport. Do a little volleying on the weekends. Live a little. Find the right guy."

"I've found the right guy." Donna smiled impishly. Karen didn't press it.

"I wish I could say the same," Karen said as she started to wrap a blood pressure cuff around Donna's arm.

"How about some nice doctor?" Donna mused, her voice upbeat, the smile now full and dimpled.

The banter continued as Karen assessed her patient. The recovery was remarkable. Karen had never seen such a quick rehabilitation in her five years of working on the psych ward. She had studied the new mind-altering drug Capricet. It was still experimental—not FDA-approved. Somehow, it effectively blocked out stressors that bombarded the frontal lobes of the brain—similar to electroshock therapy, but without leaving the patient in a zombielike state. And, unlike other, overused antidepressants, it started to act within an hour. Donna DiTullio's return to normalcy was startling.

Yet Karen wondered about it. Right now, Donna DiTullio was in a safe hospital environment, where the staff monitored her carefully, talked with her, listened, cajoled, made sure she took her medications. Each increase in Donna's level was interpreted as a sign of improvement. Maybe Dr. Broderick was correct; the new drug could be masking an underlying disorder. But she wasn't a psychiatrist. Dr. Sexton and the psych team had been meticulous in assessing Donna's progress. Donna's suicidal crisis seemed to be over. And if Dr. Sexton said Donna was ready for hospital discharge, who was she to second-guess the chief of Psychiatry? Yet, she had a nagging feeling of unease.

"You'll love the Atrium," Karen said gently as she rearranged Donna's blanket. "It's over in the Kennedy Wing, where you'll be tomorrow morning for a group therapy session. There'll be two others, whom you'll meet for the first time. They were hospitalized and placed under Dr. Sexton's care—a man and a woman, both about your age, both of whom had hit rock bottom but who are now productive—weller than well, as we like to say—the gold star of therapeutic end results.

"Dr. Sexton and Dr. Puzon will be there, as well as a psych nurse and your social worker, Joe Sousa. He'll be your contact following discharge."

They kept up the good-natured give-and-take for several minutes. Donna DiTullio leaned back into the pillows, her shiny black hair framing her youthful face. She half-closed her eyes and issued a contented sigh. The Capricet was taking effect.

"Okay, Donna." Karen reached over and snapped off the light. "You're looking good. You won't have me to ace anymore. . . . I'll check in on you just before I sign out in the morning. Good luck."

They exchanged soft smiles.

●

There were some who thought Dr. Robert Sexton should have been a talk-show host rather than a psychiatrist. His aristocratic good looks, russet blond hair, and trim six-foot frame belied his forty-five years. Unmarried—there were rumors of a youthful divorce—he was seen with some of Boston's most attractive women. Congeniality was his hallmark. He carried it with him like the ubiquitous stethoscope that dangled from his white coat pocket. He had a good word for everyone, from the nurses, orderlies, and candy stripers to the cleanup crew. Even at staff meetings and monthly peer reviews, where Phi Beta Kappa egos and professional jealousies could prove disruptive, Sexton knew how to pay deference, soothe, ameliorate—keep issues from deteriorating into collision courses. He often joked that anyone, including himself, had to be a little crazy to become a psychiatrist—and there were those on the faculty of St. Anne's who were not in disagreement with his assessment.

So there was some grumbling. Some felt he was too silky smooth, a fence-straddler, and this, coupled with the fact that he made twice the salary of the chief of Orthopedics, one of his main detractors, didn't ride too well with others on the hospital staff.

But while other department heads—in particular Dr. Max

Gelberg, chief of Oncology, and Matthew Fucci, chief of the Cardiovascular Service—were aloof, imperious, and at times arrogant with the nursing personnel, Dr. Sexton realized early on, from his med school days at Columbia, that in a hospital setting the patient's survival depended on the nurse; the nurse, not the doctor, practiced the nitty-gritty of medicine; and the nurse was never to be alienated.

—

Dr. Consuela Puzon knocked lightly on Dr. Sexton's door.

"Come in, Doctor." Sexton flashed a smile full of Anglo-Saxon charm as his assistant department head entered. He motioned with his gold-plated fountain pen for her to take a seat on the brown leather sofa next to the inlaid teak coffee table.

The early-morning sun filtering through the bronzed skylights added a silky black sheen to Consuela's Joan of Arc hairdo. Her skin, the color of antique gold, contrasted with her white tunic. She unconsciously checked her black-banded wristwatch—7:30 A.M.

Sexton liked Consuela Puzon. She was not overly attractive—a little short, even squattish—but her large blackberry eyes at times seemed to dance beneath the curtain of her forehead bangs. A graduate of Santo Cristobal Academy in Manila, she had been on the staff for over a year, having been recruited by the cardinal, who had been impressed with her work and credentials during a visit to the Philippines. Originally a resident in Neurology, she seemed to have a psychological bond with patients. For Connie, as she liked to be called, treating and sometimes curing the elusive disorders of the mind were just as important as curing cancer.

Sexton quickly recognized Dr. Puzon's superior intellect, and her practical bedside demeanor, sparked by her good humor, made his decision easy. He promoted her over Dr. Lafollette as his first assistant. And even Lafollette was impressed by her clinical ability. Puzon had instant recall, could cite the *Diagnostic and Statistical Manual of Mental Disorders* and its international classifications with computerlike accuracy, and had a diagnostic acumen that Lafollette hadn't seen since his days at the Menninger Foundation.

"We've got a pretty good mix this morning, Doctor," Sexton said as he sat down next to Connie, spreading the charts out on the table.

"That young lawyer, Marden—he's back with his old firm but not trying to make partner in six months by billing twenty hours a day."

Connie nodded. "He's a good man."

"Then Janet Phillips is coming in."

"I catch her talk show when I can," Connie said with a slight Philippine accent. "Lovely lady."

"She thinks the world of you, Doctor. She's in a pressure-cooker business. A media headliner at twenty-five, but short-circuited, and bang!" Sexton slapped her chart with the back of his hand. "She was vulnerable, insecure, once the ratings started to slide. . . . She just couldn't handle it."

Connie nodded sympathetically.

"We had a few others lined up, but I thought this would suffice for the group therapy session."

Connie Puzon looked at Sexton quizzically.

"Isn't Donna DiTullio coming over? She's being discharged tomorrow at noon."

"No question about it," Sexton said. "She's my showcase for Capricet. I'm writing her case up for the *American Journal of Psychiatry*."

Connie Puzon knew all three patients like the back of her hand. All three followed a familiar pattern. Physically, they seemed perfect specimens—handsome, athletic—but all three had tried to overachieve, Donna DiTullio at the insistence of a demanding father, Marden by chasing the Holy Grail of partnership, and Phillips by getting caught in the lethal cross fire of the ratings war. Each downward spiral was inexorable. There was weight loss at first, followed by an inability to sleep. Sleeping tablets provided temporary relief, but in time these opiates only exacerbated the problem. Next followed low self-esteem, then severe depression, with its insidious grip of frustration, isolation, and hopelessness. Finally, a psychotic breakdown overloaded the mental circuits—all three tried to escape what to them seemed to be unbearable pain and anguish. Marden crashed his Jaguar into a tree, Phillips took an overdose of sleeping pills, and Donna DiTullio slashed her wrists. All three survived, and all three ended up at St. Anne's, under the care of Dr. Robert Sexton.

"Want a cup of coffee, Doctor? We still have twenty minutes." Sexton glanced at his watch.

"Plain black would be fine, thank you."

Sexton left his office and headed for the pantry area just off the overhead passageway crossing the Atrium. For a moment, he paused and looked down over the polished oak railing. At 7:45 A.M., the main lobby of St. Anne's Hospital, five floors below, was stirring to life. The admitting office's personnel were busy warming up computers. Nurses in white tunics and aides in green scrubs gathered in small groups at coffee tables.

The Atrium resembled a Hyatt Regency lobby more than a hospital foyer. Skins of glass stretched over seven floors of pink granite. A waterfall tumbled over beds of lava rock, spritzing a coral-lined pool with a fine spray. Exotic fish of gold, white, and kōki red darted among reeds, lily pads, and tropical flora. And shooting skyward, date palms, Hawaiian koa trees, eucalypti, and giant ficus reached for their place in the morning sun.

Sexton left the passageway and entered the pantry, where Joe Sousa, a social worker, was sitting with psych nurse Elaine Adamson, both smoking early-morning cigarettes.

"Good morning," he greeted them with feigned cordiality. He detested smoking, and it was contrary to Lafollette's ban.

"We have a good group coming in this morning. A couple of graduates and Donna DiTullio, who'll be getting her sheepskin." Sexton poured coffee into two plastic cups.

"I understand Donna DiTullio will be back on the courts, perhaps in the New England Open," the psych nurse said as she ground out the remnants of her Marlboro into a Cinzano ashtray.

"She really should give up the tour," Sexton said as he poured some milk into his coffee and stirred slowly. "She's good, but she'll never be a Steffi Graf or even a Billie Jean King. And that father of hers will drive her right back to St. Anne's. We have to make her realize this."

"We'll have a good session," the social worker said. "Look at Marden and Phillips. They've cut back but are functioning better than ever."

"No one is ever out of the woods," Sexton said. "All three exhibited suicidal behavior—they're still brittle. We'll start"— he checked his gold Piaget wristwatch—"at eight. That's ten minutes from now. We go for fifty minutes. I'll lead the discussion. We want all three to ventilate their behavior patterns, personal events, frustrations, and, of course, their pain, even their thoughts and feelings about suicide."

"Isn't that a little risky?" the psych nurse said. "Talking about suicide?"

Sexton stood at the pantry door, holding both cups of coffee.

His voice was authoritative. "Not at all. Years ago, we'd have locked these people in padded rooms, dosed them with antidepressants, even done lobotomies, and hoped for the best. Now we know that their anguish must be shared.

"I'll see you shortly. Dr. Lafollette is going to join us."

—

The first session went better than the psych nurse expected. Marden, Phillips, and DiTullio seemed to hit it off. There was in the group that strange camaraderie and candor that develop among hospital patients, particularly in those sharing similar ailments. All three discussed their psychiatric illness and suicidal behavior as though they were in an instructional seminar. DiTullio admitted that slashing her wrists was a timid destructive act—that perhaps she never intended to die—but said that she had a high level of anger, directed mainly at her father, and she had expressed her anger through the suicide attempt.

The psych nurse took notes throughout. All three patients handled the session sensibly. All were upbeat, even jaunty, showing no evidence of anxiety, not a vestige of depression.

"Time!" Dr. Lafollette checked the clock on the far wall. "We'll take ten. I've got to go to my office and make a few calls.

See you back here shortly." Dr. Puzon left with him.

"Anyone for coffee?" Joe Sousa asked. Marden and Phillips raised their hands.

"I'll help," the psych nurse said. "Be right back."

Several seconds passed.

"I'm feeling nauseous." Donna DiTullio put her hands on her stomach.

"Want to lie down in my office?" Sexton asked. "There's a large sofa—"

"No. I think I'll just move around a bit. It may be the medication. I'm a bit woozy."

"You two just hang out. There are a few magazines." Sexton looked at Marden and Phillips and gestured toward the coffee table. "I've got to go over a few things in my office. Donna, I'll escort you out."

Sexton left Donna just outside the conference room. As he headed toward his office, she walked past the reception area. There was no secretary at the desk. Perhaps it was too early. She went out into the hall, then through another set of swinging doors into the Atrium passageway. She stopped at the low oak rail and fingered it lightly.

The emerald flora was dappled by the early-morning sunlight. She closed her eyes momentarily and breathed in the scent of hibiscus and plumeria.

Suddenly she was falling, hurtling down toward the palms and koa trees, plunging into a dark green abyss! She heard someone yell. Then silence.

2

Cardinal Francis Minehan was not pleased when he received the call from Sister Agnes Loretta, the hospital's administrator, saying that there had been a suicide attempt at St. Anne's by one of Dr. Sexton's patients. He had been leery of establishing a psych ward at a general hospital. He was going to close the old facility out, but against his better judgment and that of Sister Agnes, he had gone along with Dr. Robert Sexton and upgraded the department. Sexton had a dossier of impressive credentials, magna cum laude at Columbia Med, a stellar internship and residency in Neurology at Boston General. Sexton came from an old-line family in Mamaroneck, New York, his grandfather having been the founder of the Hudson Valley Copper Corporation. It was during his Boston General days that Sexton studied psychiatry, passing his national boards. After a brief stay at the Peabody Sanatorium, Sexton got in touch with the cardinal. He needed no letters of introduction. Sexton was the cardinal's nephew, the eldest son of his sister Harriet.

St. Anne's was a showpiece hospital. Five years ago, at the insistence of Dr. Robert Sexton, it had become a full-service mecca of healing.

The cardinal's initial misgivings appeared to be unfounded. Sister Agnes Loretta had nothing but praise for Sexton. His cure rate was the highest on the Eastern Seaboard and he seemed to fit seamlessly into the medical confraternity. He was the cardinal's designated spokesman on crucial medical issues, testifying before state and national congressional committees and providing the necessary liaison with Blue Cross, Medicare, and the Massachusetts Medical Society, as well as the national affiliates. It was Sexton who countered rising medical costs by piloting a bill through the state legislature partially immunizing charitable hospitals such as St. Anne's, Boston General, Beth Israel, and others from civil liability for injuries to patients. He was also a lieutenant colonel in the National Guard. With the help of Governor Stevenson, some squash-playing friends on Beacon Hill, and a friendly press decrying high-judgment awards against medical practitioners, he successfully guided another bill, artfully entitled "charitable immunity," through the legislature that exempted doctors, nurses, and other health-care providers from financial accountability in excess of $100,000 arising from malpractice claims made by patients under their care. The legal limit for personal liability would be the same as the present limit for hospitals: $100,000. But the law would not go into effect for ninety days.

At first, Sister Agnes Loretta was critical of holding group therapy sessions in the conference room just outside the Atrium passageway. But geographically, the staff offices were located at this level, and Sexton and even Dr. Lafollette felt the setting was ideal for patients who had progressed to an optimum level of recovery. The same could not be said in other departments, where patients sometimes fell off gurneys or went sprawling while hobbling to or from the commode.

—

Cardinal Minehan, Monsignor Devlin, and Sister Agnes Loretta, together with Sexton and Lafollette, inspected the Atrium passageway.

Minehan looked over the rail and shook his head.

"We never should have allowed mentally disturbed patients to have access to an open area like this." His hand swept outward. "Especially those with histories of suicidal ideation."

Monsignor Devlin and Sister Agnes Loretta nodded in tacit agreement.

"We had no indication. . . . There wasn't a sign the DiTullio girl would jump. She was in good spirits, looking forward to going home," Sexton said, his face grim. "Her chart was well documented."

"Well, I want all of these open spaces paneled with unbreakable glass." The cardinal patted the rail. "And I want the psychiatric offices relocated to the ground floor. This will be done immediately; Sister Agnes has already called the movers. You will be next to Radiology."

Sexton and Lafollette didn't protest, even though they were locking the barn door after the horse had been stolen.

The group returned to the conference room, where they were joined by Dr. Consuela Puzon, social worker Joseph Sousa, and the psych nurse, Elaine Adamson, as well as the archdiocesan legal counsel, Charles Finnerty, and a young aide.

"How is the DiTullio girl doing?" The cardinal addressed the psych nurse, who was holding a hospital chart on her lap.

"Not well." She shook her head. "Aside from smashed legs and arms and internal injuries, she has massive brain damage. She's in a coma in intensive care. Probably won't survive the week." The psych nurse spoke in candid nonmedical terms.

Monsignor Devlin spoke for the first time. "It will be a blessing. Mr. DiTullio called this morning, and he wants a meeting with everyone who was present during this . . . er, unfortunate occurrence. He's going to be accompanied by his lawyer."

"Let's run through this again." Legal counsel Finnerty nodded to his aide, who immediately flipped open his briefcase and readied a tape recorder.

"We go on the premise that none of you in attendance had any inkling that the DiTullio girl would attempt suicide."

There was a collective nodding of heads.

"We've taken the statements of the other two—Marden and

Phillips—and they back you up on this observation. But what bothers me"—Finnerty unconsciously adjusted his steel-rimmed glasses—"is that other than Dr. Sexton, no one actually saw her jump. She must have gone right past the pantry, where you two were getting coffee." He looked at Sousa and Adamson.

"Well, we were having a quick cigarette," Sousa said. "We had closed the swinging door. When we heard Dr. Sexton yell—"

"Hold it a minute!" Finnerty said. "Let's back up. Where was the receptionist? You say you and the DiTullio girl went by her station." He looked at Sexton.

"It was ten minutes to nine. The receptionist wasn't due on until nine."

"How did Marden and Phillips get to the conference room?"

"It was prearranged. They arrived in separate taxis and took the elevator to the fifth floor."

"Unescorted?"

"They had been here several times before, so they knew how to get here."

"They remained in the conference room when you left with DiTullio?" Sexton nodded.

"You'll have to speak up, so we can get this on the recorder." Finnerty's voice had an authoritative tone.

"That's right," Sexton said, his voice throaty and deep.

"Did you see Donna DiTullio go out into the passageway by herself?" Finnerty looked at Sexton.

"Yes. She said she needed some air. It's very cool and pleasant in the Atrium. I thought it would do her good."

"But you said that you saw her through the glass aperture in the passageway door. Did you stop to watch her?"

"No. I was headed to my office. But I had forgotten my notebook, which had some phone numbers in it for calls I had to make. While returning to the conference room, I happened to glance out the glass opening toward the passageway.

"I saw Donna starting to climb over the rail." Sexton's eyes began to mist; he spoke slowly, haltingly.

"I bolted through the door. I yelled at her, 'Don't jump, Donna. For God's sake, don't jump!' " Sexton's voice was a raspy whisper. "I ran toward her. She looked at me—I'll never forget that look. It was—"

"All right," Finnerty interrupted, "forget about the look. Legally, it's not relevant, nor admissible as evidence.

"Erase that last portion—about the look." He turned to his aide and gave a cutting motion with his hand.

Finnerty paused for several seconds. He and his aide exchanged nods.

"Okay, please continue, Doctor."

Sexton cleared his throat.

"I rushed toward her, trying to stop her. It was too late. . . ." Sexton lowered his head. Tears rolled down his cheeks.

No one spoke. A minute dragged by.

"You okay, Doctor?" Finnerty leapt into the silence.

"Yes, I'm fine. It was just so unexpected. She was making such progress. . . ."

Finnerty removed his handkerchief from his breast pocket and offered it to Sexton.

"No, I'm okay. Thanks just the same." Sexton dabbed his eyes with his knuckle.

"That's the theme. It was completely unexpected." Finnerty smiled politely.

"When both of you heard Bob yell, 'Don't jump, Donna. For God's sake, don't jump!' what did you do?" Finnerty looked at Sousa and the psych nurse.

"We ran through the door. We saw Dr. Sexton standing at the rail. Donna had jumped."

"All right. That's good enough for now." Finnerty snapped his fingers noiselessly as a cue to his aide. "Mr. and Mrs. DiTullio are coming here tomorrow. Just stick to the truth as you have given it here. It may suffice to ward off a lawsuit."

Sexton had regained his composure. "Dante DiTullio is the toughest nut I ever came across. We've had him in for counseling sessions. I've seen parents, especially fathers, who have an insatiable appetite to mold a child into a winner, even when the youngster has only a modicum of talent—hockey, basketball, beauty pageants—you name it. Mr. DiTullio is a classic study on the cause of youth burnout."

"Is there any chance of a successful lawsuit?" Monsignor Devlin, himself legally trained and an associate professor of ecclesiastical law at Boston College, inquired of Finnerty.

"Sure, I learned long ago never to prejudge a case. Our position seems reasonable. When we explain it to the DiTullios and their lawyer, there may not be any suit—especially if Donna DiTullio succumbs, which is more than likely."

Devlin let the matter drop. As chief legal liaison between Finnerty and the cardinal, he had authorized many settlements, some involving priests and former altar boys, and he knew that a reasonable up-front offer sometimes quashed litigation along with all its dark publicity.

Finnerty wanted to put his stamp of authority on the meeting's windup.

He addressed the cardinal. "As you know, Your Eminence, thanks to the charitable immunity law, St. Anne's is responsible for only one hundred thousand, even if its staff and employees are totally liable. But individually, as for your Dr. Sexton, in fact, all of you who were in there with Donna DiTullio that morning"—Finnerty scanned those who had been present—"for the moment, the sky's the limit."

"I thought that the law limited the liability of all health-care providers as well as health-care professionals at one hundred thousand dollars," Monsignor Devlin said.

"That's the kicker. Last year, the legislature passed the Hospital Immunity Bill. This year we took care of the doctors and nurses, but unfortunately the law applies only to suits commenced ninety days from its enactment."

"But the archdiocese has a twenty-million-dollar insurance policy protecting individual practitioners, isn't that correct, Mr. Finnerty?" Monsignor Devlin's voice was reassuringly confidential.

Finnerty merely nodded. He knew that a lawsuit was a distinct probability. And he could see a brighter side to the tragedy. The defense of any lawsuit against the archdiocese would be steered to his firm, Roper, Cranston, Peabody & Weld—a great piece of business. Then it struck him. Why split this five ways? He was getting a little disenchanted with the partnership setup, especially since his name was not on the letterhead. Perhaps it was time to form his own firm, take the archdiocesan account with him. He had thought about it over the last few months. He had a tip that a twenty-man law firm was going belly-up. Terrific location, law library, teak flooring, polished oak staircase, even Winslow Homer prints on the walls. Time to get even with his crusty partners. Yes, Finnerty could see a rainbow peeking through the gloom, and a golden pot of billable hours gleamed at the end of it.

—

Dante and Anna DiTullio were ushered into the Critical Care Unit of St. Anne's by the chief of Neurosurgery, Dr. Jensen. The room was filled with silver canisters, monitors, vials, and IV machines. A mask over the inert form of Donna DiTullio was attached to a respirator. Her body was swathed in mummylike wrappings, and both legs were suspended by pulleys to overhead metal bars.

A nurse checked the IV lines, then stood aside as Dante DiTullio moved toward his daughter. Two large eyes—doll's eyes—stared blankly toward the ceiling. There was no movement, no recognition. Dante bent forward and kissed his daughter lightly on her withered lips.

Dante started to sob, the tears spilling from his cheeks onto his daughter's forehead. Anna DiTullio merely stood by her daughter's bed, saying nothing, showing no outward sign of emotion. Inwardly, she was being torn apart. She fingered the rosary in her suit pocket.

"Can she see or hear, Doctor?" Dante looked up at the chief of Neurosurgery.

"Too early to say." His voice was somber, professional. "CAT scans and MRIs show extensive damage in the temporal and occipital lobes." The doctor touched the side and back of his head.

"Those control eyesight and hearing. We've evacuated as much clotting as we could. Right now, the brain is swollen. That's why we have those little burr holes in the scalp—to relieve edema."

"She'll come out of it, won't she, Doctor, when the swelling recedes?" Dante straightened up and looked at his wife. His once-keen eyes drooped with sadness.

"We'll follow her closely, Mr. DiTullio," the doctor said. "Right now, every conceivable facet of our art and science is being utilized. She'll have two attendants monitoring her around the clock." He gestured toward the nurse.

—

Dante and Anna DiTullio sat on the brown Naugahyde sofa in Dan Sheridan's outer office, along with their nephew, Emilio Cantone, only recently admitted to the bar. Dante smoked a cigar while Anna and the young lawyer flipped through some outdated magazines.

Judy Corwin, Dan Sheridan's secretary, had taken their jackets, then slid through a side door into her boss's office.

"Wow, you could knock!" Sheridan had been adjusting his tie, peering into the mirrored surface of a statue of Justice. He patted his reddish brown hair. "I could've been *in direlecto nudum pactum*." He turned and gave a raffish wink to his "spiritual adviser," as he called her.

"Here are my notes on the DiTullios. They're the parents of Donna DiTullio. They've suffered a real tragedy," Judy said.

Sheridan's voice switched from jaunty to sober. "I read about it in the *Globe*. She jumped five floors."

"The young lawyer, Cantone, just passed the bar. He told me on the q.t. that he'd be in over his head in a malpractice case, especially one against the cardinal."

"So he doesn't want to sue God," Sheridan mused. "I don't blame him. When you sue God, you sure'n hell better win.

"Show them in, Judy, and get hold of Raimondi. If we decide to take the case, I want him to run over to St. Anne's with me and get what hospital records are immediately available, and have him take his camera. Get some snaps before they start changing things."

Judy ushered the DiTullios into the office and closed the door with a discreet click.

—

For the next tear-wrenching hour, Dante DiTullio sputtered out the tragic events and Dan Sheridan listened.

"This drug Capricet is still in the experimental stage," Sheridan said. "I assume both of you signed the authorization for its use."

"I signed it," Dante DiTullio said.

"Did you read it before signing?"

"No, I didn't. Sexton kind of talked me into it. At first, the drug seemed to be working. We went in to see Donna a week later, and it was unbelievable. She was her old self.

"But I've been reading, Mr. Sheridan. Look at all the lawsuits over Halcion and Prozac. I think there was something in Capricet that made Donna go off the deep end."

The young lawyer spoke for the first time. "We feel, Mr. Sheridan, sir, that the Atrium—way up on the fifth floor—was no place to take a psychiatric patient, especially one with a suicidal history, and leave her unguarded."

"I want you to sue for forty million dollars." Dante DiTullio's face flushed and both fists clenched into white knots.

"We'll see. It'll be a tough road. St. Anne's lawyers will put up all sorts of barriers. Is there any person or persons Donna was especially fond of during her hospital stay?"

Anna DiTullio spoke up. "Yes, a nurse. She was Donna's night nurse. I'm pretty sure her name was Assad—Karen Assad. Donna spoke of her often."

Sheridan jotted the name on a yellow pad.

"All right, we'll do a quiet investigation. I'll review it with a psychiatrist friend of mine and let you know if we are going to take your case on."

"You come highly recommended, Mr. Sheridan. We could

have gone to one of the big firms. . . ." Dante DiTullio's voice had a testy undertone.

"I know. We'll let you know as soon as possible," Sheridan said, coming out from behind his desk. "Now, you take care of yourselves."

Sheridan returned to his desk and sat down. He hadn't tried a malpractice case in ten years. Why take on this one? Against the cardinal, no less. He studied the name of the nurse, then underlined it: <u>KAREN ASSAD</u>.

3

Sheridan met his investigator, Manny Raimondi, in front of St. Anne's Hospital. It was a busy place. Cabs were dropping patients off and picking them up. Many departing were hobbling on crutches; visitors carried flowers or stuffed animals. Three ambulances pulled up, their blue emergency lights flashing, and Sheridan watched the EMTs, the doctors, and the nurses spring into action. It didn't matter who the patient was, whether he had Blue Cross or Medicaid, or even if he was a bank robber. If a human life was at stake, the medical cadre pulled out all the stops to ensure survival. Sheridan knew that if his life was on the line, St. Anne's was where he would want to be.

They sipped coffee at a table next to the florist shop as Sheridan made a rough sketch of the foyer. There was scaffolding throughout the Atrium, and Sheridan noticed some engineer types in hard hats talking with pin-striped executives. Also in the group was a priest, plain black suit, Roman collar. Sheridan recognized him as Monsignor Devlin, the cardinal's point man. They were consulting plans and gesturing upward toward the skylights. It was clear that the open Atrium would soon be encased in unbreakable glass.

"Let's get a few camera shots from down here, Manny; then we'll take the elevator to the fifth-floor passageway. Plenty of light in here. Don't think you'll need a flash. We don't want to attract attention. And before we're thrown out, let's map the scene—the conference room where the group therapy took place, the doctors' offices, the entire layout of the fifth floor. If someone interrupts you, tell them we're from the construction crew."

Manny set his small camera for the light and started to snap the Atrium's interior. They proceeded to the fifth-floor passageway and shot it from all angles, taking pictures through the scaffolding of the foyer below.

Sheridan paused a few moments. "What do you think, Manny? Should we take this case on?" He looked pensive, uncertain, which was not like him.

"I'm no shrink," Manny said as he clicked off several more shots, "but it seems to me that this was one hell of a place to hold a sit-in for a potential suicide. If the girl dies—not much of a case. But if she survives in a vegetative state—the monetary damages will be horrendous."

"I know." For a moment, Sheridan looked off into some middle distance. "We're talking about the Catholic church. I suppose if you count the cures of Jesus, the church has been in the health-care business for two thousand years. Win or lose, a malpractice suit will damage the medical facility and any medical practitioners who wind up as defendants. The media will see to that."

"What difference does that make?" Manny knew his boss was having some misgivings. "Suppose it was Beth Israel or New England Baptist? I'm sure we'd go ahead without any qualms."

"I guess you're right," Sheridan said without much conviction.

The receptionist stopped them as they were about to enter the pantry. "May I help you?"

"Oh, we're from Clancy Brothers Construction," Raimondi said, pocketing his camera, "with the scaffolding crew. Could we use the men's room?"

"Certainly," the receptionist said. "It's down the hall there on the left, past the last row of offices."

They all exchanged smiles. When out of sight of the receptionist's desk, Raimondi completed the shoot—the conference room, the doctors' offices—Sheridan pacing off distances as they went along. It was strangely quiet. There were no patients in the waiting room. The doctors were nowhere in sight, and their inner offices appeared to be closed. The two men returned to the waiting room.

"Excuse me, Mrs. . . . ." Sheridan smiled at the portly black receptionist, who appeared to be dividing her time between a paperback novel and picking at a computer.

"It's Miss . . . Miss Davidson. They call me Hettie."

"You had a pretty bad accident up here last week." Sheridan frowned in a look of concern.

"Supposed to say nothin' about it"—she resumed her typing—" 'cept if you're from the insurance company."

"No, we're just with the rigging crew. But it must have been horrible. Were you on when it happened, Hettie?"

"No, it happened just before I came in. Way I heard it was, they all broke for coffee. The girl went out into the passageway over there and jumped." Hettie made an arc with her hand.

"Anyone with her at the time?"

"Joe Sousa and Elaine Adamson were in the pantry." She gestured ahead with her pen. "Doc Sexton yelled at her not to jump. All three, Joe, Elaine, and Doc Sexton, rushed to reach her but"—the receptionist shook her head—"she jumped."

"I'm sorry," Sheridan said.

"Do you know a nurse by the name of Karen Assad?"

"Sure, she's the night nurse on the psych ward in the Cushing Building. Nice lady. Comes over here sometimes."

Sheridan and Raimondi started to head back toward the passageway. Sheridan stopped.

He returned to the receptionist. "Do you like baseball?"

"Don't like the game myself, too slow. Red Sox aren't going no place, anyhow."

"Have to agree with you there, Hettie. But here are two box

seats for the Yankees game tomorrow night. Maybe you can give them to your boyfriend."

"Might go with my girlfriend Lucie." She took the ducats, flashed a wide toothy smile, and dropped them into her purse.

"The two others who were in the group therapy session, did you happen to know their names, Hettie? As the receptionist, you would probably have a record." It was a far-out question for a corporate type to ask—even a corporate construction type. This was privileged information, and he knew he might not be able to discover the names of psychiatric patients through legal channels, but she seemed amenable. She had noticed the box-seat tickets were priced at fifty dollars each.

"Yes," she said, bending forward and sneaking a peek left and right, "it was that TV girl . . . Phillips—you know, the one on Channel Three. And the other was some lawyer. Think his name was Marden."

"Well, enjoy the game, Hettie, and have a nice day." Sheridan gave a two-fingered salute.

Phillips and Marden. He tucked them away in the index of his mind. So far so good.

—

Sheridan and Raimondi returned to the foyer. They sat for a few minutes, toying with cups of coffee, and watched patients checking in, orderlies pushing gurneys and wheelchairs, nurses—some in white, others in green scrubs—carrying X-ray films or wheeling various apparatus that always seemed to be topped by an IV hookup. It looked like chaos, but Sheridan knew that there was a subtle order to it all.

"Manny, if I ever take a shot at home plate again, make sure I end up here at St. Anne's." Sheridan was referring to his semi-pro baseball team, on which he still played catcher on midweek afternoons.

"Aren't you getting a little old for that kind of stuff?" Manny said. "You're what—forty-six?"

"And holding. Hey, the old Chicago catcher Gabby Hartnett

was almost fifty before he hung up the cleats. Same with Ernie Lombardi of the Cincinnati Reds."

"I think you're nuts playing a kids' game with a lot of Young Turks."

"Maybe so." Sheridan laughed. "But Jesus, Manny, if they certify me as crazy, never take me to the St. Anne's psych department."

"Okay." Sheridan tossed his Styrofoam cup into a nearby bin. "We've got to make a trip to medical records, see if we can trap the DiTullio kid's chart before it starts to change."

"Can we get a patient's psychiatric chart, even with a permission slip signed by the father?" Manny said as he downed the remainder of his coffee.

"Not really. Unlike regular hospital records, psychiatric charts can be obtained only through a court summons, and even then, only with the court's permission. By the time that rolls around, all the euphemisms appear—the bullshit about the heroic doctors and nurses. The incriminating stuff mysteriously disappears.

"And what I'd really like to get is the 'incident' report—the mortality and morbidity review. Unfortunately, our courts say that report is absolutely privileged."

Sheridan and Raimondi started to make their way to the medical records office.

•

"Excuse me, Miss . . ." Sheridan smiled at a young woman behind the counter. He squinted at her name tag but couldn't make it out.

"May I help you gentlemen?" she said pleasantly. "I'm Sister Mary Ignatius, director of Medical Records."

Sheridan assessed her quickly. Close-cropped ash blond hair, large blue eyes, freckles sprinkled across her nose, good figure in her trim beige dress.

"Sister . . . Wow, you could've fooled me! Where were these nuns when we were growing up, Manny? And so good-looking!" She was Irish—probably born there. He could tell by the way she gave a charming little upward kick to the end of a sentence. Maybe he had lucked out.

"Cut the blarney," she said. Her eyes narrowed in mock scrutiny, but her smile had a pixie twist to it.

"Of course." Sheridan caught himself. "I'm here to get the hospital record of Donna DiTullio. She was admitted three weeks ago last Wednesday. I have the authorization right here." He extracted a paper from his inside jacket pocket.

"Did you say DiTullio?"

"Yes." He slid the permission form toward the nun. "It's properly signed by the patient's father."

Suddenly, the crinkly smile drained from Sister Mary Ignatius's face. "You two lawyers?" she asked, her voice now all business.

Sheridan had left his telltale briefcase back in the office. Manny had on a black leather jacket, but Sheridan's blue pinstripe probably gave him away.

"Yes." Sheridan had to level with Sister Mary, at least partly. "I'm the family's attorney, and we need the hospital record for insurance purposes, disability, Medicaid, things like that."

"I'm sorry," she said, "that's a psychiatric record, privileged under Massachusetts General Laws, Title Forty-eight, Section—"

Sheridan decided to retreat graciously. "Oh, I'm sorry, Sister, I guess I should have checked the statute. Title Forty-eight, you say?"

"We can't surrender those records except by order of the probate court."

"Sorry to trouble you, Sister," Sheridan said as he reached for the permission form and replaced it in his pocket. "It was a terrible tragedy."

"Yes, I know," Sister Mary said. "Sorry you gentlemen had to make this trip for nothing."

"Only doing our job, Sister." Sheridan saw an opening. "My cousin Eunice is a Sister of St. Joseph. Teaches at Regis College. Lovely lady."

Sometimes the chemistry is just right. Sister Mary permitted herself a half smile.

"We're Sisters of Charity here." A hint of goodwill returned to her voice.

"My favorite order." Sheridan seized the moment. "Say, Sister, there's a new Andrew Lloyd Webber musical opening at the Wang Center Saturday night. It's about the Irish uprising—sort of a Gaelic *Les Misérables*. I have two tickets I can't use." He extracted them from his wallet. "Maybe you'd like to go, take a friend or a cousin."

"Oh, that would be nice." The crinkly smile was back. He slid the tickets toward her.

"Thank you," she said. "Sorry I couldn't help you out."

⬤

"Boy," Raimondi said as they were hailing a cab, "that play is sold out. And those are Sheila's tickets. She's going to be one real sore fiancée."

"Yeah, I know." Sheridan let out a deep sigh. "But somehow I have a hunch that Sister Mary can be friendly, and down the line, we're going to need all the friendship we can get."

"Yeah, sure." Manny didn't sound convinced.

⬤

Dan Sheridan sat in Dr. John B. White's waiting room, leafing through the latest issue of *Interior Design*. A comely blondish secretary alternated between answering the phone and ushering patients into the doctor's office. He liked her reassuring smile.

Dr. White and Sheridan went back a long way—to the old neighborhood in West Roxbury, the nuns at Holy Redeemer Grammar School, Little League, and four years at St. Ignatius High School. White made All-Scholastic as a left-handed pitcher and Sheridan was the catcher—second team All-City. There were some who said that White could have made it in the majors. In fact, he had a tryout with the Chicago Cubs, but that was as far as it went. He ran up against kids from the farms, from Iowa and Kansas and the Piedmont, who could clock a fastball in the nineties. White's control and slow-breaking curves didn't seem to impress the scouts. He matriculated to Harvard, then Harvard

Med, relegating his activities on the diamond to intramural soft-
ball. Sheridan joined the marines after high school, was wounded
in Vietnam, and, despite a gimpy leg, still played catcher for the
Brookfield Giants in a semipro league north of Boston.

White, who was one of the leading psychiatrists in the Boston area, now confined his athleticism to weekend golf. He could
score in the high seventies, occasionally winning a local tournament or two.

Sheridan and White kept in touch, mostly on a professional
level. White was much in demand as a forensic psychiatrist and
often testified on behalf of Sheridan's clients, both criminal and
civil. Convincing a skeptical jury that a defendant was tempo-
rarily insane at the time he committed a homicide was not an
easy task, especially with the battery of high-profile experts available to the prosecutor. But White's testimony was adopted in
three out of four of Sheridan's defenses. He had a folksy way of
talking to jurors, reducing medical and psychiatric esoterica to
language that the truck driver, the housewife, and the hod carrier
could readily understand.

Sheridan's most recent case was on behalf of a state politi-
cian who had been left a fortune by a woman recluse. She had
renounced a prior will, cutting out some nieces and nephews and
leaving over a million dollars, the bulk of her estate, to her so-
called son, Timmy Donovan. Timmy, the state pol, on learning of
the recluse's intentions and just prior to her death, rushed to the
probate court and took out adoption papers. When an investigative reporter on the local paper learned of the ploy, Timmy,
who was also a lawyer, was dragged over the journalistic coals.
Despite open criticism in the press and a battery of high-priced
lawyers and expert psychiatrists testifying that the recluse was of
unsound mind when she changed her will, Sheridan's riddling
cross-examination, and Dr. White's lucid testimony, laced with
homespun analogies, were more than sufficient to uphold the will.
As one juror said afterward, "If the recluse had left a million to
her cat, Tabby, and then axed the Little Sisters of the Poor, then,
based on Dr. White's testimony, we still would have found that
she was perfectly sane."

Dr. White's inner sanctum resembled a den more than an office. Old volumes were encased, floor to ceiling, in three walls of fruit-wood shelving. A baby grand Steinway, its walnut grain polished to a fine glisten, was set near a bay window overlooking Boston Common and the Public Garden. When the secretary ushered Sheridan into the office, the doctor was seated at his rolltop desk, signing some letters and reports. He handed them to his secretary.

"Dan, sorry I had to have you wait so long. Fridays are always busy. And, of course, there's a full moon tonight. Sit down." He shook Dan's hand warmly. He knew that when Dan had a case needing his expertise, it was money in the bank. His fee in the will-contest case was $25,000. And for Timmy Donovan, who was skirting disbarment, it was a bargain.

"Before I give you the facts, take a look at these." Sheridan produced ten photos of the St. Anne's layout that Manny had taken a few days earlier.

White studied each thoughtfully. "This is St. Anne's." He looked at Sheridan. "The Atrium and Dr. Sexton's psychiatric department. Is this about the DiTullio girl—the one who jumped last week?"

"Yes. I've been asked to represent the DiTullio family, and, of course, the girl."

"She still living?"

"In a coma. She'll probably expire," Sheridan said.

"Dan, I know all about the case. The shrink business is pretty close-knit. Word gets around."

"Well, let me give you my side of the story." Sheridan proceeded to narrate the facts as he knew them. White listened attentively.

"John, I want you to assume the best scenario. Of course, I don't have the hospital record as yet, nor Sexton's medical notes, but what do you think? Is there a case?"

White ran his hand through his thinning hair. He paused for several seconds. "Well, the girl is only twenty-one, been in treatment for about a year. She is manic-depressive, really. Probably always was, even as a teenager. Overbearing father, and of course she is an overachiever. It's a classic case. Tries to commit suicide. Gets the wonder drug Capricet and seems to be coming around—"

"What about Capricet?" Sheridan interrupted.

"It's experimental. Turns rapacious mice into lovable Mickeys and Minnies, so the drug company says. But on humans, you've got to get special permission to use it. I've given it in isolated cases, but it's still too early to see if it works or if there are deleterious side effects over the long term.

"Let's look at the legal downside. First of all, there is absolutely no way anyone can prevent a person from self-destructing. If someone is going to commit suicide, he or she will do it. The Golden Gate Bridge has suicide netting, but the patient will find another bridge or jump in front of a train or a car, or swallow twelve Elavil."

"Well, hell, Doctor," Sheridan said, "if that's the case, if you think we're wasting our time, why not do away with nine-one-one, emergency hot lines, the suicide-prevention clinics nationwide—"

"Hey, leave that for cross-examination." White held up his hand as if to ward off further attack. "That'll be the defense attorney's ploy—'If not now, later'—and a jury sometimes buys it. And don't forget that in Catholic Boston, you'll wind up with eight out of twelve jurors who are RCs, people who think it's a mortal sin to attempt suicide, let alone asking money for doing it. That's the hidden defense. Erasing that kind of prejudice will take some artful persuasion, believe me.

"But between you and me, I think you've got a hell of a case. Not a slam dunk, mind you. When you finally get the medical charts, they'll be peppered with tinsel kudos about how well she was doing, all that baloney. Let me have a look at them. You lawyers can read what they say. I can read what they don't say— the hidden stuff. St. Anne's is responsible for allowing a suicide-prone patient access to an open area up on the fifth floor. Same for Sexton and the staff. Here the DiTullio girl was left unguarded. The most vulnerable time for any psychiatric patient with a history of suicide attempt is just before or at the time of hospital discharge, and she was on an experimental drug." White wiggled his hand. "It was sheer madness to hold group therapy up there. And we're supposed to be the sane ones.

"I know Bob Sexton, Lafollette, and Puzon," White continued. "All three have the highest credentials and reputations. It's tough to figure how they went along with that situation. It was an accident waiting to happen."

"What about the 'if not now' defense?"

"Hey, just because a psychiatric patient later does himself in doesn't mean that we can't see a patient through a crisis. Experience shows—and we can detail this statistically—that once the patient gets over the feeling of helplessness, receives proper psychological support and treatment, he or she can live a productive and meaningful life."

"You said 'we,' John. Will you testify if I take the case on?" Sheridan knew he was hitting the top of the scale in the favor department. *"It'll be against the cardinal and your colleagues."*

White steepled his fingers and peered over them. He sucked in his breath for a long moment, puffing out his cheeks as he exhaled slowly.

"Do you know what you're asking?" His eyes fixed Sheridan with a steady gaze.

"I know," Sheridan said quietly. The health-care industry was a sacred cow. A conspiracy of silence ran deep in the medical profession, particularly in Boston, with its medical schools, clinics, teaching facilities, and general hospitals. Sheridan knew it, and White had felt its sting. Testifying in a criminal case, a will contest, even an involuntary-confinement hearing, was one thing. Testifying against colleagues and the cardinal could be White's professional death warrant.

"Look, John," Sheridan said apologetically, "you don't have to testify for the record. There'll be pressures, I know that. Perhaps you can help on the q.t.—maybe find me some out-of-state shrink whose—"

"What the hell are you talking about?" White's voice had

the timbre of indignation. "Sure I'll testify! Get the medical records, and see those two patients, Marden and—what's her name?"

"Phillips."

Sheridan and White both knew that in the chit department, Sheridan now owed White—big-time. But maybe it went deeper. Maybe it went back to Holy Redeemer, where the nuns taught values, not religion, back to the old neighborhood, to White's notion that there was a wrong that needed redress.

Sheridan gathered his notes and photos and stuffed them into his briefcase. White saw him through the outer office and to the front door. As Sheridan shook the doctor's hand, there was only one thing to say.

"You've got balls, John," he said. "Real balls."

"Yeah." White tried to look appropriately amused. "I hope a year from now—if we last that long—we're not both singing soprano."

4

Judy Corwin addressed Sheridan's intercom. "Judge Davis's docket clerk just called. You are to report to her session in courtroom four-oh-three at two this afternoon. It's on that Ellison boy's rape case. Seems that Assistant DA Shirley Grant is pushing for trial and the judge wants to start impaneling Monday morning."

"Okay, Judy." Sheridan sighed. "Guess we can't continue the case forever, and it's not going to go away."

"At least you've got Lakeesha Davis on the bench—she's got some soul," Judy said, trying to sound upbeat.

"That could cut both ways," Sheridan said. "Our kid's white—prep school, all the Brahmin trimmings. Bad enough his first name is Todd. It'll be a rough ride if we have to go the distance."

"How is the plea bargaining going?" Judy inquired as she started to sort the mail.

"Not good. We got nowhere at the preliminary hearing. The new DA, Gretchen Wilder, is out for some early pelts. Before we got on the case, Ellison's dad made an offer of twenty-five grand to the so-called victim, but that backfired.

"While I'm up there, I'll drop in on young Buckley. He's waiting for a verdict on the DeVelieu case; jury's been out for two days."

Tom Buckley was Sheridan's associate, had been for ten years, since he first started practice at thirty. Judy called him "young Buckley." Now at forty, the name still stuck.

"The cash-flow ledger says we're pretty far into the red column, Dan. We could use a few fees," Judy said.

"I'll see what I can do, Judy."

Judy Corwin sat at her desk, looked at the pile of bills, and issued a profound Jewish-mother sigh. Demand letters from the lawbook company and bills for leasing, photocopy paper, and malpractice insurance were all there. As successful as Dan Sheridan and Buckley were, the practice of criminal law was a roller-coaster business, and "the nut," as she called the overhead, was a voracious money-eater. But at least Dan kept some cash around—an emergency fund to cover the tips and ducats for sports events. Some people would call them bribes, Judy thought.

And she thought about the clientele—drug dealers, money launderers, white-collar skimmers, a few charged with bank fraud, a priest accused of molestation by former altar boys, and two people accused of rape. The Ellison boy, a privileged white preppy, had gotten drunk at a sorority bash and wound up in the sack with one Sandra Martinez, a fifteen-year-old going on twenty-five. It could have been a notch on his old Delta Gamma key—something to crow about when he got to college, especially since there were some follow-up encounters. But when the girl missed her period, the Ellison kid backed off, refused letters and phone calls.

The Martinez girl, who was half-black, half-Hispanic, went to her irate father. Next, the police came knocking at the preppy's door. To make matters worse, the complainant had an abortion and the physician botched the job, leaving her permanently scarred and sterile. The prosecutor would get mileage out of this further complication. That was Dan Sheridan's two o'clock appointment.

And his partner, Tom Buckley, was defending a Haitian

man, Jean DeVelieu, accused of raping a white girl. DeVelieu misinterpreted the girl's signals, claiming that she assented to his advances.

Judy took two overdue bills from the pile. They could stall the lawbook company, since the publishers wanted the texts and fillers to keep coming. The landlord was another matter.

She buzzed Sheridan once again. "Dan, I got hold of the Phillips girl. You can meet her on Friday at the studio, after her show."

"Fine," Sheridan said. "And before I forget it, get ahold of the Martinez girl's personal lawyer—you know, Sheldon Cohen. See if he can meet me at Judge Davis's session."

———

Sheridan grabbed a sandwich and coffee at the lunch stand in the aging courthouse lobby, then made his way up rows of weathered marble steps to the fourth floor. It was a mangy place, really, littered with gum wrappers and cigarette butts. The halls were dimly lit and smoky. Groups of lawyers huddled with dour and distressed clients, at times gesturing flamboyantly or whispering enigmatically.

He saw Buckley seated on a bench with his grim-faced client. Jean DeVelieu held a moonfaced baby, who appeared on the verge of dozing off for an afternoon nap.

Sheridan nodded, then clapped DeVelieu on the shoulder. "Jury's been out two days now," he said. "That's a pretty good sign. Someone's holding out."

"Johnny Coyne, the bailiff, said it's a deadlock." Young Buckley cupped his hand to keep the bad news from his client. A mistrial would only stall things awhile; it was no real out.

"Not bad, Buck. You've done a helluva job," Sheridan said, directing the gratuitous kudos to the client's ear.

Just then, Bailiff Coyne, attired in a black suit with brass buttons and wielding a white staff, marched into view, the jurors following behind. They were returning from lunch and would swing right past Buckley, Sheridan, and the client.

"Quick," Buckley said to DeVelieu, "give me the baby!"

"What, monsieur?"

"The baby! *Donnez-moi l'enfant!*" Buckley dug up some high school French, then reached out and forcibly withdrew the baby from DeVelieu's grasp. Coyne and the jury were still fifty feet away. Sheridan saw Buckley pinch the baby on the rear end. There was a great screech. He bounced the baby and pinched it again. The baby, now wide-eyed and wailing, reached for its father. "Da-Da!" the baby screamed. Not knowing what was going on, DeVelieu grabbed the baby, bounced it several times, and made soothing sounds to calm it down just as the jury passed by. Several jurors smiled at DeVelieu, reacting to the display of fatherly love.

Sheridan, a veteran of countless courtroom wars, knew that justice, especially the criminal justice system, had some hard edges. Although he didn't approve of Buckley's ploy, he had to hand it to his associate. His charade would help to soften the rough corners. Buckley merely winked at Sheridan and Sheridan nodded.

"Good luck, Jean." Sheridan patted the baby.

DeVelieu was still in the dark. "May the saints and Obeah keep you from harm," he replied in his lilting Creole accent.

—

Courtroom 403 was hoary with age. The red linoleum flooring was cracked and crumpled, and the mahogany veneer of the judge's bench was gouged and stained. Twelve vacant hard-backed chairs sat silent and forlorn in the jury enclosure. The vaulted room was solemn and dimly lit. The cracked plaster walls were painted a grimy municipal green. No peach marble floors, red-wood rails, or fluted walnut bookcases graced this gloomy sep-ulchre of justice.

There to meet Sheridan was Shirley Grant, the assistant DA. Already she had her brief and papers spread out on the counsel table. She was young, perhaps late twenties. Not bad-looking, Sheridan thought. Her dress was corporate gray. She turned and nodded, no smile, and eyed Sheridan as if he were a heralded gunslinger. Nothing like bringing down Johnny Ringo.

Sheridan flashed a broad smile and extended his hand.

"Miss Grant, nice to see you again." She eyed him curiously. He was going to add how attractive she looked, but he could see the prosecutor was loaded for bear. Shirley Grant wasn't Irish; she was mainline WASP. And Gaelic flattery, however sincere, would get him nowhere. It might even get him a kick in the balls.

"Can't we settle this thing, Miss—mind if I call you Shirley?"

"No way!" she snapped. Her eyes narrowed in a "take no prisoners" glare. "Your Yuppie client caused this poor girl irreparable harm. She'll never bear a child, never feel the warmth of her child's hand, never see her daughter trotting across the . floor, leaping into her arms and saying, 'Hi, Mom!' "

For a moment, Sheridan glanced toward the jury rail, hoping Shirley Grant would pick up his subtle "play that for the jury" look. She didn't.

"And psychologically, she's damaged for life. Here." Shirley Grant sifted through some papers on the counsel desk. "This is her psychiatrist's report. She's a basket case; she'll probably never graduate from high school."

Cut the bullshit! Sheridan felt like saying. Your victim's a teenage whore; she's a druggie. She was flunking out of school even before the Ellison encounter. But he kept that to himself. This was not a case to try. This was a case to plea-bargain. He said nothing and counted to six.

"Okay." He sighed. "I'd like to save the Commonwealth a lot of expense and time. I know that I've got a tough case, and you're a top-notch adversary, Shirley. I've checked around."

A slight smile crept into the corners of Shirley Grant's lips.

"But, of course, it's your girl's word against my client's," Sheridan said gently. "My client has no record, not even a parking ticket."

"What do you have in mind?" she said.

●

Sheridan met Sheldon Cohen, the Martinez family's lawyer, out in the corridor, by the water fountain.

He came right to the point. "Sheldon, Shirley Grant might

be willing to entertain a reduced charge, providing we can work things out."

Sheldon Cohen, short, curly black hair, Tom Dewey mustache, bent down to the water fountain and pretended to drink.

"Mr. Martinez wants five hundred thousand dollars."

He looked up at Sheridan, birdlike, his hand still on the bubbler nozzle.

"Sheldon"—Sheridan's voice was controlled—"if I have to try this case, win or lose, even if my kid goes away, I'll make a damn good fee. You'll wind up with nothing. We have to finalize this now or never. Say I get you sixty thou. You get twenty; your client gets forty—nontaxable. More money than Martinez will see in a lifetime."

"I'm incensed!" Cohen bolted upright from the water fountain. "You're a racist, Sheridan, and you're playing a racist card!" He bent down and pretended to take another drink at the bubbler. Again he looked up at Sheridan. "Make it a hundred and we got a deal."

Sheridan nodded. It took some doing. Buckley would probably walk DeVelieu because of a pinch on his baby's bottom. Sheridan would walk Ellison for a hundred thousand. He'd later tell Judy that it was an expensive piece of ass.

———

At first, the prosecutor wanted no deal less than indecent assault, a felony conviction with six months' jail time and two years' probation. Sheridan insisted on simple assault, a misdemeanor, stating that with a felony conviction, his client would be unable to join the Marine Corps. When the plea bargaining seemed on the verge of collapse, Sheldon Cohen, sensing the $100,000, together with his fee, was in danger of evaporating, promptly joined the negotiations.

"Look," he said to the assistant district attorney, "my client stands to lose a hundred grand if this Ellison kid is sent away. Sheridan and I have an agreement contingent on scaling this down to a misdemeanor."

"I'm not interested in your agreement," Shirley Grant said curtly. "I'm here to prosecute this defendant for raping a minor.

If we have to try this case, I'm going to have eight or nine blacks on the jury. They're not going to cater to a privileged preppy by the name of Todd Thayer Ellison—the Third, no less!"

"Listen"—Cohen's voice rose an octave—"my client goes along with a misdemeanor, my client's father goes along, and I go along. And when you come right down to it, my girl has a helluva background. It could get messy. There were no blood tests fingering the Ellison kid as the father. And she may develop some memory loss, like she can't identify the defendant."

"That would be obstruction of justice!" The prosecutor's voice still snarled, but with a hint of resignation.

"You're damned right!" Cohen bristled. "Justice is a hundred grand in my client's pocket, and you're the one who's obstructing it!"

"And don't forget the Marine Corps," Sheridan interjected.

Finally, after a few calls to her superior, the prosecutor agreed, wearied from the barrage and not entirely sure that her teenage complainant could hack it on the witness stand.

"And what is it with the Marine Corps?" Grant's snappish voice now had a tinge of humor. "There must be a war on that I don't know about. You're the fifth attorney this month who's said that his kid was headed for Parris Island."

—

Sheridan was seated in the courthouse coffee shop, scribbling a few last-minute corrections on a trial brief, when a bookish-looking young man toting a briefcase approached his table.

"Mr. Sheridan," he said diffidently, "mind if I sit down? My name is Ted Marden. You left a message for me. I'm with MacAllister, Choate & Pierce."

"Oh, yes, please sit down. Like a cup of coffee?"

"No thanks. I happened to be in Judge Davis's session—I'm the next case out—and I watched your presentation. Got to hand it to you—rape scaled down to copping a feel. Like to borrow that legal wand of yours."

"Oh, there's a lot more to it," Sheridan said. "If we didn't have plea bargaining, the criminal justice system would collapse.

Case dockets would be jammed. There are only so many trial judges to go around."

Sheridan took another sip of coffee. He knew that Marden was Dr. Sexton's psychiatric patient and had been in attendance when Donna DiTullio jumped. He'd work into it slowly.

"What kind of case do you have, Ted?" He'd again try the first-name tack.

"Oh, it's a restraining order. We represent Northeast Fisheries Corporation on a breach of contract with a Canadian conglomerate. Seems the Canadians have three tugs in Boston Harbor, and we're seeking injunctive relief, preventing them from sailing. It's sort of complicated."

"Sounds like something I'd shy away from. Bet there's a lot of law involved."

"There is. International treaties and that sort of stuff. But the meter's running, as old man MacAllister likes to say. I must have ninety thousand dollars' worth of billable hours right here." Marden patted his shiny grained leather briefcase.

"I envy you guys with the big fees," Sheridan said.

"Sometimes I envy you, Mr. Sheridan. I mean, your type of practice. My firm runs me ragged. I'm a junior partner, really—they bill me out at three hundred and fifty an hour and pay me a fraction of what I bill. Several months ago, I was working twenty-hour days seven days a week, flying all over the country, living out of a suitcase. I had a complete breakdown."

"I know," Sheridan said, sensing an opening.

"You know?"

"That's why I put in a call to you, Ted. I represent Donna DiTullio."

Suddenly, Marden seemed to stiffen. "How did you get my name?" he asked guardedly.

"I understand you and Janet Phillips, the Channel Three girl, were in a group therapy session some hour or so before Donna DiTullio jumped." Sheridan sidestepped a direct answer.

"I'm not so sure I should be talking to you." Marden's early affability suddenly vanished. "Obviously, you intend to sue everyone in sight—you guys usually do."

"No, just St. Anne's and the members of the staff who were in attendance. And, like you, I'm duty-bound to investigate—see every witness and get every scrap of evidence that's relative to my case. I already have a call in to Phillips. She's agreed to see me."

"Well, what do you want from me? I'm not so sure I can help you. . . ." Marden was still defensive.

"I've already seen a psychiatrist who says it was gross negligence to hold a group therapy session up there at the Atrium, especially when three weeks before, my client had tried to do herself in."

Ted Marden was still on guard. "Look, I don't want to get involved. My law firm isn't going to appreciate this one bit. There are subtle ways they can get rid of someone. I know of a few cases."

"I can't make any guarantees, Ted, but for the present, everything will be confidential. What I'd like to know is what was said at the group meeting."

"How is Donna DiTullio doing?" Marden's voice softened.

"Not good. She's in a coma. She may not make it."

Marden shook his head. "I guess it would be a blessing," he said. His eyes misted. "I don't think I can help you too much, Mr. Sheridan."

"Call me Dan. That's okay. Just give me a rundown of what went on for the fifty minutes before the break—who said what, who went where, what you observed, how Donna DiTullio reacted. Any red flags that she was upset and might jump?"

"Well, let me give it to you as best I can," Marden began slowly.

Dan listened—no notes. But the content of what Marden related would be instantly recorded as soon as their meeting was over.

The gist was that no one suspected that the DiTullio girl would jump. The session was an open discussion of each patient's suicidal ideation. There wasn't a hint that Donna would self-destruct.

"Okay, Ted, I'm sorry to have troubled you. I hope your motion for injunctive relief is acted upon favorably."

"Listen, Dan." Marden's voice suddenly lowered. "Maybe I can help you. Maybe you can help me.

"I've busted my ass for three years. MacAllister, Choate & Pierce are paying me peanuts, dangling the carrot of partnership to keep me running. Every case I get on my own—no matter if I just write a will—I have to kick the entire fee into the firm. . . ."

"How can I be of assistance?" It was Sheridan's turn to be guarded.

"I have an automobile accident case. You handle auto cases, Mr. Sheridan?"

"Never saw an auto case I didn't like," Dan paraphrased Will Rogers.

"Well, my aunt Alice got whacked by an eight-wheeler on the Mass Pike. There's plenty of insurance coverage. She's at Mass General with a fractured hip, five broken ribs, a ruptured spleen, and a subdural hemorrhage. Good injuries, as you guys would say. Been there over a month. She's a schoolteacher. The truck driver was drunk. The way I figure it, with punitive damages, it could go for a million, even a million and a half."

Sheridan shook his head. "Is she going to make it?"

"Aunt Alice will make it," Marden said. "She's a crusty old broad, a real complainer. That was even before her injuries. What I'm trying to say is . . . would you take the case on, Mr. Sheridan?"

To Sheridan, it was a windfall, a lawyer's dream.

"Certainly," Dan said. "We'll get cracking on it. Send over your file."

"I'd rather hand-deliver it. Don't want the firm to know I'm involved." Marden permitted himself a small smile. "Can we split the fee fifty-fifty?"

"Sure," Sheridan said. They shook hands. "Fifty-fifty."

"And when the case is settled, send the referral fee to my home in Brookline."

Sheridan could almost lip-synch the next line.

"I don't want to trouble the partners," Marden said.

Sheridan watched young Marden depart. He stuffed his brief into his battered trial bag. A soft smile played around his face. It had been a pretty good day.

5

Sheridan wasn't a proper Bostonian; he was too much of a rebel to fit the mold. But he did love the city. Not a place he preferred in winter, when the streets were mired with gray slush and trees looked bare and arthritic. Yet on a bright summer day, with the scent of the sea in the air, there was no place he'd rather be.

Sometimes he'd walk from his office to take in a late-afternoon game at the Red Sox's turn-of-the-century bandbox, known as Fenway Park. Even strolling through the Common was an adventure of sorts. He'd stop to listen to some sidewalk orator, dodge skateboarders and people on Rollerblades, watch buskers and three-card monte players, vying to separate tourists from their dollars.

On the picturesque arched bridge in the Public Garden, he'd pause to watch the swan boats, which were crowded with children doing lazy eights in the willow-laced lagoon.

He loved the animated bustle of Boylston Street, and he enjoyed checking out the young models as they browsed in tony boutiques in Back Bay.

But it was the architectural jumble of Boston that intrigued him most—the downtown, with its five-star hotels and gleaming skyscrapers, interspaced with the Boston of another age, a nineteenth-century town of red brick, gas lamps, and cobblestone streets. On a foggy evening, you could almost expect to see a horse-drawn carriage.

As he headed up Beacon Street en route to his meeting with Sheila O'Brien at an outdoor café just off Louisburg Square, he thought of his grandfather Eamon, who had crossed the Atlantic along with thirty thousand other Irish immigrants, many of whom were later crammed into ugly row houses at the bottom of the wrong side of Beacon Hill.

"We were stable boys and hod carriers for the Brahmins—when they'd give us a job, that is," his grandfather would ruminate. And Sheridan knew the history, how James Michael Curley masterfully cobbled the Irish into a political force, finally ousting the Cabots and Lodges from City Hall.

"Vote early and often," Curley would exhort his constituency. And more than a few votes were conjured up from the grave.

Sheridan met Sheila a little after five and they were escorted to a landscaped cloister in a garden where it was claimed that Nathaniel Hawthorne, Louisa May Alcott, Daniel Webster, and John F. Kennedy had often dined over the years. Sheila, a former FBI agent and Fordham Law grad, was prepping for the Massachusetts Bar exam and serving her apprenticeship with a high-profile State Street law firm.

"What's happening over at Dewey, Screwum & Howe?" Sheridan peered over his menu at his companion. She pushed a strand of sandy blond hair back from her forehead and suppressed a laugh. But her china blue eyes smiled, crinkling at the corners.

Sheridan knew Sheila O'Brien was too good to be true—creamy skin, a young thirty, perky face and personality. As young Buckley described her, she had the face of an angel and a body like mortal sin. Despite the disparity in age, Judy Corwin was all for the arrangement. Sheila had taken Dan out of his moodiness and away from his one-night stands. Five years earlier, he had lost his wife and only child, an eight-year-old son, in an automobile accident. He was devastated and became emotionally aloof, fearful of any continuing involvement. Then Sheila O'Brien came onto the scene. For Dan Sheridan, she was a lifesaver. Judy had been with Dan since he first hung out his shingle fifteen years ago and had stuck with him during the hard times following the death of his family. She'd been witness to a driven, take-no-prisoners Dan Sheridan, a man with an obsession to win at all costs—whether it be handball, the law, or poker. Not that Dan would ever relent, but even young Buckley knew that as of late, Sheridan was mellowing. He had even let Buckley win a few hands.

And sitting opposite him was the reason for it all: Sheila O'Brien.

But Judy Corwin knew that Dan was vulnerable. If Sheila suddenly walked—Judy had the Jewish-mother instinct—tough Dan Sheridan would crumple like a house built of matchwood.

Right now, as Sheila parried his mild obscenity, Sheridan was secure, controlled. Just as she was about to reply, she fingered her engagement ring. It was Sheridan's ultimate hedge against rejection.

"Good news, Dan. The senior partner, Mr. Cranston, had me in the office today, offered me a junior partnership at—would you believe this?—seventy-five to start?"

"Hundred?" Dan picked up the menu and studied it.

"Thousand, Dan, thousand."

"You said you'd think it over." Dan's eyes remained glued to the menu.

"Sure." She reached over and pulled Dan's menu down. "I'm waiting for a better offer."

Sheridan sidestepped, clicking his fingers at a passing waiter. "This is a classy place, Sheila. Even the hamburgers have French names."

The black-tuxedoed waiter nodded, then scribbled the order on a small pad. "*Deux boeuf haché and deux Bud Lights*," he repeated in a fractured South Boston Irish version of French.

Dan and Sheila held hands for a long moment.

"Had a pretty good day today, Sheila. We walked Ellison and DeVelieu."

Sheila smiled and shook her head. "Now we can afford that June wedding." She held up her hand, spread her fingers, and studied her diamond.

Sheridan brushed some imaginary bread crumbs from the table. "Sheila, we walked them. I didn't say we got paid. But seriously . . ."

Sheridan knew he had booted it. The word *seriously*—it was uttered beyond recall. There were several seconds of silence. He rushed into the breach.

"Got a new case—malpractice. Your guys over at Roper, Cranston, Peabody & Weld will probably end up defending it."

"Oh?" Sheila covered up Sheridan's lapse. "Against Mass General or Beth Israel?"

"No, against St. Anne's."

"St. Anne's. That's Mr. Finnerty's account."

"I know. I've already dictated the complaint. I'm serving the hospital, members of the staff, and of course the cardinal. It's going to be kind of sticky. I may wind up being excommunicated." He gave a slight chuckle.

"Do you think . . ." Sheila looked at him.

"No, don't quit yet. If your firm gets the case, and I think they will . . . well, you know."

Sheila said nothing. Any iota of impropriety—even if unfounded—would be suspect. Conflict of interest, the bane of any law firm—of any legal practitioner. And the bar overseers hovered like scavenging vultures. If Finnerty's firm took the case, she would have to resign. She was perturbed. She'd worked so hard to get where she was. For the next several moments, neither spoke. They nibbled at their burgers and sipped their beers. But the silence was disquieting. Dan sensed that Sheila was upset.

Suddenly, she brightened.

"We all set for tomorrow night?"

"Tomorrow night?" Dan was about to take a healthy bite from his hamburger, but his hand stopped just short of his mouth.

"The Andrew Lloyd Webber show. I sold my soul for those tickets."

"Oh." Sheridan tried to manufacture some nonchalance. Somehow, he knew that his great day was coming to a frayed end. "My aunt—you remember Aunt Ginny—has this great friend, a little old nun, Sister of Charity. . . . I gave the tickets away." He bit into his burger. He didn't lie easily, especially to Sheila O'Brien.

Sheila said nothing. She took a long drag on her Bud, then smiled pleasantly and nodded her head. But somehow her eyes were not smiling, and Sheridan knew he had struck out twice in a matter of minutes.

"Wow, that was quick." Sheridan addressed Judy Corwin and young Buckley in their small conference room. "We filed suit against St. Anne's only three days ago, and *bang*—back comes their lawyer's answer!"

"The old gobbledygook—seeking sanctions for a frivolous lawsuit, and of course a motion to dismiss under Civil Rule Eleven, that we had no legal or medical basis for bringing a case." Judy Corwin's hand drew a circle above her head.

For a few moments, Sheridan studied the legal pleadings. "Kind of interesting," he said. "This is a new defense law firm, Finnerty & Associates. The letterhead lists Charlie Finnerty, his daughter Mary Devaney, and—what do you know—our old friend, the ex-DA, Mayan d'Ortega."

"Isn't Finnerty the guy who's a partner in Sheila's law firm?"

"The same," Sheridan said. "You know, I can almost see what happened. Finnerty's close to Monsignor Devlin, the cardinal's right-hand man. Finnerty thought he wasn't getting his fair slice of the pie, so . . ."

"He went south and took the cardinal's account with him," said Buckley.

Sheridan felt a wave of relief. If Finnerty had jumped ship from Sheila's firm, she wouldn't have to resign. He hadn't wanted to contemplate the long-term effect if she'd had to leave her job

because of his case. But one day, eventually, they'd be on opposing sides of the fence. Would he be willing to step aside in
her favor? He didn't know.

"Sounds like we've got our work cut out," Sheridan said.
"Finnerty's hit us with a hundred and thirty interrogatories, notices to produce documents, set up depositions for everyone and
his uncle. The meter is running—billable hours. These guys
know how to milk it."

"What else is new?" Judy Corwin said as she gathered up
the documents. "Time to play the paper chase. Want me to fire
back—let's see . . . one hundred thirty interrogatories per defendant? That's five hundred and twenty interrogatories. I'll get them
out of the form book. It'll keep them at bay for a while."

"No," Sheridan said. "The fewer pleadings, the better. Hitting the other side with a paper blizzard only serves to educate
them. Makes their attorneys overprepare. Right now, I've got to
gather as much information as I can sub rosa."

"Dan," Buckley said, "we don't handle that many civil
cases, but one thing I know. We gotta fight these guys at their
own game. Paper, paper, paper! Whack, whack, whack! It's like
duck hunting. You gotta work a lotta blinds to bring down a single
mallard."

"Maybe, maybe not. Right now, we've got to get as much
dope as we can on Sexton, Puzon, and Lafollette. Even where
they went to grammar school."

Buckley shook his head. Something was gnawing at Sheridan; he couldn't put his finger on it.

"You want us to check out the cardinal?" He looked at
Sheridan. "He might have been selling indulgences or something."

Sheridan sidestepped the remark.

"Assad," he said. "Karen Assad. She was Donna DiTullio's
night nurse. It will take forever to get the hospital record. We
have to run the whole probate court gamut—and then what?"

"The record'll be pristine," Corwin interjected, "tailored to
perfection."

"You think you can handle it, Tommy?"

"You mean the angel in white?"

Sheridan nodded.

"Piece of cake. Obviously Lebanese, olive-skinned, probably got beautiful tits like a stack of dimes."

"I'll leave you two middle-aged perverts to yourselves." Judy Corwin scooped up the papers and started to depart in a pretended huff.

"And, by the way," she said, looking back over her shoulder, "Monsieur Jean DeVelieu telephoned about our bill for twenty thousand dollars. Says he's penniless. He gave his address— someplace in Port-au-Prince."

Sheridan said nothing until Judy had departed.

"You should have collected DeVelieu's retainer up front, Tom. We'll never get paid, you know that."

"For chrissakes, Dan, what in hell's eating you? We'll be on every talk show going—TV, radio, you name it. The cases'll come rolling in. We can pick and choose."

"Nothing's eating me!" Sheridan barked.

"Okay, okay." Buckley held up his hands defensively. "Nurse Assad, you say. You want she should tell me DiTullio was scared of heights, that she put it in the record?" He jotted the name on a piece of paper.

—

Later, Buckley talked to Judy.

"What's with Dan?" he said. "We walk two guys in one day—it should be cabaret time. Not the Ritz, mind you, but hell, some waterfront dive."

Judy shook her head. "It might be Sheila," she said. "I've noticed a change in Dan in the last few days."

"Yeah. Sheila's what—twenty-nine, thirty? And Dan's edging the midway marker. Can be a crazy time."

"Tommy, there's a pretty good saying, and it applies to you and Dan. 'Love is the only game at which two can play and both can win.'"

"What's that, Judy, an old Yiddish proverb?"

"Try Eva Gabor, circa 1985."

—

Buckley checked the current nurses register but found no Karen Assad. No listing in the telephone directory. He called information, but there wasn't even an unlisted number. He knew Assad had been Donna DiTullio's night nurse. He'd try the old frontal attack. He didn't want to do it, especially at the psychiatric ward, but he'd try her at the hospital.

It was 10:00 P.M. He hailed a cab, directed the driver to St. Anne's, and, as he sat in the backseat, mulled over how he was going to get to Karen Assad. Obviously, when the suit was commenced, the red flags were up. Everyone would assume a defensive posture. The law prohibited contact with the defendants, who were represented by attorneys. But nursing personnel, those who were not named in the lawsuit, were fair game. Any attorney would be remiss in not conducting such an interrogation.

The psychiatric ward was now located on the ground floor, next to Radiology. Buckley walked across the pink granite floor, noticing that the waterfall gurgled over volcanic rock and the tropical flora dipped exotically, like in some Polynesian Eden.

The nurses in white tunics seemed to move at an easy pace, unlike the frenzied bustle of neighboring hospitals. Buckley looked up. The scaffolding he had seen in Sheridan's photographs had disappeared, and the entire foyer, reaching to several stories, had a tinted-glass effect. He wouldn't mind spending a few days here, providing the sickness wasn't too serious. Come to think of it, his back was kicking up. Maybe an MRI would be in order. He filed that thought in the recesses of his mind and returned to the business at hand.

The hallway to the psychiatric department was carpeted in light green—the nonskid variety. He checked the receptionist. Sheridan had said that she was black, pleasant, could be helpful. But this one was old-time Caucasian and looked all business as she ripped away at a computer.

"Excuse me, Mrs. . . ."

She lowered her granny glasses and peered up at Buckley.

She appeared to be in her late fifties and had a head of hair like a scouring pad. She didn't look too pleasant.

"You're going to have to sign the register," she said curtly, pointing to a book on the counter.

Buckley nodded and scrawled an imaginary name.

"Visiting hours are over. They're two to four, seven to nine." She kept drilling away at the computer. "No exceptions unless you're family."

"No, I'm here to see Karen Assad." Buckley gave a polite smile.

"She won't be in until eleven. That's fifteen minutes from now." She looked up from the computer and reached for the registration book.

"You a personal friend"—she studied the signature—"Mr. Law?"

"Look, Mrs. . . ."

"Slater. And it's Miss."

Buckley suppressed a yawn.

"I'm a reporter for the *Globe*, trying to do a piece on mental patients. Want to get down to the nitty-gritty—people like you and the nurses—the people in the trenches. It's a tough game, believe me. *You* people do a tremendous job."

Receptionist Slater suddenly lost her glacial front. She gave Buckley a demure "get my name right" kind of smile.

"The name's Miriam Slater." She pronounced it slowly. "Been here since St. Anne's opened—that's going on seven years.

"Look, Karen will be here in ten minutes or so, but she'll be really busy. Change of shift, you know. She'll have to review the charts, make the midnight rounds. In fact, some of these loonies"—the demure smile broadened—"have to be checked every fifteen minutes. Why don't you go down to the caf? Karen generally goes down for a break at twelve-thirty. I'll see that she gets the message. You got a card, Mr. Law?"

It was almost 12:45 A.M. Buckley had done the *USA Today* cross-word, plotted a few horses in the racing form, and downed his fourth cup of coffee. Except for several nurses in faded green denims a few tables away and a janitor swabbing the floor, the caf was deserted.

Buckley was about to abandon his quest when he spotted a tall, rather attractive woman in a white jumpsuit who was getting a cup of coffee at the counter. He pulled out a notebook from his breast pocket and jiggled it above his head. It worked. She nodded.

Buckley assessed his position. This was a key witness. He could get into a peck of trouble giving her the media line. It could boomerang during the trial. He could envision the defense lawyer playing the fabrication for all it was worth in front of the jury.

"Hello." She smiled. "Are you the reporter from the *Globe*?"

"Yes." Buckley rose. "Mr. DiTullio said you were Donna's night nurse. Couldn't praise you enough. Said you were a lovely lady."

He scraped a chair back from the plastic table.

"Mind if I ask a few questions?"

"You're doing a human-interest story, right?" She hesitated, avoided sitting down. "Miss Slater said you'd be here." She gave him a polite smile.

Buckley sighed audibly. He furrowed his brow in a manu-factured look of concern. He looked into her hazel eyes.

"I'm not a reporter," he said slowly. "Can I level with you?"

She returned his gaze. Her smile suddenly evaporated.

"Please do," she said, placing her coffee cup on the table and gripping the back of the chair with both hands.

"I'm Tom Buckley, Donna DiTullio's lawyer."

Karen's eyes narrowed, but she said nothing.

"Won't you please sit down, Miss Assad." Buckley motioned with his hand. "Look, I had to use that ruse with your reception-ist."

Might as well give it to her up front, he thought. But he knew the interview could collapse.

She remained standing.

"Look, Mr. Buckley, first of all, I don't like the way you scammed everyone to get me down here. Any discussion you have with me will have to be in the presence of St. Anne's lawyers." There was a peremptory edge to her voice.

Buckley nodded. This, he thought, is going to be a tough sell. This nurse had street smarts.

"I'm sorry," he said softly. "Only doing my job. I have a duty to get all the information I can in support of Donna's case, favorable or unfavorable. Only then can I assess whether she even has a case."

Karen Assad looked at him for a long moment. She cocked her head slightly, as if she heard a door closing far off.

"Okay," she said, "I have fifteen minutes."

Buckley quickly pulled her chair back farther and adjusted it as she sat down.

"I'm risking a lot just talking to you like this." Karen glanced over at a group of young interns who now occupied a far table.

"Karen"—Buckley dropped the "Miss Assad"—"I appreciate it. I'll be very brief."

"Will I be called as a witness?" She took a sip of coffee.

"I'm afraid so. Probably be called upon to give testimony by deposition."

She looked at him over her raised coffee cup. "Okay, question."

"Yes." Buckley cleared his throat. "During Donna's hospitalization, before she jumped, did she exhibit any thoughts, like she couldn't cope with it any longer—you know, suicidal ideation?"

"I talked to her every night, gave her nightly shots of Capricet. Of course, when she was first admitted, she was in rough shape. But she responded to medication and therapy—like no patient I had ever seen before. The last few days before she jumped, she was a model patient. Had a great sense of humor—even bubbly."

No time to cross-examine, thought Buckley. You get hit with an unfavorable response, you move on. Don't alienate.

"Uh, when you woke her up on the morning of her . . . er, tragedy, any inkling that she—"

"Not a bit. She took a shower. I was in her room, making up the bed. She was even singing."

"Any indication from the other nurses, the day nurses, that she was having problems?"

"I had to review her chart each night when I came on. Except for the first few days—she wasn't blueberry pie, mind you, but she was completely down-to-earth."

"This drug she was on, Capricet. What's your opinion as to how it affects patients?"

"Greatest medication since penicillin. Best antidepressant in our entire arsenal of pharmacopoeia. Better than Prozac."

"You know it's experimental—not FDA-approved."

"So?"

"Do you think it could have masked some deep-rooted problems, created a false sense of well-being? Maybe when Donna jumped, she thought she could fly."

Karen issued a short laugh and took another sip of coffee.

"Like Peter Pan?"

"Something like that."

"Look, I've got to go." She glanced at her wristwatch. "For Donna's sake, I wish you luck."

She got up from her chair and crinkled her coffee cup, then tossed it into a nearby bin.

Buckley rose almost automatically. Legally, the night was a flat zero. He wanted to ask her one last question—whether she or any medical personnel or doctor, including Sexton, Lafollette, and Puzon, even the interns and residents or other nurses, had any misgivings about holding group therapy sessions on the unguarded fifth floor of the Atrium. He studied Karen Assad. She had a trim, athletic figure. Middle East–attractive, mid-thirties.

"I know I kind of put you on the spot," he said. "I'm single."

She looked at him quizzically. It was an awkward remark. There was an uneasy silence.

"Can I see you again, Karen? Dinner, maybe? Forget the case."

Karen narrowed her eyes and fixed him with a steady gaze. "You trying to con me, Buckley?"

"Absolutely," he said. "You may even grow to like me."

They looked into each other's eyes. In that instant, there was an innate recognition. Both lacked guile.

———

Sheridan left his card with the receptionist at Channel 3. It was 10:00 A.M. He had watched the *Boston Today* show from the TV monitors. Now, as he waited for Janet Phillips, he leafed through *Entertainment Weekly*. After poring over *Rolling Stone*, *The New Yorker*, and the *Hollywood Reporter*, with several glances at his watch, he saw Janet Phillips approaching the reception area.

"I'm sorry," she said, "we had a staff meeting. It's Mr. Sheridan, isn't it?" She extended her hand. "You're here about the DiTullio woman." She primped her reddish Rhonda Fleming hair. "Mind if we sit down? Not exactly the Ritz." She had the scintillating, practiced air of a seasoned TV veteran.

They both sat on the sofa. It whooshed as they sank in.

"Yes, I'm Dan Sheridan," he began. "I represent Donna DiTullio. I'll be brief. I understand you were at a group therapy session with Dr. Sexton just before Donna jumped."

Unlike the young lawyer Ted Marden, she seemed relaxed, almost affable. She had a vibrancy about her, and she was attractive—a model's nose, green eyes, irises flecked with gold, and what seemed to be a perpetual TV-luminary smile.

"This is not a very comfortable environment," she said, glancing at the receptionist. "Do you want to do lunch?"

"Couldn't think of anything better," Sheridan said. "Can I pick you up, say in an hour? I know a little chowder and ale place on the way to the Cape. Great lobster salad."

She studied him for a few moments. She liked his rugged looks. Sometime in the past, his nose had been broken; it was kind of pug. She liked that, too. No wedding ring. She wasn't exactly crazy over lawyers, but this one seemed a little different.

"Pick me up here at the studio at twelve," she said. "I have to be back at four. Got a novelist coming in from Chicago for tomorrow's show. Have to read the first three chapters, some of the middle, and, of course, the ending. We don't overprepare," she added. "That's the beauty of the show. People laugh. Things go wrong. We wing it, mostly."

"In two hours." Sheridan glanced at his watch.

Boy, Sheridan thought to himself, what a charmer! Full of self-deprecation. But he sensed something—perhaps a whiff of danger. Maybe behind that perpetual "look at me" kind of smile lurked a super "what can you do for me" kind of ego.

6

"Where's the boss?" Young Buckley, in shirtsleeves, tie askew, had his hands propped behind his head, feet up on his desk. He made no attempt to assume a more professional demeanor as Judy Corwin tried to tidy up his desk.

"Got an interview with that TV gal—Janet Phillips," she said. "He just called on his car phone. He's headed to pick her up now. Said he wouldn't be back. Wants you to see Mrs. Gallagher. She's the megabucks lady whose nieces are trying to have her committed. Seems they got wind they're being aced out of her will."

"That's Emma Gallagher." A grin added another crease to Buckley's face. "We drafted the codicil. She's leaving everything to the Sisters of St. Joseph. What time she due in?"

"Two-thirty. And I'd straighten your tie and put your coat on. We do have some sort of dress code around here. And don't have your usual three Manhattans for lunch. This is an important client."

"I know, I know." Buckley sighed at the lecture and changed the subject.

"You know, I saw Karen Assad last night—real late. Caught her in the caf at St. Anne's well past midnight."

"I'm surprised. You'd think Finnerty and his legal minions would have gotten to her. She say anything incriminating?"

"Not yet. But I think she can be helpful. I gave her a call this morning. I'm taking her to the circus next week. Of course, her two kids are tagging along."

"The circus?" Corwin's eyes narrowed in mild disapproval. "You're not trying to do anything foolish?"

"Like get into her white pants suit?" Buckley's smile broadened into a rictus.

"Listen," she chided, "bad enough Dan has a date with Miss Celebrity—taking her down to some out-of-the-way lobster trap on the way to Cape Cod. Phillips comes across as Jeanne Crain, all sweet and proper. Little Miss Heartland."

"Back home in Indiana." Buckley snapped his fingers.

"No, try *State Fair* with Jeanne Crain, Dana Andrews, and Dick Haymes. Twentieth Century–Fox, 1945."

"How come you're so smart, Judy? You should have gone to law school."

Judy wanted to end the nonsensical banter before Buckley really got raunchy. "Seriously, Tommy, I think it's a mistake to romance a material witness. You're taking Assad and her brood to Barnum and Bailey; Dan shuttles Phillips to some seaside rendezvous. I think both interviews should have been handled by Raimondi or someone not even connected to our office. Things could backfire. And the bar overseers are just waiting for some shred of legal impropriety from this office."

Buckley knew that Corwin was right. She had an ancestral instinct, generated by centuries of distrust. But he genuinely liked Karen Assad. In that brief moment when they said good-bye, something in her eyes responded to his. And she was damned good-looking.

"I don't know about Phillips." Corwin furrowed her brow. "I'd hate to see her do a number on Dan. . . . Your case would go *pffft*." Her fingers sprang outward.

"Hey, Dan's too smart for that. And besides, Sheila's got his attention in that department." Buckley took his feet off the desk and straightened his tie.

Corwin read Buckley's subtle dismissal, but she had to get in the last midmorning zinger.

"Caitlin called in sick again," she said, referring to Buckley's secretary.

Buckley held his breath, puffed his cheeks, and blew out a tired sigh.

"Jesus, Judy, Caitlin plays me like a piano."

"You want me to dock her? She's five days over her sick leave."

Buckley gave a weary roll of his eyes. "No, but I'll be goddamned if I'll ever hire a friend of a friend's niece who lives on the beach and phones in sick every time the weather's in the nineties. And shoot a letter off to Port-au-Prince, certified mail. I'm afraid DeVelieu's stiffed us. Even Jimmy Carter couldn't collect our fee. But let's give it one last shot. The threat to go to the U.S. ambassador routine. Better still, tell him we'll stick some voodoo pins in the goddess of justice doll."

Corwin picked up some correspondence from Buckley's desk.

"Don't have any booze at lunch," she said, putting in the last word.

"Hey, Judy."

Corwin hesitated at Buckley's door.

"Did you hear the one about Jewish foreplay?"

"Three hours of begging," Judy quipped. She winked and closed Buckley's door with an audible click.

"Jesus," Buckley said to himself, "how in the world do you stump this broad?" He sighed again, a deep "why the hell do we have to have a Jewish mother controlling our lives" kind of sigh.

But he wanted to check something out. He scribbled it on his notepad: "State Fair: Jeanne Crain and Dana Andrews?"

●

Sheridan had shot back to his waterfront pad and changed into something a little more Cape Cod–ish: plaid scally cap, aviator sunglasses, Irish-knit sweater, white Polo jeans, and blue denim boat shoes. He drove up to the studio gate in his shiny red TR6 convertible and was ushered in by the security guard, who directed him to park in the visitor's lot.

Twenty minutes, then thirty minutes went by. He glanced at his watch—12:45. His fingers did a little dance on the steering wheel. He had left his briefcase back in his apartment. Couldn't do any work; simply had to wait.

At ten past one, he spotted Janet Phillips coming down the studio steps, dressed to the nines—lavender Armani suit, a splash of deep purple chiffon at her throat, white elbow-length gloves.

Sheridan was more than a little pissed. He didn't scramble out to open the passenger door; instead, he reached across from the driver's seat and pushed it open.

"I'm sorry," she said, her lips parted in a faint little-girl smile. Her green eyes shimmered like new sprouts on a ficus. "Next week, I'm doing a segment with Diane Sawyer. Had to run through the format. And Robert Dole is due on the show, too. . . . It's a crazy business."

Sheridan merely nodded.

"Oh, listen, Dan," she said, as if it were an afterthought. She pulled down the vanity mirror and applied some frosted lipstick. "I've made reservations for the Blue Room at the Ritz-Carlton."

Sheridan felt more than a little ridiculous.

"You think I can get into the Ritz in this outfit?" He flicked his thumbs toward his sweater. "Let me go back and put on a jacket and tie."

"Nonsense," she said, reaching over and clasping his wrist. "You'll be the one person they'll all notice. They'll mistake you for Dennis Connor, the yachtsman."

●

The Blue Room tinkled with good silver and smart conversation. A flaxen-haired woman picked at a harp and a pianist was playing something by Mendelssohn.

Bowing and smiling graciously, the tuxedoed maître d' didn't bat an eyelash at Sheridan's outfit. Then, strutting with velvet-backed menus, he led Phillips and Sheridan to a table overlooking the Public Garden. As he trailed along, Sheridan could almost hear the murmuring subside; even the music seemed to slide into a hesitant lull.

"May I check your chapeau, monsieur?"

"My what?" Sheridan asked.

The maître d' tapped his forehead.

"Oh." Sheridan whipped off his cap. "Er . . . no thanks. I'll keep it with me," he said, grimacing at his stupidity.

"Nice to see you again, mademoiselle," the maître d' said as he placed the menus decorously on the table and snapped his fingers silently. A waiter in scarlet waistcoat immediately appeared, together with the sommelier, medals dangling from his neck like citations on a French general. Phillips ordered a bottle of Montrachet.

"Oysters Rockefeller for starters," she told the waiter, then rattled off some Gallic names. No *boeuf haché* at the Ritz.

Sheridan glanced around. Bronzed and elegantly dressed patrons were looking at him, some whispering. They recognized Phillips. Sheridan could read their thoughts: Who in the world is that guy in the boating outfit?

Phillips was on display. Her eyes constantly darted left and right as she pretended to listen to Sheridan. She knew she was creating a stir; she loved it. She recognized Nattie Gabler, the *Boston Herald*'s society columnist, across the room. They both nodded in silent acknowledgment.

"You married, Mr. Sheridan?" A finger slowly rimmed her wineglass.

For a posturer like Phillips, Sheridan thought it was an odd opener. And yet he knew it was the age-old invitation, not even subtle. If he played his cards right, he would be in bed with Phillips before the weekend. Maybe during the weekend.

He hesitated a moment. Temptation passed through him like a sigh. Then it was gone.

"I'm engaged," he said as he broke off a piece of Syrian bread and passed the basket to Phillips.

"Oh." She greeted the news without a hint of surprise. "A

delayed vocation?" she added with a slight smile.

"You might call it that." Sheridan didn't offer any details. Phillips was smart enough not to inquire.

Between courses, Sheridan tried to work in DiTullio. But Phillips seemed to lose interest in Sheridan and his case. She drifted, as if something else was on her mind. The posturing and the nodding continued. She never asked how Donna DiTullio was doing.

Sheridan studied the bill, whistling to himself softly: $342 for lunch, including $172 for the wine. The Montrachet was good, but it wasn't that good.

"Tell me," he said as he picked out a credit card from his wallet, "was Donna DiTullio agitated during the group therapy session, any inkling that she wasn't quite with it?"

Phillips finally focused her eyes on his.

"Would it help your case if I said yes?"

"It would make the case," he replied. However, he sensed a change in her attitude. She no longer primped and beamed; her voice was pinched with displeasure.

"If her doctor was on notice that she might suddenly pull a dixie—well, you know, it was a hell of a place to put psychiatric patients—almost an invitation to jump."

Suddenly, the Jeanne Crain eyes hardened.

"You ever read Bill Styron, Mr. Sheridan?"

Somehow Sheridan knew that the "Dan" and the wrist patting were over.

"I read *Sophie's Choice*. Even saw the picture." He reached into the silver ice bucket and pulled up the Montrachet. "There's a little left," he said. "One for the road?"

She shook her head.

"William Styron is a gifted and talented writer," she said. "Won the Pulitzer prize for *The Confessions of Nat Turner* and the American Book Award for *Sophie's Choice*. One day in Paris, frustration caught up with him; the emotional walls came crashing down. He was lost, in a vise, couldn't cope. There was only one escape—suicide. He checked himself into a mental clinic. The only thing that brought him through was prolonged hospitalization and dedicated professionals like Dr. Sexton."

She delivered this with cutting rhetoric.

"I was as bad off as Styron. For me, there was no hope, no way out. I overdosed on Seconal. I wanted to end it—the pain was that unbearable. Even wrote a suicide note."

I'll bet it was sixty pages. Sheridan kept that to himself.

"You and your kind never build, never try to improve or create," she continued. "You're like jackals, feeding and living off the misery of others." Her eyes locked his with a dark intensity.

Sheridan felt like applauding. What an actress! But this is a hostile witness, he thought. What do you do with a hostile witness? Cut your losses and get the hell out. But he made the lawyer's classic mistake: one more question. At least he wasn't in front of a jury.

"You like Dr. Sexton quite a bit, don't you?" he said softly.

"You mean professionally?" Her voice was as cold as the ocean floor.

"Of course, professionally." Sheridan paused a few moments and beckoned the waiter, who hovered discreetly nearby.

He scribbled his name on the charge slip and left a healthy tip.

"Do you want to go home to your apartment, or shall I drop you off at the studio?" he asked.

She shook her head and stared at the collection of rings on her fingers.

"I've got to chat with Nattie Gabler." She smiled glassily. "Why don't you run along?"

Sheridan wanted to say something cutting. He counted to five.

"Okay." He put the credit card in his wallet and gathered up his scally cap. "Enjoyed meeting you, Ms. Phillips." He gave a short Boy Scout salute.

What a complete bust! he thought as he waited for his car to be brought up by the hotel valet. "You and your kind never build, never try to improve or create. You're like jackals, feeding and living off the misery of others." He tumbled it over in his mind. He hated to admit it, but there was more than a gram of truth in what Phillips had said, and there was no way he'd win her over. She'd try to bury him in front of a jury. At least he knew where he stood.

●

Janet Phillips had a phone delivered to her table. She punched out a familiar number.

"You say that Dr. Sexton is tied up with patients? This is Janet Phillips. . . . Yes, I'm fine, really, but have the doctor call me tonight at my home. He has the number. There's something important I think he should know."

7

"John," Sheridan said over the phone, "I don't think I can avoid getting your name into the DiTullio suit. I need your affidavit to ride out a motion to dismiss that the defense has marked up for next week. It kind of caught us by surprise."

Dr. John White was not ecstatic over the news.

"Do you have Sexton's notes and the psych records from St. Anne's?" he asked.

"I don't, John. Have to go into probate court for the psychiatric chart, and I can't get Sexton's notes until I summon him to a deposition. That's well down the line."

"Any indication that Donna DiTullio was agitated, apprehensive, said she wanted to end it all? And as a time frame I'm zeroing in on a day or two before she jumped, and preferably the subject morning."

"Haven't got a thing, John. We interviewed both patients who attended the therapy session the morning of the tragedy—a lawyer named Marden and that Channel Three girl, Janet Phillips—and came up *bubkes*. They both relate that DiTullio was upbeat, normal as any twenty-one-year-old New England tennis champ with an eye on Wimbledon."

"Not helpful, Dan. Without being able to review the psychiatric records and Sexton's notes, I would be giving an opinion without any foundation. The defense attorney will shoot my affidavit full of holes."

"Right now, that's the chance I have to take, John. If I don't, I might be out of court forever. I don't want to bore you with technical legalese. This is not a trial. By that time, I'll have taken everyone's deposition—Sexton, Puzon, Lafollette, all the interns, residents, psych nurses, even the candy stripers. But I've got to survive the defense motion to dismiss the suit. Just give me your expert opinion that it was negligence, per se, to take a psychiatric patient—who just three weeks prior had tried to kill herself—to an open, unguarded location five stories up. I have legal cases I can cite that buttress our position. All I have to do to defeat the defendant's Rule Eleven motion is produce some medical basis that I had before commencing suit. Your affidavit should do it. Then we get down to the nitty-gritty of discovery, depositions, interrogatories, the whole nine yards."

Sheridan sensed the doctor's reticence.

"John," he said, "I could discontinue the suit, but I still can't get the records without a court order, and I can't get at Sexton without being in front of the court. So if I discontinue and bring a new suit before the statute of limitations runs, I'm still in the same boat. Our legislature enacted a new law putting a cap of one hundred thousand dollars on malpractice cases, but it comes into effect in a couple of months and only applies to cases filed after that date. Fortunately, it doesn't affect my case. St. Anne's is only liable for one hundred thousand—a ridiculous sum euphemistically called *charitable immunity*. But as to Sexton and his crew, there's no cap, at least not now. But if I don't survive this motion, I'll never get another case started within the limited time I have left. And even if I did, they'd still hit me again with a motion to dismiss. I've got to ride this out and I need your expert opinion."

There were a few moments of hesitation.

"Okay." The doctor's voice softened into an annoyed form of agreement. "Fax me those law cases and a prepared opinion.

I'm not going to perjure myself, mind you. But if I think everything touches the psychiatric bases—"

"Thanks, John," Sheridan said, cutting him off. "And you know—"

"Yeah"—it was the doctor's turn to interrupt Sheridan—"I've got a pair of big ones . . . I know."

———

Dr. Robert Sexton got off at the thirty-fifth floor of the John Hancock Building and stood for a moment in front of the brushed steel portals leading to the law firm of Finnerty & Associates. He pushed on the gilded knob and the door opened as silently and effortlessly as the door of a bank vault.

"Good morning," he was greeted by the jaunty young receptionist, who seemed to have stepped out of *Vogue*. She was slim, smartly tailored—the type you would expect to see at a high-powered law firm.

"Please take a seat. Someone will be with you shortly." She beamed. "Would you like some coffee?"

Sexton sat down on the comfortable burgundy leather couch.

"No thank you," he said. He picked up a copy of *Business Week*, flipped through it briefly, then studied the surroundings. He had often visited Roper, Cranston, Peabody & Weld, mainly providing liaison with those propounding legislation exempting physicians and nurses from responsibility for negligence. Due to his efforts, they had been able to get the partial immunity bill through both legislative bodies, the House and Senate. The governor signed it into law.

Roper, Cranston was an old Yankee firm and had been in business for 135 years. Justice Oliver Wendell Holmes had apprenticed there. But the firm seemed to grow old as did the furniture; the partners appeared never to spend a dime on fixtures. The quarters were almost Spartan. Now he studied Finnerty's reception area—teak and cherry and brass, Winslow Homer prints strategically placed on the soft pecan paneling. Finnerty had spared no expense. The surroundings exuded confidence, power, and, to Sexton's trained eye, an unaffordable extravagance. He wondered if his uncle minded paying the freight.

Presently, a stunning amber-skinned woman appeared, statuesque, jet black shoulder-length hair, almost an Oriental visage. She wore a gray suit and a white shirt with lavender laces that matched her lavender shoes.

"Dr. Sexton?" She smiled easily. Her pencil-thin black eyebrows arched over hazel eyes.

"I'm Mayan d'Ortega." She greeted the doctor warmly. "Mr. Finnerty has assigned me to defend the DiTullio case. I'll be working with you and your staff quite closely over the next several weeks. Come in. I want you to meet Walter Crimmins, claims manager of Massachusetts Casualty and Indemnity Company. They insure you and St. Anne's."

If the reception area was any indication of what a blue-chip law office should look like, the interior—especially the conference room—was something out of *Architectural Digest*. Sexton was impressed. Glass-enclosed from floor to ceiling, it offered a sweeping view of Boston Harbor. The walnut conference table, a fifteen-foot oval, glistened with a high polish, reflecting the oyster-scrolled ceiling. Twenty plush swivel chairs were spaced around the table. Again, Sexton wondered if his uncle went along.

Greetings were cordial. Crimmins introduced Corey Webster, the insurance company's general counsel, and Mayan d'Ortega introduced Mary Devaney, who, Sexton knew, was Finnerty's daughter.

Mayan d'Ortega lost no time in getting down to the opening click of business, inviting them all to be seated.

"We may be able to knock Sheridan's suit out before it gets off the ground," she said. "We're arguing a motion to dismiss before Judge Barbara Mason." D'Ortega didn't mention it, but Sexton knew that Judge Mason was married to the chief of Surgery at Boston Memorial Hospital and that Dr. George Mason took a dim view of medical malpractice cases. In fact, Dr. Mason had helped Sexton draft the bill for the $100,000 cap.

"The forum looks favorable," d'Ortega continued. "Of course, Sheridan still has time left to refile his suit. If he lets that statutory time period go by, for all practical purposes, this case is history."

Sexton had heard of Mayan d'Ortega, former district attorney for Suffolk County. She had tangled with Sheridan before. He figured there was no love lost there.

"What are our chances?" he asked.

"I don't underestimate Dan Sheridan," d'Ortega said, permitting herself a small smile. "He's always thoroughly prepared. But this time, he may be a little off base. We're arguing that at the time he instituted suit, he had no reasonable medical basis for a claim that there was a deviation from a medical and psychiatric standard of care on the part of you, Dr. Sexton, and the staff at St. Anne's. I've read every case he cited in his brief. They all have one common theme. It's negligence to leave a suicidal patient unattended in a ward above the first floor. They all involve jumps and falls. But in each case, the patient exhibited continuing bizarre suicidal ideation. That's not our case at all."

Sexton liked d'Ortega's smooth no-nonsense delivery. And if the meter for billable hours was running, Crimmins, whose company was picking up the tab, didn't seem to mind. He appeared totally enthralled. She could have taken Crimmins around the block twice and he wouldn't have minded if she charged him four times.

D'Ortega gave them the downside. "They do have an ace. That's where you and Mr. Crimmins can be helpful."

"An ace?" Sexton looked at d'Ortega quizzically.

"Sheridan submitted an affidavit from a psychiatrist, Dr. John B. White, that buttresses the plaintiff's position."

Sexton was stunned for a moment. He steepled his fingers at his lips and looked first at d'Ortega and then at Crimmins.

"You know him, I take it," said d'Ortega.

"He's a colleague." Sexton shook his head. "I can't believe it. We've served on several committees together. He's chief of Psychiatry at Simmons Hospital, a private sanatorium. Also on the staff at the VA and at St. Margaret's in Fall River. That's a Catholic hospital."

"Why don't you take over from here, Walter?" Mayan

d'Ortega looked at claims manager Crimmins. Walter Crimmins, short, tan, had wispy white hair and the speck of a white mustache. He sat in a chair at the far end of the conference table, unconsciously adjusting his tortoiseshell glasses as he studied Dr. White's affidavit.

"Yes," he began, "White really has little factual basis to support his opinion, other than his belief that St. Anne's should not have been holding group therapy on the fifth floor of the Atrium. If it stopped there—under our present law, St. Anne's is responsible for only one hundred thousand dollars—a mere pittance. But if he tags you, Dr. Sexton, and the other staff members with malfeasance, the sky's the limit." Crimmins's eyes flipped toward the ceiling. "Ms. d'Ortega is arguing our Rule Eleven motion to dismiss. It'll be heard by Judge Barbara Mason. A fine judge, right, Corey?" He turned to the general counsel.

"Yes. Excellent reputation. And I think favorably inclined toward our philosophy. But it's a narrow issue. If the plaintiff's lawyer, Sheridan, had some rational belief that a case existed before he commenced suit, then he could possibly override our motion. The judge may feel constrained to go along."

Crimmins took off his glasses and held them up toward the east windows. A small smile played around his face as he pulled out his handkerchief and polished them with great ceremony.

"If we could back Dr. White off"—he lowered his voice— "get him to withdraw his affidavit . . ." He paused for several seconds, then tucked his handkerchief back into his breast pocket and replaced his glasses.

"How in the world are you going to do that?" Sexton stammered, feeling a little uneasy. "I can't—"

"Oh, we don't want you to have any contact with White." Crimmins's voice took on an authoritative tone. "Let us handle it." Crimmins looked over at Corey Webster, who nodded in approbation.

Mayan d'Ortega said nothing. She wasn't privy to such matters, nor did she care to be. But she had heard the rumors. If a local doctor testified against his own, he could suddenly lose staff privileges, or his malpractice policies would be canceled, effectively putting him out of business. After years of faithful service, a physician's record would be questioned by the hospital's board of trustees.

"Well, you guys prepare an airtight brief," Crimmins said as he started stuffing papers and documents into his cracked leather briefcase. "And, as Ms. d'Ortega so aptly put it, come Friday night, Sheridan's case may be history."

—

Sheridan studied the Massachusetts physicians directory. The bios on Sexton, Lafollette, and Puzon read like a who's who in the college of saints and cardinals. Awards, degrees, certifications, and medical publications went on for several pages. All three were doctors of medicine and had teaching affiliations, all were certified by the American Board of Psychiatry and Neurology, and all had graduated from college summa cum laude and from medical school with top honors. There wasn't a chink in their academic armor. And they were no ivory-tower theorists. All were practicing physicians day in, day out.

"Let's split up the assignments," Sheridan said to Raimondi and Buckley. "I'll take Sexton, start with his high school years at Gonzaga—that's one of those supersmart schools in mid-Manhattan, run by the Jesuits. Get hold of the yearbooks. That's a good starting point. I'll kick around New Haven. He graduated from Yale in '73. Then I'll cover Columbia Med."

"Don't you think it would be better to enlist a detective agency?" Buckley glanced at Raimondi for backup. "They know the territory, know where to press for leads, what buttons to push."

"I've thought of that, but you know, when we've done this in the past, especially with out-of-state firms, we get back a lot of gobbledygook at two hundred dollars an hour. Most of it's worthless. No, I think we've got to develop this ourselves."

"I was afraid of that." Buckley winked at Raimondi. "You get Manhattan and the country clubs. Manny and I have to draw straws for Topeka or Manila. Dan, tell me you're not serious about Manila," he said with a toothy grin.

"I'm afraid so. Puzon went to a primary school run by the Dominican nuns," Sheridan said as he calculated the geographics. "Didn't you enjoy a short stint with the Dominican sisters, Tommy?"

"Sure did. Sister Veronica used to keep me after class, eighth grade at Dominican Academy in South Boston. She was out to break her perpetual vows—and the first one was chastity."

"So you're really serious about this checking-up stuff. You know it'll cost a fortune. Ten days in Manila—what do you think, Manny?"

"Why don't Tommy and I go to Kansas? See if we can get someone at the Menninger Foundation to drop a dime on Lafollette. Although I doubt it. Word I have is that Menninger fought like hell to keep him, but the cardinal topped their salary. Probably gave him season tickets to the Bruins. He's a hockey nut, you know. Seems he treated several of the North Stars—they're crazy Canadians."

"Okay," Dan said, "let's put Lafollette and Puzon on the back burner. I'll hit the Big Apple. Know a couple of buddies who went to Fordham; that's run by the Jebbies. Maybe they can get me in a side door of Gonzaga. . . . And Tommy, what's the latest on Mrs. Gallagher?"

"She's a feisty old broad. I tried to tell her to leave her nieces a million apiece. Even sounded it out with their attorney, Sumner Katzman. He thought that was great. Two million to the nieces, ten million to the Sisters of St. Joseph—what could be fairer? The dogs are back in the kennel. Everyone wins.

"But no, she won't budge an inch. Absolutely detests her nieces, and of course their conniving husbands—who, incidentally, are lawyers. Bad year for lawyers, Dan."

"No year has treated the profession too kindly," Sheridan said.

"Well, here's how she wants it to go down," Buckley said. "She'll remember her nieces in her will all right. Get this, Dan, Manny, I think it's pretty good. At the reading of the will, it will say, 'I want to remember my nieces, Pamela and Constance. Hi there, Pammy and Connie!' "

Sheridan tried to suppress a smile. "Hey, better get her over to Dr. White. He'll do the necessary tests, say she's as sound as the dollar she isn't leaving them."

◆

Dr. John White checked his silver-blue Porsche with the valet at the Cape Cod Country Club just over the Sagamore Bridge. David Cabral, the administrator of St. Margaret's Hospital, had set up an appointment to go over next year's budget. Several members of the board of trustees would be present, also the president, Sister Gabrielle Bernadette.

White had heard that St. Margaret's, mainly an OB-GYN facility, was in fiscal trouble. It had served the community in and around Fall River, largely Portuguese, for seventy years; its staff doctors had delivered half of the present population. That was in the days of the six-child family. Now even the ethnic Portuguese were down to 1.4, church approval or no church approval. Too many unemployment lines, fishing trawlers tied up at rotting piers, and government regulations downsizing catches off the Grand Banks had caused the fiercely proud Portuguese Catholics to reassess their priorities. The result: St. Margaret's, a ninety-bed facility, had only a 40 percent occupancy rate. There were further cutbacks, Medicaid, Blue Cross. Even a heart attack victim had to be moved out in five days. Now there were empty beds and St. Margaret's operated on a deficit. What to do?

Dr. White paused for a few minutes before walking toward the clubhouse. The sun was dying somewhere toward the west and the clouds trailed lavender tendrils over Nantucket Sound. He thought for a moment. Despite vacancies at St. Margaret's, his twenty-bed psychiatric department was filled to capacity week in, week out. It was the only real moneymaker, and Medicare, Blue Cross, welfare, whatever, picked up the tab. He knew that it was politically unwise to disenfranchise the disenfranchised, especially the mentally disenfranchised. The board of trustees knew that, even Sister Gabrielle. In a smug, self-satisfied way, he was in the catbird seat. He was prepared to up the salaries of his assistants—maybe even his own.

David Cabral now was introducing the board of trustees, consisting of several prominent Fall River businessmen, two automobile dealers, a funeral director, and the dean of the Fall River Community College. He tendered an excuse from Sister Gabrielle. Seems she was engaged in other matters. They were assembled in a private room. There was light conversation. The Manhattans and martinis were served from a private bar.

The chateaubriand mixed well with the Château Rothschild, but White recognized that the group lacked its usual exuberance. Cabral droned on about some grim statistics. According to independent accountants, St. Margaret's was in dire straits. A $40 million fund-raiser was on the horizon, but Cabral wasn't too optimistic that it would fly in the hard-pressed Fall River community.

Cabral paused for several moments, underscored the profit-and-loss statement with his ballpoint pen, then pushed the document aside. He picked up his pen and studied the point, slowly turning it in his fingers as though he were examining a rare gem.

"John," he said guardedly, "it has been brought to our attention—and correct me if I'm wrong—that you're going to testify against a colleague and St. Anne's Hospital in a medical malpractice case."

The silence in the room for the next few moments was oppressive. White could feel the earlier camaraderie evaporating. He was seized with an instant anger, but he remained silent. He patted his lips with his linen napkin, said nothing for several seconds, then carefully replaced the linen next to the silver service.

"You're correct, David," he said. "I think a physician at times has to go to bat for an injured patient, even if it's against a colleague, as you say."

"We understand that your opinion is rather far-out, John," the funeral director said, "and has no real factual foundation."

"Oh?" White parried. "Psychiatric opinions tend to be that way."

"John"—Cabral cleared his throat—"we're asking you, the board is asking you, to withdraw your opinion. We don't want you to look foolish or get into trouble. You have a very good thing going for you here at St. Margaret's." Cabral nodded to the others for confirmation.

White eyed the group in sequence, returning to Cabral.

"Are you trying to threaten me?" he said, a hint of truculence in his voice.

"Now, John," the funeral director interjected, his voice now taking on a conciliatory tone, "we're only trying to help. Please listen to reason."

"No, you listen!" White's hand slashed the air. "No one's backing me off this DiTullio case. No one! I don't know who made the calls and I'd better not find out. Some *Fall River Times* reporters might be interested, maybe even the *Boston Globe*."

White rose. "Gentlemen, I think this meeting is adjourned."

●

Dr. Sexton dialed a familiar number on his private red phone.

"Hello, Janet. I got tied up yesterday. I do hope you're all right."

"I'm fine, Doctor. . . . Yes, the Capricet's doing wonders. Physically, mentally, I'm weller than well. I'm not calling for an appointment. Just that I have some information I thought you should have."

"What's that?"

"I had lunch with an adversary of yours—Dan Sheridan."

"The attorney?"

"The same. The one who's suing you, your staff, and the prince of the church."

"Maybe we should discuss this with my legal counsel, Mayan d'Ortega."

"I've got something better in mind. This Sheridan guy was going to take me to some out-of-the-way spot, ply me with liquor, and try to get me to fictionalize a scenario about DiTullio."

"I see," Sexton said after a few moments of silence. "You say he tried to get you to fictionalize . . ."

"Tried to get me to say that during the therapy session DiTullio was apprehensive, agitated, just waiting to jump."

"And . . ."

"I wouldn't go along, of course. I came to your defense in no uncertain language. Really pissed him off."

Sexton played something over in his mind. If Sheridan was trying to bag a witness, why not let him? He'd talk it over with Finnerty. Right at the moment, he was unsure of d'Ortega.

"Have you got another date with Sheridan?"

"We didn't part on the best of terms. The next contact I have with him will probably be by legal deposition." She gave a slight chuckle.

"When's your next appointment, Janet?"

"In three weeks."

"Why don't you come in after your show tomorrow? I'd like to check your blood levels, and you may be able to help us on this frivolous lawsuit. I'll send my driver to the studio to pick you up—say about eleven A.M."

"Fine, Doctor, looking forward to seeing you."

8

D an Sheridan arrived at the courthouse just as the bailiff
was unlocking the doors. Whether trying a case or arguing
a motion, he made it a point to be early. He'd schmooze
with court personnel, the clerks, other lawyers, always imparting
a friendly greeting, a word of advice, or listening patiently to some
underling's chronicle of domestic woe, or even jotting down a tip
on a horse. In between, he would try to get book on the presiding
judge——little stories or swatches of information that could determine or alter a stratagem.

"Johnny." He flashed a warm smile in the bailiff's direction.
"Clemens is starting for the Sox tonight against Seattle. Got a
couple of box seats I can't use. How would you and the missus
like to take in the game?" He reached into an inside jacket pocket
and pulled out two tickets.

The exchange was deft and quick. "Sure'n we'd love to,
Danny me boy. Have a feeling 'tis the year. We haven't won the
pennant since Billy Buckner booted that easy roller at first."

Bailiff Johnny Coyne swung the battered bronze doors open,
then kicked the door pegs into place.

"You guys did pretty good, Danny. Those were the first two

jailbirds this year who walked outta here on their own."

"Well, let's just say that justice prevailed—for a change."

"Whaddya got in here so early in the morning?" The bailiff checked his watch: 7:45.

"A motion before Judge Mason. Understand she's the governor's new appointment. Haven't been before her." He tossed it out matter-of-factly.

"For a bench rookie, she can be kinda testy. She's been on civil assignments for the past four months. Comes from some stuffy bluenose firm. The plaintiff bit the dust in the last five cases tried in front of her. You plaintiff or defendant, Danny?"

"Plaintiff. I represent the DiTullio girl, the one who jumped five stories at St. Anne's. Perhaps you heard about it?"

"Read about that in the papers. Seems to me it was a helluva place to leave a patient, especially one kind of bonkers."

"That's what I'm saying in my brief." Sheridan patted his trial bag. "Hope Mason agrees."

Sheridan mounted the worn marble stairs, then rode the tired, creaky elevator to the twelfth floor. The hallway was deserted. He resisted the temptation to study the racing form. There was a two-year-old he liked in the fifth at Suffolk named Canadian Sunset. Reminded him of the old Glenn Miller tune. Maybe he could check it out and get a bet down before post time.

Despite his years of trial experience and his knack for talking to jurors as if he was leaning over the back fence, Sheridan was always a little awed when entering the courtroom. It harked back to law school, to the ethic of Bellarmine, Jefferson, Cardozo. This morning was no exception. He pushed open the green leather-tufted doors with oval windows and made his way past the wooden spectators' benches, pausing for a moment at the jury rail. He patted it gently, like he'd tap the wrist of an old friend; then he momentarily glanced in at the rows of vacant jurors' chairs.

Courtroom 1206 had seen palmier days. The rust-colored linoleum was badly pitted. On the cracked plastered walls, portraits of turn-of-the-century jurists peered down with proper judicial disdain. But there was a grimy dignity to the place, and to

Sheridan it was the inner sanctum, the temple, and he felt a little shiver as he made his way to the counsel table.

Better check his citations for last-minute glitches, he thought. Also study d'Ortega's brief. She had distinguished each case he listed, and had added a few that were diametrically opposed.

He had read and reread each case, some for, some against. But he knew that the DiTullio case wouldn't hinge on points of law or past legal precedent. Right now, it was a narrow factual issue. Was Dr. White's opinion sufficient to justify commencing suit? There was no counteraffidavit filed by Sexton or others in an attempt to vitiate or water down White's position. It should hold up—all things being equal. But were all things equal? Would Judge Mason give him a fair shake? An appeal from an adverse ruling would get him nowhere. And the political environment, unfortunately, was anti-lawyer and antilitigation. He would have to demonstrate to the appeals court that Mason was clearly wrong, that she had made an egregious error of law. And he knew that the chances of tipping over a trial or motion judge were practically nonexistent. With time running out, he would have to win it or lose it in the present forum. He sat there for several minutes, trying to juggle his expectations against his limited options.

Judge Mason's law clerk suddenly appeared from a side entrance, carrying a stack of files. The clerk was a portly, moon-faced individual in a 1970s seersucker suit. He and Sheridan exchanged nods. Sheridan was unfamiliar with the clerk—probably another of the new appointments. He was about to get acquainted, fingering two more Red Sox tickets in his coat pocket, when he heard the whoosh of the back doors. He turned, and there was his old nemesis, Mayan d'Ortega. Neither smiled, just exchanged slight nods. The professional respect was there, but there would be no effusive greeting, no quipping, no war stories, no easy, unspoken camaraderie. D'Ortega was dressed in a sedate gray suit with black leather shoes that matched her jet black hair.

"Miss d'Ortega." He extended his hand. "So nice to see you again; it's been a long time."

She shook his hand with just the proper amount of professional firmness. "Not that long ago—maybe a year." The faint hint of a smile crept into her eyes.

Despite Sheridan's having blown out her indictment when she was prosecuting a capital case, and despite Sheridan's roguish reputation, d'Ortega found a quality of likability about him. But she quickly dismissed this train of thought. They were now adversaries. If d'Ortega lost, she'd return to fight another day. For Sheridan and his client, it would be a battle for survival. Tough odds.

Suddenly pushing through the rear door, accompanied by lawyer Charles Finnerty, was Dr. Robert Sexton. With them were Dr. Connie Puzon, Dr. Pierre Lafollette, and Monsignor Devlin.

"Son of a bitch!" Sheridan swore to himself. He had heard that Judge Mason's husband was closely allied with Sexton. He had toyed with the idea of requesting that the judge recuse herself. But he was playing a hunch that she'd lean over backward to be fair. However, now he was not so sure. He wondered if he wasn't getting bagged.

"Boy," he said to d'Ortega while he watched the entourage being seated. "You really need all those props? It's only a motion."

She threw him a dismissive look, then proceeded to shuffle through some documents on her counsel table. Sheridan knew the courteous parrying was over.

"All rise," intoned the clerk as Barbara Mason, sporting a springy blond hairdo, walked in with proper black-robed dignity and ascended the bench.

As Sheridan stood at the counsels' table, a rivulet of acid crept toward his stomach ulcer. He glanced over his shoulder at Sexton, Monsignor Devlin, and the others. Then it hit him quickly—instant anger. He was an attorney. He had to protect someone who couldn't fend for herself, a woman completely powerless, a cipher, an absolute zero. He suddenly detested his adversaries, even d'Ortega. A battle to the death had begun.

The judge studied some papers for several moments, then looked down at Sheridan and d'Ortega.

"Good morning," she said equably. "I've read your respective briefs and, of course, Dr. White's affidavit. I'll now hear arguments. Miss d'Ortega, I believe it's your motion to dismiss. I'll hear from you first."

"Thank you, Your Honor." D'Ortega rose, then paused for several seconds.

"This is an extremely important motion and my clients are here, as you undoubtedly know." She gestured toward the rear benches. "They are deeply concerned with what transpires here today.

"First of all, Dr. White's opinion is a mere conclusion without any factual foundation. He has not studied any hospital records, medical notes, or the nurses' charts. He knows absolutely nothing about Donna DiTullio's *medical* and *psychiatric* assessment during her stay at St. Anne's Hospital. . . ."

"Excuse me." Sheridan bolted upright. "I never interrupt another lawyer during argument—"

"Well, you're interrupting now!" d'Ortega said, cutting him off with a withering glance. "Please, you'll have your chance. Let me finish. . . ."

"Well, Judge, I want my sister to address the issue. Parading her clients in here and telling the Court they're concerned is a blatant attempt to prejudice the Court. . . . Sure, they're concerned about the lawsuit. Too bad they're not concerned about poor Donna DiTullio. Maybe I should have wheeled her in here and—"

"Mr. Sheridan!" Judge Mason banged her gavel. "I think you're out of order! I can see. I can hear. You will sit down and remain seated and will not interrupt or address the Court until requested!" She raised her gavel again. "Is that clear?" She added the proper judicial scowl.

Sexton and his colleagues, even d'Ortega, thought that Sheridan had blown it. The judge was pissed. D'Ortega read it in the hiss of her anger.

But Sheridan knew what he was doing. At least he thought

he did. He knew the judge would register the anger in *his* voice, the intensity of his demeanor, his advocate's stance.

"I apologize to the Court, Your Honor," he said softly, "and of course I apologize to my sister attorney, Miss d'Ortega.

"I got sort of carried away, Judge. Maybe I'm too close to my client. Please excuse me."

The judge nodded and motioned to d'Ortega to continue. D'Ortega's delivery was fluid and persuasive. She reached down into ten years of trial experience—pressing a point here, distinguishing a point there, articulating legal cases with instant recall. Even Sheridan was impressed. He now knew he had to pull it out.

The judge adjusted her robe. "Mr. Sheridan, you may address the Court."

He rose slowly but deliberately. He glanced down at some notes on his yellow scratch pad, then looked up at the judge.

"May it please the Court," he began, his voice taut. "First, let me correct some improper impressions that were advanced by Miss d'Ortega. I'm sure it was not intentional.

"Miss d'Ortega knows full well that Dr. Sexton's medical records, the psychiatric charts, including the nursing and consulting notes, were unavailable to me as Ms. DiTullio's counsel, hence unavailable to Dr. White. Her argument that the doctor failed to review these documents is completely specious. I won't say it was a fraud on the Court, Your Honor, but it came damn close." From the corner of his eye, he could see that d'Ortega was seething.

"Dr. White's credentials are outlined in his curriculum vitae, which is appended to his affidavit. His expertise in psychiatric cases and disorders of the mind is of the highest caliber. His opinion is straightforward and unequivocal. It was negligence on behalf of all defendants to allow a suicidal patient access to an unguarded elevated floor such as the Atrium. The bases for his opinion are well set out in his affidavit: one, that the patient was on an experimental drug that was still being monitored for both its efficacy and its side effects on humans; two, that she was leaving a safe and secure hospital environment, where she had

been confined for three weeks. He states that that is the dangerous time when most suicides occur. Dr. White backs this up with
reliable statistics. And finally, the patient was left alone without
any supervision, monitoring, or control."

The judge remained impassive; Sheridan couldn't get a read
on her.

"Dr. White's opinion is the sole evidence that is before the
Court," he continued. "There is no evidence to the contrary.
When you put the evidence on the scales of justice, Your
Honor"—Sheridan lifted his arms, both palms up—"they tilt in
the plaintiff's favor.

"I respectfully submit that the plaintiff has carried the day
on the narrow issue before this Honorable Court."

Sheridan paused momentarily. He felt he had done a good
job. Time to sit down.

He looked over at d'Ortega. Her eyes were coldly furious.
He had leveled some serious charges against his opponent. If he
survived the motion, the case would become a bloodbath.

●

Governor Stevenson's chief legal counsel, Thad Braxton, called
Dr. Mason from the sixteenth tee at the Commaquesset Country
Club on Cape Cod. It was Stevenson who had pushed the limited
malpractice immunity bill through the legislature, despite vigorous opposition from the state and county bar associations.

Braxton sat in his golf cart, balancing a cellular phone in
one hand and a five iron in the other.

"Hello, George," he said. "I'm down here at Commaquesset
with Senator Haley. The weather's in the low eighties. Can't say
the same for my game."

"Yes, Thad." Dr. Mason sat nursing a gin and tonic at pool-
side in the leafy acreage of his Wellesley Hills colonial. "Fine
man, the senator. The medical association is deeply grateful for
his help, and of course the governor's, in getting that splendid
piece of legislation through both houses." Mason paused for several moments, taking a sip of his drink. Governor Stevenson had
appointed the doctor's wife, Barbara, to a superior court judge-

ship—again, since she had little trial experience, with much opposition from the bar association.

"The governor's got to mend a few fences," Braxton said, reaching into the silence. "The trial lawyers' noses are a bit out of joint."

"Those jackals are finally getting their due," Mason said. "But tell the governor that not only are we in the medical sector behind him one hundred percent but, come election time, I'll see to it that we open our wallets."

"I know we can always count on you and your people, George. . . ." Braxton paused a few moments. "How is Barbara doing?"

"Barbara's fine. She's sitting in the trial session in Boston. The taxpayers are getting their money's worth, believe me. She goes in at eight in the morning and doesn't get back here sometimes until after nine at night."

"The governor counts her as one of his best judicial appointments. She keeps this up, she'll be slated for the appeals court.

"Oh, by the way," Braxton said, almost as an afterthought, "Senator Haley called the governor recently. Seems that someone very important in the party is interested in a lawsuit involving that woman who jumped at St. Anne's a couple of weeks ago, a patient of your colleague Dr. Sexton."

There were a few more seconds of silence. Dr. Mason took another sip of his drink, and Braxton knocked some mud off his cleats with his club.

"Yes, Barbara mentioned the case to me. Seems she's about to render a decision."

"Well, see if you can talk to her, George."

Again, there was a short pause.

"I'll see what I can do, Thad." The doctor's voice was artificially steady.

"Thanks, George. I know we can always count on you."

The doctor drained his glass, put on his clogs, and toweled the perspiration from his face. This had to be handled delicately. The governor was calling in a big chit.

●

Judy Corwin was always upbeat, even when she was down.

"Seen this morning's *Herald*, Dan?"

"Just got as far as the race results at Suffolk Downs. Had fifty on a horse named Canadian Sunset. Went off at five to one. Unfortunately for me, it finished at six-thirty."

"Any word from Judge Mason?"

Judy shook her head. "Mason is new," she said, "doesn't want to make any mistakes. She'll probably write a four-hundred-page decision.

"But take a look at this, Dan. The *Herald*'s 'Eye' column. Sheila faxed it over. Seems you and Janet Phillips are an item. Sheila's got a sense of humor; wonders where Nattie Gabler got ahold of your old high school year-book picture."

Dan studied the fax for a moment. There was a picture of Janet Phillips, proper angle, shading, right out of *Star Lite Magazine*. Dan's had been taken a few years back. He looked rather solemn.

Sheridan scanned the text quickly.

"Are TV star Janet Phillips and Boston's criminal lawyer Dan Sheridan getting serious? They were seen holding hands the other day at one of Boston's finest eateries." Sheridan crumpled it and slam-dunked it into Judy's wastebasket.

"Boy, what that Gabler won't do for a story!" Sheridan let out a wounded sigh. "I suppose Sheila's really pissed."

"Of course she's pissed. You give away her theater tickets, take Janet Phillips to the Ritz—holding hands, no less. I think you and Buckley handled it all wrong, contacting those witnesses. And you came up with zeros."

"Maybe, maybe not," Sheridan said testily, not appreciating Judy's midmorning lecture. "We had to conduct an immediate investigation; we had to take the bull by the horns."

"I'd say you got gored in the gluteus maximus." Judy gestured toward the wastebasket. "I'm sure Judge Mason saw the same article. Maybe the best thing that could happen is that Mason throws us out of court. For all practical purposes, the case

would be over. We could get back to the real practice of law—
defending hookers, sleazy bums, rapists. . . . That's what pays the
rent."

"Well, I really don't see how Mason can rule against us. If
she's as careful as I think she is, being newly appointed, she
won't risk getting tipped over on appeal.

"Any checks in the morning mail?"

Judy again shook her head. "Lots of bills—but no scratch.
Here are your messages. One is from the Yucatán princess." She
smiled indulgently.

Sheridan scanned the pink slips. "Hm . . . I'm sure d'Ortega
isn't calling to wish me luck. Talk about being pissed! She was
livid after the hearing. No amigo stuff—didn't even call me
gringo. She left looking as though she had bitten into a hot tamale.

"First, I gotta square things with Sheila. Maybe take her to
lunch at the Ritz." Sheridan's grin had a boyish twist.

●

"Janet, you look great." Dr. Sexton greeted his patient as a nurse
escorted her into his new quarters on the ground floor of St.
Anne's. "Here, sit down." He gestured toward a low sectional
sofa that followed the contour of a glass-and-bronze coffee table.

"We've had a few changes since we last met."

"Yes," Janet said. "I sort of miss the view."

"That'll be all, Nancy." Sexton gave a dismissive nod to his
nurse.

"The blood studies are on your desk, Doctor," the nurse
said deferentially.

"Fine."

She closed the door gently.

Sexton picked up Janet Phillips's chart and scanned the
blood cultures.

"Cholesterol's still a mite high, Janet. And I wouldn't be
drinking while you're on Capricet. We haven't got enough raw
data back from the manufacturer, so best play it safe. Medications
and alcohol never mix."

Sexton proceeded to interrogate gently, probing and observing for signs of anxiety, stress, hints of depression, sexual tensions. He followed a proven psychiatric routine, a line of questioning developed by Dr. Lafollette at the Menninger Clinic. Except for her self-deprecating charm, which covered a deep-rooted narcissism, Phillips appeared to be well on the road to normalcy.

"I think we'll reduce the Capricet, Janet. You're on a fairly high dosage—five milligrams per day. We'll cut that in half and give it a trial over the next six weeks.

"I'll give you several samples. That should last you. Just sign the dosage form that Nancy will give you on the way out."

"Doctor." She leaned toward him, her slender bronzed fingers lightly touching the back of his hand. "You'll never know how much I'm indebted to you."

Sexton pretended to slough off the compliment.

"You're one of my best patients," he said, clasping his hand over hers and tapping it benedictively.

"Perhaps you can do my show," she said. "We could run a series on psychiatry." She thought for a few moments. "Yes, I think that would be a splendid idea. It would be great exposure. . . ."

"Speaking about exposure, Janet, I read this morning's *Herald*. Seems you and my adversary—that criminal lawyer . . ." He groped and snapped his fingers noiselessly.

"Sheridan," she supplied.

"Yes, the ambulance chaser, who at the moment is suing everyone in sight." He gave her an opening.

"The *Herald* piece is just from a gossip columnist who spotted us having lunch. The 'holding hands' bit was pure fiction.

"In fact, he tried to cajole me—wanted to take me down to some hideaway on the road to the Cape. I steered him to the Ritz. It was really comical. He looked like one of the Irish Rovers."

Sexton smiled, a paternal, Marcus Welby kind of smile, paused tactfully, then worked into it slowly.

He furrowed his brow slightly. "Janet, how would you like to help us? St. Anne's, Dr. Puzon, all the nurses who cared for you, Dr. Lafollette . . . professionally, I mean."

"In the lawsuit?" As if she had anticipated him, tight little parentheses formed at the corners of her mouth.

"Yes." He cleared his throat. "I've discussed it with our counsel, Mr. Finnerty. He thinks the Sheridan guy was way off base trying to contact a psychiatric patient without permission of the Court, and without having other counsel present."

"He tried to get me to say that the DiTullio girl was agitated, depressed, delusional—the whole suicidal-ideation gambit."

"That's interesting. Too bad you didn't have him on tape." Their eyes met, locked for a moment—as if both had hit upon the idea simultaneously.

"There's a possibility I might resurrect our relationship," she said. "Perhaps we can invite some of Boston's best barristers to rehash the aftermath of the O. J. Simpson case, or whatever. Give Sheridan the limo treatment."

"Janet, you're absolutely amazing. If we could ever get Sheridan offering a bribe to solicit untrue testimony . . ."

—

Carmelita, the Mexican maid, cleared the dishes and served dessert and coffee, then discreetly retired. George Mason patted his lips with a white linen napkin, then made his way to the portable bar. "Brandy?" He held up a snifter.

"Make it a good one. Been a tough week. Being a trial judge is a lot of hard work."

Dr. Mason cracked some ice and poured the brandy from a cut-glass decanter.

"Understand you're deciding the St. Anne's case." Their snifters pinged in silent toast.

"Um." She closed her eyes and took a deep swallow. Her cheeks flushed slightly.

"Oh, the St. Anne's case. Yes, my law clerk is preparing a decision—checking all the cases. It's a very close issue."

"How are you going to rule?" George Mason jiggled the amber mixture.

"I feel constrained to allow the case to proceed."

"So you'll rule against St. Anne's?"

"That's right. It doesn't mean St. Anne's and its doctors are liable. It only means the plaintiff's case is not dismissed. There was an affidavit by a Dr. White buttressing the plaintiff attorney's position—that he has a reasonable basis for believing that a legal cause of action exists."

"But isn't this a frivolous suit?"

"I don't know," she said thoughtfully. "Suppose I tried to commit suicide—was put on an experimental drug, then three weeks later was left unattended in a wide-open area five floors above the ground. A jury might well find someone responsible."

Mason got up and poured himself another brandy. He held it up as an invitation. She shook her head. He knew it wasn't going to be easy.

"I got a call from Thad Braxton today. He's Governor Stevenson's chief counsel. He expressed great interest in preserving the integrity of St. Anne's. It was Stevenson who put our malpractice bill through, mainly at my urging."

She eyed her husband curiously. She hadn't graduated from college and law school without an intuitive intelligence that at times could ferret out problems before they even developed.

"You're not suggesting. . . ."

"I'm not suggesting a thing." Mason sipped his brandy. "We owe a lot to the governor. He stood by your appointment, despite the flak he took from the lawyers. You were jumped over a lot of Harvards and Yales. That took some real guts, believe me. And Braxton said you were one of the governor's best appointments. You might be slated for the appeals court."

"I'll take that brandy, George," she said, uncertainty creeping into her voice. Mason noted the slight tinge of resignation. He was ten years her senior and had always been able to dominate her, guiding her through law school, providing her with fluffy charitable chairs, a beautiful home, an impressive group of friends. Coming from a small town in the Midwest, reared by a wastrel father and an alcoholic mother, she had headed east after high school. She landed a job in the Memorial Hospital flower shop, where Dr. Mason, who was just coming off a stormy divorce, noticed her one day. After that, all the flowers he purchased were for her. The little girl from Ottumwa, Iowa, had struck gold.

"Let me think about it." There was a teary glaze to her eyes and she seemed to be staring into some thoughtful distance.

━

It was late that night when Dr. Mason reached Thad Braxton at his Cambridge home. They exchanged simple pleasantries.

"Tell the governor," Mason said, "it's a done deal."

9

Charlie Finnerty remained impassive when he received the news from claims manager Walter Crimmins that Dr. White couldn't be backed off. He had half-expected it. He didn't think it advisable for the underwriters to diddle with White's professional liability insurance. White, despite being in a high-risk field, had never been hit with a claim or a legal complaint. Any disturbance of White's policy coverage would stir up a hornet's nest.

But the call from the governor's counsel, Thad Braxton, was a day-maker. Ordinarily, a defendant firm wouldn't be completely happy with a case ending before it got off the ground. A summary dismissal would eliminate a barrelful of billable hours, the heart, soul, and blood supply of a defense law firm. The litigation mill, with its hungry maw of depositions, interrogatories, production of documents, motions, cross-motions, library and computer time, counsel, cocounsel, paralegal, and consultant fees, legal-brief writing, trial preparation, and augmented fees for courtroom time, as it applied to the St. Anne's case, would come to an abrupt halt. Finnerty's bill to the cardinal's insurer for winning on a motion to dismiss would be moderate at best. But the coup accomplished in the case would be well received by Monsignor Devlin. And Finnerty was looking to a lot of legal tomorrows.

The cardinal's legal work included leases, purchase and sale agreements, contract negotiation, phasing out of old properties, union problems, workers' compensation and tax litigation, defending clerics against claims of harassment or of sexual abuse—some spurious, some factual—and in general guiding the cardinal's temporal ship safely through the shoals of everyday living. This lucrative account, formerly handled by Roper, Cranston, Peabody & Weld, was now in the hands of Charlie Finnerty. Finnerty met Mayan d'Ortega as she was descending the spiral staircase leading to the law library. She was carrying a sheaf of documents.

"How do you think it went, Mayan?" There was a crisp snap to his voice.

"To be perfectly candid, I can't see the judge ruling our way. And an appeal from any adverse decision will go nowhere."

"That Sheridan guy roughed you up quite a bit in his argument—practically accused you of fraud," Finnerty said.

A slight smile played across her face. "That comes with the territory," she said. "No one told me that this was an easy business. In fact, it's a tough way to make a living. My younger brother, Benito, is a boxer—fights out of Santa Fe. Somehow, I think he has fewer scars than I have."

Finnerty gave her a paternal nod.

"I'd say Sheridan didn't lay a glove on you. For a trial lawyer, you hold up pretty well."

She accepted the compliment and continued toward her office. Finnerty traced the lyric swirl of her jet black hair as it flounced about her shoulders. He then knocked on the polished oak banister for luck. Things looked good. He knew he had one of Boston's best trial lawyers in Mayan d'Ortega. And what a beauty. The daughter of a wealthy El Paso oil man, Texas Law School grad, Bar Review, in her five-year tenure as chief prosecutor, then as Boston's district attorney, she had lost only one felony case—and that was to Dan Sheridan.

And for d'Ortega, he thought, as far as Dan Sheridan is concerned, it's payback time.

He rapped on the banister again. Yes, things couldn't look better.

—

Barbara Mason entered her judge's chamber, followed by her young law apprentice, Cindy Hodges.

"I have your decision all prepared, Your Honor. It's well written, buttressed by black-letter law. Only needs your signature."

"Just leave it on my desk," the judge said. "I may want to make a revision or two."

"I think your ruling for the plaintiff is proper," Hodges said. "As you point out in the body of your decision, there was no evidence denting the plaintiff's position, and at this juncture of the litigation, it is purely a factual issue."

"It's after three; the court docket's clear. Why don't you leave early, Cindy," the judge said as she unsnapped the buttons on her black robe.

"I should stay until closing," the young girl said. "I can go up to the law library and check the cases on that bank fraud case that was argued this morning."

"Plenty of time for that," the judge said as she removed her robe, then folded it over her arm. "Knowing municipal employees, on Friday afternoon this place will be absolutely deserted in half an hour."

"Okay, Your Honor. Have a nice weekend."

—

Barbara Mason fingered her black robe before hanging it up in the narrow closet. Black was the color of impartiality. She thought about it.

She primped her hair in the mirror on the closet door. She stopped and looked at herself for a long moment.

She thought back on her life—of growing up on the plains, the flat sameness of the land, how she'd hated it. Then there was the bitterness, her parents' constant battling. She would cry herself to sleep at night. Now she was safe, secure. She had come a long way from Iowa. But she saw something else: little dark crescents forming under her eyes. They hadn't been there a week ago. She closed the closet door gently and returned to her desk.

She clicked on her word processor and typed out a new decision. She studied it on the fluorescent screen.

> DITULLIO V. ST. ANNE'S HOSPITAL ET AL.
> In the above matter, having duly considered all of the evidence, arguments, and briefs of counsel, the Court hereby finds for the defendant. The plaintiff's case is dismissed.
>
> > Honorable Barbara L. Mason
> > Justice: Boston Superior Court

She closed her eyes and tilted her head back. There was a vault-like stillness in the room. The only sound was the muffled drone of Friday-afternoon traffic coming from outside the chamber window.

Suddenly, she reached down into some primordial preserve she didn't think she possessed. She had always tried to do what was right, and she had a certain innate gutsiness. At least she thought she did. She pressed DELETE and Page Down. Somehow, all at once she felt good about herself. Her self-respect was still intact. She wasn't so sure about her future.

—

Charlie Finnerty's computer was zeroed in on the court docket in the civil clerk's office. He almost couldn't believe his eyes when at 4:45 his computer pinged to life and sputtered out that Judge Mason had denied their motion to dismiss. He called a messenger service to pick up the judge's decision.

He spun in his swivel chair for several moments, taking in the panoramic expanse of the city as it stretched to the harbor. To the north, he could make out Mount Monadnock, a hazy purple cone on the horizon. Had to be fifty miles away, he thought. The view gave him a heady sense of power, also a fictive sense of well-being. He spun back toward his desk and picked up the phone. Reality was setting in.

"Walter," he said to Crimmins, "we've kinda been misled."

"Misled?"

"I thought everything was arranged." Finnerty's voice was curt.

"You mean . . ."

"Exactly. I just got word that Mason ruled against us!"

"Are you sure?"

"It just came in on my computer. It picks up the court docket the moment an entry is made. I've sent a messenger to pick up the judge's decision, just to make sure."

"Something's funny," Crimmins said. "We had the assurance of Thad Braxton, the governor's chief counsel, that Mason would go right down the line."

Finnerty issued a frustrated sigh. "Well, something went haywire. You can't trust these women judges; it isn't like the old days."

"Charlie, I'd take an immediate appeal. Maybe we can get a more favorable ear on the appeals court."

"That's nonsense!" Finnerty barked. "Nobody's going to tip the judge over unless she committed gross errors of law. I listened to the arguments, read the briefs. It's just not going to happen."

"Then we'll simply have to defend the case to the hilt," Crimmins said, "hit this Sheridan guy with a paper blizzard."

"It'll be expensive, Walter, believe me. I'll have to add five additional paralegals just to service this case alone."

"If only we could have stalled the case until the new law went into effect."

"For chrissakes, Walter, *only coulds* don't count in this business! Either you win or you lose. There are no ties."

"Charlie, let me check with Thad Braxton about what exactly happened. You do what you have to do. I'll get back."

Charlie Finnerty was about to get Mayan d'Ortega on the inter-com. He thought for a moment. What's done is done. Maybe Mason got cold feet. Something definitely went wrong. He reached for his private red phone and punched out Sexton's num-ber. Time to play another card—maybe the trump card.

—

Johnny Coyne, the bailiff, got word from the clerk that Mason had ruled in Sheridan's favor. Sheridan had no computer wired into the clerk's office, but Coyne called Sheridan and gave him the news not long after Mason had filed her decision.

"Well, Johnny, guess we got hit by a pitched ball, but at least we're on base. And it's only the top of the first."

"I wish you luck on the case," Coyne said.

"Yeah, think we're going to need it, Johnny, same as the Red Sox. Hope you and Patsy enjoy the game."

"What do you know," Sheridan said to Judy after he had hung up. "We survived. Mason denied d'Ortega's motion to dis-miss.

"Set up depositions of Sexton, Puzon, Lafollette, and the administrator of St. Anne's. I think her name is Sister Agnes Loretta. Tell them to bring all their notes, correspondence, med-ical charts, bills, and so on. You know the jargon, Judy. Set them up within ten days. We'll start off with the good sister, save Sexton for last; we'll interrogate him for eight or nine hours. I want every single note he has on DiTullio, every clinical assessment, going back to her initial visit."

Corwin merely saluted with her pencil; Sheridan knew the deposition notices would go out like clockwork.

"And get Dr. White on the line. Got to set up a meeting. He's got to educate me on all those psych tests—Rorschach, Stanford-Binet, the Wechsler Scales, everything they use to see what makes us tick. Have to make these shrinks think I know what I'm talking about."

—

Barbara Mason gave her pocketbook to Carmelita and checked the hall mirror. "Is the doctor home?" she asked.

"Si, señora, he eez out by zee pool."

Barbara proceeded to the pool area, and as she stepped onto the deck, she could see her husband, attired in a bathrobe and clogs, pacing, his cellular phone pressed close to his ear. Perspiration stippled his face, giving him a high and hectic color.

"George." She waved, her voice uncertain.

He looked her way and motioned with his finger.

"Yes, Thad," she heard him say, "I never tell Barbara what to do. . . .

"I know what I said, and I'm sorry the governor is put out. Barbara takes her job seriously. She called it as she saw it. What more can I say?" He gave his wife a friendly wink, then telescoped the small antenna into the receiver, snapped the phone off, and smiled at his wife.

She crumpled into his arms, sobbing.

"Hey." He ran his hand through her silky hair, then kissed her gently on her cheek, now wet with tears.

"I was goddamned foolish," he said, "trying to put the fix in. Maybe I thought I owed the governor. But you stood alone. Thank God you did the right thing. That's why I married you."

Barbara Mason's shoulders still heaved convulsively.

"Carmelita," he yelled at the maid, who was trying to look inconspicuous by straightening the deck chairs, while still remaining within earshot.

"Two Manhattans! Use the good whiskey!" he shouted. "We'll have them right here at the pool!"

"Si, señor." Carmelita tried to figure out what was going on.

"And pour yourself one"—George Mason laughed—"and join us. We might all go skinny-dipping before the evening is out."

"Señor Jorge," Carmelita mumbled to herself, "*muy loco.*" She spun her forefinger around her temple.

"You can say that again!" Mason shouted. He then scooped up his startled wife and let out an old high school war whoop.

Then, as Carmelita watched horrified, he ran and jumped into the pool. There was a great splash.

Barbara surfaced, spitting water, her blond hair matted into her eyes.

"*Muy loco*," repeated Carmelita as she downed a shot of tequila before preparing the Manhattans.

George Mason was crazy all right, crazy about his wife—and would get crazier as the night wore on. Hell, he thought, I might even break my record.

"*¡Madre de Dios!*" Carmelita gasped as she walked out onto the deck, balancing a tray of Manhattans. She switched the tray to her left hand and blessed herself. The Masons were splashing and frolicking in the pool, and now all they had on were their weekend tans.

●

Sheridan snapped open a can of Bud Light, kicked his loafers off, and settled back into his couch. Outside his waterfront condo, a full moon shimmered across the Mystic River and for several moments he watched the dark silhouette of a tanker slide silently out into the stream. He adjusted his coiled reading lamp and started paging through Donna DiTullio's scrapbook, compiled by her father, Dante. She had had a tennis racket in her hand from age three on. In pigtails, in braces, at the beach, away at summer camp—she was always on the courts. But Sheridan saw something else. In group photos, with relatives, a Fourth of July at the Cape, he could always pick her out. She was the one who was never smiling. She always had a look of grim determination. And interspersed among the clippings, the annotations, and the award citations was a jovial Dante DiTullio, sometimes smoking a cigar, sometimes in T-shirt and tennis shorts, or confecting a public image while holding up a silver trophy—basking in the limelight of a driven daughter. Sheridan could sense the oncoming tragedy as he studied the progression of photographs. At twenty-one, there was a sad, beaglelike cast to Donna DiTullio's eyes. She had paid an awesome price for her triumphs.

Sheridan clicked on the videotape of Donna winning the

New England Women's Championship at the Longwood Cricket Club. She was in against a tall, angular girl who seemed to have the fireball serve of a Steffi Graf and was as relentless as Monica Seles and who always seemed to have DiTullio in a deep hole.

But Sheridan watched in silent amazement as DiTullio fought back with smooth, graceful strokes, gliding rather than racing across the court, chipping, lobbing, catching her opponent cross-legged, then smashing down the baseline. At match point, with all the chips on the line, it was Donna DiTullio who blew an ace past her opponent.

At the awards presentation, the faint hint of a smile flickered across Donna's face before she pulled her sunglasses from her hair down over her eyes. Sheridan replayed the tape.

It was well after 1:00 A.M. before he clicked the rewind button and turned off the VCR. He took the tape, together with the scrapbook, and placed both in his briefcase. He had an appointment in a few hours to see Dr. Jensen, Donna's neurosurgeon at St. Anne's. She was about to be moved to a chronic care facility—an outmoded brick ark north of Boston. Dante DiTullio wanted Sheridan to stop the move.

"Bring some kind of injunction," Dante pleaded. But DiTullio's insurance coverage had certain limitations and the comptrollers and administrators of St. Anne's were unimpressed with Dante DiTullio's railing and Sheridan's acerbic letters.

Sheridan had never seen his client.

"She's in a near-vegetative state," warned the neurosurgeon. "You may get a little squeamish."

Sheridan was no stranger to death or to tragedy. He had witnessed it in Vietnam when his squad was ambushed and over-run at Gia Dinh by a Vietcong patrol. Only two GIs survived. A broken Dan Sheridan, his leg nearly amputated, took almost four years to recover. And then his wife and eight-year-old son were killed by a drunken driver. Often he had been called by police to identify former clients—small-time hoods, for the most part, who had skimmed on the mob or crossed the Cali connection. Squeamish was an understatement.

—

Buckley worked his way back to his seat, balancing two swirls of cotton candy and a large bag of popcorn with a paper tray holding Cokes.

"Oh my God," Karen Assad exclaimed. "Here, let me help you."

She proceeded to distribute the drinks and confections to her two boys, who watched in stark wonder as the Flying Gabriellas worked their magic high above them.

The ringmaster announced the finale—clowns in grease-paint, prancing horses, plumed elephants, tights-suited acrobats, and sequined ladies started their grand entrance. Buckley always enjoyed it. Three hours of nonstop entertainment. And it hadn't changed since he was a five-year-old, munching candied apples with his father. He recalled it with boyish animation: eleven clowns emerging from a baby Austin, the horn blaring with each egress; a tall animal trainer with Nordic blond hair cracking his whip as tigers and lions snarled and growled and jumped through fiery hoops; and the Flying Wallendas working without a net.

After the performance, they squeezed into Buckley's 1973 MG convertible and headed for Karen Assad's residence in Jamaica Plain. The boys were asleep when Buckley pulled up in front of Assad's apartment. For a few moments, neither said a word; only the drone and occasional sputtering of the ancient engine disturbed the stillness.

"You were a delight, Tom," she finally said, "and they were ecstatic." She glanced back at her sleeping children.

"How about next Saturday? Let's go down to Nantasket Beach. It's supposed to be a great weekend."

"I don't think so, Tom." She shook her head. "Now don't get me wrong. I thoroughly enjoyed the evening. And I'm afraid I might get to like you. . . . You're Irish, I'm Lebanese; we come from opposite cultures, opposite ends of the world."

"What in hell has that got to do with it!" Buckley slapped the steering wheel.

Karen was trying to let Buckley down easy, to avoid the real reason, but she could see it wasn't going to work. She sucked in her breath and looked at him, her direct gaze devoid of coyness.

"I can't help it—maybe it's intuition—but I can't dismiss it from my mind that you're still trying to con me." She glanced back at her sleeping children.

"I don't blame you." Buckley reached over and turned off the motor. "But you know, what is is. I can't change that." He glanced over at Karen. The muted light from the dashboard cast her face in a soft glow.

"Can I call you, say next week?"

There was a long moment of silence.

"Let me be perfectly straight, Tom. You are counsel for Donna DiTullio. You are suing St. Anne's. I work for St. Anne's. I like my job. I also need my job." She paused again.

"I think it's best we end everything here right now."

"Okay." Buckley issued a deep sigh, as if he'd been saving it up for years.

"You carry Kaliph—he's smaller. I'll carry Ahmed."

10

Sheridan bought a dozen yellow roses at the St. Anne's flower shop and rode the escalator to the second floor. He checked at the main reception booth and was directed to Neurology. As he walked along the white-tiled corridor, he watched an attendant rush toward him pushing a gurney carrying an inert form with an oxygen mask clamped over the face; two nurses kept pace, one holding an IV.

A young Oriental in a white coat—perhaps a resident or an intern, Sheridan thought—trotted alongside.

"You're going to be all right, buddy," he said as he bent forward to the patient. "Just hold on!"

As they scurried past, Sheridan thought about it. Each of the practitioners—the nurses, the attendant, the doctor—was trying to bring the victim through. Maybe the patient was old— perhaps it was his time to go. Maybe he had suffered a stroke or a heart attack or some traumatic accident. To those practitioners, it made no difference. There was a crisis. Pull out all the clinical and scientific stops. See the patient through—even for the night.

Sheridan watched the medical team bang through a set of doors marked EMERGENCY.

Sheridan tossed his eyes toward the ceiling, petitioning the patron of the healing arts. "Saint Luke, if you're really up there, help the poor bastard survive."

He stopped at the reception desk just inside the Neurology Department. A comely secretary wearing a white tunic told him that he could go right in, that Dr. Jensen was expecting him.

"Thank you," he said, "and here, these were for a patient, but I'm afraid she'll have no use for them." He offered the roses to the secretary.

"Thank you. They're beautiful. Is the patient deceased?"

"No, she's in a coma. I'll buy some more when she comes to. If she comes to."

——

"Here, put on these celluloid glasses." Dr. Jensen handed a pair to Sheridan.

"The MRI—the magnetic resonance imaging—of the brain that you're about to see is in color and these glasses, like the old 3-D movie specs, give them a three-dimensional effect.

"Donna's still in a coma. We're guarding against pneumonia, but her prognosis is poor. To be frank, I never thought she'd last this long." Jensen's voice was authoritative, confidential.

"She did make one slight neurological improvement," he continued. "Not much, mind you—she still has no cognition nor reaction to painful stimuli, but just three days ago when we flashed our little penlight into her eyes, they did react. The pupils contracted. Then when we put her into a darkened environment, the pupils dilated. So they reacted to light and accommodation. These reflexes were absent until a few days ago. Her other reflexes are all hyperactive and she has a positive Babinski. This means her toes fan and her big toe points upward when we stroke the bottom of her foot with a pin. When I tap her Achilles and patella tendons with my little rubber mallet, her foot kicks out in an exaggerated movement, as though she was kicking a soccer ball. These are signs of a great deal of brain damage."

The doctor clicked on the light behind the X-ray illuminator, took a steel penlike object from his pocket, and extended it into an elongated pointer.

Sheridan sat in quiet awe as the three-dimensional images came into focus.

"These are the latest in computerized X-ray technology," the doctor began. "Here in the upper-right film is Donna's brain the day of the tragedy. See, these spaces here are the ventricles, located in the midbrain. On our film, they have a purplish color. They are filled with cerebrospinal fluid. This is like a water jacket that bathes the brain and spinal cord. From what we know, she fractured the frontal part of her skull. So the impact was about here." He used his pointer. "The intracerebral hemorrhage occurred just opposite the point of impact. This is a rebound phenomenon called contrecoup. See this reddish area spiking out near the left rear of the brain? That's the hemorrhage. It punctured the white and gray matter of the brain tissue, even spilled into the ventricles. When we did a spinal tap, the cerebrospinal fluid was grossly bloody. Also, there are minute hemorrhages throughout the brain matter. These interrupt control centers for volition, eyesight, hearing. Thus the coma. Fortunately, those centers controlling respiration and heart rate were unaffected.

"Now contrast that film, which was taken on day one, with one taken this morning. This film is to the left of the film you just viewed." He again used his pointer. "This red area has receded. It's been encapsulated, and eventually, if she survives, it will be a jellylike substance called a subdural hematoma. We've already cut the skull open and evacuated as much of the hemorrhage as we could without causing further brain damage. As you can see, the hemorrhagic area has been greatly reduced in size."

"Doctor, if you were able to evacuate the remainder of the clot, would she improve?"

"I doubt it. Too many hemorrhages are scattered throughout the brain matter. We're not dealing with an isolated clot. And she sustained so many other injuries—fractures, perforated intestine—as I say, it's almost unbelievable that she survived this long.

"We're not supposed to say this, especially me, her neurosurgeon, but it would be a blessing if she died during the night. If by some miracle"—Dr. Jensen wiggled two sets of fingers— "she survives, she'll be a living vegetable, and you know what that entails."

"I know," Sheridan replied quietly.

"Doctor, I want to thank you for taking the time to explain the situation."

"Think nothing of it. Just doing my job."

Sheridan nodded. "And I'm doing mine. You know, of course, that I'm suing St. Anne's."

"Certainly I know." Dr. Jensen clicked off the illuminator button on the X-ray viewer and turned up the lights.

"Personally, I hope you get a zillion dollars. My sole interest is in the patient. There'll be some ethical questions down the line, a petition to turn off life-support systems. You know the legal jargon."

"Let's hope we both do the right thing," Sheridan said.

—

Sheridan left his briefcase at the nursing station and was accompanied by a pleasant young black woman with a lilting Caribbean accent who said she was a nurses' assistant. He could feel the icy stares of the nurses as he made his way to Donna DiTullio's room.

"She's not too good," the assistant said. "Understand she's gonna be sent out soon."

"Yes, that's what I've been told."

As he walked toward Donna's room, he passed semiprivate and private rooms, all occupied, some patients swathed in bandages and slings, some trussed up with pulleys, others lying hopeless and forlorn in their beds.

"We got some serious cases here," the assistant said as she paused at the door of DiTullio's room and gave a slight rap.

"She won't hear it, but I knock anyway."

She opened the door a crack and peeked in.

"Donna," she said in a singsong voice, "you got a visitor."

The assistant stayed in the back of the room, by the door.

Sheridan cleared his throat and fought back tears as he approached the inert form of Donna DiTullio. Her bandaged legs
were oscillating slowly over a pulsating drum. Tubes and wires
hung down from an overhead bar and crisscrossed to the intra-
venous bottles and cardiac regulators. She looked as though she
were hooked up to an old-fashioned switchboard. A respirator
wheezed and sighed. The room had a scrubbed, antiseptic smell,
in contrast to a mass of bright flowers in a vase on the nightstand.

He leaned close to his client. Her scraggly dark hair, already
streaked with gray, fanned out on the pillow, and her sunken face
was stretched taut over her facial bones. Her doll's eyes stared
blankly toward the ceiling, like two dark brown marbles lying
inert in a field of white.

He reached down and took her clammy, withered hand in
his.

"Donna," he whispered, "I went through your scrapbook.
You're a real champion. Maybe when you're well, you can work
on my backhand." He gave her hand a gentle squeeze.

There was no point in staying. As he was about to leave, he
looked into her eyes once more.

"Jesus!" he swore to himself. "Am I imagining things?" He
bent closer. The porcelain gaze still seemed lifeless, unmoving.
The lattice shades were tweaked shut, the light dim in the room,
but he could swear there was a slight glisten at the corners of her
eyes. Could she have heard him and been unable to respond? He
wanted to tell the attendant, but felt he was being guided by
emotion rather than reason. No, he would return on Monday.
Maybe bring along the scrapbook and video.

"I'll be back, Donna," he said quietly. He gave her hand
another squeeze.

●

When Sheridan returned to his office late in the afternoon, Dante
DiTullio was waiting for him. He had been sitting next to Judy
Corwin's desk, skimming through some outdated magazines,
drinking coffee, and giving Judy vacant nods as she tried to en-

gage in some banter. She recognized the shadow of melancholy in his pallid face.

"Mr. Sheridan." He jumped up quickly as Dan entered the office.

"Oh, Mr. DiTullio." Sheridan extended his hand. "We won the motion to dismiss." He was about to add, I know you and Mrs. DiTullio will be pleased, but he saw that under DiTullio's slick black eyebrows, his eyes were disconsolate and pained. The fact that they were still in court would not be registered as a plus at that moment.

"They're moving Donna to the Hampton Chronic Care facility, Mr. Sheridan," DiTullio blurted. "You've got to do something to stop them.

"They've destroyed my little girl; now they want to pack her away in that goddamned warehouse."

"I just came from seeing your daughter and talked with Dr. Jensen, her neurosurgeon," Sheridan said. "I was told that they were going to transfer her."

"I had a call from Karen Assad—you know, Donna's psychiatric nurse. She gave it to me on the q.t. She was visiting Donna and was told by the day nurse that Donna was going to be moved tonight."

"Tonight?"

"That's what Miss Assad told me."

"I was preparing a restraining order." Sheridan nodded to Judy.

"Well, you gotta stop them with an injunction or something. Call up some judge!" DiTullio grabbed Sheridan's arm, his once pallid face now flushed with anger. "They're all in cahoots— Sexton, Jensen, Sister Agnes Loretta. . . ."

"I'll see what I can do," Sheridan said. "It's too late to do anything today.

"Get that restraining order ready for my signature. Fax a copy to d'Ortega; tell her I'm presenting it to Judge Mason." He nodded to Judy, who had already started punching it out on her word processor.

"Can't make any promises, Mr. DiTullio. Unfortunately, this time, St. Anne's holds the high cards."

"I know why they're doing this, Mr. Sheridan. I haven't got major medical insurance. It's a simple matter of profit and loss to those bastards. You can't pay, you go to some cheap storage bin like Hampton. And they got hack doctors up there ... bottom-of-the-barrel nurses."

"Look, Mr. DiTullio, we'll do our best. You go home and take care of Mrs. DiTullio. It's not the end of the world." He patted the man on the shoulder. Somehow, the advice sounded hollow. Sheridan knew that Dante DiTullio's world had ended the day Donna jumped into the Atrium.

—

Sheridan again showed up early at the courthouse on Monday. As he entered the courtroom, he was met by Charlie Finnerty.

"Dan Sheridan!" As Charlie smiled, his cheeks bunched up and his pale blue eyes seemed to glitter. "Heard a lot about you, Danny me boy. Got a great rep on the criminal side." They shook hands. Finnerty pumped Sheridan's hand as if he were a long-lost brother.

"What are you doing on this side of the fence?" Finnerty's smile broadened. It looked as if it were carved in wood.

"Same thing you're doing, Charlie. Trying to make some money to pay my bar bills."

Somehow, Finnerty knew that Sheridan knew that all this phony cajolery was going nowhere. He still smiled, but the opal glitter seemed to fade from his eyes.

"Here," he said, "this is Mayan d'Ortega's brief to your motion for a restraining order, with an affidavit from Dr. Jensen, saying that it was safe and reasonable to transfer Donna DiTullio to a chronic-care facility."

"*Was?*"

"Yes. She was transferred to Hampton Chronic Care and Rehabilitation Hospital last night.

"Dan, I'm afraid your petition came too late," Finnerty said with manufactured jauntiness.

"Did Dr. Jensen really approve this transfer?" Sheridan said as he scanned the doctor's affidavit.

"Well, I'll let Mayan argue those prickly points of law, Dan. She's due here any moment. Judge Mason's clerk says we're at the bottom of the list, so it'll be a long morning. But seriously, Dan, before Mayan and you start to tangle"—Finnerty's voice was now lodge brother–confidential—"let's get rid of this case. You know and I know that your client will never live out the month.

"A wrongful-death case is worth a hundred, a hundred fifty thou, tops, you know that. Boston juries haven't been overly generous, especially in malpractice cases. And you'll get tied up in four years of litigation. But because it's you, Dan, I think we can settle this case."

"What did you have in mind, Charlie?"

"I'm authorized to offer you one hundred and fifty thousand dollars. And of course St. Anne's will assume all the costs of medical treatment to date. So let's see . . ." Finnerty feigned tumbling some figures around in his head. "There'll be a fifty-thousand-dollar fee for you, a hundred thousand for your clients. Not bad for a few hours' work."

"Well, Charlie, I'm duty-bound to relay your offer to my clients, but I'll tell you right now, the answer is *no!*"

"Look, Dan, you turn down this offer, you'll be in litigation up to your eyeballs. The church can afford it. And I'll make a mint.

"The last ten malpractice cases in Boston went defendant. Times have changed, Dan. We're not back in the high-flying eighties when juries would give the home office away. Things are tough. Half of the people on the jury panel have been laid off or are on unemployment. Nobody's giving them a handout; they're goddamned stingy. I'm giving it to you straight, Dan. You don't try these cases on the civil side. I do."

Finnerty spotted d'Ortega coming through the swinging doors.

"Dan," he said quickly, "because it's you and only because it's you, I'll exceed my authority. You tell me your clients will accept two hundred thousand and I'll see to it that St. Anne's insurer honors my commitment."

"Charlie, I appreciate what you're trying to do for me, I really do, but let me give you a counteroffer."

"What's that, Dan?"

"Make it twenty million and we've got a deal."

"Hey, Dan, what have you been smoking?" Finnerty gave a chortling laugh. "Let's get serious. You tell me you'll accept two hundred thou and I'll have the check cut right away. Send it over with the releases. That's how much I trust you guys."

"Charlie, I couldn't be more serious." Sheridan held both hands up, spread his fingers, and pumped twice.

"You're crazy, Sheridan." The wooden smile suddenly drained from Finnerty's face and was replaced by little tics of resentment. "Crazy . . ." He shook his head and heaved an exaggerated sigh.

"So I've been told."

"Okay, ordinarily I'd withdraw the offer forthwith . . . but take it up with your clients. As you say, ethically, you're duty-bound to do so. They can use the money, and we're just trying to do the right thing. Get back to me within three days and I'll keep the offer open."

"Charlie, I know my people. If my little girl lives, she'll need constant care for the rest of her life, and this is the sole responsibility of your clients."

Finnerty cut him off. "Dan, save that kind of stuff for the jury. You fight this case and you'll be in over your head, believe me. You handle criminal cases. There you get your money up front. This is a different ball game. Your costs on this case could run a hundred, a hundred and fifty thousand. Your client, your Mr. DiTullio, is broke. He's a four-flusher. We've checked him out. Couldn't even pay for major medical insurance. We can afford this type of litigation; you can't."

Sheridan caught a glimpse of Mayan d'Ortega out of the corner of his eye. She remained discreetly out of range. "Hey, Charlie, we play the cards we're dealt. Withdraw the offer; I'm not interested."

The hearing before Judge Mason went as Sheridan had expected. D'Ortega stressed Dr. Jensen's opinion that Donna DiTullio had irreversible brain damage and would probably exist in a coma until her support systems failed. He didn't expect her to survive and felt that the state-run chronic-care facility could adequately attend to the needs of the patient, where the cost to the DiTullios would be a tenth of that charged by a private hospital such as St. Anne's.

Sheridan thought it strange that the chief of Neurosurgery omitted mention of the neurologic improvement in the patient's pupillary reflexes. He had liked Jensen. Now he wasn't so sure. Obviously, someone had gotten to him.

He wanted to rebut d'Ortega's argument by narrating his discussion with the chief of Neurosurgery, tell the judge about his own observations, the tearing in Donna DiTullio's eyes. But his courtroom intuition told him that his motion for a restraining order was a lost cause. He'd save that for another time. Instead, his arguments was pure emotion, and as he expected, Judge Mason ruled against him. She didn't even take the matter under advisement. She ruled right from the bench. Maybe she owed d'Ortega. He thought about it. He still wasn't sure.

He shook d'Ortega's hand, gathered up his documents, stuffed them into his trial bag, and made his way toward the courtroom exit.

"See you in court, pal." Charlie Finnerty stood behind the bar enclosure and gave a wave in Sheridan's direction, his toothy grin radiating insincerity.

Sheridan wanted to toss back some demeaning barb, but he merely nodded and pushed his way out through the swinging doors.

—

Janet Phillips okayed her producer's format, "Doctors and Lawyers: The Killing Fields."

"Sounds catchy," she said. "I think our show needs a little

more controversy, audience participation. Ricki Lake sort of stuff."

The producer pushed her horn-rimmed glasses up into her hair.

"We'll tape certain segments," she said, "but for the live portion, we'll have three noted doctors and three local lawyers.

"We've lined up Dr. George Mason at Memorial Hospital, Dr. Friedman, president of the AMA, and Dr. Gilman, the head of the Mass. Medical Society.

"On the lawyer side, we've three of the best malpractice lawyers in the state."

Janet Phillips scanned the slate of participants.

"Jennie," she said, "do me a favor. Drop one of the lawyers and invite Daniel Sheridan. He's mainly a criminal lawyer, but he's the one who is suing St. Anne's and Dr. Sexton."

"Isn't that your doctor?" the producer asked, hesitation creeping into her voice.

"Yes. I'd invite Dr. Sexton to be on the show, but I think the forum will be lively enough. Wouldn't want Sexton and Sheridan to start rolling around on the floor."

"Might not be bad for the ratings—same thing happened on *Geraldo*," the producer said.

"Well, get this Sheridan guy on the show. Give them all the limo treatment. You know the score, Jennie."

The producer formed a circle with her thumb and forefinger, and gave her hand a little shake.

"It should be quite a show," she said.

11

Sheridan caught the last Delta shuttle to La Guardia, took a cab, and checked in at the New York Hilton. He had called ahead to meet an old friend, New York lawyer Neil Kennedy, who had served with his unit in Vietnam. Kennedy was the medic who had kept him alive as he was flown by helicopter from Gia Dinh to the hospital camp at My Tho, south of Saigon. Kennedy grew up in Queens, and after the war he joined the New York Police Department, went to NYU nights, and finally graduated from Fordham Law School. He now practiced with a small firm in the Bronx, taking any type of case that came to the door. Sheridan and Kennedy had kept in touch.

"I thought you'd like the place. Not the Palm Court, mind you, or the Plaza bar, but it's my favorite Second Avenue hangout." Kennedy almost had to yell, as the crowd was stomping out some Irish national song. No "When Irish Eyes Are Smiling" or touristy ditties at the Blarney Stone.

"Boy, some of these Irish girls look kind of tough." Sheridan laughed as he sipped a pint of Guinness.

"Yeah, can't exactly say they look like Maureen O'Hara or even Shana Delaney," Kennedy said, draining his Jameson.

"These aren't the secretarial types. Some are on the police force; some construction workers. And, believe it or not, some are IRA."

"IRA?" Sheridan looked quizzically at Kennedy. "I thought that was the last chauvinistic preserve on the face of the earth."

"No." Kennedy signaled a buxom waitress for another round. "You see that girl over my left shoulder, sitting with those two guys who look like Victor McLaglen?"

Sheridan surveyed the trio. "I'd say she's the best-looking one in the place."

"Well, that's Meaghan Dwyer—she served time in Reading—same place they incarcerated Oscar Wilde. They say while screwing some British colonel, she grabbed his pistol and blew his brains out. Tried in the Old Bailey, but the boys in the white wigs couldn't make it stick. She claimed sexual harassment, the self-defense bit.

"Understand she's got a green tattoo on her rear end; real national slogan."

"Something like *Erin go bragh*?" Intrigued, Sheridan took another look at the group.

"No, something like up yours," Kennedy added with a grin.

They sat and drank and watched until the Fife and Fiddle Boys took a short break and the place seemed to lapse into a conspiratorial stillness. The only sounds were whispers and shared confidences.

"What brings you to the Big Apple?" Kennedy asked as he nodded to a few acquaintances.

"I've got a med mal case up in Boston. Could go for zero, could go for millions—depends upon my client surviving."

"Must be good injuries, as we lawyers like to say."

"My girl jumped five floors from a psycho hospital atrium and right now she's in a coma. Touch and go. Prognosis, zilch. Might not last much longer."

"Those are tough cases," Kennedy said. "We had a case; one of the city's top lawyers put his heart and soul into it, spent a fortune on expert witnesses, not to mention his time. It was on Court TV."

"I recall it," Sheridan said. "*Gahan* v. *New York Hospital*."

"Yeah, a wrongful-death suit. Plaintiff's lawyer, an old Fordham grad, claimed his client was given the wrong medication. Left a million-dollar offer on the table; jury came back with one hundred twenty-five thousand."

"That's the problem. I just rejected two hundred thousand. If my client dies—and I think she will—the insurer will offer zero. But if she survives, with her health-care needs, personal-care attendants, loss of future earnings, ten million dollars is conservative."

"Dan, how can I help? Let me guess. Conspiracy of silence. You can't get a Boston doctor to testify against the local shrink. You want I should find you a doctor who wears Gucci shoes, Turnbull & Asser shirts, drives around in a five fifty SL? I think I've got just the guy; we're handling his divorce. Wasn't it Ben Franklin who said when they were drafting the Declaration of Independence that we'd better hang together or we'll all hang separately?"

Sheridan laughed. "Fortunately, I've got a doctor who's not suffering from *indigeo testicularis*. Already survived a Rule Eleven motion to dismiss."

"Rule Eleven"—Kennedy sighed—"the bane of every attorney who tries to sue R. J. Reynolds or the Dragonwyck Corporation."

"I'm really down here to get book on the chief defendant, a Dr. Robert Sexton. He was at a group therapy session, left my girl unattended. She got up, went to an open railing, and jumped."

"And she's still living?" Kennedy shuddered.

"This Sexton guy grew up in Mamaroneck, New York."

"Nice neighborhood. The only way a kid like me from Queens Boulevard could get in there would be to deliver the groceries."

"Well, Sexton comes from the polo-playing Sextons. Grandfather founded Hudson Valley Copper. But strange as it may seem, old man Sexton married his housekeeper, Harriet Minehan, who raised the kids Catholic. And Harriet is the sister of our present Cardinal Minehan. And the cardinal owns the hospital, so he's a codefendant."

"Boy, you sue God, Sheridan, you sure'n hell better win!" It was an old lawyer joke that could travel. Kennedy signaled for another round of drinks.

"What I need is some info on Sexton," Sheridan said, "something that might affect his credibility. As a kid, did he steal hubcaps from Rolls-Royces or knock up some Presbyterian vicar's daughter? I thought with your connections at the NYPD, you could get me a lead or two."

"Mamaroneck is in Westchester County, outside the Metro's jurisdiction. I can get their crib sheet, if there is one. But I'll bet your Sexton was head altar boy, Eagle Scout, whatever. Where'd he go to high school?"

"Gonzaga, in midtown Manhattan."

"Gonzaga! You gotta have a one ninety IQ even to apply. They graduate one hundred percent to Harvard, Georgetown, Yale, Holy Cross. Kids even go to Oxford. Not exactly Brooklyn Trade."

"Well, he went to Gonzaga, undergrad Yale, then Columbia Med.

"I'm scheduled to take his deposition next week. What I need is background, stuff that doesn't appear gilded—right now, anything."

"I do know a Father Cahill. Think he's the dean of studies at Gonzaga. Used to have him for Greek history back at Fordham Prep. I'm sure if you go in blind and ask to see Sexton's folder, the Jebbies will call the cops. Let me set up a meeting. How long are you going to be in town?"

"As long as it takes.

"How about Columbia?" Sheridan said.

"We may be able to help you there. I defended one of the associate professors of surgical oncology in a sexual harassment suit. Seemed he flunked some young med student and she claimed he was tapping her—it was a Mexican standoff. Went before the Board of Medicine. She was twenty-two, a body you wouldn't believe. My client, old Doc Webster, was seventy-one;

couldn't get it up if it was encased in plaster of paris. She agreed to a passing mark; he was reinstated. Easiest forty-thousand-dollar fee I ever earned."

—

The call to Father Cahill opened all the doors.

"Here," he said to Sheridan as he handed over Sexton's folder. "As you can see, he was one of our brightest pupils. Student body president, National Honor Society, straight A average, valedictorian. Of all the students who ever graduated from Gonzaga, he's the exemplar of the Jesuit ethic."

"Sounds good to me, Father," Sheridan said. "You've got quite a school here, Padre," he added.

"Well, we try." Father Cahill had a baffled-professor mien. "The church is under attack these days." A smoldering fire started to kindle in the old mentor's eyes, and Sheridan knew he was in for an ecclesiastical journey.

"I remember the way it was in the old days—*ratio studiorum*; the classics—Euripides, Plato, Seneca, Ovid. . . . You know, back in '53, there was a—"

"Father"—Sheridan looked at his watch—"I've got to catch a six o'clock plane to Boston." He reached over and shook the old priest's hand.

"You've been very helpful. I'm going to recommend Dr. Sexton's candidacy to the Governor's Council on Right to Life Legislation." Sheridan bit his lower lip. He didn't lie easily, especially to a Jesuit.

"Hope you make your plane," Father Cahill said, "and say hello to Bob Sexton. . . ." He closed his eyes, as if to recall some elusive line from Aristophanes.

—

It was close to midnight when Sheridan checked into the Blarney Stone. The late-night patrons spilled out onto the street and wound around the corner. Sheridan had to slip a beefy doorman a twenty to get through the crowd milling around the entrance. He made his way past the bar, smiled at Meaghan Dwyer, who was surrounded by a coterie of scally-capped toughs who eyed him coolly. The fiddlers and pipers were in full swing and the crowd was singing "The Wild Colonial Boy."

Kennedy stood up and waved from a corner table. Sheridan picked his way carefully. He didn't want to jostle a patron and accidentally knock a beer out of someone's hand. It was no place to have an altercation.

He shook hands with Kennedy, pulled a spindly wooden chair back from the table, and sat down. The buxom waitress quickly appeared as the fiddlers segued into "The Rising of the Moon."

"Thanks for the contact with Father Cahill," Sheridan began. "Quite a character. I'd be there yet if I hadn't manufactured the 'got to catch a plane' bit."

"I can't imagine him being dean of studies, especially at Gonzaga," Kennedy said. "He was a little foggy even when I had him at Fordham Prep."

"Well, he showed me Sexton's four-year record—four-oh average. Nothing but sterling accolades," Sheridan said.

"Kind of interesting," Kennedy said just as the fiddlers finished with a zingy flourish. "There was absolutely nothing in Mamaroneck. Sexton was a star pupil in grammar school, won the CYO medal for academic achievement. Also played in Little League, apparently was quite a skier, and of course was an Explorer Scout. I called in a favor with the NYPD, a Detective O'Halloran, who's been on the force for thirty-four years. Comes from my old Queens neighborhood. Absolutely no criminal record on Sexton. But Sexton had a live-in girlfriend while he was at Columbia Med."

Kennedy bent closer to Sheridan.

"A young chick from Staten Island, haven't got her name. They lived near Columbia, on West One Hundred Sixteenth."

"What's so interesting about that? I assume they married and later became divorced or separated."

"Divorced, no. Separated, yes.

"According to O'Halloran's memory, from working on the case peripherally, she had gone out jogging in Central Park—

late afternoon in the winter—when it was fairly dark. Ended up
in a clump of bushes near the Conservatory Pond. The body was
spotted by another jogger. Robbery was the apparent motive; her
wallet was missing, as well as a silver bracelet given to her by
her live-in boyfriend—your Robert Sexton. ID was made by a
key ring.

"Girl was twenty or twenty-one. The police investigation and
coroner's report ruled it a homicide. Case was unsolved. Sexton
was in class at the time. Of course, we've had a lot of muggings,
particularly of joggers and tourists in Central Park."

"Can you get me a printout of the investigation and coroner's
report, Neil?"

"Might be hard to come by. That stuff's over twenty years
old. May or may not be in storage somewhere. I'll check with
O'Halloran.

"How is that going to help you in a malpractice case? Seems
to me it's immaterial. You couldn't even question Sexton about
it in a deposition."

"You're probably right, Neil. But see if you can get it for
me. I really don't know where I'm going. If it's unavailable, have
your detective friend give me the name of the investigating officer."

The music makers had returned from break. It was nearing
closing.

"This seems a good time to cut out, Neil," Sheridan said,
tossing two twenties on the table to cover the tab. "We'll grab a
cab. Drop me off at the Hilton and I'll pay your fare to Queens."

"No, this is definitely *not* the time to cut out," Neil said as
he eyed Meaghan Dwyer and her Victor McLaglen look-alikes.

"They're getting ready to sing 'The Soldier's Song.' See all
those glasses raised? That's the Irish national anthem. You start
walking out now and, believe me, you won't be walking for the
next few months."

"Up the Republic!" came a chorus from the raised glasses.

"Up the Republic!" shouted Sheridan as he jumped to his
feet and raised his Guinness as high as it would go. He chanced
a glance over his shoulder and gave a big wink to Meaghan

Dwyer. She either blew him a kiss or gave him the finger. He wasn't about to find out which. And he wondered if her tattoo was kelly green or emerald green. He wasn't about to find that out, either.

●

The next morning, Sheridan took the New England Express out of Penn Station, got off at New Haven, and took a cab to the Yale campus. He got nowhere with the administration office. Red Sox tickets were of little value in Connecticut. A visit to the Sterling Library was uneventful. A kindly librarian directed him to the college yearbook section. He paged through the 1973 yearbook, and under the S's there was a serious, handsome lad: Robert Cushing Sexton. His achievements were awesome. Summa cum laude, premed major, winner of the Yale Science Award, Drama Society I and II, captain ski team. "Could be seen on the slopes of Vail, Aspen, and Stowe" was an added quote.

No waiting on tables down at Morey's for this Eli Blue, Sheridan thought.

He made a photocopy of the page and folded it into his inside pocket. He considered visiting the New Haven Police Department but then thought better of it. He was dipping back over more than twenty years. And Sexton probably never even got a parking ticket.

12

A distraught Dante DiTullio, this time accompanied by his wife and the young lawyer Emilio Cantone, was waiting in the small reception area the day after Sheridan returned from New Haven. Judy Corwin did her best to listen to Dante's litany of woes, nodding her head in tactful commiseration. She served coffee from a new carafe that she had purchased. She made excuses for the Styrofoam cups, reminding herself to buy dinnerware cups and saucers at Jordan Marsh.

Sheridan greeted them as cordially as the moment would allow. Judy ushered the group into the conference room and joined Sheridan in his office.

"Why are they here?" Sheridan asked. "They keep popping in without appointments."

"I suppose it's because you represent them," Judy chided. "Mrs. DiTullio seems to be holding up pretty well, but Dante's falling apart. Seems they visited their daughter up at the Hampton facility. She's not even in a private room. I know about Hampton. It's an outdated brick ark where the elephants go to die. The words *Rehabilitation Hospital* on the end of it are a farce. Frankly, I wouldn't take a sick parakeet up there.

"Dan"—she furrowed her brow—"you've got to be a little more understanding with the clients. We're not dealing with some two-bit criminal or trying to beat a drunk-driving charge. These people are devastated."

"Look," Sheridan said testily, "I'm giving this case every working moment. They have to understand that. Sure, they think it's my fault we lost the motion for a restraining order. But that's the reality they've got to face. And if I let clients get under my skin, I'd lose my objectivity. I wouldn't be able to function. Do you think every surgeon who is about to operate starts wailing and telling his assistant, 'These injuries are simply terrible'? No, the DiTullios have to realize these things take time. Litigation is no cakewalk. It's more like picking your way through a mine-field."

"How did things go down in Gotham?" Judy asked, tactfully changing the subject.

"They have some great Irish bars down there." Sheridan gave Judy a quick smile. "But as for Sexton—at Columbia, Yale, even in high school—he was a superachiever. While he was in med school, he had a live-in girlfriend, a young filly from Staten Island. While Sexton was away at classes, she went for a late afternoon jog, got robbed, and was fatally beaten.

"The police investigation and coroner's report ruled the death a homicide. I don't even know the girl's name. An attorney friend of mine got the info from a detective. I'm trying to get a printout—if one even exists."

"How is that going to help in the DiTullio case?"

"Frankly, Judy, I haven't got the vaguest idea." Sheridan stood up and straightened his tie in the reflection of his office window.

"Don't jump all over Dante DiTullio when he tries to vent his anguish."

Sheridan merely nodded.

●

Sheridan listened patiently, first to Dante DiTullio, then to Can-tone. There was a mild threat that the DiTullios might be better served by engaging one of the larger firms. Sheridan did a slow burn at the suggestion, but he merely responded that the Di-Tullios were free to go elsewhere if at any time they felt they were receiving inadequate representation.

"No," Cantone interjected, perhaps seeing a referral fee in jeopardy, "you seem to be on top of the case, Mr. Sheridan. It's just—you know, the legal system creeps at a snail's pace, especially in malpractice cases."

"I don't deny that. But I've already scheduled four depositions for next week. We're leading off with the hospital administrator, Sister Agnes Loretta."

"Is there anything that can be done to get Donna back at St. Anne's?" the young lawyer asked. "We feel that she's receiving substandard care at Hampton. When we were up there, the nurses didn't respond to the call button, and when they did, they couldn't have cared less about medical treatment. All they do is chat and gossip and prattle among themselves."

"I can't go back into court unless I can document the substandard care. Even then, I doubt we'd get Donna back into St. Anne's." Sheridan knew never to gloss over the facts of a case or make illusory promises to a client. Later, if by some stroke of legal luck he was successful, then he was a prince. But the line between prince and bum was rather thin at times.

He looked at the DiTullios. "Tell me, have you noticed any cognition at all in your daughter, any tearing when you mention her name?"

"Not a thing." Dante shook his head disconsolately.

"Who is her primary physician at Hampton?"

"A Dr. Brockelman," the young lawyer said. "Has to be in his late seventies. Kind of doddering. Probably good on growling stomachs, constipation, and ingrown toenails. But frankly, I wouldn't want him to cut into me."

"I plan to go up there tomorrow." Sheridan wrote Brockelman's name on his yellow scratch pad.

"One last order of business," Sheridan said. "The counsel for St. Anne's has offered to settle Donna's case for two hundred thousand dollars."

"Two hundred thou—" Dante's face flushed and he started choking.

"Here." Sheridan handed him his coffee. He swallowed, choked again, and started to sob. He looked at Sheridan with tearful beagle eyes.

"You gotta be kidding," he blurted, struggling to control his voice. "That's an insult! It's ridiculous! Those bastards destroy my daughter and think they can buy me off for a few lousy bucks!"

Sheridan waited for Dante DiTullio's anger to run its course.

"I couldn't agree with you more," he said, his voice soft with understanding. "It's just that I'm duty-bound to communicate any offer. The offer is to remain open until the close of business today."

"Tell them to shove—" Dante glanced sideways at his wife. "Tell them they know what they can do with their offer!"

"That will be done forthwith," Sheridan said.

"After we take depositions from the defendants over the next few weeks, of course you and Mrs. DiTullio will be deposed by the other side. They'll have a court reporter there and you'll both testify under oath. Since this is a psychiatric case, the questions could get quite personal and sensitive.

"I want both of you to keep your cool, so I'll have you in at intervals before your depositions. I'll act as the defense attorney and cross-examine both of you. In that way, you'll have heard most of the questions and we'll go over your answers so you'll both be viewed with empathy and understanding. Okay?" Sheridan extended his hand to Dante DiTullio.

●

"You have a special invite from the producer of *Boston Today* to appear on their show," Judy Corwin said as she sorted the mail. "And of course a note from Janet Phillips thanking you for the lunch at the Ritz, et cetera, et cetera."

Sheridan was studying the invitation as young Buckley came out of his office.

"Any checks, Judy, from Cap Haitien or Santo Domingo— whatever?" he said.

"A raft of bills, a lot of lawbook flyers, and a petition from the Yucatán princess seeking two thousand dollars in attorney's fees. Seems she's invoking a section in the new law where the losing party in any civil case or motion has to pay the other side's legal fees."

"What?" Sheridan looked quizzically at Corwin. "When in hell did the legislature slide that one by us?"

"It's part of Governor Stevenson's package," Judy explained.

"Governor Stevenson's sellout," Buckley added.

"We lawyers can only blame ourselves for what's going down." Sheridan shook his head. "It's bad enough that malpractice cases are limited to a one-hundred-thousand-dollar cap, but this nonsense about paying the opponent's legal fees will force us all out of business."

"That's the way they do it in Merrie Olde England," Buckley said, not appearing dismayed at Sheridan's dismal reflection. "Talked to a barrister friend of mine in London. They have no such thing as contingent fees, and the losing party could get whacked for one hundred, one hundred fifty thousand pounds, depending on the case. Makes a person think twice before getting involved in litigation."

"Well, what they're doing," Sheridan said, "is precluding the middle class from access to the courts. Guy's not going to sue if he has to put the homestead up as collateral."

"You know," Buckley said, "thank God we've got a criminal practice, and, of course, Mrs. Gallagher's estate."

"Yeah, but what bothers me is that they'll chip away at everything—product liability, automobile cases. No one will be held accountable anymore," Sheridan said.

"This new law limiting awards on malpractice cases hasn't gone into effect yet. How come d'Ortega's trying to stick us with costs under a section of a law that's not even on the books? Our case was brought under the old law."

"I dunno, think you'll have to take that up with the Mex. You might have caught her off base," Buckley said as he collected his mail from Judy and thumbed through it quickly. There was a small envelope from Karen Assad. He put that in his pocket.

"How did things go in New York?" he asked as he was about to head to his office.

"About as expected. Seems Sexton was a junior Albert Schweitzer, Jonas Salk, and Paul Dudley White all rolled into one. Guy's got more honors and awards than a Bolivian general. But there was one thing a little out of line, but I'm not sure where it fits or whether it's even relevant." He tapped Janet Phillips's invitation in the palm of his hand.

"Sexton was living with some young girl while he was going to med school—gal from Staten Island."

"Staten Island? That's not exactly Westchester County," Buckley said.

"Haven't got the girl's name. A lawyer friend of mine who used to be a cop is trying to get me the NYPD printout."

"Printout on what? Did Sexton and his friend dip into the Phi Epsilon bank account?"

"Seems the girl was bludgeoned to death while jogging in Central Park. Sexton was in class at the time."

"How in hell is that going to help us?" Buckley hesitated at his office door. "You try to interrogate him in his deposition on a domestic tragedy years ago and d'Ortega will find another hidden section to hit you with triple costs."

"I suppose you're right," Sheridan said. "No sense stirring up a hornet's nest. But it might be interesting to find out how come Sexton of the Mamaroneck Sextons got hooked by a girl from Staten Island."

"Perhaps her father owned all the breweries on the island," Buckley mused.

"Or it could have been love." Judy raised her eyebrows and pursed her lips in feigned disapproval. "You male chauvinist barristers ever think of that one?

"And how about the Phillips invitation?" Judy asked. "It'll be good exposure. Things will be on the up-and-up. At least you won't be trying to romance a material witness."

"Funny," Sheridan said as he studied the invitation again,

"this Phillips gal did a complete one-eighty. We didn't exactly part under the best of circumstances."

"Well, don't wear your Irish Rover outfit on her show," Judy said. "Wear your dark blue suit, the one you wear when you give your final argument to the jury—your integrity suit."

"When is the show?" Sheridan put the invitation in his coat pocket, as Buckley had the note from Assad.

"Two weeks from today," Judy said, scribbling the appointment in the diary.

"You want to get a couple of brewskies after work?" Buckley said. "Why don't you call Sheila? There's a little dockside café on the waterfront. We could make it a threesome."

"I could use a couple of lagers," Sheridan said. "These sessions with DiTullio are draining. . . ."

The fax machine suddenly erupted with a staccato rhythm. Sheridan watched as it spilled out a memo from Neil Kennedy. He picked up the three pages and scanned each quickly.

"Well, I'll be damned," he said. "The girl from Staten Island was named Emanuela Rivera."

"Rivera?" Buckley furrowed his brow. "That's definitely not Westchester society."

"Death was ruled a homicide. Never solved. The investigation was handled by a Capt. Mike Ahearn, since retired and presently living in Fort Lee, New Jersey."

"Do you want Raimondi to check it out, Dan? Track down the Rivera girl's family, talk with the captain? You've got enough problems juggling the DiTullios and preparing for next week's depositions."

"No, we've got plenty of time. After my Andrew Lloyd Webber fiasco, I promised Sheila a trip to Manhattan, a little shopping at Saks and Bergdorf's. We could take in a show, and there's a quaint little Irish tavern I found. They play the fiddle and sing the real maudlin stuff, 'Rose of Tralee,' 'Galway Bay,' serve soda bread. Sheila might enjoy it."

Buckley read the note from Karen Assad. She thanked him for the great evening at the circus. "Perhaps we could meet just one more time. Give me a call. K."

●

Sheridan pulled into the parking lot of the Hampton Chronic Care facility. A light rain shrouded the area and the mist billowed about the sparse lighting at the entrance. It was late—almost ten o'clock—perhaps too late for visiting hours. He hauled up his oversized trial bag, which contained a portable VCR, Donna DiTullio's tennis tapes, and her scrapbook. He also gathered up some yellow roses, which were wrapped in silver foil. He had purchased them from a roadside florist.

There were only a few cars in the parking lot. He looked up at the moldering brick square in front of him. It resembled a grim prison more than a hospital, and as he made his way toward the dimly lit entrance, he knew his spirits could use a good shot of bourbon. Maybe later, he thought.

The inside was not much of an improvement—walls of gray plaster, gray linoleum flooring, harsh lighting. A janitor mopped the hallway and a beefy-looking receptionist in a nursing cap and a white pants suit sat at a small desk, working a crossword. It was an end-of-the-line state facility with a low-budget Medicare decor.

"Boy, it's mean outside." Sheridan shook himself, stamped his feet, and ran his fingers through his damp hair. The nurse looked up and was not too pleased at the small puddles Sheridan was leaving on the floor in front of her station.

"Can I help you?" She managed a fake little smile.

"I'd like to see Miss Donna DiTullio. Just a short visit." His voice had the proper note of apology. "I know this is a late hour. . . ."

"You a relative?" She eyed the trial bag suspiciously.

"No. I'm her lawyer."

Her cheeks bunched up into a smirk. She checked the chart. "Visiting hours are from two to four and six to eight," she said.

"Those rules are strictly enforced. This is a chronic-care facility. People are gravely ill here."

"I know," Sheridan said softly. He knew he had to take the lecture. He thought of handing her a ten. She looked as though she could use it. But she had a tough Irish face. It might boomerang.

"Tell me, Miss uh . . ." Sheridan held up his hand, his forefinger and thumb forming a circle.

"It's Mrs.—Mrs. Cooney," she interjected quickly.

"Yes, Mrs. Cooney. Is Dr. Halberstadt still here?"

"Heavens no! No!" she said. "He was chief of Orthopedics, but he's now with the VA someplace out in California. Hasn't been here for over a year." She was starting to sound chummy.

Sheridan was well aware of Halberstadt's history. He had become addicted to morphine, had a proclivity for night nurses, and it was Dan Sheridan who had saved his license before the Board of Medicine and arranged for his transfer to more temperate climes.

Sheridan and Mrs. Cooney were now on common ground.

"I've come a long way." Sheridan shrugged.

"Look," the nurse said, "Miss DiTullio is on the second floor. Let me call to find out if you can see her. She's in a ward with three others—terrible cases. Perhaps we can draw a curtain."

"Mrs. Cooney, I do appreciate this." He drew one of the roses out of the foil wrapper and handed it to her. She smelled it, hugged it briefly, and smiled.

"Go right up, sir. The elevator's broken, so take the stairs. First bank on the right. See Betty Evans, the super on the second floor. I'll call and tell her you're coming."

●

Sheridan was ushered in by the night nurse. He had parted with another rose and the nurse had promised to put the rest into a nice vase for Donna. She added that Donna was one of their best patients. Sheridan wondered about that one. To his inquiry as to whether Donna registered any cognition, there was a negative response.

The place had the smell of impending death. The room was silent. Sheridan made out three forms in the dimly lit interior, mere clumps on metal bed frames. One woman in the terminal stages of old age, hair scraggly white, slept with her mouth open. Another snored in fits, while the third followed him with her eyes, lonely eyes in a shriveled face, as he walked toward Donna's curtained enclosure. The nurse pulled the curtain open.

"Donna," she said softly, "you have a visitor.

"I'll leave you two. Only thirty minutes, Mr. Sheridan. It's against regulations."

"Thank you," Sheridan said. "I won't be long."

He cranked up the bed to put Donna almost in a sitting position. Her hair, unkempt, was a gray cobweb on the white pillow. Again he noticed the sunken cheeks, the blank gaze.

"Donna, it's me, your friend Dan Sheridan. Got a lousy forehand, a lousier backhand, the world's slowest serve. But I could beat Pete Sampras in a one-on-one. I mean at basketball."

He was inches from her face, plumbing her vacant eyes. And there it was! The tearing, this time welling and slowly easing down her cheeks.

Good Mother of God! he swore to himself, I think she can hear me.

There wasn't much room in the curtained enclosure, but Sheridan pulled out the VCR from his bag and put it on the nightstand, adjusting it to Donna's eye level.

"Got a little surprise for you, Donna. You were the best in New England. I want you to see how it was." He clicked on the set.

For twenty minutes, he watched the gutsy Donna DiTullio charge, scamper, sidestep, float with graceful agility as she put her opponent away in the final set.

Now the tears slid down Donna's cheeks into her mouth. Sheridan took a facecloth and gently dabbed her face.

"Donna," he said, "I think you can hear me." Her eyes still stared blankly.

Sheridan clicked off the set and glanced at his watch. The night nurse would be back at any moment.

"If you can hear me, Donna," he said, bending closer to her face, "blink your eyes. Can you hear me, Donna?" He raised his voice.

Slowly the eyelids fluttered. There was more tearing. Then she closed her eyes, and after several seconds, reopened them.

It was primitive, but it was a sign of cognition.

She may be petrified of the doctors and nurses, Sheridan thought, but why didn't she respond to her parents?

He smiled and gave her cold, limp hand a gentle squeeze.

"I'll be back tomorrow," he said.

Now he had to convey the fact of her response to someone, the night nurse, Dr. Brockelman. He had to get her back to St. Anne's. He'd talk to her neurosurgeon, Dr. Jensen. He might even pay a call on the cardinal.

13

As usual, Sheridan made an early entrance into the court-room. He was surprised to see Mayan d'Ortega seated at the defendant counsel table and Charlie Finnerty with his hand resting on the judge's bench, kibitzing with Judge Mason's law clerk. Apparently, they were sharing a light moment. The clerk laughed and Finnerty, who had caught Sheridan's entrance out of the corner of his eye, put on his best Cary Grant smile.

D'Ortega rose from her seat.

"*Buenos días, señorita,*" Sheridan greeted her warmly.

"Good morning, Mr. Sheridan," she replied coolly. She seemed to take the Spanish salutation as a put-down.

Catching the tone of her voice, Sheridan didn't extend his hand.

Charlie Finnerty patted the clerk on the shoulder and gave Sheridan the lodge-brother treatment.

"Danny me boy," he said as he pumped Sheridan's hand, "let's settle this thing and all go home. I'm sure we have better things to do. . . ." He paused a few moments.

"You talk over our offer with your clients?"

"Funny you should mention that, Charlie. My clients thought you were joking. They still want twenty million."

"Well"—Finnerty's smile began to fade—"you gotta lay off those mushrooms." He glanced at his watch. "I've got to be in Judge Thompson's session at nine. I'll let you and Mayan argue out our petition for costs."

"Are you serious about trying to tag me for two thousand dollars for bringing a motion to prevent Donna DiTullio from being dumped on a trash heap?" Sheridan's voice hovered between ridicule and disbelief.

"Hey, I told you, Dan. You mix with us, you're in a dogfight. This is civil litigation. We don't pitch underhand in this league."

"Look, Charlie, the new law doesn't go into effect for two more weeks. *The loser pays* might be the law in England, but we're in Boston, not the Inns of Court."

"Dan, you obviously misread our petition for costs. We're not going under the new law. But even under the existing law governing this case, the judge, in her discretion, can allow legal costs to the prevailing party. See, Dan, you criminal lawyers don't try enough civil cases to appreciate the nuances of civil procedure."

"Hey, Charlie, don't lecture me. I didn't ride into town on a truckload of turnips." Sheridan paused, trying to sheathe his anger.

"And if you want to play this kind of game," he said, "you seem to forget that I prevailed on your Rule Eleven motion. I can bring a petition for costs, say for four thousand dollars."

Charlie Finnerty beamed, and his cheeks bunched up into rosy little knots.

"Dan, before this case is over, you'll get some lessons on civil procedure that you'll never forget. You must bring a motion for costs within ten days or they are deemed waived. Simply stated, Dan, you've misread the statute, probably never read it at all. . . . Look, I've got to run. Judge Thompson is a stickler for punctuality."

"Do you really need the two thousand dollars, Charlie? I

mean, don't you think Judge Mason will think you're being kind of chintzy?"

Charlie picked up his briefcase. "Hey, Dan, that's up to Judge Mason. All we're doing is invoking the law . . . and, Dan, I may be able to stretch the two hundred thou, make it three. Take your fee right off the top. A third goes into three very easily. It's short division."

You know what you can do with your offer, Sheridan was tempted to say, recalling Dante DiTullio's reaction. This seemed like an opportune time to spew out something obscene. Sheridan merely gave a slight wave of his hand.

"Have a good day, Charlie," he said.

—

The session before Judge Mason was brief. The judge did think the two thousand dollars was a little on the steep side. Mayan d'Ortega countered with her time sheets, the fact that she had employed two paralegals, and added, "Since we knew our opponent to be a formidable adversary, we needed all the extra research and legal assistance we could get."

"The defendants' petition for costs is allowed." The judge gave a slight rap of her gavel.

Sheridan took it as graciously as he could. He knew that Charlie Finnerty's paper chase would now begin. But he had more important things on his mind, and his first priority was to get Donna DiTullio back to St. Anne's.

—

Buckley picked up Mrs. Gallagher to drive her over to Dr. John White's office. She insisted on bringing along her Saint Bernard. Aptly, he was called Barney. They succeeded in stuffing the huge furry creature into the small back space of Buckley's MG, and all during the trip Barney slobbered on the back of Buckley's neck.

Dr. White put Mrs. Gallagher through a battery of psychiatric tests designed to evaluate her intellectual functioning and her current mental and emotional state. Buckley waited in the reception area with Barney, who panted and drooled, to the dismay of the doctor's nurse.

"Aren't I supposed to lie down on a couch, Doctor?" Mrs. Gallagher said as she brushed some imaginary specks off the arms of the leather chair in front of Dr. White's desk. "That's what Bette Davis did in the movie *Now, Voyager*. You remember that scene where Claude Rains was the psychiatrist. He had his little notebook."

"Yes, I remember." Dr. White smiled indulgently. "Wasn't Anthony Perkins in that picture?"

"No, you're thinking of *Psycho*, with Janet Leigh. That was much later and nowhere near as good."

"You're right.

"Well, I don't have a psychiatrist's couch, no gold watch and chain to try to hypnotize you, no tape recorder. We're here simply to establish that you are of sound mind," he said as he scribbled in his notebook.

"Just complete a few sentences for me and give me their meanings." White and Mrs. Gallagher exchanged conspiratorial smiles.

"A penny saved—" White began.

"Isn't worth the trouble," Emma Gallagher interrupted.

"No. A penny saved is a penny earned. What is the meaning of that old adage?"

"Oh, it has something to do with frugality, but I still say it's not worth bothering about. Now, if you ask me about saving a couple of million, then, Doc, I think you'd be onto something."

Boy, this is a crusty old broad, thought White. She may be closing in on ninety, but she's still cooking on all cylinders. Buckley had told him her nieces were trying to have her involuntarily committed. White would make certain that would not happen.

"Who is presently attorney general of the United States?" White read from a printed form designed to test the patient's knowledge of current events.

"Damned if I know." Emma Gallagher gave a lazy shrug. "Who *is* the attorney general?"

White thought for a moment, then looked at his notepad for the answer. "Edwin Meese," it read. He knew that wasn't correct. Time to update the questionnaire. Who was the attorney general now? He hadn't the foggiest idea.

"I'd say you covered everything pretty well, Emma." White slapped the notepad shut and came out from behind his desk.

"Doc, I need a good shot of whiskey," she said as she gathered up her pocketbook.

White escorted Mrs. Gallagher to the reception area. Barney bolted and jumped up joyously on both of them, almost knocking them to the floor. When order was restored and Buckley, Mrs. Gallagher, and Barney were safely out of the building, White reached for the bottle of Dewar's in his desk drawer. He poured himself a stiff one. Like Emma Gallagher, he needed it.

—

By day, the Hampton Chronic Care facility seemed to lose some of its seediness. The lawns were trim and the drive tree-lined. But the stark brick square of the building with its black tiled roof and corroded green copper gutters didn't instill confidence in the visitors, let alone those consigned there with long-term disorders.

Sheridan met with Dr. Brockelman, who headed up Neurology. Lawyer Cantone's assessment had been accurate. The doctor was tall but bent into a permanent stoop. He wore rimless glasses with a cord that looped over his ear, then connected to a buttonhole of his starched white coat. He had a kindly, florid face and a great mane of shaggy hair the color of dry ice.

They sat in the doctor's small office, which was cluttered with multicolored charts depicting the brain, spinal cord, and other facets of neuroanatomy. A full-sized skeleton dangled from a metal stand, and there were volumes of medical books, some displaced on the floor. Sheridan noticed in and out boxes on the gunmetal desk, with documents, memos, and correspondence equally distributed. Everything looked generations old. Sheridan suspected that if he were to return in a week's time, nothing would have changed.

"As far as we can tell, Mr. Sheridan, the patient is unre-

sponsive and still comatose; she doesn't react to painful stimuli."
From his bent position, he looked up at Sheridan, his head
cocked at a birdlike angle.

Sheridan told him about the tearing and blinking, but
Brockelman tended to brush it off.

"Must be pure reflex," he said. "I review the chart each
morning and there's no change in the patient's status."

"I have Donna's scrapbook here." Sheridan patted his briefcase. "Somehow, she responds to me, especially when it relates
to her tennis achievements. I really think she can hear but can't
communicate. It's an awful thought, Doctor, but she may be encased in her own body and trying desperately in some primal way
to let us know that she really has cognition."

"Most unlikely," Brockelman said.

"Well, would you allow me a little experiment, Doctor?
Bring along your best neurological resident or nurse and let me
see if I can't get through to Donna."

Sheridan and a reluctant Dr. Brockelman made their way to
the second floor, thunking up a metal staircase with turn-of-the-
century grillwork. The doctor apologized for the elevator being
out of order.

"It should be fixed in a day or two," he said.

The duty nurse looked up from her crossword and greeted
the doctor. She handed him Donna DiTullio's chart and he leafed
through it quickly, his brow furrowed in a look of authoritative
concern.

"There's been no change.

"Can you page Nurse Jennings?" Brockelman asked as he
scratched his initials on the chart. Sheridan noticed that his hand
had an obvious tremor.

"Good morning, Donna," Nurse Jennings said with manufactured buoyancy as she entered the room. "We have visitors."

There had been three other patients in the room when Sheridan was last there. Now there was only one emaciated woman,
and she emitted a muffled moan as they made their way to Donna
DiTullio's bed.

Donna's eyes were still blank and unmoving, fixed on the ceiling.

The nurse was about to draw the gauzy curtains when Sheridan noticed that the IV bottle on a stand above Donna's head was crumpled inward and completely empty.

"For Christ's sake!" Sheridan blared. "How in the hell did that happen?" He pointed to the IV. The nurse and Dr. Brockelman both looked startled.

"She could get a fatal embolism. All that thing's doing now is sucking air." Sheridan was enraged.

Jennings quickly shut down the IV. "I'll get the duty nurse," she said, and left abruptly.

"These things happen," Brockelman apologized.

"Well, damn it, Doctor, they shouldn't happen!" Sheridan made no effort to curb his anger.

—

A nurse's attendant hooked up a new IV and Nurse Jennings checked the drip.

"Everything's okay." She smiled.

Brockelman listened to Donna's heart with his stethoscope.

"Heart, respiration are fine," he said. "We have to make sure this doesn't happen again." He looked at Jennings and put on his best authoritative scowl.

After the crisis had abated, Nurse Jennings cranked Donna into a sitting position, and Sheridan bent down to within a foot of her face.

"Donna, it's me, Dan Sheridan," he said gently. "I want to show you something." He held out a newspaper clipping. Nurse Jennings and the doctor peered over Sheridan's shoulder.

"Here you are with a tennis racket at summer camp. I think that's Lake Winnipesaukee, up in New Hampshire. You won your first tournament. It says you were in the first grade."

There in black bangs was a wide-eyed tyke receiving a Paul Revere bowl. Tears now welled in Donna's eyes. Sheridan, Nurse Jennings, and the doctor moved closer.

"Do you remember that day, Donna?" Sheridan spoke louder. "If you do, blink your eyes."

"My word!" Brockelman exclaimed as Donna's eyelids fluttered, almost like a butterfly taking flight, then blinked several times. Tears now bathed her cheeks.

"Donna, do you remember I showed you some videos?" Sheridan thought he'd refine the experiment. "If you remember me playing the video, blink your eyes *once*." Again the eyelids fluttered, and she did as Sheridan requested.

"Do you know the name of the nurse?" Sheridan nodded toward Jennings. "If you do, blink once. If you don't, blink twice." There came a double blink.

"How about the doctor? Do you know his name? Blink once if you do, twice if you don't." Again two blinks.

"I can't believe this." Brockelman sighed, looking bewildered. "We'd better get this down on the chart. She seems to be communicating.

"Nurse, get in touch with Dr. Malcolm Stuart." He turned to Sheridan to explain. "He heads up Neurology at the state medical hospital.

"I want to arrange a consult and have Stuart do a series of scans. It could be that her cerebral hematoma is resolving. But let's not get too hopeful. The semblance of cognition can disappear overnight."

⬤

Sheridan called Judy on his car phone. The depositions were scheduled for the next day in his office, starting at ten, leading off with Sister Agnes Loretta, followed by Paxon, Lafollette, and Sexton. They would continue daily thereafter. Mayan d'Ortega, Finnerty's daughter, Mary Devaney, and two paralegals would be in attendance for the defendants.

"It's going to be a few long days, Dan."

"It'll be longer for Sexton," Sheridan said. "And how did Buckley make out with Emma Gallagher?"

"He called in," Judy replied. "Said he was taking Mrs. G. and her pooch down to Port of Last Call on the waterfront. Seems they all needed a drink."

14

Mayan d'Ortega had spent the better part of the day going over the expected deposition testimony with Sister Agnes Loretta, Dr. Sexton, Dr. Puzon, and Dr. Lafollette. There would be no surprises; d'Ortega had seen to that. She had covered every conceivable question that Sheridan could raise.

"What you say now is under oath," she said. "We can't deviate from it later on. Be consistent. Just tell the plaintiff's attorney what happened—no more, no less. Don't volunteer information. If the attorney asks for a yes-or-no answer, keep it brief. I'll be there with each of you, and if I think the questions are not relevant or go into territory that is improper, I will advise you not to answer."

When the coterie of legal talent showed up at Sheridan's office at 10:00 A.M., they were prepared and the witnesses well schooled.

Sister Agnes Loretta was in her mid-fifties. Her reddish hair was cut short and she had a kindly Irish face and a disarming smile. She wore a plain gray dress. A small cross was embroidered onto the left sleeve near her shoulder.

The court reporter set up her recording machine and

d'Ortega and her group took their seats around the small conference table, their yellow scratch pads at the ready.

"Sister Agnes Loretta," Sheridan began, "you are well represented by counsel. I'm going to ask you a series of questions. If you can't answer the question or don't understand the question, just ask me for clarification. Fair enough?"

"Fair enough," Sister Agnes Loretta said evenly.

"Okay. Would you administer the oath to the witness?"

"Raise your right hand," the court reporter said. "Do you swear to tell the truth, the whole truth, and nothing but the truth, so help you God?"

"I do," Sister Agnes Loretta replied.

Sheridan understood the exact purpose of a deposition. It was not a vehicle for cross-examination, nor designed to trip up a witness or make the witness look foolish. It was simply a means to gather as much information as possible that could make or break a case. It also gave the interrogator a chance to appraise the witness. Is he or she arrogant, imperious, hesitant, ambiguous, or cagey, or does he or she come off as truthful, informed, and empathetic? Sheridan could see from her responses to preliminary questions that Sister Agnes Loretta would come off looking like the saint she probably was.

No, she had never been arrested, never married, became a Sister of Charity shortly after graduating from New Rochelle College. She then became a registered nurse, held various administrative posts, including dean of St. Anne's School of Nursing, and for the past six years had been St. Anne's chief administrative officer. Technically, she supervised all departments, including Psychiatry. She answered only to the cardinal and she agreed with Sheridan's characterization that she was Dr. Sexton's boss.

"Sister Agnes Loretta"—Sheridan looked up from his scratch pad and eyed the good nun sitting across from him—"prior to the accident involving the patient Donna DiTullio, were you ever critical of the practice of holding psychiatric group therapy sessions on the fifth floor of the Atrium at St. Anne's Hospital?"

"Critical?" There was a wariness in her voice. "Of whom?"

"Critical of Dr. Sexton, first of all, for locating his offices on the fifth floor, where psychiatric patients had access to an open area. Second, critical of the cardinal and the entire Psychiatry Department for going along with the arrangement. And last of all, critical of yourself."

"Just a minute!" Mayan d'Ortega voiced a loud objection. "You are asking Sister a question that calls for an expert opinion. She is here as a factual witness only. If you want to ask her what happened on that tragic day—"

Sheridan cut her off. "Look, Sister Loretta is the chief executive of the hospital. I've got every right to interrogate her on hospital protocol, good or bad."

"Again, I voice my objection to this and to any line of questions calling for an expert opinion."

"Fine, object." He turned to the court reporter. "Put that down in the record. Now, Sister, if you would please answer my question."

"No. I'm not going to allow Sister Agnes Loretta to answer. Again, you are not entitled to elicit expert opinions from factual witnesses. That's black-letter law, in case you didn't know it, Mr. Sheridan."

"Are you telling me that in front of a jury I couldn't pose this question?"

"This is a deposition."

"I understand that. Look, I'm going to ask all of the defendants about the standard of psychiatric care as it pertains to this case. You keep this up, Mayan, and we'll be here for three weeks."

Sister Agnes Loretta remained calm as Sheridan and d'Ortega hammered each other with points of law. The others in the room sat at parade rest, tight-lipped, their pens poised at their yellow pads, waiting for the legal hostilities to abate.

"We'll take this up with the judge," Sheridan shot back as he tried to move on.

He then proceeded to interrogate the sister on purely factual details: where she was when she received the initial report of the accident; whom she talked with; what was said; what she did in response to the tragedy. Sister Agnes Loretta supplied the answers without objection.

"Whose decision was it after the accident to move the psychiatric ward to the ground level?"

"It was my idea initially," she answered. "The cardinal and Dr. Sexton agreed."

"And whose decision was it to enclose the Atrium with unbreakable glass?"

"I'd say that was a joint decision of His Eminence, Dr. Sexton, and me."

"Now just sticking to your part in that decision-making process, Sister, did you feel that it was necessary to glass in the Atrium for the protection and safety of the hospital's patients, especially psychiatric patients?"

"Mr. Sheridan!" Mayan d'Ortega snapped, her angry eyes raking his face. "We've been over this ground.

"Sister," she said, her eyes still fixed on Sheridan, "I instruct you not to answer. And Mr. Sheridan, if you persist in this line of inquiry, we're going to suspend right now."

Sheridan bristled. "Look, I'll conduct this deposition in my own way." He counted to five. "Okay, you've instructed the witness not to answer. I'll reserve my rights on the propriety of your instruction. The judge may order the good sister to answer.

"And, Sister"—Sheridan thought he'd get in the last aside— "at trial you'll be asked that very question in front of the jury, and at that time and place, your counsel can object to her heart's content."

Sheridan next inquired what had happened at the meeting with the cardinal, Monsignor Devlin, Charlie Finnerty, and his staff lawyer. Again, he ran into a stone wall. Mayan d'Ortega claimed everything discussed at that meeting was privileged information under the aegis of attorney-client privilege and instructed Sister Agnes Loretta not to answer.

Question after question met with the same protective objection.

"A few more questions, Sister." Sheridan glanced at his notes.

"When the accident occurred, did you notify the Boston Police?"

"Did I?"

"Yes," Sheridan said. "After you learned of the horrible tragedy, did you call the police so that they could make an immediate investigation?"

"No." She shook her head.

"Did Dr. Sexton call the police?" Anticipating d'Ortega's objection, he added, "If you know."

"I don't believe so," she said, hesitation creeping into her voice for the first time.

"How about the hospital's security? Did anyone from that department call the police?"

"No, Mr. Sheridan, we were too concerned with the patient."

"Sister Agnes," Sheridan dropped the "Loretta," "no one, in fact, connected with St. Anne's—not you, not Monsignor Devlin, not Dr. Sexton, not anyone connected with security—no one called the police. Isn't that a fair statement?"

"No one called the police," the nun replied, her voice almost a whisper.

"And as a result, no police investigation was ever conducted, even to this day, is that correct, Sister?"

"It was an accident. . . ."

"I appreciate that, Sister. I didn't ask you whether or not it was an accident. No investigation was ever made. Not on the day of the accident, not ten days later, not then, not even now—isn't that correct, Sister?"

"That's correct." Her voice was subdued.

"No call was made to the police, Sister, because you, Monsignor Devlin, Dr. Sexton, Dr. Puzon, and Dr. Lafollette were too busy circling the wagons, trying to get your stories straight."

"Mr. Sheridan!" Mayan d'Ortega bolted upright. "This deposition is at an end. In fact, there'll be no depositions of Dr. Sexton, Dr. Puzon, or Dr. Lafollette. I intend to seek a protective order preventing you from taking further defendant depositions. You can limit your discovery to set interrogatories." Her eyes and voice were coldly furious.

"Sister," she said, then turned to the others, "this meeting is over."

Sheridan said nothing as he watched d'Ortega and her assistants gather up their documents. The audible clicking of briefcase clasps signaled that the meeting was over. The leave-taking was awkward. Civility, collegiality, were completely blown away. Neither d'Ortega nor any of her assistants looked his way as they filed out of the conference room.

"Good-bye, Sister," Sheridan said.

Sister Agnes Loretta turned slightly. Their eyes met and held for a moment, then moved away as if by agreement. Something in her expression responded to his. Was it a sense of regret?

"Good-bye," she said softly.

●

"Well, what was that all about?" Judy entered the conference room after the court reporter had departed. "When they all stormed out of here, they were steaming. Didn't even ask for the key to the ladies' room."

Sheridan loosened his tie and draped his coat over a chair.

"I don't know whether I did the dumbest thing or the most brilliant. D'Ortega and I got into a pissing contest. When I was drilling around the nerves, she wouldn't let the nun answer. Then *bang!* She calls off all depositions. Says she's going to insist on sanctions. Someone will get fined. No question!

"But, you know, somehow I get the impression that Sister Agnes wanted to answer. And if she did, she'd tell the truth, and those great walls of infallibility would come tumbling down.

"And you know, Judy, as Charlie Finnerty said, 'We don't pitch underhand in this league.' "

He clasped his hands behind his head and put his feet up on the conference table.

"Yep," he said, more to himself than to Judy, "I think we had a pretty good inning."

●

Charlie Finnerty commended Mayan d'Ortega as he studied Sister Agnes Loretta's deposition testimony.

"Not only was this Sheridan guy completely off base," Finnerty said, "he wasn't even in the ballpark. We have a brief in progress on our motion to preclude plaintiff from taking further depositions. The paralegals are working on it now. We can punch into our new Lexis and get every case on point in a matter of minutes."

Mayan returned to her office and checked the morning mail. Restlessly, she dictated memos on several files, then started to complete her time sheets, allocating four hundred dollars an hour portal-to-portal on the St. Anne's case. But she couldn't concentrate. She got up from her burnished rosewood desk and took in her surroundings for a few moments. No one could ask for more luxurious quarters than her oversized corner office with its pegged hardwood floor and rich burgundy accent rugs. She studied her gold-framed diplomas from Rice University and Texas University Law School. Then there was the treasured family photo: her father, tall, silver-haired, aristocratic; her mother, dark, sloe-eyed, an enigmatic smile etched into her proud Indian face; the young Mayan and her brother, Benito, both teenagers, hugging their pony, Pacheco.

Again she looked about the room. At age thirty-one, she seemed to have everything. But some sense of loss, a lack of fulfillment, gnawed at her. She had had boyfriends, some high school jocks, the captain of the football team at Rice, but the relationships were short-lived. Now she was too busy, too driven, to have time for lovers.

Then, oddly, she thought of Dan Sheridan, her archadversary. She tried to revive the hiss and spit of her anger but found it impossible. Sheridan had a likable quality—she couldn't deny it. And physically, she was drawn to the square cut of his jaw, his pug nose, and his ocean blue eyes, eyes that could laugh yet change quickly to steely blue.

She thought of Charlie Finnerty's remark that Sheridan wasn't even in the ballpark. Sheridan was in the ballpark all right, and he was throwing nothing but smoke.

She shook her head, blinked a few times, and quickly returned to her present assignment. She logged in 3.7 hours on the aborted depositions.

She paged her secretary on the intercom. "Susan, I think I'll take the rest of the day off. My dictation is on the machine. Prepare our motion to preclude and I'll sign it and file it tomorrow morning."

"Can I tell Mr. Finnerty where you're going? He wants a conference of all personnel at four."

"Yes. Just tell him I'm taking a drive to the Cape."

15

"I've talked with Malcolm Stuart at the state university hospital." Dr. Jensen drummed his fingers together as he spoke with Dan Sheridan. "Told me he reviewed Donna DiTullio's latest CAT scans; seems the hematoma is now encapsulated, confined to the occipital area of the brain." The doctor touched the back of his head.

"The small hemorrhages scattered throughout the brain apparently have been absorbed. This is a rare phenomenon, but it does account for some neurologic improvement.

"Mr. Sheridan, the brain is a delicate organ," he continued, "but mysteriously, it can survive a great deal of damage. Destroy one part of the brain—say the temporal lobe"—Jensen touched his left temple—"other portions take over. There have been cases in medical literature where a person's frontal lobes were completely ablated, and other than being a little more irascible, he or she carried on and lived a fairly normal life."

"What about Donna's ability to communicate? I assume you've spoken to Dr. Brockelman."

"I only just got the confirmation from Dr. Stuart. As I said before, her eyes do react to light and accommodation. But this is pure reflex. Cognition depends on the integrity of what we call 'cerebral gray matter,' that part of the brain that allows us to think, move, harbor thoughts of love. Take an orange—the gray matter of the brain is the skin, or the peel. In relation to the brain, it's about that thick.

"But when Stuart visited the patient at Hampton, he couldn't elicit any form of cognition. He did confirm your blinking experiment with Dr. Brockelman, and Donna does now react to painful stimuli. Stuart jabbed the palm of her hand with a pin and there was a withdrawal response. Again, this is reflex. You put your hand on a hot stove and you whip it away damn quick. You don't even have to think about it."

"Well, she is making some sort of progress, is she not, Doctor? A hell of a lot more than when we first met."

"Very little—only minimal improvement."

"Which leads me to my next question, Doctor."

"I was afraid of that." Dr. Jensen gave a dismissive glance at his watch.

"When you signed your affidavit recommending transfer to Hampton, you said that the patient had reached an end result, that improvement was unlikely."

"Look, Mr. Sheridan"—irritation crept into Jensen's voice—"I can't get involved in the politics of your lawsuit."

"Doctor, I'm asking you to come up with me to Hampton. Let me demonstrate that Donna hears, can communicate, can answer simple questions. Then you decide for yourself. . . ."

"You want me to go back on my affidavit?"

"Of course not. At the time you signed that document, we all thought, myself included, that Donna was doomed."

"I can't intervene," Jensen said in a voice that brooked no argument. "Miss DiTullio is no longer my patient. How would you like it if some lawyer showed up at your office and started interfering with one of your cases?"

Sheridan eyed him carefully. "Dr. Jensen, you know and I know that Hampton is a third-class dump. It's a disgrace! And Brockelman shouldn't have gotten past veterinary school. Look, I'm asking you—with your reputation and expertise—yes, to intervene. Because a human life is at stake, and you can turn it around. I'm asking you to get her back to St. Anne's, under your medical care and treatment."

"You're putting me in one hell of a position, Mr. Sheridan. You're suing St. Anne's. I understand you skewered Sister Agnes Loretta pretty good the other day."

"Forget about the lawsuit. I'm coming to you as one human being to another. Donna DiTullio needs help. You're the department head. You give the word and she's back here." Sheridan paused for several seconds. "Make this one of your special cases. Bring Donna DiTullio back from a living hell."

"I'm sorry, Mr. Sheridan. You're playing the sympathy card. We're both professionals. We can't let emotion override judgment. . . . And if you'll excuse me, I'm scheduled for surgery in"—he glanced at his watch again—"in twenty-eight minutes."

Sheridan got the cue. Further discussion would be unproductive. The meeting was over.

"Okay, Doctor." He picked up his briefcase. "Thanks again for seeing me." He shook the doctor's hand.

"I'm going up to Hampton next Thursday at ten A.M. I could swing by and pick you up."

"Mr. Sheridan"—Jensen gave an exasperated sigh— "enough is enough! You lawyers have a way of twisting things, saying black is white and getting the legally uninitiated to believe it."

Sheridan nodded. "I hope the surgery is successful, Doctor. Good luck." He paused at the door.

"I'll be outside your office Thursday morning at ten, just in case you're interested."

The Nordic curl to Jensen's lips was a coiled spring.

"Get the hell out of here, Sheridan," he blurted, "before I call Security!"

❧

After picking up Karen Assad at her apartment, Buckley drove to an outdoor café on the waterfront. He duked the headwaiter a twenty and they were escorted to a table overlooking the pier. It was a picture-postcard day; gulls wheeled overhead, squawking like rusty hinges. The harbor was dotted with white sails, and clouds floated through the blue sky like herds of puffy white elephants.

God, she's a beauty! Buckley thought as he assessed Karen Assad's olive-skinned breasts, which seemed to spill out over her low-cut lemony dress. He had a pretty good hunch that Karen wasn't here to give him the "conflict of interest, I can't see you anymore" bit.

They tripped through the niceties. Ahmed and Kaliph had really enjoyed the circus. Ahmed, a Cub Scout, wrote an essay about it. Unfortunately, one of the den mothers criticized the circus owners for exploiting and cooping up the whole menagerie.

"Hmm . . . never thought of that," said Buckley, "but what the hell, you know those seals that bounce the beach balls . . . when they're munching on mussels and tuna, I'll bet they think they never had it so good."

Buckley and Karen Assad picked through chilled oysters and crab Louis.

"Want some strawberries with Grand Marnier sauce?" Buckley said as the waiter appeared. "I know you have the night shift, but even a pilot has an eight-hour bottle-to-throttle factor."

"No thank you, Tom. . . ." She waited for a long moment.

"Are we on the same wavelength?" Her eyes lingered in his.

"Karen," he stammered, "forget about the goddamned case!" He closed his eyes momentarily.

He reached over and held her hand. "For once in my stupid, miserable life—maybe it's out of the blue—who gives a god-damn? I think I'm nuts about you."

It was now on the table. In a way, to Karen, it was a little scary.

Karen Assad had an innate wariness, born out of centuries of distrust, betrayal, crunching for existence, survival. But some-how, she knew Buckley wasn't trying to con her. And she knew that at age thirty-six, divorced from a deadbeat dad, two kids, this might be her last chance. Buckley was a little overweight, balding, not exactly Omar Sharif, but she wasn't going to blow it.

"I have some information about your case that I think you should know," she said as she finished her coffee.

"Look, Karen, whatever it is, keep it to yourself. Sheridan's deposing practically everyone at St. Anne's who had any contact with Donna DiTullio, probably will depose the cardinal. He'll develop whatever information he needs."

"How is Donna doing? I haven't seen her since she left St. Anne's."

"Only so-so. But it's strange, the brain hematoma may be resolving. Sheridan says he can communicate with her. It's kind of primitive; she blinks her eyes in response to his questions."

"God, that's remarkable!" Karen said. "If by some miracle . . ."

"It'll take more than divine intervention," Buckley said. "It'll take the best medical treatment possible. If she stays at Hampton, she'll regress fast, believe me."

"I know." Karen nodded ruefully. She looked at the waiter, who hovered discreetly out of range.

"Here"—she withdrew her hands from Buckley's—"allow me." She beckoned the waiter.

"No." Buckley grabbed the bill from the waiter's hand. "You can't buy me for twenty-six dollars and ninety-five cents."

●

Buckley dropped Karen off at her Jamaica Plain apartment. As he drove back to the office, somehow the case, Mrs. Gallagher, and the law seemed to be in a remote corner of his universe. His only thoughts were of Karen Assad. Was he crazy? He tilted down the rearview mirror. His face was too puffy. He'd lose weight, cut down on the scotch, start playing tennis. He looked again, then reset the mirror. He failed to notice a nondescript car following. It had been tailing him from the waterfront café.

●

The "confreres," as they were called, met in the makeup room of Channel 3. The doctors and two lawyers wore well-tailored business suits. Dan Sheridan was dressed in his "integrity blue." The introductions were affable. In between the coffee and Danish, the technicians dabbed and dusted, adding facial highlights and color to deflect the cameras' bright support lights. It was to be a one-hour show with audience participation, arguing the pros and cons of the new malpractice law, which had recently been enacted by the legislature.

Jennifer, the producer, had issued a preshow format, but she told the group that it could deviate from the printed questionnaire if anyone felt he could liven up the show.

"I don't want you throwing scalpels and lawbooks at each other," she said, "but if you have a chance to get in a few good zingers, go right ahead. Nothing like spontaneity to spice up a program. Janet Phillips knows how to get the audience whipped up. And I think you'll all get a kick out of your performance. You'll all receive videos of the show."

"Ready in ten minutes," a voice boomed over the intercom.

Applause greeted the group as they were led into the studio. An audience of some thirty people sat in elevated tiers.

Janet Phillips, stunning in an elegantly tailored Escada suit, pastel pink with a hint of lavender, beamed as the cameras focused, angled, elevated; the technicians and engineers were carefully watching the monitor.

The show went reasonably well. There were a few rhetorical bricks thrown. Someone used the Shakespearean cliché "Let's kill all the lawyers."

Dan Sheridan corrected the speaker, saying the quote came from *Henry VI*. The dialogue was between two anarchists who were contemplating tyranny. One, Cade, the rebel, said, "I will make it felony to drink small beer," and Dick the butcher replied, "The first thing we do, let's kill all the lawyers."

Dr. Friedman, an erudite spokesman and president of the AMA, heralded the Massachusetts statute as a forerunner of things to come nationwide.

"Defensive medicine, ordering unnecessary tests out of fear of being sued," he concluded, "is skyrocketing medical costs."

Sheridan countered that in his opinion, the law was unconstitutional, citing that it favored one privileged segment of the population, the medical profession, over those permanently and tragically disabled due to medical errors.

"In our system of justice," he said, "all people should be treated equally. Somehow, Dr. Friedman overlooked the Harvard Medical study done just last year, where it was found that more than ninety-five thousand Americans were killed annually due to medical malpractice, and three hundred thousand seriously injured, and only one in eight such incidents resulted in a legal claim.

"And he overlooks the AMA's mandate put out in 1975.

" 'Defensive medicine, like defensive driving, is good medicine.'

"And speaking of costs, last year individuals in this country spent six point four billion dollars on dog and cat food, twelve billion on CDs and sheet music. The tobacco companies spent two billion dollars in advertising and promotion to induce smokers to commit slow suicide, and, incredible as it seems, the cost is tax-deductible. Only five billion was allocated to medical malpractice. That means when you go to the doctor and pay for a forty-dollar visit, only twenty-six cents is allocated for medical liability insurance. In fact, of our total health-care costs, less than one-half percent is allocated for malpractice.

"And where are Dr. Friedman and the government focusing their knives? On the catastrophically injured and debilitated, who are most in need of support and rehabilitation.

"You know"—Sheridan looked directly into the camera as it zeroed in—"in the Roman Forum, there's an ancient inscription. *'Salus populi suprema lex.'* 'The safety of the people is the first law of the land.'

"The Romans knew that two hundred years before the birth of Christ. Somehow, I think we're all forgetting it."

Janet Phillips led the applause. It was effusive, prompted by several plants sprinkled throughout the audience.

"You were marvelous, Dan," she said as she later escorted him out to the silver stretch limo. "You're powerfully persuasive. I can see how you win over juries."

Sheridan felt a little foolish as he surveyed the ostentatious vehicle.

Janet fondled his arm with a firm grasp, then kissed him lightly on the cheek.

"I was completely out of character at our first meeting, Dan." The soft green eyes, now misty, looked into his. "I was on a lower dose of my medication. I'd really love to see that oyster bar of yours. Can we get together next week, some afternoon after I've finished taping my show? I'll wear some faded jeans and a yellow slicker, sneakers, the whole nautical bit. We'll make it a full day."

"I've got a pretty tight schedule," Sheridan said as he was about to enter the backseat of the limo. The driver, who had opened the door, stood at stiff attention. "My fiancée and I are going to New York tomorrow."

"See if you can squeeze me in, Dan." She gave his arm another tug. "I think we can have some *real* fun, and I've got some information on your case you should know about."

"Okay," he said, "I'll call you when I'm in a better position to know when my diary says I can goof off."

Riding back to his office, he told himself he wasn't going to get involved with Janet Phillips. She was beautiful all right, and a charmer. Her whole world was based on confected charm. And she threw out more than a little carrot. "*Real* fun," she had said, putting the emphasis on *real*. And that tidbit about information. He didn't know which intrigued him more.

—

The private investigator sat in Charlie Finnerty's office. He was smoking the tail end of a cigar and leafing through his notebook.

"I followed this Buckley guy and he picks up Karen Assad, a psychiatric nurse at St. Anne's Hospital, picks her up at her apartment at"—the investigator glanced at his notebook—"twelve forty-six P.M. and drives to the Dockside Restaurant on the waterfront. They had lunch. I sat three tables away. Believe me, they were friendly."

"How friendly?" Charlie Finnerty sat on the edge of his desk, arms folded about his chest.

"Very friendly. They were hunched over during the entire meal, holding hands and playing kissy-face."

"You say Buckley's female companion was Karen Assad, a nurse on the psychiatric ward at St. Anne's. How did you determine that?"

"After Buckley drops this gal off back in Jamaica Plain, I wait outside her apartment for eight and a half hours."

"Eight and a half hours?"

"That's right. It was ten-fifteen. She comes out the door, has on a raincoat; it was open in front and I could see her white nurse's uniform. She takes the subway a block from her house. I leave my car at the locus and get on the same trolley. She gets off at the St. Anne's stop, and I see her enter the psychiatric wing."

"How did you find out her name?"

"We have our ways, Mr. Finnerty. I figured there would be only a few psych nurses arriving at eleven; I called a friend of a friend."

"She wasn't tipped off that she was being tailed?"

"Absolutely not. We're professionals."

"Okay, Jim, you did a good job." Finnerty picked up an envelope from his desk and handed it to the investigator.

"There's twenty one-hundred-dollar bills in there, Jim."

The investigator slid the envelope into his inside jacket pocket and ground the remnants of his cigar into the green marble ashtray situated on a polished walnut credenza.

"Do you want us to do the Sheridan guy, Mr. Finnerty?"

"Not yet. For the moment, just wait until you hear from me."

●

Charlie Finnerty called Dr. Sexton from his private red phone and caught the doctor just as he was leaving for his late-afternoon rounds.

"Do you know a psych nurse by the name of Karen Assad?" Finnerty asked.

"Yes, she's on the eleven to seven shift. I seldom see her, due to the hours."

"Would she have tended Donna DiTullio?"

"I would assume so. The nurses are on rotation. Why do you ask?"

"Oh, just a gut feeling I have, Bob. I'll let you know if I develop anything."

Finnerty waited for several moments.

"I think it's time we invoked plan B." He spoke elliptically. But Sexton knew what plan B would involve. He wanted to avoid it if possible.

"Can't this matter be settled, Mr. Finnerty?"

"Bob"—Finnerty disciplined his voice into a conciliatory tone—"as I look at it now, you and your staff are absolutely blameless. We've made a good-faith offer, but this Sheridan guy is pigheaded. You might say he's a holdup artist. So what do you do with punks like that? You teach them a lesson, right?" Finnerty had dealt with clients for decades, employing his own brand of forensic psychology. Some had to be massaged, some lectured, some disciplined, but none ever alienated—especially when they were footing the bill.

"If you say so," Sexton said, but his voice seemed to lack enthusiasm.

16

Sheridan and Sheila O'Brien caught the Senator out of South Station, had breakfast in the club car, then watched the small bosky towns whiz past as the train clicked along the Connecticut shore.

"We're staying at a little hotel on Madison Avenue, the Westbury. Got tickets for *Sunset Boulevard*. We'll have a late-night snack, then catch Bobby Short at the Carlyle." Sheridan was trying to make amends.

Sheila leaned back against the club-car chair and gently closed her eyes. Now that Finnerty had started his own firm, she didn't have to worry about conflict of interest—not until the next time at least.

"Hope you didn't run into much trouble getting Monday off," Sheridan said.

"We both have trouble getting Mondays off, but let's make the most of it."

She opened her eyes and for a moment watched the front diesel engine snake along a curve trestling over a marshy cove.

"How is your case coming along?"

"So-so." Sheridan swiveled his chair toward Sheila. "It's

sad, really. The DiTullio girl's making some progress. I can actually communicate with her. But Dr. Jensen, her neurosurgeon at St. Anne's, has washed his hands of her case. He seemed to be in my corner when I first met him, but he subsequently did a one-eighty. And all he has to do is snap his fingers, and she'd be back at St. Anne's."

"Is the place she's in now so bad?"

"Bad? You wouldn't believe the Department of Health allows that slag heap to remain open. I think they still use chloroform up there for an anesthetic. Might even use whiskey or make the patient bite on a bullet."

"Why are we staying over on Monday? . . . Don't tell me." Sheila gave him a crinkled smile. "It has to do with your case."

"Tonight and Sunday, we do the town." Sheridan patted her hand. "Understand Bergdorf's opens at ten, and I've got plenty of plastic on me."

"I can certainly use a couple of outfits for court. All my old stuff makes me look like an undergraduate."

"Monday, I'm going over to Staten Island. You can stay back at the hotel or hit Bloomingdale's. But I could use your help."

"Staten Island?"

"Sexton comes from some fancy town in Westchester County."

"That's the cardinal's nephew?"

"The same. Well, a good friend of mine, Neil Kennedy, a lawyer from Queens, got a read on Sexton's living arrangements when he was at Columbia Med. He was living with a girl from Staten Island named Emanuela Rivera. Unfortunately, she went for a run in Central Park. Was fatally mugged. Sexton was in class at the time.

"Rivera's mom and dad still live in the Port Richmond section of Staten Island."

"What do you hope to learn from them?" Sheila couldn't quite follow Sheridan's investigative slant.

"I don't know. Neil set up the appointment. I thought if you came along, it wouldn't spook them.

"We'll grab the Staten Island ferry, feed the gulls, take in the Statue of Liberty, the whole tourist bit.

"On Monday afternoon, I'll take a cab over to Fort Lee, New Jersey. It's a blind call, really. A retired New York police captain named Mike Ahearn conducted the investigation into the Rivera girl's death. Case was never solved, but I'd like to ask a few questions anyway."

"Want me to come along?"

"I don't think so. I may be spinning my wheels—but I've done that before. You can finish up your shopping." ⸱

⬤

Saturday night, after enjoying *Sunset Boulevard*, they walked up Broadway, had corned beef sandwiches at the New York Deli, parted with a hundred-dollar bill for the maître d' at the Carlyle. A candlelit table suddenly opened up down front and they held hands while listening to the piano magic of Bobby Short.

Sheridan considered taking Sheila to the Blarney Stone, but then thought better of it. They wouldn't be singing "Too-ra-loo-ra-loo-ral," and he just had a hunch that Meaghan Dwyer might be a little pissed at him, saying to her hooligans, "Look at himself now, sportin' some young thing half his age," or maybe even tossing out some verbal insult. Best to let the dulcet tones of Bobby Short bring the evening to a romantic close.

⬤

Sheila wasted no time on preliminaries. While Sheridan put on the HIS terrycloth bathrobe provided by the Westbury and lay on the bed watching the late news, she showered, took a quick look in the mirror, peeked around the bathroom door, and, with a towel wrapped turbanlike around only her head, ran and leapt at Sheridan. For the next hour and a half, it was raunchy madness. As always, they tore into each other like feral animals—it lasted and lasted. Sheila's idea of Irish foreplay was "Brace yourself, Bridget."

The meltdown, the sighing, Sheila's sandy blond hair matted, spread on Sheridan's heaving chest, his muscular arm cradling her gently, the sweat of their bodies, the aftermath—that was the inner peace, the contentment, the real sexual embrace.

"You know, my friend"—her finger traced little circles on his hairy chest—"you were good," she said.

Sheridan didn't respond. She propped herself up on one elbow and inched toward his face. He was completely gone, sound asleep.

—

Sheila dragged a reluctant Dan Sheridan to Mass at St. Patrick's Cathedral. Sheridan, raised Catholic, parochial grammar school, Xaverian Brothers at St. Ignatius High School, had started to question his faith when he was in Vietnam. He had grown cynical over the years, a feeling especially intensified when his wife and young son were killed.

"I think I was sold a bill of goods," he told Sheila in a weak moment. "My parents, my grandparents—slaves really to the Catholic ethic. Maybe I deny God not because he allows tragedies to happen to his chosen people; I deny God because of reason. Love is the only certainty."

It wasn't the trappings—the marble columns, the gilded altar, the priceless mosaics, the "Ave Maria" sung by the choir robed in white and scarlet, the cardinal's retinue of clergy swinging thuribles of incense at the elevation of the Host—that moved Sheridan; it was the congregation going to Communion, some tourists, some Manhattan aristocrats, numerous Hispanics, Haitians, Mexicans, a mix of Slavs, various Europeans, some plain Americans—maybe fourth-generation families. Sheila joined the line of people headed toward the altar rail. Sheridan demurred. He shook his head as he watched Sheila coming back to the pew, hands clasped, head bowed.

Jesus, he swore irreverently to himself, this has got to be the greatest hoax of all time. But oddly, he thought of Lincoln, a saint of sorts. "You may fool all of the people some of the time; you can even fool some of the people all of the time; but you can't fool all of the people all of the time." Had all these people been fooled for two thousand years? he began to wonder.

—

Early Monday morning, they caught the Staten Island ferry at the Battery, fed the gulls, spotted and waved at the tourists at the Statue of Liberty parkside. They landed at St. George's Point. From there, they took a cab, getting off at a three-story building on a side street just off Jewett Avenue.

Sebastian and Santurce Rivera welcomed them into their modest second-floor apartment. After introductions and explanations that Sheridan was involved in a malpractice case against Dr. Sexton, and that they were merely checking on his background, they sat in the living room. Santurce served tea and Sebastian smoked a cigar.

"These are our children." Santurce pointed to several photographs adorning the walls and sitting on the mantel.

"This was our daughter, Emanuela." It was a First Communion picture, now quite faded, but in an ornate silver frame.

"She was a beautiful child." Sheila picked up the photo, studied it, then passed it to Sheridan.

"Yes, she was very special," Sebastian said quietly.

"It must have been a terrible loss," Sheridan said as he looked at an angelic dark-haired child veiled in white, hands laced with rosary beads.

"We'll never get over it." Santurce sighed. "But we know she's with the angels. We pray to her each day."

"How did your daughter and Dr. Sexton meet?" Sheridan asked as he got up and replaced the photo carefully.

"They met on Long Island. Emanuela was a waitress at a restaurant out on the East End." Santurce's voice choked and she began to weep. She paused for several seconds, then took out a handkerchief and dried her eyes.

"This Sexton fellow had just graduated from Yale," she continued. "His folks had a summer place in Wainscott. He saw a lot of Emanuela, and one day she moved in with him when he started school at Columbia."

"They ever marry?" Sheridan knew he was touching a nerve.

"No," Sebastian said disconsolately. "And they were both Catholics."

"But he was good to Emanuela, and she was completely in love with him," Santurce interjected. "They were so beautiful together."

"Tell me"—Sheridan looked at Sebastian and tried to avoid Santurce's teary gaze—"when they lived together in New York City, was . . . er . . ." He cleared his throat. "I know this is sensitive, and if you don't want to discuss it, you don't have to."

Sebastian laid his cigar down on a standing ashtray. The smoke curled toward the ceiling. His eyes were wet. He had anticipated Sheridan's question.

"Yes," he said, his voice husky, "she was two months' pregnant at the time. It was discovered by the pathologist."

There was a long silence.

"Look, we've taken up too much of your time," Sheridan said. "I want to thank you for being so open with us." He and Sheila rose. "And thank you for the tea."

"One last thing," Sheridan said. "Were you satisfied with the police investigation?"

"Oh, yes." Sebastian chewed on his lower lip and his eyes brimmed with tears. He shook his head. "Bad place, Central Park. I wouldn't walk there, even in daylight.

"And the Sexton boy was devastated. He remained at her grave and was still standing there when we all departed. She's buried in Groves Lake Cemetery."

"In fact, he was very thoughtful," Santurce said as she permitted herself a thin smile. "He gave us an envelope with five thousand dollars in it. We didn't want to accept it, but he insisted that it was something he wanted to do in Emanuela's memory."

"Thanks again." Sheridan shook Sebastian's hand and kissed Santurce lightly on the cheek.

"Here," Sebastian said as he showed Sheridan and Sheila to the door. He handed Sheila a small prayer card with a sepia picture of Emanuela surrounded by a rosary. "You can pray to her. She intercedes for us quite often."

Sheridan left Sheila back at the Westbury and took a cab

over the George Washington Bridge. He told the driver to drop him off at the center of Fort Lee. Sheridan went into a drugstore and ordered a cup of coffee, then asked for a telephone directory for Bergen County. This was going to be a blind call. For all he knew, Mike Ahearn could be in some trailer camp in Fort Lauderdale. There were several Ahearns in the directory, no Michael, two with the initial *M*. He finished his coffee, then dialed the first *M* listing. No answer. One o'clock on a Monday afternoon—he wondered if he had really expected a contact. Call two—*bingo!*

"Is this Capt. Michael Ahearn?"

"Yes," came a gravelly voice. "Who's this?"

"My name is Dan Sheridan. I'm a lawyer from Boston."

"A lawyer?"

"Yes, I'm a former police officer, Boston PD. Went to law school nights."

"Whaddya want?"

Kennedy had said he could use Lieutenant O'Halloran's name, so he chalked one up on the plus side of Kennedy's chit docket.

"I'm a friend of Lieutenant O'Halloran, NYPD. I'm down here investigating a medical malpractice case I'm handling up in Boston."

"Madge," Ahearn shouted, "turn that thing down. I'm on the line here.

"Well, what can I do for you, me being down here and your case up in Boston?"

"The defendant whom I'm suing is a doctor—actually, a psychiatrist."

"Yeah?"

"He went to Columbia Medical School fifteen plus years ago. I'm just trying to get some background information on him."

"Well, why call me?"

"Lieutenant O'Halloran, who retires this month, said that you investigated the death of the doctor's girlfriend."

"What? What was her name?"

"Emanuela Rivera. She was living with a Robert Sexton. Seems she was fatally ambushed in Central Park."

There were several seconds of silence.

"Yes, I remember," Ahearn said.

"Can we meet, Mike? Say for a half hour or so? I'll pay you for your time."

"Look, where are you now?"

"Corner of Main and Palisades, a drugstore."

"Take a cab to O'Doul's. It's a small bar. Just say the name; the driver will know where it is. Meet you there in fifteen minutes."

—

Mike Ahearn was a badly preserved sixty-seven. Potbelly, sagging jowls, droopy eyes like a Saint Bernard, wearing wire-rimmed glasses that seemed to hang on the end of his porcine nose.

They took a seat at the rear of the bar. The bartender brought over two Bud Lights and Sheridan tossed a twenty on the table, telling him to keep the change.

Sheridan passed Ahearn an envelope with five one-hundred-dollar bills. "Here," he said to Ahearn, "I know this is an imposition. But for your time." Ahearn tweaked the envelope open with his thumb and forefinger, smiled a leprechaunish kind of smile, and stuffed the envelope into his inner jacket pocket.

"Well, Mr. Sheridan, what can I do for you? Keep in mind that it was well over fifteen years ago—maybe close to twenty. But I remember the case."

"Was it ever solved—I mean were you able to develop any leads?"

"As I recall"—Ahearn paused and took a swig of beer—"girl was Puerto Rican, came from Staten Island. Sexton guy was a med student from Mamaroneck. I remember speaking to his parents. They were fine people, aristocratic. This Sexton kid was part Irish, on his mother's side."

"Harriet Minehan," Sheridan added. "In fact, Harriet Minehan's brother is the present cardinal up in Boston."

"Well, we did a thorough job. Coroner, pathologist, statements from everyone. Sexton was in school at the time it happened. Kept the case open for three years. Couldn't find a clue. Unresolved homicide. Case closed. That's about par for ninety percent of homicides in Manhattan."

"Do you have any of those statements, Mike?"

"Naw. Probably destroyed after seven years. Or in some dusty archive somewhere."

"Did you know that the Rivera girl was pregnant at the time?"

Ahearn thought for a few moments.

"Yeah, come to think of it, I remember seeing something to that effect in the pathologist's report."

"Okay, Mike." Sheridan shook Ahearn's hand warmly. "I'll grab a cab back to the big city."

"Anytime. Think I'll just hang in here for a while." He signaled the bartender for another beer.

●

Mike Ahearn wasted no time in getting to the pay phone. He made a call to Boston.

"Dr. Robert Sexton?" he said, his voice cracking like frozen leather. "Not in? Yeah, have him call Mike Ahearn in New Jersey. It's important." He gave the secretary his number.

17

Judge Mason listened patiently to Mayan d'Ortega's motion to preclude the plaintiff from taking further depositions. She appeared impressed with Mayan's fluent presentation.

"I have no problem with Mr. Sheridan eliciting factual data from the deponents, but he has no right to attempt to elicit expert-opinion testimony. This line of questioning should be reserved for depositions from the designated experts. Mr. Sheridan has already listed a Dr. John B. White as his psychiatric expert. And I expect to list our experts: Dr. L. Tyler Richardson, chief of Psychiatry at the Kennedy Center; Dr. Saul Goldenbach, professor of clinical psychiatry at the State University Medical School; Dr. Charles O'Rourke, chief of Psychiatry at the Veterans Administration Hospital; and Dr. Mesak Segarian, chief of Psychiatry at Memorial Hospital."

"Boy," Sheridan said to himself, but audibly enough for all to hear, "talk about touching all bases."

Judge Mason was unable to suppress a smile. Even Mayan d'Ortega arched her pencil-thin eyebrows and gave Sheridan a favorable "you scored on that one" nod.

"Mr. Sheridan." The judge looked down at both counsel.

"I'll hear you as to why you believe you should be able to interrogate the defendants on standards of psychiatric care."

"Judge, there is no case in Massachusetts on point, but our rules are based on the federal rules, and I have listed several cases in other jurisdictions favorable to the plaintiff's position. I won't rehash my brief. Suffice it to say, I appeal to Your Honor's judgment and pure logic. The defendants aren't designated experts, but they are experts in the field of psychiatry. Sister Agnes Loretta is expert in hospital administration. Certainly I should be able to interrogate them in their respective fields. All I'm asking is whether or not, in their judgment, considering the nature of the illness, these defendants should have been conducting a group therapy session with a suicidal patient on an open fifth-floor location—on the edge of a cliff, no less—and leave the patient unattended. Now, all I want is their answer. If these doctors, and that goes for Sister Agnes Loretta, feel that their conduct comported with good psychiatric practice—fine. Let them say so under oath. It's the same question I'll ask them when they're on the witness stand, in front of a jury.

"Judge, let me put it another way. If a defendant is going fifty miles per hour in a school zone, runs a stop sign, and hits a child pedestrian on the crosswalk, then, if you follow Ms. d'Ortega's reasoning, I have no right to ask him if his conduct was negligent, irresponsible, even reckless."

D'Ortega was quick to rise. "You can't equate the complexities of psychiatric medical practice with an ordinary automobile case! That's completely ludicrous!"

"That's what I'm doing, Judge, despite Ms. d'Ortega's gratuitous characterization."

"When can all depositions be concluded, assuming I allow Mr. Sheridan to interrogate the defendants as he suggested?" the judge asked.

"Oh, I'd say within three months, Judge," Sheridan replied. "I just received an order from the probate court granting permission to obtain my client's psychiatric record while she was at St. Anne's."

"All right," the judge said, "I'll set a time limit—all depositions to be concluded within ninety days. Do you intend to list any psychiatric experts in addition to Dr. White?" she asked Sheridan.

"No, just Dr. White."

"How is your client, Mr. Sheridan?" the judge asked.

"Not good, Your Honor. She's at Hampton Chronic Care and Rehabilitation Hospital. I wish I could get her back to the Boston area, even to St. Anne's." Sheridan looked out of the corner of his eye, trying to gauge the effect of his last remark on Mayan d'Ortega. Nothing registered.

"Well, I'm going to overrule your motion, Miss d'Ortega," the judge said evenly, "and hopefully you two can resolve future differences lawyer-to-lawyer, without the need of judicial intervention."

"No question about it, Your Honor." Sheridan looked up at the bench. This judge might not be bad to try this case in front of, he thought. She seems to have a sensitivity that some judges lack. Not imperious or arrogant, traits that appear to be infective when a lawyer suddenly dons the robe.

Mayan d'Ortega was not happy with the judge's ruling. But an appeal would be a useless gesture. She would advise Finnerty against it.

She pretended to engage Mary Devaney in some light legal banter, not bothering to acknowledge Sheridan's slight wave. But she watched him as he left the courtroom, and she felt a slight pang of regret that she didn't know him other than as an unfriendly adversary. She wondered what he thought about her.

—

Dr. Robert Sexton was surprised when his secretary said that a Mike Ahearn had called from somewhere in New Jersey. In fact, the secretary thought that it was some relative, perhaps with bad news. Sexton declined her assistance in placing a return call.

"It's an old friend," Sexton told her. He jotted the name and number on a notepad and told her to refer the afternoon patients to Dr. Puzon.

He walked past the receptionist and headed for the lobby

pay phone. Mike Ahearn was a voice from the past, going back fifteen or more years. His contact did not augur well. Sexton fumbled with several quarters, then gave the operator his card number.

"Hello, is this Capt. Mike Ahearn?" Sexton bent forward, his eyes unconsciously checking the lobby traffic.

"That's right." Ahearn's sandpaper voice had the high pitch of a prizefighter who has caught too many to the head and throat.

"Mike, good to hear from you after all these years. How's the missus?"

"Fine, just fine."

"And your children? You have two, I believe."

"Three. All grown up. Got 'em all through college. Unfortunately, two are back living with me."

"Well, those things happen, Mike." There was a short pause. "What can I do for you?"

"Had a visitor the other day. A lawyer from Boston."

"From Boston?" Sexton's voice was hesitant.

"Guy named Dan Sheridan. Says he's suing you for malpractice."

"Oh, yes," Sexton said with manufactured nonchalance. "It's a frivolous suit, believe me." There was another long pause. "What in the world took him down to New Jersey to see you?"

"Said he wanted some background information."

"Background?"

"Look"—Mike Ahearn's voice rose an octave—"he was asking a lot of questions about you and your girlfriend."

"What in the world . . ."

"Listen, Doc, that's what I'd like to know."

"It's harassment, pure harassment, that's what it is, Mike," Sexton stammered. "This lawyer is a two-bit shyster."

"Maybe, maybe not. Guy said he was an ex-cop, wanted to get the investigation report on the girl's death, statements, that sort of stuff."

"The investigative reports? Weren't those . . . you know."

"Look, Doc. I've got my retirement; after thirty-five years on the force, it adds up to a good monthly stipend. Now me and

Madge got this place in Jersey and a condo down in Vero Beach. We go there for the winter."

"Well, I'm glad you called, Mike. I assume you told him the results of the investigation."

"Yeah, and that's why I'm calling. Seemed kinda funny to me he'd be trying to snoop into something from that long ago. And Doc. . . ."

"Yes?"

"I don't want him down here prying around. Understand?"

There was an unmistakable warning in Ahearn's throaty growl.

"Okay, Mike. Let me know if you need anything."

"I don't need nothin'. Just don't want this guy showing up at my doorstep again."

"Don't worry, Mike. No problem. Say hello to Madge and the kids for me."

Sexton hung the receiver up slowly. A bit of a complication, he thought, nothing to worry about. He stood at the phone for several seconds. This Sheridan's got to be dealt with. He'd call Charlie Finnerty.

—

"I'm thrilled you'd go out with me again, Dan, especially after that horrid time I gave you. And you were really marvelous on my show. We got an eight point four viewer rating on the Nielsen."

Janet Phillips sat in the front seat of Sheridan's 1976 TR6, fluffed her hair, which was now spun gold, put on oversized sunglasses, and snuggled as close to him as the low bucket seats would allow.

Sheridan had on his customary scally cap, a plain white T-shirt, khaki shorts, loafers, no socks.

They engaged in light banter as Sheridan's polished red roadster thrummed along the Cape Cod highway. At Barnstable, he cut left, turning into a leafy road, and headed toward the bay. They sped past weathered clapboard houses, half-hidden by Scotch pine and bayberry heath, and then crunched into a lane of crushed oyster shells and pulled up in front of a small water-front restaurant. A sign in the shape of a dolphin read MARJORIE'S CHOWDER HOUSE.

They were escorted to a table outside, where a lunchtime crowd sat under bright yellow umbrellas and picked away at lobsters, mussels, and corn on the cob.

"Dan, it's good to see you again," the proprietor said as she came over from the cashier's booth.

"This is Marjorie," Dan said, introducing her to Janet Phillips. "Not only is she a direct descendant of Priscilla Alden but she also serves the best clam chowder on the Eastern Seaboard."

"Janet Phillips! I love your show," Marjorie said with exuberance. She had wrinkled, weather-beaten skin the color of the lobster traps that decorated the entrance. But she had a pleasantly rustic voice and an engaging smile.

"Let me cook up something special," she said. "You two just sit back and drink in the bay and a couple of martinis." She flicked her fingers for a waitress. "Leave the rest to me. I'll give you the Cap'n Ahab special."

They started with clam chowder and topped it off with bay scallops, lobster, oysters on the half shell, with a complement of crusty French bread and ice-cold ale.

Unlike the meeting at the Ritz, this time Janet Phillips was calm and the green eyes focused only on Sheridan as she listened to him, as if what he said was the most important thing in the world. Sheridan was beginning to like this other side of Janet Phillips. Maybe he had her all wrong.

"How is your case coming?" she asked.

"Oh, it'll run its course; we're a long way from trial. Right now, I'm tracking down a few leads. Got a raft of depositions coming up. The defense lawyers will make a fortune."

She furrowed her tanned creamy brow in a look of concern.

"How can I help?" she said, bending closer to Sheridan. Her hand reached for his; Sheridan didn't pull away.

"Oh, I'll be taking your deposition within the next few weeks. When I do, just tell the truth—no more, no less."

"Would it really help your case if during the session Donna

DiTullio was agitated, picking at her dress, distraught, even if the others said she exhibited blueberry-pie normality?"

"It sure would," Sheridan said. "The case would be a slam dunk."

"A woman can pick up things a man often would miss— nuances, a tone of voice, fidgeting with a ring, things like that.

"Supposing I were to say in my deposition that Donna was edgy, her knees were shaking, her voice seemed far-out. . . ."

"You picked all that up?"

"Well, I could . . . uh . . . embellish it a little. I've thought it over. I feel so terrible about that poor girl. We could give a hyped-up version. I'm sure if I came across favorably to your case, the people you're suing might settle."

Sheridan steepled his fingers under his chin and looked into Janet Phillips's green ficus eyes. Was he hearing correctly? There was an oh-so-subtle implication.

"You'd be under oath, testifying under the penalties of perjury, you know that."

She nodded.

"Well, if in your judgment Donna was distraught, voice spacey, as you say—even if the defendants say otherwise—it would be for the jury to decide who's telling the truth. They are the triers of fact. I could argue that you are completely disinterested, no ax to grind, unlike the defendants. As a witness, you'd come across as quite credible."

"How much are you suing for?"

"Oh, if my client survives, I'll have a medical expert who will give an opinion on her life expectancy. If she gets over these next few months, she might live for another twenty years—in a near-vegetative state, mind you. Then my economist will testify that she will incur at least six million dollars in future healthcare costs over that twenty-year period."

"Six million?"

"Those are what we call 'the special damages'—what it's going to cost just to keep Donna alive. On top of that, we factor in her loss of earning capacity. I'm not saying she could've beaten Steffi Graf or Monica Seles, but she would have been up there.

That could go four to five million dollars. Then there's her pain, suffering, loss of bodily function, humiliation. We'll let the jury put a monetary figure on that."

"My." Phillips feigned a gulp, spreading her hands over her breasts. "You're really talking a lot of money. I'm adding it up; you're up around twenty million."

"Something like that."

"Well, let me see if I can help you, Dan. Let's meet again, say shortly before my deposition."

"That would be fine. I really appreciate this, Miss Phillips."

"The name is *Janet*." She smiled her impish, doe-eyed Audrey Hepburn smile. "And Dan, would you like to do the Vineyard? My producer has a place in Chilmark, right on the beach. Let's spend a weekend. That'd be a good time to prepare for my deposition."

Sheridan thought for a few moments.

"I think we'd better keep this strictly professional," he said. "After all, you are a key witness."

"Oh, don't be such a goddamned straight arrow. I know you're engaged, but a little weekend romp is good for the soul. Hey, we hit it off in the sack, I bury these guys you are suing.

"And don't worry. I'll leave a little piece of Dan Sheridan for your—what's her name?"

"Sheila. Sheila O'Brien." Sheridan reddened. The conversation was getting a little crazy.

Janet Phillips excused herself. As she headed for the ladies' room, he paid the bill and left the waitress a thirty-dollar tip. He passed the time kibitzing with Marjorie.

Janet Phillips took off her white poplin jacket and disengaged the tiny microphone from a stickpin holding her lavender kerchief about her slender neck. She looked at the cassette and noted that it was almost finished. It had caught the entire conversation. She checked herself in the mirror, smoothed her hair, wet her finger with her tongue, and slicked her eyebrows. Funny, she thought, how a guy like Dan Sheridan, with his reputation as a tough guy, was really so frail and brittle. She brought the cassette to eye level, gave it a little shake, then dropped it into her purse.

●

Karen Assad waited until she saw Sister Mary Ignatius, director of Medical Records, head for the executive lunchroom. She then told the clerk at the medical records desk that she wanted to check on a patient's chart. It was one in the afternoon, and Karen wasn't due on the psych ward until eleven. But she showed up at Medical Records in her full nurse's outfit.

The clerk seemed a little flustered, asked the patient's name, and said she'd need a doctor's authorization.

"Oh, Ruby." Karen gave her best caregiver's smile after having checked the girl's name tag. "I used to work in Medical Records." It was an angel-in-white fib. "Only have to check a hemoglobin notation on the patient for Oncology." She waved a notebook.

"You know your way around back there?" the clerk asked. "It's a real maze. What's the patient's name?"

"Davis, Juanita Davis."

"Lovely name, Juanita," the clerk said. "My aunt's name is Juanita." They exchanged "we're on the same team" smiles.

"Just go straight ahead. Gotta take a left at the sign saying FOR OFFICIAL USE ONLY. That'll bring you into the D's. They're all in swing-out cabinets. Davis shouldn't be too hard to find."

Karen followed directions. She slid out the D cabinet, and there it was, "DiTullio, Donna."

She had at least twenty minutes. She knew Sister Mary Ignatius ate like a bird; Karen had followed her lunchtime routine during the last couple of days. She pulled out the file and laid it on top of the cabinet. It encompassed the three weeks of psychiatric treatment prior to the accident and the weeks of hospitalization following the accident. There were nurses' notes, blood chemistries, radiology reports, electrocardiograms, electroencephalograms, CAT scans, MRIs, the entire gamut of medical esoterica. But Karen wasn't looking for these. She had a hunch, maybe far-out. She had been intimately connected with Donna

DiTullio—had taken her vital signs, assessed her medical and psychological condition, studied her medical charts. She had a pretty good idea that when Donna DiTullio jumped that near-fatal day, she was pregnant. Karen skimmed through the psychiatric records, but they were of no value. She next scoured the record of Donna's St. Anne's hospitalization following the tragedy, which covered confinement in Neurology. She glanced at her watch; Sister Mary Ignatius would be back in four minutes. Jesus, she thought, it's got to be here!

With less than two minutes' leeway, she found it. She knew it had to be there, unless it had been extracted by design. The pathology report. She looked around. Nothing but walls and walls of cabinets. She read it quickly. "Dr. Rashi Diwali, pathologist. There is a 2 × 3 cm mass, definitely fetal." This was followed by a pathologic breakdown—enzymes, coloration, tissue analysis, diagnostic conclusions. The period of gestation was estimated at three months. The mass had been removed surgically.

Karen glanced again at her watch. It was too late to ask Ruby for a photocopy of the record, and Ruby would think it very odd that the name on the record was DiTullio and not Davis. If only she had a camera. She knew it was time to go. She could come back.

"Thank you, Ruby." She breezed past the receptionist's desk, pushed the swinging doors open, and made her way down the hallway.

"Good afternoon, Sister." She gave Sister Mary Ignatius a pleasant greeting as the head of Medical Records suddenly appeared from a side entrance. Karen kept going. She was fairly certain the sister hadn't seen her emerging from the records department. But it had been close.

18

D an Sheridan grabbed a cab to St. Anne's Hospital, taking with him the probate court order authorizing release of Donna DiTullio's psychiatric records. He would wait while the record room staff photocopied both the hospital and the psychiatric records. He had a blank check in his briefcase; he knew it would be expensive.

There was another purpose to his mission, and this was a little dicey. He wanted to see Sister Agnes Loretta without her legal cadre being present. He was violating more than a few ethical codes, but he thought he might be able to plead his case for getting Donna back to St. Anne's. The lawsuit wouldn't be mentioned. But he could be in a pack of trouble, particularly with the bar overseers, if Sister Agnes Loretta took his approach the wrong way. It was a chance he was willing to take. And there was the strong probability that, coming in unannounced, the sister wouldn't see him at all.

Sheridan was directed to Sister Agnes Loretta's office, which was located in Administration, on the seventh floor of the glassed-in Atrium. A pleasant secretary said that Sister was in but quite busy at the moment. Sheridan gave her his card, said that Sister wasn't expecting him but that he hoped he might have a brief interview, ten minutes at most.

"Who do you say wants to see me?" Sister Agnes addressed the intercom as she balanced a telephone in the crook of her neck and reached for some documents on her desk.

"An attorney—Daniel O. Sheridan," the secretary said, looking at his business card.

Sister Agnes Loretta hesitated for a moment.

"Yes," she said into the telephone, "have Dr. Sanders call me back." She then hung up the phone and returned to the intercom.

"Where is Mr. Sheridan now?" she asked her secretary.

"Right outside. Said it would be a brief visit."

"Call Attorney Charles Finnerty. If he's not in, I'll talk with Attorney Mayan d'Ortega. And tell Billings in Security to send someone up right away."

"What will I say to this Sheridan fellow?"

"Tell him I'm tied up for the entire day."

The secretary reentered the reception area.

"Excuse me," she said to Sheridan, "I have to take a call in the other office."

Just then, the intercom buzzed.

"Betty," came the voice, "have Mr. Sheridan come in. Forget about those calls."

The secretary shrugged. "You're lucky," she said to Sheridan. "Sister said she'll see you. She's *really* busy. The diocesan auditors are due tomorrow—you know how hectic that can be."

"I never liked accountants, IRS agents, or bank examiners." Sheridan gave the secretary a sardonic wink as she led him to Sister Agnes Loretta's office. "But you've got to admit, they all have a great sense of humor."

—

"Sit down, Mr. Sheridan." Sister Agnes Loretta half-rose from behind her modest walnut-veneer desk, which was crowded with envelopes and documents. "As you can see, it's paperwork week—and the cardinal's overseers are due in shortly to see if our existence is justified." Her open hand swept sideways.

"Thank you for seeing me, Sister. I'll take only a few minutes of your time."

She looked at him curiously. "I'm not legally trained like Monsignor Devlin, but your coming here like this is a little unusual, is it not, Counselor?"

"Very." Sheridan fixed Sister Agnes with his steady blue eyes. "In fact, it's not quite ethical. But I felt I had to see you."

"I was about to call Mr. Finnerty and Security. You're on the other side of our litigation and you know full well that I have legal representation. I could have you reported."

"I know," Sheridan said evenly. "I'm not here to discuss the lawsuit, Sister. If I did that . . . well, disbarment might be a modest censure."

Sister Agnes Loretta studied Sheridan for a few moments. She hadn't attained her position as chief executive of Boston's largest hospital without being capable of judging the intricacies and nuances of human character, and she had an innate feeling that Sheridan, whatever his mission, was sincere, not intending to do any harm or to gain any undue advantage. And she liked his pug Irish face, his habit of hunching his shoulders, and his ocean blue eyes. Sincerity etched his face too deeply to be fabricated. And why would he risk his license on a chance visit?

"Let me say at the outset, Mr. Sheridan, we're legal adversaries. You really have no right being here. Now, what is it you want?" Her voice was soft but authoritative.

"Sister, I'm not here as a lawyer, and God knows I'm breaking all the rules, but I'm trying to get Donna DiTullio back where she can receive proper neurological treatment. Right now, she's wallowing in a run-down state facility called Hampton Chronic Care and Rehab."

"Hampton?"

"The same. The leper colony of medical outcasts."

"How is Donna?"

"Not too good. I've seen her several times. Somehow, I've struck a recognition chord; I'm able to communicate with her. She answers my questions by blinking her eyes."

"Well, how can I be of assistance?" The nun looked concerned.

"Donna doesn't have a chance at Hampton. I've ignited a little spark. If it isn't nurtured, it will soon die out. She needs vigorous neurologic care, constant monitoring, around-the-clock nursing." He hesitated for several moments. "Sister, I'd like to get her back here at St. Anne's."

"Mr. Sheridan"—the concern in the nun's face deepened— "aren't you putting your legal case into an obvious conflict? You're suing St. Anne's, alleging bad medical practice. Now you want your client to return here."

"I'm saying that the Psychiatric Department breached its duty of care. I made no mention of the medical service. In fact, the medical care is the best that can be had. That's why I want her back here."

"I'll speak with Dr. Jensen." She offered a slight opening.

"I've already spoken with Jensen. He's the one who signed her transfer papers to Hampton. And we didn't part under the best of circumstances."

"You know, Mr. Sheridan, St. Anne's is a private hospital. A room here can run two thousand dollars a day. Medical charges can double that. I'm familiar with our reasons for transferring your client. The family had no adequate insurance or funds to pay for Donna's hospitalization. At least at Hampton, state and federal funds come into play."

Sheridan risked being curt. "I know all this. I'm asking you to make an exception, assume the costs, get her back to St. Anne's. Pretend the hospital's name is Good Samaritan."

A faint smile flickered on Sister Agnes Loretta's lips.

"Let me review this matter with Monsignor Devlin, and I'll let you know. But I have to tell you up front that in all probability your request will be turned down. It's—"

"I know"—Sheridan stood up—"it's a question of economics."

"Not entirely, Mr. Sheridan." She extended her hand. Sheridan cupped her hand in both of his. Time for one last plea.

"They tell me that Mother Teresa took in outcasts off the

streets of Calcutta and operated her hospice, sometimes with her own funds and from whatever donations she could scrounge."

"Unfortunately, Mr. Sheridan, I'm a businessperson in a tough enterprise and can't match the celebrity or the fund-raising ability of the good Mother. And you come at a very inopportune time. The archdiocesan auditors will be checking every debit, every billing."

"Okay, hope to hear from you favorably, Sister." He was going to add that he would light a votive candle and say a rosary for some divine intercession, but so far his luck had held, so he let it go.

"And I want to thank you for seeing me," he said. "And maybe in that upcoming audit, on the charitable side of the ledger, there'll be room for Donna DiTullio."

—

Janet Phillips played the tape for Charlie Finnerty and Dr. Sexton.

"It's on the edge." Finnerty wiggled his hand. "Not outright subornation of perjury, but the intimation is there. This Sheridan guy is coming awfully close to the line.

"Now, Bob, I think Janet's done enough. Let me take the tape and put it away in the safe. Of course, if Sheridan succumbs to your Vineyard invitation, Janet, give me a call. I just received notice from his office that he intends to take your deposition in two weeks. And Janet, I want to thank you for your cooperation. I watched your show the other day—the lawyer-doctor bit. You really should be on a national network."

"Janet, would you kindly wait outside?" Sexton said. "I'll be only a few minutes. I want to go over something with Mr. Finnerty."

"Sure." Janet gave a demure smile. "Perhaps we could all make the Ritz for lunch."

"Perhaps," Finnerty said as he escorted Janet Phillips to the door.

—

Charlie Finnerty took out a long silver-foiled cigar from a gold case, then offered one to Dr. Sexton, who refused. He noticed the tight, disapproving set of Sexton's lips and thought better of lighting up.

"Interesting woman, your Janet Phillips," Finnerty said as he snapped the cigar case shut. "That tape shows where Sheridan's headed. But he's cute; he didn't quite commit himself. Of course, if he goes to bed with Janet, then it's a whole new ball game. He's a kind of maverick, doesn't enjoy any real status in the bar associations. And the bar overseers would love to pounce on him. I'm on their board of trustees, and believe me, if we ever bring charges, he couldn't find a single friend up there."

"I'm a little troubled about the way Sheridan's conducting his investigation," Sexton began.

"Listen, Bob, we're well aware of his sneaking around, contacting people on the side. We've got our private investigators working on it."

Finnerty lowered his voice to a conspiratorial whisper.

"We'll catch him passing money to witnesses, trying to induce them to manufacture a story. If he or his associate, Buckley, try to contact you or Dr. Lafollette or Dr. Puzon, let me know. I'd like nothing better than to see this guy removed from practice. And that goes for Mayan d'Ortega, too."

Sexton changed the subject. "I've never really looked at my professional liability policy. If worse comes to worst, how much am I insured for?"

Finnerty issued a slight chuckle. "You're covered for twenty million dollars. We've got this case reserved at a million dollars. And even that's too much money. Jurors, especially Boston jurors, are tightfisted. No one's giving *them* any freebies. In fact, for them, times could never be worse. Believe me, juries are downright stingy. And if the DiTullio girl dies, which she probably will, Sheridan will grab a hundred grand quick."

Sexton seemed reassured.

"Say hello to the cardinal for me," Finnerty said. "And please, let me, Mayan, and our staff do the worrying."

●

Charlie Finnerty sat at his desk after Sexton h̶~~...~~
the Phillips tape was useless. Phillips was doing a̶~~...~~g.
And he hadn't told Phillips and Sexton that it wa̶~~...~~minal
offense to tape someone's conversation without that p̶erson's authorization or knowledge. He got out his cigar, pulled out his
silver Dunhill lighter, and was about to enjoy the rich taste of a
Cuban panatela when his secretary buzzed and told him that
Sister Agnes Loretta's receptionist was on the line.

"Well, I'll be damned," Finnerty swore softly to himself.
"You say that Attorney Dan Sheridan showed up at Sister's office
this morning? And he was closeted with her in her office? . . .
You have his business card? . . . Interesting. No, don't trouble
the good sister by telling her you called me. Just fax me a copy
of the card."

Finnerty put his feet up on the desk and drew deeply on his
cigar.

After savoring the rum-flecked smoke for several minutes,
he placed a call on his private red phone to Jim Ward at the
detective agency. They exchanged pleasantries.

"Jim," Finnerty said, "I think it's time we expanded our
operation. Put a tail on Dan Sheridan.

"Yes," Finnerty said. "For the next ten days. Make it a
twenty-four-hour surveillance."

●

Sheridan and Buckley studied the record of Donna DiTullio's
three-week confinement at St. Anne's psychiatric ward. It was
voluminous, over three hundred pages. Judy Corwin had made
duplicates, and each studied his copy independently of the other.
Both underscored, made notes, and attached yellow tabs to des-
ignate sections deemed important.

Nothing popped out. Apart from day one, there were no red
flags, no indications that Donna might try to self-destruct.
Donna's condition was "guarded" upon admission, but with each
passing day, there was marked improvement, well documented

doctors' and nurses' notes. Sheridan told Judy to send a copy of the record to Dr. John White. Maybe he could decipher the psychiatric esoterica and find something they couldn't quite put a finger on.

Next came the St. Anne's Neurology record, dating from the day Donna jumped to her transfer to Hampton. Again, the record was extensive. Again, Sheridan and Buckley pursued independent reviews. The listed injuries were horrendous. Donna was in a continuous coma. Sheridan and Buckley held the CAT scan and MRI films up to the east windows, but the radiolucent images were just an opaque mix of lights and shadows. Even comparing the radiologist's reports with the X-ray films was of no value. Again, the chronology of medical treatment, consultations, pharmacology, doctors' orders, nurses' notes, even the medical history, gave no indication as to what motivated Donna to jump, or even indicated that she intended to jump. Not a clue, not a hint. It was as if a normal, happy-go-lucky twenty-one-year-old suddenly decided to jump in front of a freight train. It just didn't figure.

"What do you think, Buck?" Sheridan put down his pencil and wiped his eyes with the back of his wrist.

"Well, one thing looks a little funny to me."

"You mean there was not a sign, a single shred of evidence, that Donna was agitated, upset, depressed, or spaced-out just before she jumped?"

"No, I'm sure someone seriously contemplating suicide doesn't go around carrying a sign saying 'I'm going to jump' but it's the records themselves that bother me. Not an interlineation, not an erasure or a deletion, not a word crossed out. Even the nurses' notes—perfect handwriting."

"Nah." Sheridan shrugged. "You're trying to tell me this is a tailored job? All this stuff, *except* what's handwritten, has been transcribed." Sheridan shook his head. "I think we're stuck with what's in front of us."

Karen Assad smiled at Ruby, who was on the desk at Medical Records.

"Want to check one more lab study in that Davis file for Dr. Kelley."

It was again a little past one. Sister Mary Ignatius was at lunch. This should be easy.

"Sure, Karen," Ruby said after squinting at her name tag. "You know your way to the *D*'s. Straight ahead, first aisle on your left."

Karen pulled out the DiTullio file on the cabinet runners. She checked her 35-mm camera, pushed a few buttons to activate the flash and align the proper distance, then leafed through the record.

Hm, she said to herself, must have missed it. She started again, this time carefully noting each page.

The pathology report—where the hell is it? She was sure it had been somewhere in the initial pages—maybe three or four days after the accident. The pathologist was a Dr. Diwali. She waded through it again. No path report! She remembered that it was on a single page. Early on in the hospitalization. What the hell? Where was it?

She started at the beginning and again scoured the record. No luck. She glanced at her watch. Sister Mary Ignatius was due back just about now. Time was up. She made a quick exodus.

She smiled at Ruby, then passed Sister Mary Ignatius in the corridor.

No, she said to herself as she hurried along. No, I'm not imagining things. The path report is missing.

Sister Agnes Loretta sat at a coffee table with Monsignor Devlin and Charlie Finnerty in the monsignor's chancery office.

"I'm asking you, Monsignor, and you, too, Mr. Finnerty, to make a special allowance and take Donna DiTullio back into St. Anne's, under Dr. Jensen's service."

"As your legal counsel, I strongly advise against this," Finnerty said with an officious scowl. "All sorts of conflicts can arise.

Dr. Jensen will be put into the difficult position of being called as a witness for the plaintiff against his own hospital. Things could get very awkward." The monsignor sipped a cup of tea and listened carefully.

"I'm inclined to agree, Charlie," Monsignor Devlin said thoughtfully. "The DiTullio girl is, after all, getting free medical care at Hampton. We're a private hospital. The auditors will be dead set against it. We'd be assuming costs of over a half a million dollars a year. And Mr. DiTullio has indicated that the family has no means of paying, and he told us in no uncertain language that he has no intention of paying for the past hospitalization, which, I might add, runs to over a hundred thousand. And"—he looked at Sister Agnes Loretta—"if some state charitable funds don't kick in, this is an expense we're going to have to eat."

"The insurance company's chief underwriter said that a move like this would skyrocket your liability insurance premiums for the next fiscal year," Finnerty added.

"Well, we should shoulder some responsibility," Sister Agnes Loretta said, slight perturbation entering her voice. "After all, the patient was in our care, custody, and control when she jumped."

Charlie Finnerty felt he had to shut down this line of reasoning quickly.

"What prompts this concern?" he asked.

The nun cocked her head and thought for a few moments.

"I think we have an ethical responsibility to take in a certain number of charity patients. This is done by Boston Memorial, Massachusetts General, and Beth Israel."

The monsignor finished his tea, as did Sister Agnes Loretta. She and Finnerty declined another cup.

"Let me take it up with His Eminence," the monsignor said. He pushed a button for the housekeeper. "I'll let you know our decision in a day or two."

Charlie Finnerty and Sister Agnes Loretta got up to leave.

"Can I see you, Monsignor, on some nonrelated business?" Finnerty said.

"Will you excuse us, Sister?" He addressed the nun politely.

"I'll say a prayer to St. Anne," she said, "that we make the right decision." Her voice was as soft as down feathers.

—

"How well do you know Sister Agnes Loretta?" Finnerty asked the monsignor.

"How well? What do you mean?" The monsignor's brow furrowed.

"Well, let me tell you that I don't think Sister was completely candid with us when I asked her what prompted her concern for Donna DiTullio."

"You're not questioning Sister's probity!"

"No." Finnerty paused for several moments. "But I heard that this attorney Dan Sheridan happened to visit her at her office on the q.t."

"Oh?" Irritation crept into the monsignor's voice.

"This is an egregious violation of the code of legal ethics," Finnerty said. "I'm sure Sister Agnes wasn't cognizant of the breach, but Sheridan was well aware of it. You simply can't talk to a defendant without his or her attorney being present. And we, as Sister's counsel, had no knowledge, absolutely none, that Sheridan would do this sort of thing. He should be reported to the bar overseers."

The monsignor listened patiently. "What do you want me to do?" he asked. "Sister Agnes Loretta is the best hospital administrator in the archdiocese—in fact, the best in the Boston area, and that includes Mass General and Beth Israel. Salarywise, she could command a half million a year on the outside. And you know, Charlie—she knows it."

"All I'm saying, Monsignor, is that this Sheridan guy will go to any extreme to win over a witness or win a case. We happen to know he's approached another witness. Wined and dined her at a private hideaway."

Finnerty paused to gauge the impression of his last words.

"Sister Agnes Loretta should be forewarned that she can't discuss any details of the case ex parte. And the decision should be firm that this DiTullio girl remain at Hampton, or wherever, but under no circumstances should she be readmitted to St. Anne's. We weaken on this point and Sheridan will make further demands. And believe me, he'll bring a wrongful-death case against all of you, including Jensen, if the girl dies, which I understand is a ninety percent probability."

"All right, Charlie." The monsignor again pressed the button for his housekeeper. "Realistically, what'll it take to settle the case?"

"Probably a million dollars."

"Well, that's comfortably within our insurance policy limits, is it not?"

Finnerty's lips thinned out into a straight line, signaling his disapproval.

"Monsignor," he said, "with all due respect, we have only a twenty-million-dollar liability limit. You never know what a jury's going to do. Sometimes they feel so sorry for the injured person that reason and the evidence fly right out the window. There are such things as runaway juries. If for some crazy reason the plaintiff hits for forty million, with the twelve percent legal interest stacked onto the award, you could be looking at over forty-four million dollars, forty million of which the church and the archdiocesan parishioners would have to pick up. You'd put St. Anne's in hock, and all the second collections in the world wouldn't bail you out."

The monsignor held his chin between his thumb and forefinger and thought for a few moments. The calculations were sobering.

"All right," he said finally. "No need to trouble the cardinal. I can see the logic of it all. I'll speak to Sister Agnes."

19

Sheridan's conference room was small and Spartan, the rosewood-veneer table was badly scratched. With three lawyers, the witness, the court stenographer, and a frayed bamboo palm in the corner, there was little elbowroom.

Sheridan had decided to pass on Sister Agnes Loretta's deposition. He was still awaiting her decision on Donna DiTullio. Also, he was scheduled to drive to Hampton the next morning. He'd drop by St. Anne's and page Dr. Jensen on his car phone, just in case the doctor had had an unlikely change of heart.

"Dr. Puzon," Sheridan said, "we're here today to take your deposition testimony. I'm going to ask you a series of questions under oath and I want you to give me the answers. You're represented here by your attorneys, Mayan d'Ortega and Mary Devaney. Okay?"

Puzon nodded agreement.

Sheridan swung through the preliminaries—Dr. Puzon's early schooling and medical training. He had studied her curriculum vitae, which was impressive. She, like Sexton and Lafollette, had outstanding credentials. Also, like her colleagues, she had contributed numerous articles to prestigious medical journals, and she was working on a textbook on the principles of clinical psychiatry. It was a 685-page tome scheduled for publication the following spring by a respected medical publishing house.

Next, Sheridan established the doctor-patient relationship between Puzon and Donna DiTullio. Although Dr. Sexton had been DiTullio's primary physician/psychiatrist, she and Dr. Lafollette attended morning rounds and visited Donna DiTullio often, sometimes two or three times a day. Dr. Puzon had also checked Donna's chart regularly, noted clinical consultations, radiology reports, CAT scans, electroencephalograms, electrocardiograms, blood chemistries, vital signs, medication records, and nursing notes. The chart, she said, gave a running commentary on the patient's progress.

These were Sheridan's jack-in-the-box inquiries, the answers popping up in the questions. Nothing tricky, no dangerous terrain. Dr. Puzon handled them professionally and with intelligent articulation. No need for either side to impress. There was no jury here.

Next came the hard questions. Judge Mason had ruled that Sheridan was entitled to question the defendants as to whether their conduct comported with the acceptable standards of psychiatric care existent in June of 1996, when Donna DiTullio met with her near-fatal accident. For the record, d'Ortega would object, but this wouldn't prevent Sheridan from eliciting answers. Somehow, Sheridan sensed that Consuela Concepción Puzon, schooled by the Dominican nuns, wouldn't commit perjury or try to stonewall the interrogation. He would lead into the tough terrain by a series of seemingly innocuous questions.

"Dr. Puzon, in your review of the medical chart, you noted that Donna DiTullio exhibited gross forms of suicidal ideation, is that correct?"

The doctor thought for several seconds.

"No, that is not correct," she said firmly.

"Why do you say that is not correct?"

Mayan d'Ortega was about to object but waited as Dr. Puzon answered.

"The word *gross* bothers me, Mr. Sheridan. Donna attempted suicide on one isolated occasion."

"You don't call the action of a twenty-one-year-old girl who tried to slash her wrists and bleed to death *gross*?"

"I don't," she said. "As a matter of fact, the wounds would not have been lethal. Psychologically, it was an overt act of defying her parents, directed mainly at her father. It was what we psychiatrists call 'a suicidal gesture,' but not designed to be fatal."

"Now wait a minute, Doctor," Sheridan stammered. "You don't call slashing one's wrists a *serious* suicide attempt? She could have bled to death slowly, and quite painfully."

"Many people make token acts of committing suicide, knowing that others are present to intervene.

"The DiTullio girl's wounds were superficial, Mr. Sheridan. Upon emergency admission, the coagulating factors had already stanched the flow of blood."

"Yes, Doctor, but these relatively nonlethal actions, or suicidal gestures, as you call them, are not to be taken lightly." Sheridan scanned his notes. "In fact, the great clinical psychiatrist Karl Menninger stated as early as 1938 that such a person is communicating that he or she is upset and thinking about suicide, and even if he or she was not planning to die, a suicidal gesture represents a *cry for help*. Do you agree with that statement, Dr. Puzon?"

"I've read that," Dr. Puzon replied testily. "But the wristcutting in this case was a mildly destructive act."

This witness is being difficult, Sheridan thought. Might as well move on.

"Now, are you familiar with the drug Capricet?"

"Yes, quite familiar."

"You were aware that Dr. Sexton prescribed initial doses of five milligrams intramuscularly three times a day. In fact, Dr. Puzon"—Sheridan again glanced at his notes—"you yourself renewed this prescription on the seventh admission day and initialed 'Same dosage.' "

"That's correct."

"You know the drug is not FDA-approved."

"That's not exactly correct. It's been approved by the FDA for human studies. We had both the patient's and her parents' authorization to administer the drug under FDA guidelines. The clinical results were most remarkable, I might add."

"You are aware, are you not, Doctor, that statistically the recurrence of suicide attempts is more prevalent in the twenty-to-thirty age group, especially among patients recently hospitalized for psychiatric disorders?"

"It's only a general statistic."

"I didn't ask you if it was a general statistic," Sheridan said dryly. "I asked you if you were familiar with the statistic."

"I am familiar with the statistic," Puzon said softly, but with a cold undertone.

"And Donna DiTullio fitted into that group statistic, did she not?"

"She did."

"And you will agree with me, Doctor, that a young female that age presents a risk of suicide ten percent greater than her male counterpart."

Puzon shook her head. "No, I will not agree."

"Why not?" Sheridan's questions were now rapid-fire.

"Your statistics are outdated. I have done recent exhaustive research for my book, and by today's statistics, male and female are about even."

Sheridan thought for a few moments. Not a question to ask in front of a jury, but on deposition might as well find out the case's downside.

"Doctor, during the Middle Ages, suicide was regarded as a mortal sin, and this view held serious implications for one's soul."

"Are you asking me a question?"

"Let me put it this way, Doctor. Are you a Roman Catholic?"

"*Please!*" Mayan d'Ortega's voice and look spewed indignation. "You're not in front of a jury. Mr. Sheridan, let me be blunt. I'm going to object to this *toro excremento*, this bullshit!

Your whole line of questioning of Dr. Puzon has been pure bullshit!"

Sheridan admired the frankness of her anger. "Excuse me." Sheridan feigned surprise, knowing from d'Ortega's alluvial rhetoric that he had her on the run.

"Ms. d'Ortega, the term *toro excremento*, is that Hawaiian? I think in Hawaii they say, 'You're in deep MuaKahKah.' "

D'Ortega threw her head back and issued a slight "Oh, my dear Jesus!" kind of sigh.

"Okay," Sheridan said, "let's get back on the record. Strike the last question." He smiled at the court stenographer. The tiff was over.

He'd address this kind of prejudice at trial time. The majority of the jurors would be Roman Catholic, whether Irish, Italian, Polish, Hispanic, or even black. You commit suicide, you go straight to hell. That was ingrained from the first grade on. But he'd let Dr. White handle it. He continued his questioning.

"Now, the modern function of psychiatric therapy is not to cure the disorder but, instead, to remold the premorbid personality so as to enable it to cope once the disorder is lifted. This is especially applicable to suicide attempts. Isn't that sound psychiatric reasoning, Dr. Puzon?"

"That's fairly sound reasoning."

"Now, Doctor, the past is the best predictor of the future. You'd grant that premise, would you not?"

"That statement is a little too broad."

"Well, you do know, Doctor, that prior to admission to St. Anne's, Donna DiTullio tried to kill herself. In fact, that's why she was admitted."

"I'm well aware of why she was admitted. But her subsequent clinical course was remarkable. Her depression had lifted. Following her initial episode, there was *absolutely* no suicidal ideation, and this assessment was consistent up to the day of the group therapy session."

"But isn't it true, Doctor, that among women wrist-cutters you find the risk of eventual suicide greater than among non—wrist-cutters?"

"I can't agree with that premise. You would have to show me those statistics."

"Well, isn't it true, Doctor, that Karl Menninger was convinced of the pervasiveness of the self-destruction impulse in humans and saw self-mutilation as a manifestation of this drive, albeit in a milder form?"

"I'm not sure I understand your question," Puzon parried, "but Menninger did note that some people destroy a part of their body rather than take their lives. In mythology, when Oedipus discovered that he had unwittingly murdered his father and married his own mother, he blinded himself. Menninger concluded that some people focus self-destructive impulses on one part of the body, enabling the whole to survive. Menninger," she said forcefully, "called this 'focal suicide.' "

Boy, Sheridan thought, this Filipina is one cool papaya; in front of a jury, maybe the best cross-examination would be no cross-examination. She's got all the answers.

"Dr. Puzon," Sheridan continued, "upon her admission to St. Anne's, did you classify Donna DiTullio as a high risk for suicide?"

"She was a moderate risk. Identifying high-risk patients is difficult. Today in the United States, only one in one hundred thousand persons a year commits suicide. It's rare."

"Let me see if I follow you, Doctor." Sheridan again studied Puzon for a few moments.

"Suicide is irreversible, is it not?"

"It's a terminal event. That's not the case here."

"Now, Doctor. In the hospital environment, the patient is medicated, carefully watched, given support. Then suddenly, when the patient is going to be discharged, all props are about to be taken away. And won't you agree, Doctor, that the most vulnerable time for a suicidal patient is upon hospital discharge?"

"It's a vulnerable time."

"When the suicidal drive is strong, Doctor, then you will agree with me that home is no place for the patient."

"The suicidal drive in this case was nonexistent."

"Well, the patient did jump from the *fifth* floor. This was no mere gesture, isn't that correct, Doctor?"

"There was no indication at any time during the therapy session that Donna would jump."

"If the clinicians, such as yourself, Dr. Lafollette, and Dr. Sexton, failed to note that Donna DiTullio was nervous, apprehensive, fidgeting during the therapy session, there's no question in your mind, Doctor, that this would constitute bad medical and psychiatric practice, especially when holding the therapy session on the *fifth* floor of an open atrium?"

Strange, he thought to himself. Here I am, paraphrasing Janet Phillips.

Mayan d'Ortega was about to voice an objection, but she held off while in a strong, even voice Dr. Puzon answered.

"You're assuming facts that have no basis in reality. I observed and listened to Donna very carefully during that fifty-minute therapy session. She was bright, articulate, her mood was normal, even a bit elevated. Her energy level was increased. She looked forward to the future, to resuming tennis."

"Fine, but humor me for a moment, Doctor. Assume my facts to be true, then answer my question."

"Your facts are not true. At these group therapy sessions, I assess the patient. The problem confronting me on that morning was whether Donna DiTullio had gotten over her suicidal crisis and whether she showed any signs that she would attempt suicide in the immediate future. Donna's mood had improved, her depression had lifted, there was no weight loss, her appetite was good, there was no insomnia, and she had focused her thoughts on the future."

"Doctor, were you, as the number-two person in charge of the psychiatric unit at St. Anne's, concerned—were you just a little fearful about these patients' safety—when you were holding psychiatric group therapy sessions on the fifth floor of the open Atrium of St. Anne's?"

"Did I voice any concern?"

"No, I said *were* you concerned? Did you see any problem?" Sheridan manufactured an exasperated sigh. "Let me put it this way. Did you ever say to yourself, Wow! We've got patients up here who may be suicidal. Way up on the fifth floor, in a wide-open atrium. We, who should be watching these vulnerable people, are all going for a break and leaving them unattended for ten minutes or so while we go sip our coffee. Did you think, Gee, maybe we shouldn't be doing this?" He leaned close to Dr. Puzon and plumbed her liquid almond eyes.

She hesitated, then glanced at Mayan d'Ortega, who gave a barely perceptible nod.

"Certainly we are concerned with the safety of all our patients. But this group was carefully screened. This isn't the 1800s, Mr. Sheridan. We no longer manacle patients and shoot them full of morphine, turning them into zombies. I have often taken patients more severely deranged than Donna DiTullio on outdoor excursions to Vermont and Maine. We even climbed Mount Monadnock. Sure, someone might bolt from the group and run out into the road, but in all my years at St. Anne's, we've never had one fatality."

Sheridan was going to applaud. It was a heartrending speech, well scripted, well rehearsed. And Puzon gave it with the special conviction she had learned from the Dominican nuns. It would be effective in front of a jury—no question. He withheld his sarcasm.

"Do you think you've honestly answered my question, Doctor?" There was a cynical edge to his voice.

"Yes," she replied.

He had intended to get into what happened after the jump, what was said when the cardinal's investigative team interviewed those in attendance, did Puzon have any input in glassing in the Atrium and moving the psychiatric ward to the ground floor. But he thought he'd wrap it up. Robert Sexton would be his target for this line of interrogation.

"I think that's all I have," he said to the stenographer.

"Oh, one last question." He waited several seconds.

"When you led that group up Mount Monadnock, Doctor, you didn't use the Red Trail, with its precipitous drops and narrow footpaths, did you?"

She looked at Sheridan, bemused.

"No. We took the Orange Trail."

"I hiked the Orange Trail as a first grader at Holy Redeemer. Sister Vincent de Paul was our trail guide. That trail's a piece of cake, even for a six-year-old, wouldn't you agree, Dr. Puzon?"

"Piece of cake?"

"Oh, never mind."

—

Karen Assad again met Tom Buckley at the Dockside. The setting wasn't seaside idyllic this time; a weather front had moved in. It was hurricane season, and someplace in the horse latitudes a big storm was brewing, aiming for Cape Hatteras and the outer stretches of New England.

They were escorted to an outside table, but the wind picked up and started rumpling the beach umbrellas as though they were toy balloons. As the rain spattered onto the patio, Tom and Karen beat a hasty retreat to the inside bar. The waiter carried their drinks, and as Tom doubled back to retrieve his briefcase, something caught his eye. The same man—middle-aged, checkered sport coat, gray slacks, yellow jersey, aviator sunglasses, gray fedora—who had been seated a few tables away also made his way to the haven of the bar. It was the gray fedora—who in the world nowadays wears a snap-brim gray fedora like he's a young Dick Nixon? And in this heat. He dismissed it and nestled into a bar stool next to Karen.

"Sorry about the rain." Buckley spread his arms, palms up. "Think we're in for 'a bit of a blow.' "

"That's New England." Karen laughed. "What did Mark Twain say? 'If you don't like the weather in New England, wait a minute.' "

They went through the "how're the kids" routine and "what's doing at St. Anne's." Buckley told Karen about Mrs. Gallagher and the Saint Bernard. They ordered another round of drinks and oysters, to be followed by grilled sole.

"September's an *R* month," Buckley said. "Never eat oysters in a month that doesn't have an *R* in it."

"Why's that?" Karen asked, bemused.

"Damned if I know." Buckley whacked down another shot of scotch.

"Seriously, Tom"—she reached for his arm—"I think I came across something you should know about . . ."

Buckley looked to his left as he held up two fingers, signaling the bartender to bring another round. Out of the corner of his eye he caught the fedora with the sunglasses three bar stools away. Why did this guy bug him? He had to come in out of the rain just like they did, and he had to sit at the bar. Tom turned to Karen.

"Look, Karen, let's not talk shop. Sheridan's obsessed with the case, not me. Right now, I'm concerned about a lovely Lebanese girl who's got two kids, happens to be an RN, and I think she kinda cares for me. Might be someone you know?" He belted down another scotch.

"Okay." Karen nodded. "But listen to me." She bent closer to Buckley. "I checked Donna DiTullio's hospitalization record for the weeks before she was transferred to Hampton."

"You're not supposed to do this," Buckley said.

"I know, but I did it, okay? I became attached to Donna. She was not just a patient; she was someone special."

"Okay." Buckley unconsciously looked to his left. Gray Fedora had moved a seat closer. Buckley thought a moment, then again returned to Karen Assad.

"What's so important?" he said.

"I found something very unusual. Donna was three months' pregnant when she jumped. I suspected it all along. Her blood studies, temperatures. It was confirmed by the path report."

"She was three months along?" Buckley said. "Maybe her old man knocked her up. I always had bad vibes about him."

"Whatever. But when I returned to Medical Records with my trusty Minolta, the path record was missing."

"Missing?"

"As if it had never existed."

"Are you sure?" Again he unconsciously glanced to his left.

Gray Fedora was sipping his drink, eyes glued to the overhead television.

"I'm positive!"

Buckley thought for several seconds, again glancing to his left. Gray Fedora was still eyeing the set. Some reporter from CNN was talking about Bosnia.

"Excuse me, buddy," Buckley said, leaning toward the stranger, "can you pass me the pepper?"

"What?" The man seemed startled.

"The pepper?" Buckley pointed to the condiments on the bar.

"Oh . . . sure," Gray Fedora said, smiling a toothy grin as he slid the pepper shaker toward Buckley.

Buckley got a quick imprint of the guy—thin, pale lips, pug nose (almost like Sheridan's), fiftyish, a bit overweight, like himself. Somehow, Buckley could sense it: This guy looked like a cop.

"Thanks, buddy," Buckley said. He hated pepper, especially on lemon sole, but he shook the shaker vigorously. Then he bent close to Karen and lowered his voice.

"Look, let's eat up. The fact that she was pregnant could actually hurt our case. Maybe she was too humiliated to tell anyone about it, even her psychiatrists and the nurses, particularly *you*, Karen, and you said that you were closer to her than anyone on the nursing staff. Maybe some guy dumped her and she couldn't face it. Maybe she was going to take the only way out— she was going to jump, and she wasn't going to let a soul know about her intentions. And I can see her manipulating all of you— Puzon, Sexton. She'd feign being upbeat, making a remarkable recovery—she threw everyone off."

Karen nodded. "I see what you mean, but . . ."

"I didn't say what you discovered is unimportant." Buckley again caught Gray Fedora out of the corner of his eye. And again Gray Fedora seemed mesmerized by the overhead television and was munching some pretzels. But this time, Buckley noticed something he hadn't noticed before. Gray Fedora was glued to the television all right, but his head was tilted, maybe only slightly, but tilted toward them.

God, Buckley thought, I'm getting paranoid.

"Karen"—he glanced at his watch—"it's one-thirty. I gotta be in court at three. Could you come into the office, say about ten in the morning the day after tomorrow? You've never met Dan Sheridan; I think you'll like him." He lowered his voice. "We've got all the hospital records from St. Anne's. Maybe you could review them, particularly the psych records. We really can't make out the mumbo jumbo. And tell Dan about the missing pathology report. The fact that it's missing could be more important than the fact that Donna was pregnant."

—

Buckley paid the bill and escorted Karen to his car in the parking lot. As he was about to back out, he checked the rearview mirror. Sure enough, Gray Fedora had also checked out and was in a black Ford Taurus. Buckley pulled slowly out of the lot, took a left on Atlantic Avenue, and headed toward the Storrow Drive overpass. A quick glance in the rearview mirror confirmed his suspicions. The Taurus was trailing behind, with three or four cars in between. Could be coincidence, he thought. He was about to make sure by taking a right over the Longfellow Bridge and doubling back along the Cambridge side of the Charles River. But this move might alert Gray Fedora, if in fact he was actually tailing them. And it might spook Karen, since she'd know they were heading in the wrong direction. So he nonchalantly continued at a sensible early-afternoon pace, drove down Boylston Street, headed for Kenmore Square.

"You think Ahmed and Kaliph might like to take in a Red Sox game, maybe next week? The Tigers are in town. It's one of those rare afternoon games. I could get tickets," he said to Karen as he checked the rearview mirror. Gray Fedora's Ford was still lagging behind.

"I'm sure they'd love to go," Karen said. "They're both in Little League, but neither plays too well."

"Hell, when I was a kid, we had a pickup team," Buckley

said. "I was always the last one chosen, and they'd stick me in right field.

"Hey, it's a done deal for the Sox," he added. "We'll make an afternoon of it, hot dogs, you name it. I'll show the boys how to keep score."

They kept up the chatter until he parked in front of Karen's apartment. It was in a quiet tree-lined area of modest three-deckers. He escorted her to the front door.

"Want me to pick you up the day after tomorrow morning and drive you to the office?" he asked as she pressed a few buttons unlocking the security system.

"No, I'll take a cab. Be there about ten." She gave him a light peck on the cheek.

As he went down the stairs, he nonchalantly glanced at the row of cars parked in the street. The Ford Taurus was nowhere in sight. But it had followed him from the Dockside, and he'd last seen it about two blocks from Karen's street. He knew it was a tail.

He pulled out and headed back into town toward the office. He checked again in the mirror. Nothing unusual—just ordinary traffic. He was about to get Raimondi on his car phone but then thought better of it. If whoever was tailing him was a real pro, his call could be intercepted quite easily. He'd take it up with Raimondi and Sheridan when he got back to the office. Raimondi was good at this subterfuge stuff. He'd put a tail on the tail.

●

To Charlie Finnerty, Mayan d'Ortega was a rainmaker's dream—tireless, patient, churning out briefs, spending innumerable hours preparing for depositions or for trial. Tactfully aggressive, she seemed to have a zest for litigation unmatched by anyone he had ever encountered. Mayan had a way with clients, too. She had a steady firmness, her entire demeanor lacked guile, and even the most impossible clients quickly recognized that her time and her advice were the best that money could buy. Finnerty knew this, and it was reflected in the weekly pay envelope, the small courtesies, and the fresh flowers he sent daily to brighten her desk and her day.

But of late, Mayan seemed to be harboring some inner disquiet, manifested in the way she blew up at Sheridan during the depositions of Sister Agnes Loretta and Dr. Connie Puzon. It was unlike Mayan. Maybe she felt—as lawyers often do—that she would have preferred to be on the other side of the litigation. Perhaps she was listening to some faint echo heard not too many years ago in law school—that she, Mayan d'Ortega, could make a difference.

At five to six, she called it a day, telling the evening receptionist that she would leave for the health club. She felt the slight padding about her thighs and knew it was time to leave one treadmill and get on another—this time for a long-overdue workout.

The de Milo Fitness Spa, located next to the Harvard Club on Commonwealth Avenue, was an upscale athletic club run exclusively by and for women. Skipping dinner, Mayan was thankful that only a few members were there at this early-evening hour, running on the overhead track, riding bicycles, lifting weights, and generally trying to keep mortality at bay.

Dressed in black spandex tights and white Adidas training shoes with orange trim, she worked the Nautilus and StairMaster, then topped off her workout with eight laps in the marble-tiled pool. Feeling more relaxed than she had in months, she wrapped herself in an oversized towel and headed for the steam room, where she occupied a redwood bench. Through the swirling vapor, she was barely able to make out a toweled figure seated in the far corner. But she knew who it was, and she also knew that this was not the kind of situation where she could pretend not to see or recognize her. It was Sheridan's fiancée, Sheila O'Brien. Although they had never met, each knew the other by reputation. Mayan remembered that when she was working at the district attorney's office as chief prosecutor, Sheila had been an FBI agent investigating, of all cases, Dan Sheridan for possible mail and wire fraud—a government sting that fell apart with the suicide of Mayan's boss, District Attorney Neil Harrington.

"Hi." Sheila leaned forward, peering through the mist. "Nice to see someone else in here. Not good to be broiled by your lonesome. . . . You're Mayan d'Ortega. I'm Sheila O'Brien, a friend of your current adversary, Dan Sheridan."

Mayan peered back at Sheila. It was an awkward meeting in an awkward setting, but she was curious about the girl sitting across from her, the girl who had captured the man about whom she herself had ambivalent feelings. She noted Sheila's sandy blond hair, now damp and matted; and her blue eyes, which seemed to glint with a misty sparkle. And she was surprised that Sheila was a good deal younger than she had expected.

"He's quite an advocate," Mayan said with a hint of apology. "It's too bad we have to be on opposite sides of the fence."

"That's the trial lawyer's lot," Sheila said pleasantly. "Sheridan speaks quite highly of you."

Mayan felt herself warming to her unexpected visitor, and it wasn't the 110-degree temperature.

"The DiTullio case is a real tragedy—so much is at stake." Mayan still spoke guardedly. "But on the defense side, we can't pick and choose. We're like the cabdrivers. We have to accept the fare regardless."

"I know what you mean." Sheila took a small towel and mopped her face. "I work over at Roper, Cranston, Peabody & Weld. Even the senior partners put in ten-hour days. And the way things are nowadays economically, we service anything that comes in the door."

Neither mentioned Charlie Finnerty, although both knew that Finnerty had taken a huge chunk out of Roper, Cranston's clientele base.

"Are you a lawyer, Sheila?"

"Member of the New York Bar," Sheila said, "took the Mass Bar exam last April. Should be hearing something in a few months."

"You going in with Mr. Sheridan?"

"No, I think I'll stay with Roper for a while. Dan's work is grueling, and right now he's too preoccupied to focus on anything but the case. That's why I enjoy coming here and working out."

"I should do this more often," Mayan said, still feeling friendly toward Sheila O'Brien.

"Understand you and Mr. Sheridan are engaged. Have you set a wedding date?" Mayan asked as she noticed Sheila's diamond.

"Probably we'll end up at City Hall." Sheila smiled. "You know how hectic this business can be."

"You're telling me," Mayan said with a hint of resignation.

The conversation had been polite and, in the atmosphere of the steam room, impersonal, almost anonymous. In fact, neither could see the other too well through the mist.

"I think I've lasted my ten minutes." Sheila stood and tucked her towel tighter around her breasts. "It was nice meeting you, Mayan. Maybe we can get together sometime, have a drink or lunch."

"Perhaps when this case is over," Mayan said. "Good meeting you." Neither woman offered to shake hands.

A slight pang of regret stirred somewhere deep inside Mayan as Sheila departed—and just a twinge of jealousy. She didn't know whom she envied more, Dan Sheridan or Sheila O'Brien. She closed her eyes and leaned back against the wall.

20

S heridan drove to St. Anne's, tipped the security guard a
ten-spot, and parked in an area reserved for the medical
staff.

"Dr. Jensen, please." He called from his cellular phone,
giving his name to the receptionist. Several seconds passed and
Jensen finally came on the line.

"Look," Jensen said, his voice agitated, "I've taken the matter up with Sister Agnes Loretta. She said the monsignor is dead
set against readmitting the DiTullio girl."

"Okay," Sheridan said, not evincing any surprise at the
news, "but what about *you*? Would you come up to Hampton and
see for yourself? I just want to demonstrate that Donna's improved. She can carry on a pretty good conversation with me, in
her primal communicative way. You'll see. It's an hour's drive.
We'll spend a half hour with her, say, then I'll get you back in
no time. If we can't get her into St. Anne's, maybe you can arrange
to get her into State University Med on Dr. Stuart's service. I've
just got to get her out of Hampton."

Frustration etched Jensen's voice. "Okay. I'll meet you out
front in, say, ten minutes. Sister Agnes Loretta isn't going to like

this one bit! Do you have it arranged with Dr. Brockelman? I would be stepping on his toes, you know."

"Absolutely." Sheridan risked a white lie. "Got it all set up. I'm sure he'll be impressed to see you."

"Ten minutes, right out front," said Jensen.

—

Sheridan and Dr. Jensen checked in with the receptionist at Hampton. Jensen looked around, obviously uncomfortable with the surroundings.

"We're here to see Donna DiTullio. We've met before."

"Sure," the receptionist said, "you're Miss DiTullio's lawyer. How's the lawsuit coming?"

"Okay," Sheridan parried. "This is Dr. Curtis Jensen, chief of Neurosurgery at St. Anne's. He saved Donna's life, really."

"Pleased to meet you, Doctor," she said pleasantly. "I'll page Dr. Brockelman."

Jensen merely nodded.

"I'll also buzz Nurse Jennings on the second floor. Elevator's still out of order. It was repaired last week, but it's on the fritz again."

They climbed the cast-iron stairway and checked in with Nurse Jennings, who escorted them to Donna's room.

"Mr. DiTullio is in with Donna now," she said. "Been there all morning."

"What?" Sheridan was perturbed. "The receptionist didn't tell us her dad was with her. Is Brockelman in there also?"

She nodded. "Donna isn't having a good day, Mr. Sheridan," the nurse said. "She just stares at the ceiling—no response, no cognition. I think she's regressed since your last visit."

Sheridan stopped a few doors from Donna's ward. He could sense that with Dante DiTullio and Brockelman present, Donna was manufacturing a blank that would persist during Jensen's visit. It would only strengthen Jensen's resolve to keep her at Hampton.

The nurse rapped lightly on the door, then let both of them in. Donna was propped up in the bed, and Brockelman was in the process of listening to her heart with his stethoscope. The usual IVs and tubes dangled from overhead plastic bags and canisters. Dante DiTullio was hunched in a molded plastic chair, tears running down his cheeks. Donna was now the only patient in the room. Three bed frames devoid of mattresses and patients were pushed against the wall. Sheridan had watched the census deplete with each visit, and he knew it would not be long before Donna became another Hampton statistic. But at least now she had a private room.

"Dr. Brockelman," the nurse said, "this is Mr. Sheridan."

"Yes?" Dr. Brockelman turned toward the visitors, still listening to Donna's heart.

"And he has a colleague with him, Dr. Jensen from St. Anne's Hospital. Dr. Jensen was Donna's original physician."

Dante DiTullio looked up as Dr. Brockelman cracked a broad smile and rose to meet Jensen. The doctor removed his stethoscope from his ears, allowing it to dangle around his neck.

"Well, well," Brockelman greeted Jensen, "this is a pleasant surprise. I'm honored, really, that you'd take the time from your busy schedule to drop in on us. Other than Stuart at University Med, we are seldom graced by such a visitation." He shook Jensen's hand, somehow overlooking Sheridan.

Dante DiTullio was still hunched in the chair, and he dried his eyes with his handkerchief. He looked befuddled, not knowing what had prompted Jensen's visit. But he felt it didn't augur well.

"I only want to check on the patient's condition, Doctor— if you don't mind, of course. I haven't seen Donna since she left St. Anne's.

"May I?" He pointed to Brockelman's breast pocket, which contained a brace of pens, one an ophthalmologist's light.

"Certainly." Brockelman beamed as he pulled out the pen-shaped light and passed it to Jensen. For the next few minutes, Jensen peered into Donna's eyes, viewing the vitreous humor, the retinal artery and vein, the optic nerve, and the general contour of the recesses of her eyes.

"Blood vessels are clearly delineated, optic disk isn't

choked, no sign of papilledema," he murmured. He snapped the light off and bent over Donna, blocking the overhead glare.

"Eyes react to light and accommodation," he said with an authoritative purr. "She looks much better than when I last saw her."

But Donna's eyes were vacant, staring into some distant void. There was no tearing, no sign of recognition.

"Donna, I'm Dr. Jensen," he said softly. "I operated on you after your fall. I think you're coming along better than expected.

"See if you can follow this pen." He held the pen-shaped light about a foot from her nose and moved it first right, back to center, then left, then up and down. Donna's eyes remained blank, unmoving.

Next, Jensen asked the nurse for some cotton, tore off a small piece, and touched the cornea of Donna's eye. She blinked.

"Well, the corneal reflex is present. Fifth cranial nerve is patent. But it's pure reflex, nothing volitional.

"If you can hear me, Donna," Jensen said, "please blink your eyes."

Dante DiTullio, Dr. Brockelman, and Nurse Jennings huddled over Jensen's shoulder. There was no response—just the blank stare. Jensen shook his head. He tried again. Nothing.

Sheridan stood in the background. He knew that any hope of getting Donna back to St. Anne's, or even to State University Med, was fading fast.

Next, Jensen asked the nurse to uncover Donna's feet. This time, he used a ballpoint and scratched the sole of Donna's foot. The toes fanned out and the big toe pointed upward. Jensen again shook his head.

"That's a positive Babinski," he said. "Neurologically, she still has a great deal of brain damage."

Dante DiTullio issued a muffled moan and sank back into his seat. Tears welled in his eyes. Sheridan patted him on the back, then followed Jensen and Brockelman to the nurses' station.

Jensen picked up Donna's chart and leafed through the last several days.

"Other than that time you witnessed the patient and Mr. Sheridan supposedly communicating, Dr. Brockelman, is there any entry by you or any of the nurses or residents that she has any cognition?"

Brockelman was quick to answer. "None whatsoever."

Sheridan had his own theory as to why this experiment had failed. For one thing, men and women in white petrified Donna, and with her father present, there was such an inner source of resentment that some cognitive screw got out of synch—an impenetrable veil snapped shut, closing her off from the outer world.

—

The ride back to Boston was not a happy experience. For the most part, neither Sheridan nor Jensen spoke. And Sheridan knew that Donna would remain at Hampton.

He dropped Jensen off at St. Anne's front entrance. It was a busy place—ambulances, taxis, patients being wheeled toward waiting automobiles, some hobbling on crutches, others being carried in on stretchers, accompanied by emergency techs, medics, and nurses.

Sheridan jumped into the embarrassing silence.

"Want to thank you for coming up with me, Doctor. This wasn't Donna's day, I guess."

"Guess not," Jensen said tersely. He got out on the passenger's side and shut the door with a decisive thud. He merely nodded, then walked toward the entrance.

With the slam of the door and Jensen's departure, the tiny window for Donna DiTullio had been effectively shut. And Sheridan had no cards left. He had played out his hand.

—

Buckley greeted Sheridan and Raimondi in the small coffee room, which also housed the Xerox and fax machines. Judy had brewed some decaf and had also spread out Donna DiTullio's hospital records in the conference room. Karen Assad was due in about an hour. Buckley had already filled in Sheridan on the pregnancy bit. Sheridan, like Buckley, felt this could harm rather than help

the case. It could have moral implications, which would not be
lost on a jury. Jurors could be admonished by the trial judge to
eliminate any biases and prejudices from their deliberations, but
as a practical matter, both Sheridan and Buckley knew that any
such judicial injunction would be like trying to tell someone to
sit in a corner and not think of a white bear. In fact, jurors would
be meticulously selected based on prejudice and bias, whether
economic, cultural, ethnic, political, religious, or dictated by gen-
der or age. The demographics would be exploited by both sides.
And all the judicial admonitions in the world couldn't sweep away
ingrained prejudice.

"When you took Jensen up to Hampton," Buckley said to
Sheridan, "did you have the feeling that someone was tailing
you?"

"Tailing me?"

"Yes, that you were being followed."

"Never entered my mind. Only glanced in the mirror to
check for the State Police cruisers. As you know, I'm a little heavy
on the pedal. Didn't notice anything unusual."

"Well, I'm sure I was followed when Karen and I had lunch
at the Dockside. I spotted a guy a couple of tables away. Had a
funny feeling about him. We leave the Dockside, he leaves. I
drive Karen to Jamaica Plain, he's tagging along several car
lengths back."

"Did you catch his license plate number?" Raimondi asked.
Buckley shook his head.

"Karen's due in here shortly," Buckley said. "She hasn't
seen or heard from her ex-husband in three years. Moved to Lou-
isiana someplace. Pays no alimony, not even child support, so
this tail can't be from the deadbeat. Got to be something to do
with the DiTullio case."

"How's Karen getting here?" Raimondi asked.

"I gave her money for a cab. She'll pull up out front"—
Buckley checked his watch—"in about half an hour."

"Why don't you and Dan get things set up in the conference
room?" Raimondi said. "I'll just meander around outside, stay

out of range, and kind of keep an eye on who's coming, going, or staying when Karen pulls up."

—

When Raimondi left for downstairs, Buckley poured the morning coffee—straight black for both of them.

"Dan," Buckley said after taking a good sip of Sanka, "we've got other stuff besides the DiTullio case—Mrs. Gallagher, and we've got five criminal cases coming up in November. That Larson kid, he was doing his Christmas shopping a little early—three-thirty in the morning at Bloomingdale's—when they caught him. And, Christ, I think you're forgetting Carmine Perez. Comes from a fine aristocratic family in Medellín, Colombia. Picked up on Route One with four million dollars' worth of heroin in his golf bag. Claims it was planted. Dan, the U.S. attorney is hitting us with all sorts of motions. We're going to be defaulted—and Perez is not a happy camper, believe me. He's being held without bail, and the Perez family is getting a little uptight. Got a call from his uncle, 'El Dragone,' the other day. Wants to know what we're doing on his nephew's case. Reminded us that the family paid us a twenty-five-grand retainer."

"For chrissakes, Buck!" Sheridan snapped. "I know all this fucking stuff! I'm not going to let clients run me, understand? You got to realize this. Never let the client tell you what to do. You tell the client what to do. You're flying the airplane. Don't even let the client in the cockpit! Got that?"

Buckley had heard it all before.

"Sure," he said, "but these Colombian clients—they say cross-examine, you cross-examine. They're not Mrs. Gallagher, God bless her. We take on this type of client, then we're in bed with them, like it or not."

"Look," Sheridan said, his voice edged with displeasure, "fuck the Colombians! They wait in line like everyone else. So Perez is languishing in jail. Maybe it'll teach him a hard-earned lesson. We get to his case like any other. Colombians, mafiosi, drunk drivers, prostitutes—they all deserve a defense. We'll give it to them. You defend these guys, but believe me, as Edward

Bennett Williams once said—and he defended the capo of capos, Frank Costello—'You don't run with them.' "

"Enough said." Buckley downed the Sanka.

Sheridan crumpled his plastic cup and threw it into the wastebasket. "You know, Buck, you could be right. I am getting a little too obsessed with this case. I'm losing my objectivity. But I have a premonition that the DiTullio case is going to make or break me."

"What in hell are you talking about?"

"I really don't know." Sheridan shook his head. His voice seemed distant. "I don't know—it's like I'm at some crossroad. I do the right thing, we're all heroes, basking in notoriety—the legal sunlight. But I've got kind of a gut feeling—and it's not good. The DiTullio case may drag a lot of people down, including us."

"Chrissakes, Dan!" Buckley almost exploded as he leaned against the watercooler. "Are you all right?"

"Hey, Buck, never felt better."

Buckley issued a pent-up sigh. "Jesus," he said, "I certainly hope so. Let's go in and get ready for Karen."

—

Raimondi joined a group of tourists at the Old Granary Burial Ground, his telescopic camera strapped over his shoulder. They walked along the footpaths while a young woman guide in a park ranger's outfit, complete with a Smokey the Bear hat, pointed out the graves of Paul Revere, Ben Franklin's parents, and Sam Adams. Raimondi checked his watch and moved closer to the worn grate fence bordering Tremont Street. It was about five to ten. He twisted the camera lens and, in between a few practice shots at some lichen-covered headstones, kept an eye on the front entrance to Sheridan's office building. He had a pretty good read on Karen Assad—mid-thirties, jet black hair, olive skin—a tall Lebanese beauty, as Buckley had described her. The guy in the gray fedora—perhaps mid-fifties, on the chubby side—but Buckley didn't have much more.

At about five after ten, a yellow cab pulled up and Raimondi watched as Karen Assad paid her fare and then walked into the building's front entrance. Sure enough, five or so seconds later, a gray Chevrolet pulled up. The car waited at the curb about two car lengths from the front door. There was a female driver, mid-twenties. A young man alighted from the passenger's side. He had on a white windbreaker, blue jeans, Reebok sneakers. A small camera case dangled from his neck. He definitely was not Gray Fedora. He paced up and down for a minute or two, then took several snaps of the building's foyer. Raimondi watched through his camera range finder as the stranger clicked off a few more shots and then entered the building. Raimondi could see him chatting with the security guard, then saw him aim his camera at the index register, taking several quick shots. All this time, the girl driving the Chevy waited at the curb.

Raimondi got as near to the fence as possible and tried to get a shot of the vehicle's license plate. Unfortunately, the Chevy had only a rear plate and Raimondi couldn't get a good angle on it. Instead, he took several pics of the driver seated in the car, then managed to get a fairly good close-up of the guy in the white windbreaker. Then, oddly, White Windbreaker, or Whitey, as Raimondi noted him mentally, talked briefly to the girl, then exchanged his camera for one quite like Raimondi's, complete with a telescopic lens attachment. The Chevy drove off and Raimondi made a quick mental note of the plate number, 695-021. Then, as luck would have it, White Windbreaker, his sophisticated camera slung over his shoulder, made his way into the Old Granary Burial Ground.

Raimondi again melded in with the guided tour. He changed the lens on his camera and started shooting more worn gravestones. Whitey was sitting on the low brick wall surrounding the Franklin family monument, keeping his eye on the foyer entrance across the street. Raimondi aimed several shots in Whitey's direction.

The tour group made its way to some more graves—John Hancock and that of Elizabeth Goose, known the world over as the Mother Goose of nursery rhymes. When the group departed down the old granite steps, Raimondi went with them. He took up a new station on the steps of the Park Street Church, where abolitionist firebrands William Lloyd Garrison and Wendell Phillips had launched their crusade against slavery, fanning the flames of discontent that engulfed the country in the conflagration of civil war.

Karen Assad would be spending the better part of the morning with Buckley and Sheridan, but Raimondi was sure that White Windbreaker was part of a team that was tailing Assad. He hunkered down at the top of the granite steps, partially concealed by a white wooden pillar at the church's entrance. He could see Whitey, who was still sitting on the wall at the Franklin monument. It would be a long wait.

After several minutes, Raimondi pulled out a portable phone from his camera bag and poked out a number.

"Rosa," he said, "Cousin Manny here. How're things at the Registry of Motor Vehicles? I'm on a job right now. Trying to get a lead on a hit-and-run case we got in the office." There was a brief exchange.

"Rosa, the license number is Mass six-nine-five-oh-two-one. Yeah, call me back on my mobile phone as soon as you can." He gave her the number. "I'll be right here for the next hour or two," he said. "And how's Tia Maria?"

"Auntie Maria's fine, Manny. I'll call you back."

—

Karen Assad sipped her coffee as she went through Donna DiTullio's extensive psychiatric record. Sheridan sat next to her and Buckley leaned on the conference table, hovering over her shoulder.

"It's a complete factual record," she said. "Everything's been noted." She didn't place too much significance on Buckley's theory that the record looked too trim. She said that the doctors' notes were sometimes handwritten but might also have been dictated and the medical secretaries did the editing. The nurses' notes were also complete and unvarnished. She recognized her own.

"Donna was in the Psych Department for three weeks. Her

menstrual period was due some ten days after her admission, but none was noted. So the inference was that she missed her period.

"I had a hunch she was pregnant, although she never told me about it—and she did share her most intimate moments, especially when the Capricet was making her feel good. You'll also note that her temperature was slightly elevated each morning and that her appetite had increased. There was no mention of morning sickness by any of the day nurses, but that could be due to the Capricet.

"As I recall," she said, "the pathologist was a Dr. Rashi Diwali. Let me see if I can get a read on him. The report that I read said the mass was fetal, with a gestation period of about three months."

"The fact that she was pregnant and concealed it, both from the doctors who were trying to help her and from the nursing staff, particularly you, Karen, could harm her case," Buckley said. "It could have severe credibility overtones that a jury might hold against her, not to mention the moral sanctions. Lay jurors, particularly Catholic lay jurors, can be pretty tough on a plaintiff who has committed mortal sin."

Karen Assad looked amused and shook her head.

"We're stepping into the twenty-first century," she said. "So the girl was pregnant. Can't you give the jury your Mary Magdalen spin?"

"We'll do our best, naturally," Sheridan said. "But some jurors can be downright mean, especially to their own. They'll know DiTullio is Italian, and Italian means old family values, and old family values tend to ostracize the fallen woman; no one reaches down to help her. It's a reality we've got to face. Maybe it's best to let this sleeping dog lie. We forget about the pregnancy."

"But why would someone, obviously in the hospital's employ, lift the path report? Someone wanted it deleted." Karen didn't want the matter brushed away so easily.

"I don't know," Sheridan said. "Could that person be Dante DiTullio? He couldn't have had access to the psych records, but the record of the hospital admission following her accident was more available to him than to me."

"No, I know the Medical Records Department. First of all, he could only get a copy of the original. The original record was kept in the record room. He couldn't have access to where it was kept."

"Yes, but as you say, you gained access despite your lack of authorization."

"I know, but I did this through a pretty authoritative subterfuge."

Karen thought for a moment, as did Sheridan and Buckley.

"We're not thinking the same thing, are we?" Buckley blurted.

Karen hesitated. "You don't think for a moment . . ."

Sheridan nodded. "I'm thinking it. But it's just too implausible."

"You think that Dante DiTullio might have impregnated his daughter?"

"God," Buckley said, "I'm on the same wavelength. Perhaps, Karen, we should forget about Diwali and his path report. It could be a minefield; best we go around it."

—

Raimondi was sitting on the top step of the Park Street Church, trying to look nonchalant as he kept his eye on Whitey. Like Raimondi, Whitey resembled an out-of-towner, milling with the tourist group as they ambled around the old cemetery. He, too, had a magna-lensed camera and was shooting pics of headstones and old grave markers, as Raimondi had done. He also was equipped with a portable phone, which he used several times. No question, this guy and the young woman driver were private eyes. And their interest was in Karen Assad.

Close to noon, Raimondi's phone beeped its audible signal. He glanced at Whitey, who was now seated on a granite slab near the cemetery gate and had primed his camera and had it aimed at the front entrance of Sheridan's building.

"Hello, Manny." The voice was hushed, almost conspiratorial.

"Yeah," Manny said, still keeping an eye on Whitey. "Is that you, Rosa?"

"Yep." The voice brightened a bit. "Got the info you wanted. I'm calling from a pay phone outside the Registry.

"Six-nine-five-zero-two-one is registered to Ajax Rental, Logan Airport. Your defendant might be an out-of-towner."

Hm, Raimondi thought, this could pose a problem, getting the Ajax records to see who rented the car. These guys are smart.

"Ajax Rental, Logan, you say, Rosa?" He logged it into his mind.

Just as he clicked the off button, Karen Assad emerged from the front entrance of the building and hailed a cab. Whitey was quickly alert. He aimed his camera and clicked away. Raimondi did likewise, aiming at Whitey. *Click! Click! Click!* They were keeping Kodak executives in silk shirts.

As Karen Assad entered the cab, the gray Chevy with the young girl driver pulled up almost on cue. Whitey got in and away they went. Raimondi shot one last photo of the Chevy as they drove past his position. Ajax Rental, Logan Airport. He had to find out who had rented the car. This wasn't going to be easy.

21

D r. Sexton was looking forward to the weekend. It had been several months since he had taken time off. And with the crush of relocating the offices, the DiTullio suit, and Captain Ahearn's unsettling call, he anticipated the next four days with relish. Ever since his stint as a lieutenant colonel in the National Guard and a brief tour of duty in Desert Storm, he had developed a keen interest in guns and ammunition. He had become an experienced sharpshooter with all types of weapons— from low-caliber carbines to 28-gauge shotguns, even a .45 automatic. Although he had signed up as a medical officer, he had opted for combat training, and he always welcomed the two-week encampments at Camp Drum, New York. And lately, the short sojourns at the Lake George Rod and Hunt Club, where the guests would track anything from moose to lynx to boar, almost replaced his winter skiing safaris to Aspen and Sun Valley.

"You taking the Beretta and the Bauer?" the groundskeeper asked cheerily, realizing he and Selma, the cook, would have free run of the house for the better part of the week.

"I'll pack both and the laser sights in my gun slings," Sexton said. "I want to bring my own ammo. We're going after some of

the meanest boar in upstate New York. We're out there by ourselves—no dogs, no backup, just the trusty Bauer. You miss and
you climb a tree damn fast. Two members got mauled pretty bad
last season."

"Okay, Doctor, I'll bring the Caddy around. . . . Think I'll
drain the pool while you're gone, and work on that leak in the
main skimmer."

"Fine," Sexton said, "and you know the lodge number. But
don't call unless it's absolutely necessary, and that includes my
staff—even Sister Agnes Loretta. I'm really going to rough it for
the next few days, get back to where it all began."

Sexton unlocked the small anteroom in his mahogany-
paneled den, and for a few minutes he studied his gun collection.
There were ten rifles in the rack, the stocks richly grained: Moss-
berg 590s, Mausers, Bauers, Berettas, Brownings, a Finnish Sako
and a 12-gauge Russian Baikal. He selected the Beretta 390 and
the Bauer, carefully inserting both into the olive green gun bag.
Although he wouldn't use it for moose, elk, or boar, he selected
a telescopic day and night sight, examined it, then inserted it
into the sling's side compartment. He'd get in some long-range
practice at the club's target area. Next, he selected two boxes of
ammunition, one .357 Magnums, the other Van Zandt bullets, a
special brand manufactured in Holland, capable of bursting upon
impact like a Fourth of July cherry bomb. A hit in any area—a
leg or an arm—would detonate like a hand grenade; even a flesh
wound would prove fatal. Illegal and unavailable on the U.S.
market, they were too messy to use on live game. When he was
out on the hunt, he would use the regular Magnums, which
pierced with a clean wound. He'd save the Van Zandts for the
remote target areas, against partially sunken logs or an otter or
two that might be frolicking in one of the many ponds and streams
that dotted the club's acreage.

Sexton drove to Hanscom Field, a small airport west of Boston, and was met by a young pilot wearing blue jeans and a faded
brown leather jacket. The pilot introduced himself as "Normie"
and proceeded to carry Sexton's luggage, including the gun
slings, to a waiting single-engine Piper 180.

"Got over five hundred hours." The pilot smiled beneath his Ray•Ban shades as he watched Sexton inspecting the plane somewhat anxiously. "Never had an accident. Not even a near miss." He stored Sexton's equipment in the backseat and they scrambled aboard.

"You familiar with the course to Glens Falls, New York?" Sexton felt embarrassed asking, but the pilot looked all of twenty-one, maybe younger. They'd be crossing the Green Mountains, mostly a pine-forested, sparsely populated expanse. Planes were known to have disappeared in that dense wilderness, never to be found.

"Flew there last week," the pilot said as he ran through his checklist. He revved the engine, rolled onto the tarmac, and taxied into position for takeoff. Cleared by the tower, the Piper zoomed down the runway and lifted off.

After a smooth two-hour flight in a perfect azure sky, they touched down at Glens Falls Airport. A white-haired old-timer met them and packed Sexton's bags and gun slings into a vintage station wagon. They headed along remote back roads to Catskill Bay on Lake George.

The Lake George Rod and Hunt Club had an exclusive membership. Exactly one hundred white male professionals, mainly Manhattan doctors, lawyers, and stockbrokers, paid the $25,000 annual fee to engage in a good round of drinking, congeniality, marrying off a daughter or two to the well-connected clientele, and of course killing the preserve's animal population for sport. The lodge's taxidermist did a brisk business, mounting moose heads, stuffing partridges, and making bracelets out of boar ivory.

Before retiring that night, Sexton examined the Van Zandt 7-mm bullets. The slugs had spiral grooves, tips slightly blunted. The brass cartridge seemed longer than ordinary 7-mm ones. He wondered about accuracy and recoil. He'd be out on his own for about eight hours in a remote corner of the reservation. He'd test the Van Zandts, but not on the boars or black bears; game that was blown apart might be tough to explain. And if he was caught using illegal ammo, he faced expulsion from the club.

The four days went quickly. No calls from Boston. He'd bagged two black bears, four deer, and one boar. He didn't want souvenirs. The bearskin, the boar, and the deer meat were turned in to the club.

On the last day, when the guide deposited him in a jungle of Scotch pine and thick underbrush, Sexton used his map and compass and made his way to an algae-infested pond. He watched several otters slipping into the water, their brown heads bobbing along, diving, then resurfacing. He fixed the telescopic sight onto the Bauer, then loaded it with a full complement of Van Zandts. About five hundred yards out on the lake, a loon skimmed low over the water. Sexton aimed and squeezed the trigger. The bullet exploded upon impact. A few floating feathers were all that remained of the loon. Sexton next aimed at a slender birch across the lake, had to be half a mile away. *Bang!* An orange explosion and the tree splintered and toppled. Despite the grooves, the bullet's accuracy was uncanny, and best of all, there was minimal recoil. He then turned his attention to an otter whose head was making a small wake in the water, again more than half a mile away. He aimed, had the little head in the crosshairs. He waited several seconds. The target was greeted by another otter. They disappeared, reappeared, seemed to somersault out of the water. Slowly, Sexton lowered his gun.

"You're lucky, my little friends," he said as he smiled. The Van Zandts were all they were cracked up to be. He wondered about the many terrorist groups using this lethal contraband. If there were "smart bombs" for missiles, for bullets the Van Zandts were reasonable facsimiles.

The setting sun was casting long shadows across the brown-marbled lake. Sexton pulled out his map and compass. It would be a fifty-minute trek back to the lodge. He headed southeast along a small footpath. He had reloaded his Bauer with straight ammo and slung it over his shoulder. He didn't intend to end up as bear meat or being gored by a boar.

Raimondi took a cab to Logan Airport and was dropped off at the Ajax Rental lot. It was a small area of about fifteen cars, niched between Hertz and Avis. He didn't know if he could pull it off. There seemed to be a sole attendant, who at the moment was leaning against one of the cars, apparently engrossed in a tabloid newspaper. Raimondi spotted the Chevy, license plate 695-021. He could rent the car, but he decided to see if the doors were unlocked. They were. He glanced at the attendant, who was maybe fifty feet away. A row of cars blocked a clear view. No sign of movement. He opened the driver's door as quietly as possible and stuffed a pair of sunglasses under the seat. He closed the door slowly with a muffled click. Next he went to the small cinder-block office. No question, Ajax was a no-frills operation. A plumpish girl in a red jacket with white epaulets was at the counter, talking on the telephone. Raimondi waited as she concluded a personal call. Business was definitely slow; the girl and the lot attendant were the sole signs of human life. He reminded himself not to buy stock in Ajax.

"Can I help you, sir?" The girl gave Raimondi a slightly annoyed look. Obviously, he had aborted her friend's call.

"My, you're a sight for sore eyes. *Very attractive.*" Raimondi dragged it out as he flashed his handsome Latin smile.

The girl appeared flustered.

"Thank you," she said after several seconds.

"I'll bet you're a college girl," Raimondi said quickly. "Let me guess. Smith, Wellesley? Maybe Mount Holyoke. Yes, you got class. I'd say Mount Holyoke."

"Mount wha' . . ." the girl said with an amused stammer.

"That's a college out in South Hadley. Classy ladies there, believe me. I used to date one."

The girl unconsciously brushed her hair back with her hand.

"Jeez no," she said. "I only graduated from East Boston High in June. Been here now for two months. Hope to get a job with Hertz this December."

"Well, you deserve it." Raimondi looked left, then right. He caught the attendant still reading the paper. Probably studying the morning line at Suffolk Downs.

"Can we get you a car, sir? We're having a weekend special on midsize Toyotas—free gas with the first two hundred miles."

"No. I'm here trying to help someone out. My cousin rented a car from you guys yesterday. . . ." Raimondi took out his wallet and pulled out several credit cards, placing them on the counter, all top of the line, Visa Gold, American Express Platinum. He carefully extracted a piece of paper that was buried among a wad of hundred-dollar bills. The girl noticed.

"A Chevrolet, Mass. license plate six-nine-five–oh-two-one. My cousin's sure he left his sunglasses under the front seat. He wouldn't mind, but they're five-hundred-dollar Guccis."

"Five hun . . . " The girl grinned. She was warming up to Raimondi. He was dark, good-looking. She liked his shiny black leather jacket.

"Anything turned in? As I said, he rented the car yesterday—probably had it out in the early morning and returned it late afternoon."

"Sure, I remember," the girl said. "That was your cousin?"

"Yes, I'm trying to help him out."

"Well, your cousin's a she, not a he."

"Did I say *he*? I meant *she*. And listen," he added quickly, "you need a reference to Hertz. I know the vice president in charge of personnel in New York."

"Wow," she said, "that would be great! . . . Nothing was brought in, but I remember the girl. It wasn't too busy yesterday. Name was Kelly . . . Kelly Monahan. You say you're her cousin?" She again assessed Raimondi's dark Latin countenance.

"By marriage," he said. "My mother's sister was Portuguese, married a guy named Monahan."

"Wait a minute, Mr. . . . ."

"Ricardo. Ricardo Oliveira."

"Okay." She went to the door.

"Billy!" she yelled, startling the attendant. "Take a look in that Chevy—six-nine-five–oh-two-one. Is there a pair of sunglasses under the driver's seat?"

It was almost too perfect. Billy came in with the glasses.

"Look," Raimondi said, "Cousin Kelly recently moved. Could you give me her current address?"

The girl seemed to hesitate. Raimondi could read her thoughts. Cousin One asks Cousin Two to fetch her sunglasses from a rental car, and Cousin Two doesn't even know her address?

"Look, here's a twenty-dollar bill for your trouble." He laid it on the counter. "And write your name on your card. I'm going to get hold of my man at Hertz."

Still the girl hesitated.

"I shouldn't do this," she said as she picked up the twenty, "but seeing you're cousins . . ."

She punched out a few keys on the computer. *Kelly Monahan, 1069 Allston Avenue, Brighton.*

"Want her operator's license, Mr. Oliveira?"

"No, just the address will be fine." He jotted down the information in his notebook. "I want to thank you. Kelly will be pleased, believe me. You lose a pair of Guccis like this"—Raimondi held up the glasses—"and you lose a little bit of yourself." He nodded, smiled, and turned to leave.

"Mr. Oliveira . . ."

"Yes?"

"My card. The Hertz VP!"

"Oh, God, most certainly." He took the card, glanced at it.

"Mary," he said, giving the card a jiggle above his head, "good luck at Hertz!"

●

It wasn't difficult for Raimondi to connect Kelly Monahan with Commonwealth Investigations and Security, Inc., located in the Prudential Building in Copley Square. All private investigators had to be licensed by the State Police. A friendly call to headquarters got the information. Monahan was employed by Commonwealth, along with twelve other operatives, including James Ward, Commonwealth's chief executive.

Checking around, Raimondi learned that Commonwealth was a fair-sized operation with blue-chip clients. Jim Ward was

a former CIA officer. Raimondi briefed Buckley and Sheridan.
They were to be on their guard.

—

Dan Sheridan arranged the yellow roses in a chipped porcelain
vase provided by the nurse. Except for Donna, the room was
vacant, the same three steel-framed beds rolled against the wall.
Again Sheridan thought, As rooms go, at least it's private. Perhaps the nurses would be somewhat more attentive to Donna's
simple needs. He recalled the incident with the empty IV bag.
It was midafternoon, and the nurse told him that Dr. Brockelman
had gone for the day but that the resident, Ishmael Pahloor, could
be summoned if Sheridan or Donna needed assistance.

Sheridan shut the door and tweaked the slatted shades to
allow more light into the room. The shades refused to open. The
overhead light sputtered and flickered as though it was about to
expire. Obviously, maintenance was not top priority at Hampton.

"Hi, Donna, it's your friend Dan Sheridan." He leaned toward her inert form. Her eyelashes fluttered slightly. A good sign,
thought Sheridan.

"I'm going to crank you up a bit." He found the handle and
ratcheted the head of the bed several notches.

"Got some lovely roses for you, Donna." He picked one from
the vase and laid it on the night table, then swung the table in
front of Donna. Again, her eyelashes fluttered and tears trickled
down both cheeks.

"They treating you all right, Donna?"

Except for the tearing, her eyes were unmoving.

Don't want to start confusing her, Sheridan thought. Got to
keep it basic. No mental machinations, only stuff calling for a
simple yes or no.

He noticed her hands were folded in front of her. Her wrists
still had a shiny pallor, but her bony fingers were less clawlike.

"Donna, I'm going to ask you one or two easy questions. It's
like a game, really. Like we did before, blink once for yes, twice
for no." Sheridan waited several seconds.

"I'm Dan Sheridan, your friend. Do you recognize me, Donna?"

There came a long, slow slide of her eyes. They closed for a moment or two, then opened. There was also a slight twitching of her lips.

God, Sheridan thought, is she trying to say something? The twitching was an entirely new phenomenon. He wanted to call the nurse, maybe the resident, but he was afraid they would scare Donna and she'd retreat into her deep freeze. But there definitely was facial movement apart from the eyelids. This was a first. He had studied Lord Russell Quigley's text on neuroanatomy. Facial movement, particularly of the lips, was controlled by the seventh cranial nerve. And this couldn't be dismissed as pure reflex. There was some vitality along the nerve's pathway, some regeneration.

"Donna," he said, "has Dr. Brockelman been in here today?"

There were two blinks.

She does have some memory, however primitive. Sheridan tried to calculate. Memory was stored in a tiny section of the brain known as the hippocampus, which was part of the larger cerebral cortex. The circuits and pathways of this system were connecting, however imperfectly, and some slim strand was open. From his studies, he knew that when brain tissue died, it was lost forever; it did not regenerate. He thought of Jensen's hypothesis—that when one portion of the brain becomes irreversibly damaged, another part can take over.

He looked up for a moment and checked the IV bottle. It was almost empty. He'd call this to the nurses' attention on his way out. And he'd make sure he impressed them with the necessity of keeping it filled and functioning.

"Donna, I don't want to tire you out." He returned to the patient. "You're looking better." He reached over and patted one of her hands. They didn't seem as cold and lifeless as on prior visits.

"I noticed you moved your lips," he said softly but clearly. "That's a good sign. I'll be back in a day or two. Do you want me to bring some pictures again? Of you playing tennis?"

Again the single blink.

"Good-bye, Donna, for now." He kissed her forehead. There were still the deep purple crescents under her eyes, the sunken cheeks had a grayish pallor, but again her lips seemed to tremble. If he didn't know better, he'd swear she was trying to smile.

●

As Sheridan got into his TR6 in the Hampton lot, he noticed a young woman parked in a gray Chevy that fit the description supplied by Raimondi. He pulled out of the lot slowly, turned onto a rural roadway, and then continued for several miles before getting on I-95 heading south toward Boston. Periodically, he checked the rearview mirror. Sure enough, the Chevy was tagging along at a five- or six-car interval. No sense trying to shake the tail, Sheridan reasoned. In fact, might as well make it interesting.

Just before crossing the Tobin Bridge, he veered off into Charlestown and pulled up in front of St. Francis de Sales Church. He couldn't recall when he'd made such a visit, probably not since he was a schoolboy. He wasn't sure it would help, but he thought he'd say a few prayers that Sister Agnes Loretta would come through for Donna DiTullio. On leaving St. Francis, he called Judy on his car phone and got directions to the Poor Clares convent. He next stopped at a roadside produce stand on Morrissey Boulevard in Dorchester and loaded up with baskets of fruit, vegetables, steaks, and a spray of fall flowers. He even purchased a bottle of Christian Brothers brandy.

As he pulled into the convent driveway, he noticed the Chevy idle up and park across the street. He stole a quick look at the girl he felt was Kelly Monahan. She was young, mid-twenties, auburn hair, Irish face. Her fingers drummed on the steering wheel as she tried to look nonchalant.

A housekeeper answered the convent bell and directed Sheridan to a quiet screened cloister. Behind it, a nun introduced herself as Mother Mary Joseph, the convent's superior. She stepped out from behind the dimly lit screen. These were no modern nuns. She wore the traditional headdress, white bib, brown garb. But her eyes danced and her smile was genuine 1996. Sheridan had noticed the little bronze clapper bell outside the convent door. For food, money, and clothing the Poor Clares relied strictly on donations. If contributions were light, one of the nuns would toll the bell. Sheridan knew that the bell hadn't been tolled since the Poor Clares moved to their location at the turn of the century.

He spent a good twenty minutes with Mother Superior, and as he was about to leave, he gave her a hundred-dollar bill.

"Oh, no." She shook her head. "The food is enough. The cook will have a field day. And we have taken a vow of poverty, you know."

"Mother"—Sheridan gave her an impish grin—"a hundred dollars is not going to put you above the poverty line. This is for you. Send it home, waste it, or buy a little Chardonnay for the good sisters. You know when you labor in the vineyards of the Lord, Mother, you have a right to some of the grapes."

"All right." She took the bill and it disappeared quickly into her sash pocket. "God bless this day and you, Mr. Sheridan, and keep you well."

Sheridan got into his TR6 and glanced through the iron grille that fenced the grounds. Kelly Monahan and the Chevy were nowhere in sight. But as he turned the corner and headed toward the Jamaicaway, a white van seemed to be following. Sure enough, when he pulled up into his office parking lot, the van eased into the curb half a block away. Maybe he'd walk down to Chinatown, make a visit to St. James.

No, hell, he thought. Had enough religion for today.

22

Sheridan read the letter from Sister Agnes Loretta. It was concise and to the point. She regretted that Donna could not be taken back to St. Anne's. She cited that the hospital was not a chronic-care facility and their insurer would not support the proposal. "Yours in Christ," the letter concluded.

"Well, I'm afraid Donna's stuck at Hampton for the duration." Sheridan handed the letter to Buckley. "I almost thought the sister was going to make an exception." He shook his head.

Buckley tried a change of pace. "This tailing stuff is getting a little ridiculous. I told Karen Assad that I had to go out of town for several days. I don't want her involved."

"Speaking of Karen Assad—and this goes for Janet Phillips and Ted Marden, too—I think we've got to distance ourselves from all three." Sheridan's voice was all business.

"What?" Buckley stammered.

"These are material witnesses. We can't get involved with them other than on a professional basis. I know we've got Marden's aunt's case, but Judy is right. Eventually, we're going to split a referral fee with him. Right now, we have to be like Caesar's wife; even the suggestion of an impropriety would bring the bar overseers sniffing around. And how would it look on cross-examination if d'Ortega grills Marden and it comes out that he split a three- or four-hundred-thousand-dollar fee with us? How do you think the jury would see that? We lawyers have a bad enough image as it is. I'll call Marden at his home, tell him about our second thoughts. I'll recommend a couple of good personal-injury guys. I'm sure he'll understand."

He looked at Buckley. "I'm sorry, Buck, but that also goes for Karen Assad."

Buckley wasn't ready for that. He thought for a long moment. When Judy gave them the benefit of her Jewish-mother intuition, he should have heeded it. His lips tightened. It was easy for Judy to give advice. He wasn't sure he was going to follow it.

—

Charlie Finnerty took a moment to review the copy of Sister Agnes Loretta's letter to Dan Sheridan. At least that problem was shortstopped.

"Cigar, Jim?" He flipped open the antique gold box and extended it toward the detective.

"No thanks, Mr. Finnerty, but if you don't mind, I'll have one of my Marlboros." He reached into his vest pocket, took out a pack, tapped it on the back of his wrist, and extracted a cigarette.

Finnerty unwrapped his Cuban cigar and ran it under his nose, inhaling deeply. He reached forward with his Wedgwood desk lighter and offered the detective a light. After puffing his cigar into ignition for several seconds, Finnerty removed it, studying it as the blue smoke curled toward the ceiling.

"Nothing like a good cigar," he said. "Sometimes, Jim, I don't know which I enjoy better—a good bottle of Jameson or the fine taste of a prima Havana.

"Well, what good news have you got?"

The detective took a long drag on his cigarette, then laid it on a nearby green marble ashtray.

"Kind of funny," he said as he picked up a blue-backed folder.

"Funny?"

"Yes, Mr. Finnerty. We got a ten-day surveillance here." He tapped the folder. "Except for one day when the Assad girl visits Sheridan's office, there's little else."

"You sure?" Finnerty did not look pleased.

"I had my best operatives covering Sheridan and his associate, Buckley. Apart from going to court each day—and it was mundane stuff—arguing motions, mainly—that's all there is. We had our people sit in the back of the courtroom. That consumed seventy, eighty percent of their time. Buckley played a couple of sets of tennis at the Commonwealth Courts in Brookline, Sheridan shot a few rounds of golf, coached a Pop Warner football team two nights after work. He went to Hampton one day to see the DiTullio girl, then made all sorts of visits to churches and convents. Even took a group of Ursuline nuns to a Red Sox game. And on a couple of occasions, he met his girlfriend, Sheila O'Brien—she's with your former firm, waiting to hear from the bar exam. Well, as I say, they jog two days a week, early evenings in the Blue Hills."

"What about Karen Assad? She ever make another contact with Buckley or Sheridan?"

"That's what's kind of strange," the detective said. "Other than the lovey-dovey stuff at the Dockside and her trip to Sheridan's office—and we got several pictures of her entering his office building—there was no further contact. She just comes and goes, takes care of her kids, and shows up for work each night. About ten every evening, a baby-sitter comes in—an older person, could be her mother. We know this, since Assad drives her home when she packs the kids off to school.

"You want us to continue, Mr. Finnerty? Say, another week?"

"No. For now, just shut the operation down."

"Here's the entire report, Mr. Finnerty, if you care to read it. It's quite thorough."

Detective Ward was going to present his bill, but he thought better of it. It was expensive—$16,800. He'd send it in due course, maybe shave it a little.

"Okay, Jim," Finnerty said with a dismissive tone. "These were your best operatives, you say?"

"Best in the city."

"Did it ever cross your mind that Sheridan and Buckley were onto you from the get-go?" Finnerty again studied his cigar. "Karen Assad shows up at Sheridan's office. Buckley and Assad are a twosome. Now you're on the scene. Suddenly, no more contact. Sheridan's visiting churches and convents, working and performing all sorts of charitable acts. Not even one venial sin."

Charlie inhaled deeply, then sent a column of smoke billowing toward the ceiling.

"I've thought of that," the detective said.

"You're going to send a bill, of course." In the area of economics, Finnerty now held the high ground. "I trust it will be modest. I have to pass it on to the cardinal, you know."

"Certainly, Mr. Finnerty." The detective took a last drag on his cigarette and ground it into the tray. "Modest? Yes, by all means, it will be modest."

●

"Karen, I was in Detroit for the last several days," Buckley lied, cupping the phone with his hand, although he was alone in the office.

"Well, I was wondering why I didn't hear from you. Your office told me you were out on some case. How did things go?"

"Oh, as well as could be expected. Depositions, you know. These can go on and on."

"I thought maybe you'd call," she said. Buckley sensed the hurt in her voice.

"Believe me, we worked night and day out there. We're suing a major car manufacturer on a rollover case involving one of their vans. Had to depose their experts—bunch of metallurgists and mechanical engineers. Unless you're thoroughly prepared, those guys can really bruise you."

Although the air conditioner was purring at maximum cool, Buckley began to perspire. He had never been good at bending the truth, especially to someone he cared for.

"Well, I'm glad you're back in one piece," Karen said.

There was a lull in the conversation. Buckley was thinking of something safe to say.

"Do you want to come over Friday night?" Karen said. "Ahmed and Kaliph will be away. They're going up to their aunt Sophia's in Vermont. She's got a farm near Rutland. The boys go there for a week each year at this time.

"I'll cook an old-fashioned Lebanese meal, tabbouleh, baba ghanoush, hummus, and kibbe. And if you want something Irish, you can bring a six-pack."

Again, there was an embarrassing lull. Buckley wanted to tell Karen about the tail, but he didn't want to involve her. He wanted to tell her that the Detroit trip was a complete fabrication, like their initial encounter when he tried to pass himself off as a *Globe* reporter. He knew it wouldn't work. She'd slam the receiver down and that would be it. To her, he would be a complete fraud. He took a deep breath.

"I want to level with you, Karen."

"Level . . ."

"I can't make it Friday night."

"Well, what about Wednesday?"

"I've got to fly to Manila," he blurted. "Sheridan wants me to check out Dr. Puzon. Got to leave tomorrow. I'll be gone for at least a week." There was a long silence.

"Buckley"—her voice was mild, but with a skeptical undertone—"there's something else, isn't there? You're not going to Manila. I can detect it in your voice."

"Listen, I have to explain."

There was an audible click.

Buckley sat at his desk, not moving for several minutes. His shirt was mottled with sweat. Maybe he had done the right thing but in the wrong way. And he knew that in the league of human relationships, there was no such thing as three strikes. He reached for the bottle of bourbon in his lower left-hand desk drawer.

23

During the next two months, Sheridan juggled clients and cases as best he could. Perez still languished in jail, increasingly unhappy. Motions, cross-motions, and memoranda of law besieged Sheridan and Buckley from all directions—Mayan d'Ortega, the U.S. attorney's office, dictatorial judges, opposing counselors. There was no letup. Sheridan and Buckley, a two-man operation, without even a paralegal, realized they were woefully understaffed.

Although the DiTullio case was only a few months old, Sheridan moved for a speedy trial under a special section of the Massachusetts law allowing indigents or totally disabled litigants early access on the trial docket. He had sidestepped Marden's and Phillips's depositions, as well as the nurses', including Karen Assad's. He would summons them and elicit their testimony at the time of trial before the jury. Buckley didn't agree with this tack.

"It's important to know in advance what the witness is going to say," he told Sheridan. Sheridan brushed it off.

"Phillips will say DiTullio was the model patient; so will Marden. We'll take it from there." It was a cavalier approach, which Buckley didn't appreciate. Marden had refused to place his case with the lawyers Sheridan had recommended, said his firm would handle it.

Despite vigorous opposition by Finnerty and d'Ortega, Judge Mason ruled favorably on Sheridan's motion for a speedy trial, and she set the case down for the third week in November.

Both Sheridan and d'Ortega agreed that only a few preliminary details remained prior to trial: the deposition by Sheridan of Dr. Robert Sexton and d'Ortega's depositions of Dante and Anna DiTullio. Although Anna DiTullio had been a tower of strength at the outset, Sheridan noted that now her eyes were downcast, and her lips, devoid of lipstick, seemed thin and withered. She was withdrawn, seldom spoke, and physically she was bent over, and shuffled like an old lady. And as Anna DiTullio appeared to age before his eyes, Dante DiTullio seemed to have regained his earlier bluster.

"What are we suing for?" he asked Sheridan, who was prepping both in his office for upcoming depositions.

"Well, there's a twenty-million-dollar insurance policy covering St. Anne's and its practitioners."

"The case is worth more than twenty million dollars!" Dante DiTullio spewed. "Look what they done to my poor Donna!"

"It's a case to settle if we can," Sheridan offered gently, looking first at Anna DiTullio, then returning to Dante. "A trial is the last resort. And you never know what a jury will do."

"No jury's gonna turn my Donna out in the cold, believe me, Mr. Sheridan." Typically, Dante DiTullio was hearing only what he wanted to hear, effectively blocking out any warnings Sheridan was trying to deliver.

"My cousin Sal tells me that out in California a jury only last week gave a quadriplegic five hundred million dollars against a boiler manufacturer on a product liability suit. And how about that law firm in San Francisco—jury hit them for seven hundred million just for getting rid of a secretary. And you tell me you're going to settle Donna's case for twenty million?" Dante's voice now seemed belligerent, adversarial.

"My case alone"—he thumped his chest with his forefinger—"for all the pain and suffering I'm going through, is worth twice, three times that figure." Sheridan noted that DiTullio failed to mention his wife.

But Sheridan had dealt with this type of client before. This was DiTullio's one big chance to grab the economic brass ring. And Sheridan knew that neither parent had visited Donna recently. Sheridan suspected that Dante DiTullio was somehow abusing his wife, maybe not physically, but with the little mental cruelties he was capable of perpetrating. Having handled domestic cases, Sheridan could recognize the subtle telltale signs. Anna DiTullio, who had shown a certain aristocratic bearing when she and Sheridan first met, was fading quickly. Sheridan knew that time was not on his side, nor on the side of Anna DiTullio.

Sheridan also knew never to gloss or overbuild a case.

"You have to understand," he said as forcefully as he could without pushing any panic buttons, "that the insurance company has offered only three hundred thousand dollars."

"That's an insult!" snapped Dante.

"I know it is," Sheridan said, "but if they start offering anything reasonable, say two to three million dollars, we've got to consider it seriously. We could structure the settlement; two million in guaranteed payments prudently invested over twenty years could amount to six or seven million dollars in the long run."

"Look, Mr. Sheridan," Dante interjected, "if they want to pay me the policy limit, twenty million, on my claim alone, I'll consider it. But on Donna's case, I want you to sock them for all the bastards've got!"

"Okay." Sheridan decided it was senseless to prolong the discussion about settlement. He changed the subject.

"Did Donna ever use drugs?" Sheridan avoided Anna DiTullio's eyes and looked squarely at Dante.

"Drugs? You mean painkillers, stuff like that?" Dante DiTullio suddenly looked perplexed. "She had a bad elbow for a while. Her orthopedist injected something to relieve the condition. I think it was cortisone."

"No, I mean the hard stuff—cocaine, maybe marijuana. She ever smoke?"

"Of course not!" Dante's voice suddenly turned hostile. "Look, Mr. Sheridan, whose side are you on, anyway? Donna was an athlete—a superb one. She didn't smoke, drink, or fool around. As I say, she was given injections of cortisone when her elbow was acting up."

"You'll both be asked this question at your depositions. I want you to handle it just as you've given it to me now.

"How about boyfriends?"

Anna DiTullio was about to speak, but Dante cut her short.

"She didn't have time for boyfriends," he snapped. "Tennis was her whole life."

Sheridan felt it inadvisable to tell the DiTullios that Donna was three months pregnant when she jumped. Dante might go off his rocker, and for Anna it might be the last straw. Sheridan knew she needed help. He would find a way to discuss things with her privately.

—

Robert Sexton's deposition was scheduled for the following week. It would continue for two days. Sheridan had met for several hours with Dr. White, who had studied Donna's psychiatric and medical records. White had scripted twenty-two germane questions for Sheridan's interrogation of Sexton. Sheridan wouldn't be as easy on Sexton as he had been on Dr. Puzon and Sister Agnes Loretta. This would be his final chance to pin Sexton down to a position he'd have to maintain during trial.

Sheridan was in his office, going over the hospital records and mulling over the missing path report. He could make a surprise visit to Dr. Diwali, maybe take his deposition. But again, the fact that Donna had been pregnant could be a detriment rather than a plus. Though John White could educate jurors on any moral censure they might invoke against one attempting to commit suicide, the prejudice would be there, especially among Roman Catholics. Being single and pregnant would be tough to explain. Best leave it alone.

Judy interrupted his solo strategy session. "Attorney Neil Kennedy from New York on line three."

Sheridan stacked the medical records in separate piles. He'd go through them again. He punched the phone button.

"Neil," he said, "how's the gang down at Forty-second Street?"

"Been replaced by massage parlors and adult bookstores," Neil said.

"And how's my Druid goddess, Meaghan Dwyer? Still holding court at the Blarney Stone?"

"Still there," Kennedy said, "and that was late last night. You know, I think she kind of misses you," Neil teased. "But seriously, Dan, I had a long chat with Detective O'Halloran. Bought a table for my fellow attorneys to his retirement party at the Hibernian Hall up here in Queens. Cost me two grand. I think you should make it down. He's got some interesting info on that old Rivera case."

"Oh? He's located the police report, the witness statements?"

"Not that good. But O'Halloran was thirty-four years on the force, still a detective, and he'll retire as a captain. And he survived six commissioners and five administrations. Made a lot of contacts, in the department and, of course, out on the street. The official records, particularly closed cases, are stored in vaults up on East Twenty-third. As a special favor to me, he sniffed around a bit, gained access to the vaults, and guess what?"

"I think this is going to cost me some retirement tickets," Sheridan hedged.

"I'll get into that," Kennedy said. "But there was no police report."

"No report?"

"No report. It was destroyed, incinerated, in accordance with regulations."

"Well, why is that going to cost me a few ducats?"

"Because they're supposed to be reduced to microfilm."

"And that wasn't done." Sheridan anticipated Kennedy's pattern.

"So O'Halloran sniffs around a bit more, out on the street this time. Calls in a few favors. As I said before, he was peripherally connected with the Rivera girl's case. Mike Ahearn was the detective in charge of the investigation."

"Any love lost between Ahearn and O'Halloran?"

"Not much. O'Halloran knew that Ahearn was on the take. Chicken stuff—bookies, pimps, roving crap games, small-time hoods.

"Shortly after the Rivera girl's death, Ahearn gets promoted from lieutenant to captain, takes an early retirement. Sends his kids to college, owns a home in Fort Lee, New Jersey, and pays cash for a condo in Vero Beach. Living the good life.

"Look, Dan, I don't think we should be discussing this over the phone. I think you ought to come down for O'Halloran's retirement party. You'll get what he's uncovered firsthand."

"Okay, Neil. Put me down for three tickets. You say they're two hundred and fifty apiece?"

"Did I say a few, Dan? I told O'Halloran you'd buy out a table."

Sheridan gave an exasperated sigh. "Sure, a table. I'll bring Buckley and Sheila. She went to your old alma mater, Fordham. Maybe she can distribute the extra tickets."

"Send your check for two grand, and on any unused tickets, the funds go directly to O'Halloran."

There was a short silence. "Okay, Neil. As they say, 'The check's in the mail.' "

"You'll have a helluva time, Dan. Nothing like a retirement party made up of New York's finest. And, Dan . . ."

"Yes?"

"I'd leave Sheila O'Brien back in Boston. This isn't a meeting of the Holy Name Society, if you know what I mean."

"Sure," Sheridan said, "who ever heard of strippers at the Holy Name Society's annual outing? I kind of know what you mean."

24

Sheridan parked in his usual spot at the Hampton facility, gathered up the yellow roses he had purchased en route, and made his way toward the reception desk. With each visit, despite the depressing surroundings, he was getting more upbeat about Donna's progress. Although his last visit had been over a month ago, her communicative abilities were improving. One of these days, he expected her to break into a smile. And maybe, just maybe, this was the day.

"How's Donna doing?" he asked, smiling at the nurse. He picked out a single rose and gave it to her.

"Oh, thank you," she said, smelling it.

"Donna? Well . . ." She hesitated. "Not doing too good. It's sad, really."

Sheridan nodded. "I know, but you never can tell. You've got to have faith in the guy upstairs." He threw his eyes toward the ceiling.

"You're right." The nurse placed the rose in a small vial on her desk. "But I'm afraid she's going downhill."

She glanced at the chart. "She's developed pneumonia; lungs are filling up. And she's got bedsore infections all over. I'm afraid it won't be too long."

"*What?*" Sheridan blurted. "When did all this happen?"

"Within the past week," she replied defensively.

"Where's Dr. Brockelman's office." It was more a demand than a question.

"On the third floor, room three-oh-five."

Sheridan stormed off, taking the cast-iron steps two at a time. Approaching Brockelman's office, he slowed down, straightened his tie in the reflection of a dusty windowpane, and tried to calm down.

Stopping at a simulated oak fiberboard door that was partially open and had a faded sign—ERNST BROCKELMAN, M.D.—Sheridan knocked gently. No answer. He knocked again, slightly louder. Nothing. He pushed the door open. The room was still a mess, books and periodicals on the floor, files and boxes everywhere. And there was Brockelman, chief of Neurology, in a lounge chair, two o'clock in the afternoon, catching some after-lunch siesta, mouth agape, snoring the afternoon away. A half-lit cigarette, still alive, emitted smoke, fortunately from an old-fashioned stand-up ashtray. Spread on his lap was an open magazine. Sheridan entered a few steps into the room, issued a few ahems. No response from Brockelman. Sheridan looked at the magazine. It wasn't the *New England Journal of Medicine.* On the open page, two models cavorted in the altogether. And Sheridan shook his head. These were not some young chicks fronting a girlie magazine. They were two males.

—

Sheridan made his way to Donna's room. Again he knocked quietly.

"Donna," he said as he opened the door, "it's me, your friend Dan."

The room was dark and clammy. The broken light tube still sputtered overhead, the same vacant beds were rolled against the wall. No replacements. Thank God, Sheridan thought.

"I brought you your favorite, yellow roses." He held up the spray.

Funny, Sheridan thought, no response. No fluttering eyelids, not a speck of recognition, nothing. And her face had sunk in. Her lips were thin and milky, cheeks hollow vacuums, hair now scraggly gray.

"Good God," Sheridan said, "what the hell has happened?"

He bent within a few inches of her vacant eyes. "Donna, it's me, Dan. Your friend Dan Sheridan."

There was no response. Another try. Nothing. Donna Di-Tullio's face was a blank slate.

Then he noticed the IV bottle dangling overhead. It was empty, crumpled inward like a piece of discarded cellophane.

He dashed out to the nurses' station.

"Are you the nurse in charge?" he yelled.

She glanced up quickly. "No. That's Miss Jennings. She's on relief."

"Look, I don't give a fuck where Jennings is! You're the nurse in charge of Donna DiTullio, and her IV is completely empty!"

The young nurse was startled into action.

"I'll call Dr. Pahloor and page Nurse Jennings."

"Forget about Jennings. You get your ass down to DiTullio's room right now and get that IV started," he stormed. "I'm going to get Brockelman down here on the double."

The nurse and Sheridan scampered in different directions. Sheridan took the stairs three at a time.

No gentle knocking at Brockelman's door this time. He burst in. "Brockelman," he yelled, "your patient Donna DiTullio is in extremis. You'd better sound a code blue or something." Brockelman, startled out of a sound sleep, looked bewildered; the magazine in his lap dropped to the floor. Then, seeing Sheridan, his mouth curled in professional disdain. He blinked several times, adjusted his glasses, which had slid to the end of his nose, and glared.

"Who let you in here?" he finally blurted.

"Listen, you goddamned impostor," Sheridan shouted, "Donna DiTullio, she's your patient, you fucking goldbrick! You're sleeping the afternoon away, reading some boy porno magazine, and your patients are losing their lives."

"What's the meaning of this?" Brockelman feigned righteous indignation.

"Look," Sheridan barked, "Donna DiTullio has lapsed into a complete coma. Her IV bag is empty. I just checked. What the fuck is the matter with you guys! You better get your ass down there quick, Doc, because if Donna goes, you go!" He picked up the *Gay Guys' Guide* and handed it to Brockelman.

"Well, we'll see to this! These nurses . . ." Brockelman manufactured a veneer of concern as he followed Sheridan down the staircase toward Donna's room. "They're the bottom of the barrel!"

Three nurses were gathered around Donna. The IV bag was now full and running.

"How long was the IV bag empty?" Brockelman's voice was only mildly critical. It was obvious that the nurses knew that he, like themselves, had been hiding out. A pretty good deal: a medical sinecure where no one, not even the state medical board, bothered to do any checking.

"Only a few minutes," Nurse Jennings said. "Nothing serious."

"These things happen," Brockelman said soothingly. "We check on the hour, and of course the patient has a call button." He pointed to the button signal on the night table.

Sheridan was about to explode. This Brockelman was a space cadet. How in hell could Donna signal the nurses, and what in Christ's name did she know about an IV? He left the room abruptly and made his way to the lobby pay phone.

"John," he said to Dr. John White. "I'm up at Hampton. That last spark in Donna that I was trying to keep alive might be extinguished. . . . I gotta get her the hell out of here right now!"

White was silent for a few moments.

"It may be too late," he said.

"John, I didn't call you for your goddamned philosophical advice," Sheridan snapped. "I gotta get Donna out of this snake pit. Forget the goddamned case. Can you help me?"

Again, several seconds of silence. "Well, there's a private place in Vermont, Greenbriar Lodge, formerly a Mary Hitchcock hospital, staffed by Dartmouth grads. It's at White River Junction, on the Connecticut River. All the bigwigs from Manhattan and Long Island go up there. The patients aren't exactly on Medicaid. But for tough neurological cases, it's the best on the Eastern Seaboard, maybe the best in the country.

"But, Dan, they're not going to accept Donna DiTullio, believe me. They'll want fifty thousand up front before she can even get a room."

"John, call the director of admissions right now. I'll get an ambulance. I've got a few blank checks on me and forty thousand in my Keogh plan. That should cover it. Tell the director I'll have the rest within a week."

"This is not going to be easy, Dan." White sighed. "We're going to get opposition from the state and from Brockelman."

"We'll have no trouble from Brockelman. You do the necessary. I'll handle this end. You vouch for the hospital, John?"

White avoided the answer. "You really want to do this, Dan?"

"You're goddamned right I want to do it."

"You know, if Donna dies, your case dies," White said. "No economic projection, no future medicals. . . . You thinking of the case, Dan, or are you thinking of Donna DiTullio?"

It stung. "John, for chrissakes," he said in a bitter undertone, "call Greenbriar. Make sure they know she's coming. I'll get her there!"

—

Dan followed the ambulance as it sped up Interstate 89. It was an Indian summer day, the kind that visits the rolling countryside of New Hampshire and Vermont just before the first gentle snows herald a long winter. The bucolic scene, with its quilt of stone walls and white church spires on distant hillsides, made no impression on Sheridan as he trailed directly behind the white-and-orange ambulance, its blue overhead lights flashing and occasionally its siren opening a lane through the traffic.

It was a three-hour journey to Greenbriar, and it was dark when they pulled up. The EMTs pumped up the gurney and

Sheridan watched as they strapped Donna into place, checked the IV, and wheeled her in through the emergency entrance.

Sheridan liked Dr. Elliot Sagall the moment he saw him. He stood a few feet away as the doctor, accompanied by two nurses, talked briefly with the EMTs. The doctor signed some transfer papers. They nodded quickly and departed. Immediately, Sagall made a quick study of the patient.

"Get hold of Dr. Neal Weinstein in Radiology," he said to his nurse. "I want a full set of MRIs. We want impressions within thirty minutes. And alert Dr. Ashe and Surgical Two Beta. I want that room ready to go, fully staffed. It may be last-resort surgery. The patient's ninety percent gone."

Sheridan was impressed. He didn't introduce himself. That would come later.

Odd, he thought, no one asked whether she had Blue Cross or whatever, or who was going to pay. There are places like this, but not many.

It was well after eight o'clock. He sank into the plush leather lounge chair in the glassed-in lobby. It reminded him of the Atrium at St. Anne's. He sat there for several minutes.

"You thinking of the case . . . or are you thinking of Donna DiTullio?" He recalled Dr. White's words.

"Why am I here?" He sighed. But then he thought for a few minutes. Maybe White was a little more intuitive. If DiTullio survived, even in a vegetative state, his case could be worth a fortune. One-third of a fortune was still a fortune. If Donna DiTullio succumbed, Sheridan knew, it might be three hundred thousand at best.

He pulled a blank check out of his wallet and wrote it out for forty thousand dollars. He'd tell the admissions director it was as good as gold.

Sheridan waited several more minutes before asking for directions to the admissions office. He again thought of Dr. White. The case? Donna DiTullio? What *was* his chief concern? He wanted to invoke some lost saint, Michael the archangel, Jude, Chrysogonos, maybe those of his grandparents—Brigid and Brendan. But he thought these were fairy tales.

He went to the head man, not really believing it would alter the course of events, but maybe playing the odds.

"Jesus," he said to himself, "let us both do the right thing."

●

Sheridan was roused by a gentle tap on the shoulder. He opened his eyes slowly, to be greeted by a young nurse, who smiled at him.

"Mr. Sheridan," she said, "I was on last night when you came in with Donna DiTullio."

"Oh my God!" Sheridan glanced at his watch: 6:05 A.M.

"You were exhausted," she said. "You went out like a light in the chair. I checked several times during the night—thought I'd let you sleep."

Sheridan got to his feet unsteadily, blinking several times to get his bearings. The lobby at Greenbriar was flooded with sunlight that spilled like molten marmalade over the peach tile floor. At six in the morning, the hospital was stirring to life. The nurses were checking in for the day shift, and some were leaving. There seemed to be a controlled order about the place, unlike the hectic pace at St. Anne's. From a massive tinted glass window, Sheridan could see that Greenbriar sat on a bosky knoll overlooking the Connecticut River.

"Donna is in critical condition," the young nurse said. "Along with all her other problems, she's badly infected with bedsores and"—she hesitated a few moments—"she's had a thrombosis in her femoral vein, the inside of her leg, and she's thrown several clots—we call them emboli—some have lodged in her lung."

From the sound of the nurse's voice, Sheridan knew that this condition was life-threatening.

"Will she survive?" he asked, a hint of resignation in his voice, thinking maybe it was best the Lord take her now.

"The next seventy-two hours will tell," the nurse said. "She's on a full-strength heparin drip—unfortunately, it can't affect the lung clots. Pulmonary embolism is sometimes fatal even in healthy patients. And Donna is so decompensated, her resistance is pretty low. But Dr. Sagall is in charge of her case." She tried to sound professionally upbeat. "He's the best neurosurgeon in New England. She'll get superb treatment. Are you a relative, Mr. Sheridan?"

Sheridan was now fully awake.

"We're very close," he said, rising to his feet. "Can I see her?"

"She's in the critical care unit. Strictly no visitors. We've just got to pray and wait it out."

"Okay," Sheridan said. "What time does the administration office open? I have to cover the admission charges."

"In about three hours. Why don't you go back to Boston. Lovely city, Boston." The nurse gave a courteous smile. "I trained there at St. Anne's School of Nursing."

Oh, boy, Sheridan thought. She might even be related to Sister Agnes Loretta. Best not to ask.

"Can I give you this envelope? It has a forty-thousand-dollar check in it payable to Greenbriar for Donna's admission."

"I know Mrs. Cole in Accounts," the nurse said. "I'll talk to her. You keep the check." Her youthful face was covered with concern.

"Donna might not survive," she said. "No sense in complicating things."

25

Sheridan got back to Boston shortly after noon and was greeted by Judy Corwin and young Buckley. He had called ahead on his car phone to fill them in on the Greenbriar transfer, saying that he was most impressed with the medical staff but that Donna was pretty far gone.

"Dr. Sexton's deposition is scheduled for Wednesday," Judy said. "D'Ortega wanted a continuance, claimed Sexton had to attend a niece's wedding in East Hampton, on Long Island. Seems he's in the wedding party. Buckley nixed it. The wedding isn't until Saturday. D'Ortega was going to move for a protective order before Judge Mason, but then she called back and said Dr. Sexton would accommodate us, provided the deposition was taken in their offices. Believe me, she wasn't too happy."

"Okay," Sheridan said, "it doesn't give us much time to prepare, but I've got a good questionnaire scripted by Dr. White, and we'll see what kind of a witness Sexton will make. More important, I want to get hold of his private notes. He's got to produce everything—notes, bills, correspondence, tapes."

"What are Donna's chances?" Buckley asked.

"Not good. I'm afraid she's terminal," Sheridan said.

"You know, Dan," Buckley said, "if Donna doesn't look as though she can survive, I think now's the time to make the best deal we can to settle the case. Without a viable plaintiff, we can't project future economic damages, a lifetime of pain and suffering, medical maintenance. And you said it yourself—Boston juries are penurious . . . We could probably get Finnerty to go to four fifty."

"What in hell are you talking about?" Sheridan barked. "Whatever happens, the case is going to be tried to a conclusion. I'm not interested in the goddamned fee! Understand that, Buck!"

Judy stepped into the breach. "Dan, you've often counseled clients that in civil cases the law can't give them back their broken limbs, only compensation in dollars and cents for their injuries and losses. And I've heard you say that the courtroom was invented so people wouldn't throw stones at one another. Now it seems you're using that very forum for target practice."

There was a steely edge to Sheridan's voice. "Judy, I'm calling the shots around here! Not you. Not Buckley. This case is going to be tried. The jury's going to decide one way or the other. Both of you get that straight. If you want to leave . . ."

"Sure, Dan," Buckley said quietly. He knew Sheridan wasn't his old sure self. He looked drawn, tired. His eyes, of late, had taken on a melancholic cast.

Judy tactfully changed the subject. "Sheila called while you were gone. Wants to go for a jog in the Blue Hills when you get off. Said she'd meet you at the Wampanoag trail at six. A three-mile run might do you a world of good." She paused a few moments. "Reminds me of my uncle Max when he was training for the Boston Marathon. Of course, he couldn't break five hours if he was on a motorcycle. Went out one night for his evening jog and never came back. Left Aunt Sarah pretty well-off, though. That was three years ago. She's afraid he'll show up at the door someday."

Sheridan suppressed a smile. "Hey, you guys." He embraced both of them, wrapping his arms around their shoulders. "Please . . . uh, I know I haven't been the easiest guy to live with these past few weeks. Bear with me. I just gotta treat this case like any other. We get too close to the client, we lose our objectivity, our ability to function properly." He tightened his lips and shook his head. Strange, he thought, he was parroting Dr. Jensen.

"And I haven't spent any time with Sheila since our last run." He left for his office and shut the door.

Unlike him, thought Judy. He never closes the door unless he's closeted with a client.

"Not a good time to try this case, Tom." Judy looked at Buckley.

"I know." Buckley, too, could read the tensions. Sheridan was trying to do it all, journeying to New York, battling with Sister Agnes and the governmental morass of Hampton. He was getting sidetracked into legal minutiae, losing the trial lawyer's focus.

"Of course, we could ask to continue the case," Buckley said. "We'd look kind of foolish, since we were the ones pressing for a speedy trial. And we prevailed despite opposition by d'Ortega. We opt for a continuance now and the defense will smell a weakness. And what do we use as an excuse? That Sheridan's not up to trying the case?"

"Well, I've seen Dan bounce back before." Judy tried to sound upbeat. But even she thought she didn't sound too convincing.

—

Charlie Finnerty, Mayan d'Ortega, and Mary Devaney met with Dr. Robert Sexton in the firm's conference room, prepping the doctor for the next day's deposition.

Sexton had selected tapes of his therapeutic conversations with Donna DiTullio. They listened intently. No one spoke. Even for several seconds after the tape finished, *not* a word, *not* a sound.

What they had just heard was almost unbelievable: Donna DiTullio revealing her innermost secrets and terrifying fears. And the greatest fear of all was of her father, Dante DiTullio. Not only did he berate her and overwork her on the tennis courts but, according to Donna, he had sexually assaulted her on several occasions. The details were as graphic as they were horrifying.

To add insult to injury, her father had given her a mysterious drug from China called *ging-hai-sing*. It was a performance enhancer used by Chinese athletes, especially women distance runners. She would take the drug some five hours before a tennis match. And, unbeknownst to her father, she had used cocaine on several occasions, usually after she encountered defeat on the court.

"Boy," Charlie Finnerty finally said as he shook his head, "Dante DiTullio is a party plaintiff, coconservator with Mrs. DiTullio of the estate and person of Donna DiTullio. This stuff is dynamite!"

"How will we use it legally?" Mayan d'Ortega already knew its extortional effect.

"Well, before Sheridan starts with the doctor's deposition tomorrow, we're going to let him hear the tapes."

"He'll make a motion *in limine* to suppress them," d'Ortega said.

"No judge in a million years would allow his motion. These aren't just the doctor's notes, where it boils down to Dr. Sexton's word against DiTullio's. This is the voice of the patient. These conversations were held to assist in therapy." Finnerty glanced at Sexton. "Right, Doctor?"

"Absolutely."

"And the criminal complications are earthshaking," Finnerty added. "Can you imagine a jury hearing this volatile stuff? They'd ask the judge to call in the DA. Sheridan's entire case would collapse.

"We could bring an action for contribution and indemnification against the parents." Charlie's cheeks bunched up in tiny knots and his bright squirrel eyes beamed with merriment.

"We got extra copies of this, Bob?" He motioned toward the audiocassette.

"Three duplicates are in my safe."

"What a windfall!" Finnerty chortled. "And I can't wait to see the expression on Sheridan's face when I tell him the three hundred thousand is off the table." His grin had a malicious glint. He now held the high cards.

He looked at Mary Devaney. "You and Mayan continue to prep Bob, just in case Sheridan thinks he's going to prevail on a motion to suppress. But this bombshell . . . boy-oh-boy!" He flicked his hand outward. "We're going to blow Sheridan and his case right out of the water!"

—

Sheridan waved at Sheila as he drove up in his TR6. She was wearing a black spandex running suit, orange warm-up jacket, and white running shoes. Her sandy blond hair was clipped short in a brush cut. She was limbering up by doing stretches, grabbing the heels of her long, shapely legs.

"Well, stranger"—she looked up from her bent-forward position—"I was wondering if I'd see your face on the back of a milk carton."

"I know." Sheridan tried a boyish smile. "I've been playing golf, sunning myself in Bermuda. Those pink beaches are delightful."

"You might try calling. You do have my number." She bent forward and stretched her leg, grabbing again at the heel.

Sheridan had on a crumpled pair of green shorts—a holdover from his YMCA days—and a tattered T-shirt with some faded logo. He laced up a pair of gray sneakers that had seen better days.

Sheila saw the grainy weariness in his face. Her blue eyes shimmered as she jumped to her feet. She hesitated, almost shaking his hand.

"Got a great path picked out," she said. "It's about two miles up, on a slight incline. We head through the woods. Trail's kind of snaky, but the terrain is fairly even. At the two-mile marker, there's a stream that cascades between several boulders. There's a large isolated rock with some ancient Indian imprints. Seems King Philip, the chief of the Wampanoags, used to hang out around here. Then from King Philip's rock back to our starting point—it's downhill. The loser pays for dinner."

Sheridan was beginning to feel better. Sheila was a tonic. He knew it. A lesser woman would whine or pout. He had to see her more often, do more jogging, even if it was only one day a week.

"You're on," he said.

A few more deep knee bends, some diagonal stretches, and they were off. They breezed along the trail at an easy pace, running shoulder-to-shoulder. It was dusk, but the trail was on the western side of Big Blue. Shafts of orange sunlight mixed with the purples and moss greens of the forest floor. As they rounded a twist in the trail, a few deer skittered into the woodlands ahead of them.

At the halfway mark, they rested at King Philip's rock. Except for their labored breathing, there wasn't a sound—no birds chirping, no scuffling in the bushes. Nothing moved. The silence was eerie. Sheridan ran his fingers along the ancient Indian glyphs. It was holy ground; both Sheridan and Sheila could sense it. The great sachem of the Wampanoags was an awesome phantom to wrestle with. Best they get going.

On the run back, Sheridan filled Sheila in on the legal jousting, the battle to get Donna DiTullio out of Hampton, Raimondi's finding out that someone had a tail on them. He avoided mentioning Janet Phillips and her invitation to the Vineyard.

To Sheridan's surprise, he wasn't in bad shape. At the three-quarters mark, Sheila picked up the pace. Sheridan went with her. As they rounded the final turn, seeing their cars ahead in the rest area, Sheila lengthened her stride. Sheridan accelerated. They hit the last hundred yards and Sheila gave it her final kick. Sheridan now felt as though he were running on *E*. His legs were cramping up; a deep burning sensation seared his chest as he sucked for air. But he hung in with Sheila. She glanced over at him, a sly smile on her face. Sheridan grimaced back. Was she thinking the same thing? It was almost like intercourse. Sheila cranked up the pace and Sheridan knew he couldn't match her final sprint.

Later, back at Sheila's apartment, after a coed shower, they skipped dinner. In Sheila's bed, the undulating pace went on all night—a fun kind of race that Sheridan wasn't going to lose.

—

Sheridan showed up in the office at 8:00 A.M. Judy and Buckley were having a cup of coffee and were startled by Sheridan's effusive greeting. He hadn't slept a wink, but he seemed to have lost his sallow complexion. He hadn't looked this well in months. The tenseness was gone from his jaw; his ocean blue eyes seemed much more alive.

"I'm famished," he said. "Can you throw in a bagel or two with my coffee, Judy? Nothing like a four-mile run. Does wonders for the appetite," he added with a boyish grin.

Judy stirred the coffee and put a good helping of cream cheese on the bagel. She stole a glance at Buckley. She felt that Sheridan was on his way back. They exchanged knowing nods. Maybe not all the way back, but it was a good sign.

"Running almost beats sex," Buckley quipped.

"Oh, I wouldn't go that far." Sheridan took a healthy drink of coffee and wolfed down the bagel. "But it's a lot like the practice of law."

"Running?" Judy asked, knowing that the conversation would start going downhill.

"No, sex." Sheridan drained his cup.

"How is sex like the practice of law?" Judy's lips were pursed in disapproval.

"When it's good, it's great. When it's bad"—Sheridan paused for several seconds—"it's still pretty good."

—

Sheridan and Buckley were ushered into Charlie Finnerty's oversized corner office. Mayan d'Ortega sat on the plush burgundy leather couch with Mary Devaney.

They exchanged greetings with professional courtesy.

"This is Walter Crimmins, claims manager of Massachusetts Casualty. They insure St. Anne's and the defendant staff members," Finnerty said. "You gentlemen mind if he sits in on Dr. Sexton's deposition?"

"Perfectly all right," Sheridan said as he shook Crimmins's hand.

"Dan," Finnerty said, as if it were almost an afterthought, "the court reporter called. She'll be a mite late, and she'll need time to set up in the conference room. Dr. Sexton is in there now."

"Charlie," Sheridan said, "take all the time you want. It's going to be a long day."

"Yes," Finnerty said with a mirthless smile. "But before we get started, Dan, I want you to listen to those tapes you requisitioned in your deposition notice."

"Tapes?" Sheridan was on instant alert. Any documents or evidence adverse to Sexton's position would have been deepsixed long ago.

"Yes. Every psychiatrist records his patient's conversations. I'm sure your Dr. White cued you in on this. It's de rigueur in the profession.

"And I'm doing this as a special favor to you, Dan." He motioned to Mary Devaney, who set up the audiocassette.

"I think what you're going to hear will be quite interesting." Another signal from Finnerty to Devaney. She clicked a button and the tape began to play. Sexton's voice was soft, modulated, the ultimate counselor. Each conversation was dated, the time sequences of the sessions carefully identified. The tapes, excerpted to include Donna's relationship with her father, went on for three-quarters of an hour. What came through was a terrifying litany of horror: Donna's tirades against her father, sobbing, her voice sometimes deathly quiet, sometimes shrill, her lack of self-esteem, her total degradation.

A good minute passed. No one spoke.

Finnerty reached into the silence. "What do you think, Dan? You still want to go ahead with the lawsuit?"

Sheridan started to speak, but Finnerty cut him off.

"Oh, I know you're going to bring a motion to suppress, Dan. But even Judge Mason wouldn't rule in your favor, you know that."

Sheridan had the urge to punch Finnerty out. He eyed Mayan d'Ortega. Her slanted Indian eyes were devoid of emotion.

Sheridan knew it was blackmail: Drop the suit or we go to the DA.

"Seems to me, Charlie," he finally said, "that it's funny, in tapes covering thirteen months of treatment, Sexton never once mentioned to Donna DiTullio that he was taping her conversations."

"Oh, don't give me that, Dan. These were made in a therapeutic environment. Even your trusted pal John White will tell you that. And Dr. Sexton will testify that he advised the DiTullio girl that he was taping their conversations."

"You got that in the doctor's notes?"

"It's in there."

"Strange, Charlie. Why would he put it in his notes and not include it in the tapes?"

Finnerty grimaced in obvious displeasure.

"Dan," he said, "let's quit beating around the bush. I was going to withdraw the offer of three hundred thou, but, hell, you've put in a lot of time on the case. I never want to see a lawyer go away empty-handed. Three hundred thousand, Dan. It's not pocket change."

He turned to the claims manager. "Okay with you, Walter? The three still on the table?"

Crimmins nodded his assent.

Sheridan counted to five in an attempt to sheathe his anger.

"You got an extra copy of this tape for me, Charlie?"

"You betcha, Dan. Mary, give Dan the tape in the cassette. We have some backups."

"You want to go ahead with Dr. Sexton's depo, or maybe you want to consult with your client Mr. DiTullio?"

Sheridan looked at Buckley. Buckley passed a "let's get the hell out of here" nod.

"All right, Charlie, we'll suspend with Sexton for the time being. I'll talk it over with Donna's parents."

Buckley and Sheridan picked up their briefcases and headed through the reception area, then stood at the bank of elevators in the green-marbled lobby. Neither spoke.

Finnerty came out to see them off, his voice now full of bonhomie—fellow-lawyer camaraderie. "Dan, I know you're in a hell of a spot. You represent Donna DiTullio, but you also represent her father. You can't abandon one in favor of the other. Absolutely unethical, like representing two defendants accused of the same crime. Lawyers have lost their ticket for less.

"And Dan, I just talked to Walter Crimmins. The three will be on the table until noon tomorrow. You call me."

Dan again said nothing. Buckley noticed Sheridan's fists clenched at his sides, and he grasped Sheridan's right arm with a firm grip. He sensed that Dan was close to doing something absolutely foolish. The elevator indicator lit and the doors pinged open.

"Until noon tomorrow, Dan." Finnerty's plastic smile and syrupy voice grated on Dan Sheridan like fingernails scratching a blackboard.

They stepped into the elevator. A cross-examiner never ends on a weak note. It's the trial lawyer's eleventh commandment. You have to get in the last shot. But Sheridan and Buckley knew they were in a gross legal bind.

"Yeah, Charlie," Sheridan said as the doors started to close. "I'll be in touch."

26

Sheridan and Buckley were expecting the DiTullios that evening, but Dante canceled, claiming an important business meeting.

Sheridan had almost forgotten Neil Kennedy's invitation. He consulted his watch; it was close to five.

"We'll figure this out, Buck. Might have to get both parents to withdraw as conservators; appoint some near relative to prosecute the suit. Anna DiTullio is close to the breaking point. You know, adversity is supposed to toughen people, bring them together. But that's for storybooks. I've seen just the opposite. The victims resort to backbiting, little cruelties, grow further and further apart, until the relationship is gone.

"Let me think over what we're going to do." Sheridan checked his wallet, making sure he had enough for a round-trip to New York. "I've just got time to get the six o'clock shuttle out of Logan. I'll take a cab from La Guardia and be in there by eight."

"The Big Apple?"

"Oh, cripes, I forgot to tell you. Neil Kennedy called me a few days ago, said a retiring Manhattan cop has some info on

Sexton's girlfriend's death. Name's Joe O'Halloran."

"You gotta go tonight?"

"Cost me two grand. It's a retirement party."

"*Two grand!* Where is it being held, the Waldorf-Astoria?"

"Queens. Hibernian Hall. I would've asked Sheila, but it's one of those parties. I doubt Cardinal O'Connor will be in attendance. That'll come later."

Buckley weighed his words carefully. "Dan, why are you going off on this tangent? Why try to dredge up some remote and irrelevant event?"

Buckley expected another Sheridan outburst. Instead, Dan cracked his boyish grin.

"Haven't been to a good stag party in years, Buck. Want to come along?"

"You serious?"

"Sure I'm serious."

Buckley glanced at his watch. "C'mon, man," he almost shouted, "we'll miss the plane!"

—

Hibernian Hall was packed with New York's finest, rank and file, higher echelon, even the commissioner. No one was in uniform, and Sheridan noticed that it was an all-male preserve. He and Buckley checked in at the outside desk. An old-timer smiled at them as he noted the two-thousand-dollar contribution, gave them stickum name tags, and assigned them to table 43.

"We got Lance Robinson of *Eyewitness News*, and Sally Caruso from the Comedy Connection. Boy, she's something. And some gals from the Merry-Go-Round bar on West Forty-second Street." He gave Sheridan and Buckley a long, slow insider's wink.

Sheridan, being an ex-cop, night-school law grad, mixed in with his table as though he had always belonged. Buckley swapped baseball stories with guys named Donelan, Cahill, Lombardi, Sanchez, and Koslowski. There weren't too many guys with three names at Hibernian Hall, even in a Republican administration. The police commissioner was a Fordham grad, a Democrat no less, named Tesconi.

Toastmaster Robinson made at least twenty introductions, lacing his recognitions with smarmy encomiums. Commissioner Tesconi tried a serious tack. Sheridan could see that he was reading his prepared talk. Tesconi paused for a moment. The audience, now well liquored, applauded courteously. He resumed. They shouted for him to sit down. He did. Later, Sally Caruso had the boys reeling, slapping their thighs, as she zipped through her raunchy routines.

The Merry-Go-Round girls—billed as the Tall Texans—attired in spurred leather boots and little else, went through their paces, high kicking, grinding, lap-dancing, Sally Caruso adding encouragement as the girls extracted twenty-dollar bills from the audience as though it were play money. Sheridan wasn't turned off by it all.

"The poor sons of bitches," he said softly to himself, "a night with a babe who pretends he's the most important guy in the world. Even if it's a sham, it beats Bob Hope. They love it." And he knew he was one of them. He tucked a fifty-dollar bill in the gun belt of a busty beauty who was gyrating at table 43, and Buckley matched it.

Later, when the singing and raucous laughter died down and the boys were lined up to shake O'Halloran's hand and congratulate him on his retirement, Sheridan and Buckley stood in the background with Neil Kennedy. They were finally alone, except for a janitor, who started folding chairs and moving tables.

"Couple of more minutes, Sam." O'Halloran gave the janitor a two-fingered sign.

"Joe, this is Dan Sheridan and his partner, Tom Buckley. Dan's the lawyer from Boston I was telling you about. Ex-cop from Boston, went to law school nights."

Joe O'Halloran had a beer-barrel gut, wispy gray hair, a tough cop's countenance, but his bright brown eyes were cautiously alert, like a squirrel taking a kernel from your hand.

"Pleased to meet a brother." He shook Sheridan's hand with a firm no-nonsense grip, then Buckley's.

"Dan bought out an entire table, Joe." It was a nice opener, not lost on O'Halloran.

"Neil tells me you're suing Robert Sexton in a malpractice case up in Boston."

"Yeah," Sheridan said, "scheduled to go to trial in three weeks. Did Neil tell you the circumstances, how our client was under Sexton's psychiatric care and jumped from an open atrium, some five stories?"

O'Halloran's jaw tightened, his mouth a thin horizontal line. He nodded.

"She still living?" he asked.

"Just barely. Might not survive the next few days."

"Neil says you're checking into the circumstances of Emanuela Rivera's death." O'Halloran glanced at Sam, who was mopping the floor in the back of the building, then hunched closer to Sheridan.

"Neil told me the records of the investigation hit the shredder and were never reduced to microfilm, contrary to regulations."

O'Halloran nodded. "I'm telling you this in strictest confidence, you guys being friends of Neil. Case was closed as an unresolved homicide."

"I've talked to Captain Ahearn," Sheridan interjected.

"That son of a bitch." O'Halloran's lips curled with disdain. "Well, Ahearn and me, we were both lieutenants, working out of Precinct Twenty and Twenty-four, covering the West Sixties all the way up to a Hundred and Twenty-fifth Street, Lincoln Center to Harlem. I was initially on the case, doing the routine stuff, interviewing her landlord, tenants, the jogger who found the body, even Robert Sexton. He was in his last year at Columbia Med.

"Well, suddenly—bang!—like that." O'Halloran snapped his fingers. "I get zapped from the case. The commissioner calls me in, Ahearn takes over. I give him my notebook, all the stuff I collected."

"Did you retain anything?"

"Nada! Not a thing. Keep in mind, this all happened like fifteen to twenty years ago.

"I tells Ahearn that the Sexton kid first gives me a story that at the crucial time he was at his anatomy and physiology class, with Professor Munson or Munster, something like that.

"Well, I checks with the professor. Kind of tweedy guy, I recall, but had a memory like an elephant. Knows that Sexton wasn't in class that afternoon. Didn't take any formal attendance, but seems the classroom was an elevated semicircle, kind of like a Greek theater. He looks up at the students. There were only a dozen or so in his class, and on that day, Sexton wasn't one of them. He was certain on this point.

"I recheck with Sexton. Now he remembers he was in the library. I check with the librarian, middle-aged woman, mother-hen type, knew all the students. She couldn't recall seeing Sexton *at all* that day.

"So I tells all this to Ahearn. Tell him Sexton's really got no alibi.

"But, as you know, Dan, whether you do or don't have an alibi doesn't amount to a row of pins. Look at the O.J. case."

Sheridan nodded in quiet understanding.

"Well," O'Halloran continued, "the case gets closed, unsolved. Of course, Sexton's family had a lot of juice with the commissioner, Patrick Minehan. Now things break kinda fast. Ahearn suddenly makes captain, takes an early retirement. Buys a winter place in Vero Beach. And that's the last I hear of Sexton until Neil asks me to check on the case."

Sheridan ran a hand through his hair. "Anyone ask Sexton to take a lie detector test?"

"Not that I'm aware of. As I say, I was broomed off the case and that was that."

"When you interrogated Sexton, did he have a lawyer?"

"No, not during my initial interview. He was broken up, though. I remember that. Looked shell-shocked. That's why I didn't place too much significance on his error about the anatomy class."

"Did you ever confront him with the librarian's information?"

O'Halloran shook his head. "No, that's when I was taken off

the case. The commish makes it clear he doesn't want me making any waves."

"Thanks a lot, Joe." Sheridan shook O'Halloran's hand, and Buckley did the same.

"I've probably run into a dead end, but I think I'll have one more talk with Mike Ahearn, if it's okay with you. I don't want to upset any applecarts."

"Hey, what the fuck do I care. My pension's vested, even my Blue Cross. And Mike Ahearn is a goddamned conniver. He grew up in Queens, just like me and Neil. We were both cops, Irish, same ethnic values. He retires on a boosted-up captain's pay; I keep slugging it out. Only made captain on retirement. . . . And you didn't see him show up here tonight . . . cheap bastard."

The hall lights suddenly blinked.

"Okay, we're coming, Sam." O'Halloran gave a wave of his hand.

Sheridan and young Buckley decided to stop over at the Westbury for the night. Buck could take the 8:00 A.M. shuttle back to cover the office, and Sheridan would make another pass at Ahearn.

—

Mike Ahearn was not pleased when he answered the phone and Dan Sheridan said he was in town and asked if they could meet at O'Doul's that afternoon.

"Well, well." Ahearn manufactured a smile as he greeted Sheridan at the same corner nook they had occupied before. "If it ain't the legal beagle from Bahston." He gave it the New Yorker's arrogant inflection. "Thought you disappeared with the Red Sox. Think they finished up somewhere in the want ads."

Ahearn's pugilistic voice seemed piped to a higher pitch than on the previous visit. He scraped a chair up to the gnarled table and sat down facing Sheridan.

"What brings you down to Fort Lee this time?" He eyed Sheridan warily.

The bartender arrived and wiped the table.

"Two light beers," Ahearn said, holding up two fingers.

Sheridan was wryly amused that Ahearn automatically ordered for them both.

O'Doul's at midafternoon on a weekday in Fort Lee, New Jersey, was practically deserted. A few stragglers sat at the bar, downing some shooters and watching a TV audience-participation show.

"I was at Captain Joe O'Halloran's retirement party last night." Sheridan threw it out with studied nonchalance.

Suddenly, the smile drained from Ahearn's face. He had dealt with lawyers before, but he wasn't sure what game Sheridan was playing, if indeed there was a game.

"Listen, Sheridan." He leaned toward his visitor, his squinty eyes now as cold as Siberia. "Are you trying to blackmail Dr. Sexton or something?"

Sheridan feigned surprise. "Not at all, Mike, but Captain O'Halloran says that the records of the investigation involving the death of Sexton's live-in girlfriend were destroyed, and not reduced to microfilm, as required by regulations."

Ahearn's ruddy complexion turned ashen gray. In fact, he looked as if he'd just been told he had terminal cancer.

"What are you implying?" He looked up at Sheridan from under his whiskery eyebrows.

"Not *implying* anything, Mike. I'm *telling you.* O'Halloran said he checked on Sexton's 'alibi,' and guess what? No alibi. You told me Sexton was at school at the time of the accident. . . . *He wasn't.*" Little beads of sweat were forming on Ahearn's forehead.

"Your beers, gentlemen." The bartender placed two steins on the table. "Need any pretzels?"

Ahearn shook his head. He waited several seconds, then downed half his glass. He wiped the foam off his mouth with the back of his hand. Their eyes collided and held.

"Look, Counselor, that was years ago. The investigation's closed, understand? Closed. *Kaput!*" His hand slashed the air.

"You're smelling around for something that just isn't there. And guys who poke their noses into something that doesn't concern them—hey, they could wind up like Jimmy Hoffa." The bleak, mirthless smile returned to his face.

"I think our business here is finished," Ahearn said as he drained his glass.

Sheridan stood up. "Guess you're right, Mike. Thanks for your time." Neither extended a hand.

Sheridan stood, hesitating before he turned to leave.

"You don't suppose for a moment, do you, Mike, that Sexton might have hidden in wait for the Rivera girl . . . say, because he had knocked her up? She was a poor spick from a working-class borough, and that wouldn't look good for a Phi Beta Kappa Yalie with a promising medical career, would it?"

"Get the fuck outta here!" Ahearn stormed. "You come nosing around here again, Sheridan, and you're going to end up as part of the Jersey Turnpike."

"Sure, Mike." Sheridan threw a twenty-dollar bill on the table. "Like the Red Sox, I'm gone."

—

It didn't take Mike Ahearn long to get in touch with Dr. Robert Sexton. He called from the pay phone at the end of the bar, next to the men's room.

Sexton's secretary parried the call as best she could, but she finally told the doctor that the caller was insistent.

"Okay, Stacey." Sexton issued a wounded sigh. "I'll take it on my private line." Even the secretary couldn't listen in.

"Mike," Sexton said guardedly, "what's up?"

"I'll tell you what's up," Ahearn fumed. "It's that fuckin' lawyer-cop Sheridan, the guy who's suing you."

"Oh, that's going to be resolved very shortly. My attorney has agreed to settle."

"Don't fuck with me, Doc! You gave me that crap weeks ago!"

"Well, what's the problem?"

"The problem is that the fuckin' jerk just left here. Sheridan comes to see me unannounced . . ."

"Yes?"

"Someone gives him info that you had no alibi when the Rivera girl died."

Sexton shivered inwardly. A cold knot began to form in the pit of his stomach. He hesitated for several seconds.

"What is he trying to do, engage in some sort of extortion, trying to up the amount of the settlement? Maybe you should report him to the district attorney."

"District attorney my ass!" Ahearn spewed. "You take care of this situation right away. Am I making myself clear? *Right away!*"

Sexton sat in his chair for several minutes after Ahearn had hung up. He fumbled with the push buttons on his telephone, trying to reach Charlie Finnerty. Unable to control his trembling hands, he hung up after two short rings. He unlocked his bottom desk drawer and withdrew a small vial. He poured a glass of water from the silver pitcher on his desk and popped two Valiums. He knew what he had to do.

—

Sheridan managed to catch the five o'clock Delta back to Boston. He was relieved to see that young Buckley was still in the office, catching up. Sheridan described the events of his day.

"I still don't see how you're going to get the circumstances of that girl's death into evidence," Buckley said. "If you try asking questions on this stuff at trial, I can see d'Ortega jumping to her feet screaming, 'In the name of decency, Your Honor!' And the judge will ream you out right in front of the jury."

"Well, something's funny about that death," Sheridan said.

"So, it's funny. The mere fact that Sexton had no alibi doesn't mean he committed the homicide. Hell, two-thirds of our criminal clientele have no alibis, and most of the time we walk them."

"Still, why should this Ahearn guy threaten me?"

"Who knows?" Buckley replied. "Maybe he's pissed off you're snooping around. Probably knows he booted the investigation and wants to protect his pension. Big deal."

Sheridan closed his eyes. He wondered how Donna DiTullio

was doing up at Greenbriar. Then he realized there'd be fireworks with Dante DiTullio. But there was no question Dante would have to be removed from the case, including his claim for loss of consortium.

Suddenly, Buckley asked, "What exit?"

"What?"

"What exit?" Buckley repeated. "The Jersey Turnpike. Where Ahearn says you'll end up. Might want to pay my last respects. That's a long stretch of roadway. Gotta know the exit."

Sheridan shook his head. "How did we ever wind up together?" But he had to admit young Buckley was a good guy to have around—like the neighborhood bar, kind of softened the rough edges of life. He gave his partner a weary smile and headed for home.

Buckley returned to a letter he was writing to Karen Assad, attempting to explain his disappearance. He shook his head as he read it through. He crumpled it up—it wasn't going to work. He'd wait until the case was over. But that might be too late.

27

Charlie Finnerty made a call to the assistant clerk of courts, Terrence Fahey. Terrence was his aunt Kate's boy. After Terrence had been bounced by one of the Beacon Hill firms, Charlie had been instrumental in getting the head clerk, "Chic" Mahoney, to take him on. Terrence had a soft and safe sinecure, if he didn't screw up. He had shuffled a few papers and eventually was promoted to assignment clerk. This was an important post, since on the civil side of the ledger, it was the assignment clerk who designated what case would be tried before what judge. And as all trial lawyers knew, the black robe worn by judges did not always signify impartiality. There were plaintiff judges and defendant judges, and maneuvering the case to be heard before the "right" judge was an art form.

"Terry." Finnerty's voice was chipper. "How's Katie?"

"Still in the nursing home, Charlie. Not doing too well, the Alzheimer's, you know."

"Yes." Charlie's voice dipped to a somber tone. "Sad, real sad. My mother, God rest her soul, said Kate was a fine lady. I must send her some flowers. . . . House of the Good Shepherd over in Roslindale, you say." Finnerty scratched down an address.

"I'll get them right out, Terry, might brighten her day." He paused.

"Tell me, Terry, is Judge Mason still assigned to the case of *DiTullio* v. *St. Anne's Hospital et al.*?"

"As far as I know, Charlie. Let me check the docket."

Several seconds passed. "Yes, she'll be the judge."

"Fine judge, Mason," Finnerty said. "Been on the bench only about a year, and handles herself real well. We've had several preliminary matters before her.

"But, you know, Terry, the St. Anne's case is highly technical, and of course there's a lot at stake. I think it calls for the judicial temperament and expertise of someone who has experience in these difficult matters, someone like, say, Judge Irving Samuels."

"Let's see." Terrence consulted the court docket and turned a few pages. "Yes, Samuels. He's sitting on criminal cases. But let me see what I can do."

Terrence Fahey didn't have to figure it out. Uncle Charlie, as he was known in the family, was calling in a big chit. And he also knew that Samuels, schooled in the big law firm mentality, was a "defendant's" judge who hated to see a plaintiff's attorney make a score. He was also well aware that it was Charlie Finnerty who headed the judicial nominating committee and had sponsored Samuels's appointment to the bench.

"Yes, I kinda agree. Mason isn't mature enough for this sort of case. It'll take some doing. . . ." Terrence threw it out to strike some semblance of balance in the favors department.

"I'm sure with your ingenuity and capability, Terry," Finnerty said, "and in the interest of both sides to the litigation, knowing that this case needs Samuels's expertise, you can make the necessary arrangements.

"And by the way," Finnerty said before hanging up, "I was talking with Chic Mahoney the other day. Tells me the first assistant's job is opening up. Seems Tom Harkins is retiring. I told Chic you'd be a natural for the spot."

"Thanks, Charlie."

"Don't mention it," Finnerty said.

—

Sheridan's TR6 thrummed along New Hampshire Interstate 89. He had left Boston at 4:00 A.M., and now as he neared White River Junction, the first rays of sunlight glimmered over the White Mountains. Below, the Connecticut River was wrapped in a gray shawl of mist.

Greenbriar in daylight had a roseate warmth as the sun glinted off copper-toned glass that stretched over five stories. Sheridan parked in the visitors' lot, closed his eyes momentarily, and soon was fast asleep. He was awakened by an ambulance siren somewhere in the distance. He blinked several times, trying to get his bearings. He had slept for two hours.

Slightly stiff, he made his way to the peach-marbled reception area at the main entrance. A pleasant middle-aged woman in a pink jacket checked the patients' register and told him Donna DiTullio's condition was guarded, that she was confined to a special critical care unit. She then gave him directions to Dr. Sagall's office on the third floor.

Sheridan was impressed with the sparkle and vitality of Greenbriar. The nurses, attendants, and medical personnel seemed to stride along with a brisk cadence. Perhaps he was imagining it, or perhaps he was comparing it to the lethargy and incompetence of the medical staff at Hampton.

Dr. Sagall's waiting area held its share of unfortunates—herniated-disk cases; a slight, fragile woman in the initial stages of multiple sclerosis; others who chatted about diagnostic tests and upcoming or past operations.

"Dr. Sagall will be in surgery until one," the secretary said as she eyed Sheridan with naïve curiosity. Sheridan's tie was askew, and his rumpled suit looked as though he had slept in it, which was the case.

"I'm Donna DiTullio's legal custodian," he said as he tried to suppress a yawn. "I drove most of the night from Boston. Would it be possible to see Miss DiTullio, just briefly?"

"She's in a special room in Critical Care. Let me call Dr. Ashe; he's the chief Neurology resident. If he gives the okay . . ."

After a brief telephone conversation with the resident, the secretary pinned a visitor's card on Sheridan's lapel.

"Donna is in the Mary Hitchcock Wing. It's a little complicated getting there. Tell you what. I'm due for my break. I'll escort you.

"Betsy," she addressed the intercom, "please take over for fifteen."

—

The secretary stood at the door as Sheridan entered the Critical Care unit. Unlike the gloomy gray cloister at Hampton, in this space the sunlight spilled onto the pink tile floor and toffee-colored walls like molten honey. The yellow roses that Sheridan had wired ahead added a slight perfume to the room's antiseptic smell. Donna was propped up in bed, her vacant eyes staring into some unseen distance. But her hair had been washed and brushed and there was a slight color in her pale cheeks. The IV was full and running, and an EKG sent blips and squiggles across a fluorescent screen as it monitored Donna's heartbeat.

"She's on a heparin drip," the secretary said. "Dr. Ashe feels the immediate crisis is over. The embolism lodged in the left lung, but it seems to be dissolving. But she has such terrible injuries. She's not out of the woods."

Sheridan nodded, took a yellow rose from the vase, and, as he had done in the past, held it out to Donna.

"It's me, Donna, Dan Sheridan. Got your favorite flower." He held it just under her nose. She breathed in ever so slightly.

"My God!" Sheridan said. "Another first."

"Donna." He looked into her opaque brown eyes. "Do you hear me, Donna? Blink—"

Before Sheridan finished his message, she closed her eyes slowly, then opened them quickly. The brown eyes glistened.

"You're going to be all right, Donna! We've got the best doctors in the world. . . ." Sheridan choked up, his eyes rimming with tears. "You're going to be all right."

Donna almost smiled. At least Sheridan, now bleary eyed, thought she had. Again, she blinked and tears welled, then slid down her cheeks. Sheridan extracted a tissue from the box on the bedside table and daubed her face gently.

"God," he swore softly, "she just might make it."

—

Later, Sheridan had a short discussion with Dr. Sagall, whose supple surgeon's hand took notes as Sheridan explained who he was, the details of the lawsuit, and why he had practically kidnapped Donna from Hampton.

Sagall nodded in understanding. "She'll need around-the-clock care," he said. "I've never seen such atrocious bedsores; I doubt they ever rotated Donna the entire time she was there. I have to agree, it was substandard medical care."

"Doctor," Sheridan said, "you and your staff come highly recommended. Dr. John White said to say hello."

He then explained the communication he was able to have with Donna and the most recent incident, just prior to their conversation.

"Interesting." Sagall looked up from his notebook. "Her brain is badly damaged, yet if what you say is true, she has the abilities of storage, encoding, retrieving, and emoting.

"I don't want to get too technical," he said. "Part of the midbrain could have been destroyed, but a portion known as the reticular formation could have been spared.

"You study the classics, Mr. Sheridan? Alexandre Dumas, say?"

Sheridan wiggled his hand.

"Well, her condition could be like that of M. Noirtier de Villefort in *The Count of Monte Cristo*. The patient is awake but has lost all power to communicate except with her eyes. 'A corpse with living eyes.' Although unable to move—what we call akinetic—and totally mute, the patient does not suffer from the syndrome of akinetic mutism, in which the patient is unconscious and makes no appropriate response."

Sheridan explained the way Donna froze when confronted by Brockelman, even by Dr. Jensen.

Sagall nodded. "That could be due to psychogenic or cata-tonic unresponsiveness.

"By the way," he said, "Jensen's a fine neurosurgeon, top-flight credentials. We were undergrads together at Cornell. He was summa cum laude."

"And how about you, Doctor?"

"I was lucky to get by. After Cornell, I thought I'd try my hand at law school."

"Glad you're here at the helm, Doctor. There are just too many lawyers out there."

They shook hands. Sheridan liked Sagall. If Donna had an outside shot, he knew it was here at Greenbriar.

Driving back to Boston, he pondered the next crisis: Dante DiTullio. This was not going to be easy.

—

"Son of a bitch." Buckley slapped the notice from the clerk of courts. "Irving Samuels has been assigned to the DiTullio case."

"Samuels? Are you sure?" Judy was as surprised as Buckley was angry.

"The worst trial judge in the whole goddamned system," Buckley spewed. "Hates my guts, and he and Sheridan had a donnybrook last time we appeared in front of him, threatened Dan with contempt."

"Can't you and Dan file a motion to have him recuse him-self?"

Buckley shook his head.

"Dan tried that in the Butler case. Samuels denied the mo-tion in his own imperious manner. Said the jury, not he, was going to decide the case. Then he charged the jury, practically railroading us out of court. Jurors look to the judge for guidance, hold him as a father figure. I never forgot what Samuels told that jury.

" 'If you want to believe Mr. Sheridan's client,' he said, lofty-like, 'that's up to you.' And the son of a bitch throws his eyes toward the ceiling and his mouth gapes open—the old 'cock-and-bull story' nuance. Sheridan takes exception to this chicanery, but naturally, we go down the drain. When the appeals court reviews the cold record, devoid of the facial grimaces, they rule that the jury charge was perfectly proper.

"Boy, Dan isn't going to like this one bit. Not exactly a day-maker, Judy. By the way, when is Dan due in?"

"He called en route from Vermont. Donna took a turn for the better. Seems Dan was able to get through to her again.

"Said he might not be in until tomorrow morning. That's when the DiTullios are coming in."

"Well, we've really got our hands full," Buckley said. "A joint pretrial memorandum is due before Samuels in ten days. Doesn't give us much time."

—

After the seven-hour round-trip to Vermont, Dan's internal motor was running in overdrive. He knew it was important to relax, especially in preparing for trial, but the adrenaline kept kicking in.

He had called Sheila at her office, filling her in on his trip to New York. He related his suspicions about Emanuela Rivera's death, but omitted mention of the veiled threat from Mike Ahearn. As always, she offered sympathy and support. He asked her to meet him at the Wampanoag trail at the Blue Hills Reservation for a run, but she demurred, since she had a brief to get out on a case involving patent infringement.

"Seems a guy named MacDonald," she said, "opened a pizza parlor and duplicated the golden arch logo, right down to calling his pies Big Mac Pizzarinos."

—

Sheridan parked his TR6 in the trailside rest area. It was starting to get dark and there was a chill to the air. The area was deserted. He laced up his shoes, slipped into a warm-up suit, and proceeded with limbering exercises, deep knee bends, hand-to-toe diagonals.

He covered the first stretch at a steady uphill pace. This was only his fifth run, but he could see why Sheila enjoyed her weekly workouts. As the trail leveled off and he approached King Philip's rock, he lengthened his stride. The only sounds were his heavy breathing and the slap of running shoes on the dirt trail. At the stone escarpment, he stopped, checked his watch. Not bad, he thought. Fifteen minutes. He leaned back against the rock. Only the gurgle of a small stream disturbed the stillness. He straightened, then turned to start the homeward leg.

Suddenly, a loud clap rang out from somewhere in the woody hillside to his right. By raw instinct, honed by months of patrol in Vietnam, he dove into a small ditch to his left. His fingers dug into the rocks and dirt as he hugged the bottom of the gully, his head as low and flat as it could possibly go. Another clap, then another. He didn't look up, just tried to burrow deeper. He could hear the dull thuds as slugs hit the ground behind him. His heart raced, his body shuddered, and a tight knot gripped his viscera. Someone was shooting at him; he had to get the hell out of there. He could hear trees splintering, then three more shots. Thank God it was getting dark. He lay motionless for several minutes, breaking into a cold sweat, trying not to breathe. Suddenly, it was deathly quiet. He was tempted to lift his head and peek out of the ditch, or perhaps bolt into the woods behind him. But again, ingrained from Vietnam, especially when someone had the drop on you: do nothing, lie completely still—play dead. Ten, fifteen minutes passed. There wasn't a sound; nothing stirred. Slowly, he began inching backward, his head still flat, his body scraping the ground. He stopped after a few feet, waited several minutes, and again slid backward. He kept this up until he was well into the woods. It was now completely dark. Again he lay motionless and listened. The only sound was his heart thumping. Unsteadily, he rose to a squat position, ducked behind a tree, then surveyed the trail, some fifty feet distant. He could make out King Philip's rock silhouetted against the purple darkness. He darted from tree to tree; twigs snapped, leaves crunched as he moved parallel to the trail. At a clearing, he got down on one knee and checked the trail as it converged into the rest area. He saw his car some one hundred yards ahead. He again waited at the edge of the rest area for several minutes. He thought of leaving his car, perhaps walking to the reservation exit, then calling a cab from a filling station he remembered about a mile distant.

He thought better of it. He crouched down, left the wooded area, and slowly made his way toward his car. The thought crossed his mind that the car might be wired, but he'd have to chance it.

He held his breath, started the car, and slowly exited the rest area, not turning on the lights until he reached the main road. He pulled up to a Gulf station and sat in his car, trying to collect himself. He was just as frightened now as he had been on patrol in Vietnam. The Blue Hills Division police barracks was just down the street. He pulled out his cellular phone, about to call Buckley at home. Was it the Colombians? They weren't too happy that Perez was languishing in jail. Maybe it was Mike Ahearn—although as an ex-cop himself, he tended to dismiss that thought. Mike was all bluff and manufactured bravado.

He drove to the police station and was about to pull into the parking lot when he decided otherwise. Somehow, he was going to have to figure this out by himself. He'd have a talk with Perez.

28

Sheridan was still shaken when he showed up at Raimondi's apartment on Hanover Street in Boston's North End.

"Jesus!" Manny looked at Sheridan when he answered the door. "You look like you've been embalmed."

"Not quite, but almost," Sheridan stammered. "I could use a stiff one."

"Bourbon?"

"Make it a double, straight."

Manny cracked some ice and poured out five ounces for Sheridan and an ounce for himself. Sheridan took a quick sip, another, then drained the glass. The amber liquid seared his chest and rushed to his head.

"What is it, Dan?" Manny asked.

"I was shot at tonight."

"*Shot?*" Manny pointed a finger at Sheridan with his thumb cocked.

"Someone tried to kill me."

"*What?*"

"About an hour ago. I was jogging in the Blue Hills, along the old Wampanoag trail."

"Jesus, could've been a hunter." Raimondi tried to gloss over the gravity of the situation.

Sheridan shook his head. "Who hunts at night? No, someone meant to take me out."

"You report it to the police?"

Sheridan again shook his head. "No. It'd make the papers. I don't need this kind of ink—not now. Gotta figure this out myself. Could be Perez's group. He wasn't overly friendly when I visited him in jail last week. Thinks we're sloughing off on the job. Wanted me to spread some ice with certain government officials. I threatened to withdraw from the case if he ever mentioned that kind of stuff again. He wasn't pleased.

"And you know the threat from that Mike Ahearn guy—and of course anyone following us the past several weeks pretty well knew our routine."

"Yeah, but we mixed it up. And you and Buck felt that the tails were off." He thought for a moment. "I was in the office when you called in during your trip from Vermont. You filled us in that Donna was holding her own and you were going to try to get hold of Sheila to go for an evening jog in the Blue Hills. Remember?"

"Yeah?"

"Cellular phone conversations are the easiest to tap, those and fax transmittals. Unfortunately, the scrambling technology hasn't been perfected. Anyone could have bugged that call, been waiting on the trail. Ideal location to take someone out. The park's deserted, especially this time of year. Bodies have turned up in those woods. Mob hits, usually."

"I don't know, Manny. I'm goddamned scared, like in Nam. And Sheila could have been with me tonight." He jiggled the ice cubes, signaling for a refill.

Raimondi poured two more ounces of bourbon, then added water.

"I still think you should go to the police."

Sheridan again shook his head. "It boils down to two probabilities. Perez, or it has something to do with the DiTullio case."

"You don't think . . ."

"No. Not Dante. He's a bully all right. But bullies are essentially cowards. And besides, he's too goddamned stupid. Whoever organized tonight's hit has intelligence and is a pretty good marksman."

Sheridan again drained his glass, then shook his head with quick motions, like a prizefighter trying to survive a knockdown blow. The bourbon had taken effect.

"I thought it over on my way back to Boston, and I'm not going to remove Dante DiTullio as conservator or as a party litigant."

"You're not?"

"No. D'Ortega and Finnerty think they hold the aces. But this dovetails with my theory. So Donna was abused, used cocaine. It goes to prove that she was on the edge, a suicide waiting to happen. The Capricet only masked the symptoms. She required more diligent care, not less."

"Gee, I don't know." Raimondi scratched the back of his head. "Dante thinks he'll make millions on this tragedy. If I were on the jury, given the best scenario you could muster, I wouldn't give him a dime."

"That's just it." Sheridan now sounded hyper, his voice keyed higher. "D'Ortega will kick the stuffings out of Dante, no question. I'll let her."

"What about Finnerty's threat to go to the DA?"

"Thought of that, too. I'll argue my motion to suppress before Judge Mason. If I prevail, fine. If not, I think I can handle it in final argument, to our advantage."

"Mason?" Raimondi looked at Sheridan quizzically.

"Yeah, not a bad gal. She's the trial judge."

Raimondi thought for a few moments.

"Got bad news, Dan, and worse news. Which do you want first?"

"What?"

"The bad news is that Mason's been removed from the case. The assignment order from the court clerk came in while you were away."

"Oh? Well, that happens." Sheridan shrugged. "She's been

ruling in our favor so much, maybe she thinks she owes d'Ortega a makeup call.

"What could be worse?"

"Judge Irving Samuels has replaced Mason as the trial judge."

Suddenly, Sheridan's face reddened. The events of the past days, even the shooting, were forgotten.

"Son of a bitch!" he swore. "You gotta be kidding! How 'n hell did that happen! He's a goddamned submariner! Tries to sink us every chance he gets!"

"Dan, I think you better stay here tonight."

"Jesus Christ!" Dan threw his head back and closed his eyes. He heaved a deep sigh.

"Guess you're right, Manny. I'm in no shape to drive. I'll sleep on the couch." He motioned with his head toward the settee.

"But do me a favor. Set the alarm for five. There's something I've gotta do."

—

"Have another cup of coffee, Dan. Wherever you're going, it's pretty dark out there. It'll stick by you while you drive." Raimondi eyed Sheridan from across the breakfast table.

"No thanks, Manny. I'll grab a second cup back at the office. We've got Dante coming in at ten."

"Can I ask where you're going at this ungodly hour?" Raimondi glanced at the kitchen clock—5:30.

"Just a hunch." It was an elliptical response. "I'll fill you in later."

"Want my thirty-eight? Nothing like packing a little insurance."

Sheridan shook his head. "Haven't carried a gun in a long time. Swore off it for good. Besides, I haven't got a permit. The gendarmes catch me, there's a mandatory one-year prison term. That would take a lot of fixing, believe me. No . . . I'll be all right."

"I hope so." Raimondi's voice lacked conviction.

—

Sheridan got into his car, which he had parked behind Raimondi's apartment. It was unseasonably warm and thunder rumbled in the distance. Traffic was sparse as he drove along the Mass Turnpike, cutting off at the Neponset Valley Parkway, finally reaching the Blue Hills Reservation. A scribble of lightning sizzled in the dark western sky, and by the time Sheridan parked at the entrance to the rest area, a teeming downpour had commenced. He waited for several minutes until the rain eased, then slipped into a warm-up jacket retrieved from the backseat. Next, he removed a tire iron from the trunk. Retracing his way along the Wampanoag trail, he felt certain that his would-be assassin was long gone. When he reached King Philip's rock, the first hint of daylight filtered through the trees. But in the forest, nothing seemed to stir. From the rock, he surveyed the woods. The shots had come from up on the hillside.

He next studied the ditch into which he had scrambled. In the mud, he could make out where he had landed and where he had inched away following the attack. He poked around for maybe half an hour. The rain had abated, misting into a soft drizzle. Holding his thumb out at arm's length, he eyed the possible trajectory of the line of fire. He then noticed several trees had been splintered just beyond where he dove for cover. He dug with the tire iron in the loose earth for the next half hour, finally extracting a flattened slug embedded at the base of a tree. After studying it, he slipped it into his pocket. He knew there had been five or six shots, but in the next twenty minutes of probing and digging in the dense scrub, nothing turned up. From the splintered trees, he again surveyed the trajectory of the bullets' paths. Using King Philip's rock as a focus, he figured whoever had shot at him had had to be up on the hillside, maybe twenty, twenty-five yards beyond.

He paused at the rock. Again not a sound disturbed the stillness. He slogged up the hillside, snapping bushes and branches, until he came to a slight clearing.

Sure, he thought as he looked down the hill toward the trail, a perfect vantage point. This had been the position of the killer. Poking around in the mud and leaves, it didn't take Sheridan long to uncover three brass cartridges. The markings were unfamiliar. He slipped them into the same pocket with the slug, then checked his watch—five after seven. He stroked the stubble of a beard. Pretty grubby. He'd go back to his apartment, shower, spruce up a bit, pretend, at least to Judy, that it was going to be just another day at the office. But he dreaded what might happen. Dante could go ballistic over the tapes. Buckley, on hearing the turn of events, might go south, even threaten to quit because of the conflict between his interest in Karen Assad and his continued representation in the St. Anne's case. Sheridan would turn over his collection of ordnance to Raimondi. Maybe Manny could get a feel for whom and what they were dealing with.

As he drove back along the Southeast Expressway, he tried to put the jumble of events into some kind of perspective. Perez, Mike Ahearn, Dante DiTullio. Nothing figured.

●

Dante DiTullio didn't evince any emotion when Judy Corwin ushered him into Sheridan's office. He greeted Dan cordially, making excuses for his prior cancellation.

"I want you to listen to a tape we subpoenaed from Dr. Sexton's records. It's going to pose a bit of a problem." Sheridan checked the cassette and adjusted the tone.

DiTullio sat unmoving as the recording spilled out its litany of abuse. Even after the tape was finished, he remained still, showing no emotion.

"What does it all mean," he said finally, "as far as the lawsuit is concerned?" His voice was soft and steady, almost conversational.

"Well, we could have you removed from the case and name Mrs. DiTullio or substitute a near relative." Sheridan studied DiTullio.

"It's not true, you know," DiTullio said. "Donna was under a great deal of stress and that's why we consulted Dr. Sexton in the first place. You can tell she's fantasizing."

Sheridan said nothing for several moments.

"I'm going to make a motion before the trial judge to suppress the tape; I'll argue it's inadmissible evidence. I need your affidavit that Donna's testimony is untrue."

"If we lose the motion . . . what then?"

"Then we'll proceed to trial, you and Mrs. DiTullio will remain as coconservators, and we'll weather the storm as best we can. I may be able to use the tape to our advantage."

"Will there be any criminal accusations? The sexual abuse stuff, I mean."

"I don't know." Sheridan pushed the recorder's rewind button. "We're playing in a tough league, Dante. They don't pitch underhand. In fact, they fire them at your head."

"Well, I wish you luck on your motion, Counselor." Dante DiTullio got up, shook Sheridan's hand, and left.

Sheridan pondered DiTullio's reaction. He hadn't gone ape, nor had he crumbled, as might have been expected. In fact, it was his utter calm that bothered Sheridan.

29

Sheridan was still wondering about Dante DiTullio when young Buckley and Raimondi came into the conference room. Raimondi closed the door.

No sense in complicating the situation, he thought. Best to keep Judy out of it, at least for the present.

"Guess you heard?" Sheridan said.

"I did." Buckley nodded. "Dan, don't you think this is a police matter?"

"Probably—but here." Sheridan handed over a small plastic bag to Raimondi. "This morning, I went back to the Wampanoag trail, retraced my steps. Was able to pinpoint the location from which the shots were fired. Dug around with a tire iron for the better part of an hour and recovered a slug and three shell casings."

Raimondi removed the bullet and cartridges from the bag.

"Haven't seen anything like this before." Raimondi held the slug between his thumb and forefinger. "It's flattened and splintered almost like a dumdum bullet. And the cartridges are brass, longer than regular seven millimeters. Odd markings—*VZs*."

He thought for a moment.

"Sure, Van Zandts. Can't get them in the U.S.—manufactured in Holland. A flesh wound can be deadly. Used by terrorist groups, mainly.

"These were featured in a recent article in *Soldier of Fortune*. . . . You were lucky, Dan."

"Do you think Perez's group would have access to this stuff?" Sheridan looked at Buckley, then at Raimondi.

"No question about it. But I think if they were really disenchanted with you, they'd take you out with a car bomb. And you haven't crossed them; you're doing the best you can for Perez. He may growl and make unpleasant noises, but he knows he's getting the best representation available."

"Don't you think, Dan, you should get a gun permit?" Buckley said. "I've got a connection at City Hall. Can get it for you overnight. . . . Hell, maybe we should all get permits, Judy included."

"It might come to that. Right now, Manny, take this ammo and see if you can get a read on where it can be bought sub rosa in and around Boston."

"Will do." Raimondi replaced them in the plastic bag, sealed it, and tucked it into his jacket pocket.

"As if we had nothing else to worry about," Buckley said with forced jauntiness. "And speaking about trouble, how did the meeting go?"

"I don't know. DiTullio's usually boisterous, arrogant, on the defensive. I expected he'd explode with outrage. Instead, he shrugged, wished me luck on my motion to suppress, and left here as if he hadn't a care in the world. He's a real enigma."

Judge Irving Samuels had been on the bench for almost a decade. He viewed himself as a legal scholar, having coauthored a text called *Legal Procedure*. But of late, most of his literary efforts were letters to the editor, sent to the *Globe* and the *Herald*, extolling the abilities of the Massachusetts judiciary and trumpeting the need for a judicial pay raise.

But he was a cantankerous and high-handed arbiter, often

berating lawyers in front of juries, and more than occasionally levying fines and reporting attorneys to the board of bar overseers. And he held little love for Dan Sheridan and young Buckley.

Sheridan, as usual, showed up early for Samuels's session.

"What do you have?" the judge's long-suffering law clerk, Kate McDonald, asked.

"A motion to suppress."

"Criminal?"

"No, it's a civil matter. *DiTullio* v. *St. Anne's Hospital et al.*"

"Oh, yes." The clerk shuffled some papers on her desk in front of the bench.

"The judge is in chambers, has a copy of your motion. He's a hard worker, you know."

"I know," Sheridan said. "Kate, do you think we could be heard right away? I'm submitting a supporting brief." He reached into his briefcase and handed the document to the clerk.

"Is the other side here?"

"Not yet. But it's Charlie Finnerty and Mayan d'Ortega. If they arrive before the judge is on the bench, maybe you can put us at the top of the list. The hearing should take only about ten minutes."

"I'll see what I can do," she said.

At exactly nine o'clock, Charlie Finnerty and Mayan d'Ortega came through the tufted green courtroom doors. There was now a full complement of lawyers awaiting the call of the list. Most shuffled their feet nervously—Samuels was known to have a short fuse—and even if the law was on their side, it didn't always ensure judicial relief. In fact, Samuels's rulings were regularly overturned by the state supreme court.

Sheridan recalled being present when one timid advocate had tried to digest Samuels's adverse ruling.

"You're wrong, Judge," the lawyer had ventured guardedly. "The case of *McVey* v. *Electric Boat* is directly on point."

Samuels had scowled down from the bench. "Fine, take your appeal. Maybe two or three years from now, the appeals court might say you're right. Then you can come back in here, young man, roll up the parchment with the Court's ruling on it, and hit me over the head with it. . . . Next case!"

And Samuels kept a list of those who had the audacity to appeal his edicts, especially successful appellants.

"All rise," Kate McDonald intoned as Judge Samuels, attired in his black robe, strode like a martinet toward the bench.

"Be seated," she said. Then she read from a card the message that hadn't changed since the Mayflower Compact.

" 'Everyone having to do business before the Right Honorable Irving Samuels, justice of the superior court, sitting in Boston, draw near, give your attention, and you shall be heard. . . . God save the Commonwealth of Massachusetts.' "

And God save us from this unctuous curmudgeon, Sheridan added to himself, smiling first at Kate McDonald and then up at the bench, sending up a "Good morning, Your Honor" greeting.

"Case nine-seven-three-one, *DiTullio* v. *St. Anne's Hospital et al.*" McDonald turned toward the judge. "All parties are present, Your Honor. Counsel for the plaintiffs says it'll take only ten minutes of argument."

Sheridan stood.

Samuels had carefully coiffed pearl gray hair, sported a Boca Raton tan, and wore half-lens glasses, which he pushed to the end of his nose, peering over them at Sheridan, taking his measure.

"I've heard that one before," he quipped. Thirty-some lawyers erupted in forced laughter.

"It's an unusual motion, Mr. Sheridan," Samuels said after waiting for the laughter to subside. "I'll hold you and Mr. Finnerty for second call at eleven. Okay with you, Mr. Finnerty?"

Finnerty, who was being paid by the hour, chimed in quickly as he rose to his feet.

"Good morning, Your Honor." He gave a slight bow. "Eleven o'clock, that will be fine."

"The next case, Your Honor." Kate McDonald started to read from the docket. "*Northeast Petroleum Corporation* v. *City of Boston.* . . ."

—

Sheridan was inwardly steamed at the delay. He glanced over at Finnerty and d'Ortega.

"Can I see both of you outside?" he said.

A good ten minutes later, Finnerty sauntered out, meeting Sheridan next to the water fountain in the hall.

"Danny me boy." He extended his hand. "Mayan's tied up. Got three more motions to argue." He paused for several seconds. "I'm really disappointed in you, Danny, I really am. Here I got claims manager Crimmins to keep the offer open for twenty-four hours, and you didn't even render us the courtesy of a call. Not good, Dan. You have a duty to your clients, you know. It'll take some doing, but I may be able to revive the offer."

Sheridan was tempted to say, Don't lecture me, you oily bastard! But he thought better of it.

"I was preoccupied, Charlie. I've got more than one case, you know."

"You let your client DiTullio hear the tape?"

"He heard it all right."

"Well?" Charm lay on Finnerty's lips like cyanide.

"You're not really serious about using those tapes as evidence."

"What are you talking about?" Finnerty responded. "You haven't got little bleeding heart Mason hearing this motion. You know and I know that Samuels will broom you out on this one."

"I know," Sheridan said softly. "Here we are, Charlie, you and I, in the halls of justice. I think it was Lord Coke, the famous English jurist, who said, 'The only justice in the halls of justice is in the halls.' On second thought, maybe it was Mickey Spillane."

"C'mon." Finnerty's mouth flattened. "What's the point, Sheridan?"

"The point is, Charlie, you use that stuff against my clients, I'm going to cross-examine Sexton right out of the courtroom."

"Now, wait a minute. . . ."

"No"—Sheridan leaned toward Finnerty—"you wait a minute. Did it ever occur to you—and I trust you took it up with *your* client—that Sexton was aware of criminal offenses being perpetrated—forced incest, no less—and for almost a year, he didn't do a goddamned thing to intercede or prevent it by going to the authorities? For almost a year, he was running up a bill at two hundred dollars an hour."

Finnerty was startled, but only momentarily.

"Dan, you've done your homework, got to hand it to you. But let me tell you." He jabbed a finger in Sheridan's direction. "Whatever Dr. Sexton became aware of during his therapy sessions with a patient is privileged information. Like when your client levels with you, says he actually pulled the trigger—same as the sins confessed to the priest in the confessional. Where would we be if the priest suddenly runs out into the street and calls the cops? No, Dan, Mayan will tear Dante DiTullio to shreds—and your case with him!"

Finnerty glanced at his watch. "If you want the three hundred thou—" He held up three fingers.

Sheridan cut him off. "Charlie, shove the three hundred up your ass!"

Finnerty looked at Sheridan with disbelief. "Nasty, Dan, nasty. Not the way for a fellow advocate to act."

"Yeah, Charlie, real nasty."

———

The clerk called their case at five minutes to one.

"*DiTullio* v. *St. Anne's Hospital et al.,*" she intoned. "All parties are present."

Sheridan rose. "Your Honor," he began.

"Judge." Charlie Finnerty snapped to his feet. "After due consideration"—he nodded toward d'Ortega—"the defendants withdraw their opposition to the plaintiffs' motion."

Samuels looked perplexed. Again he slid his glasses to the end of his nose and peered over them at Finnerty.

"You mean you are agreeing to Mr. Sheridan's motion to suppress Dr. Sexton's tapes as evidence?"

"That's correct, Your Honor."

Samuels was surprised, but not as surprised as Sheridan.

"All right," the judge said in his officious manner. "The trial is scheduled for mid-November. Can both of you be ready?"

"We'll be ready, Your Honor," Finnerty said with professional assurance. "We do have Mr. and Mrs. DiTullio's depositions slated for later this week, but that should pose no problem to Your Honor's trial schedule."

"Mr. Sheridan?" The judge peered down at Sheridan.

"I'll be ready, Your Honor," Sheridan said with a pretense of bravado. Then he thought about it. Maybe his threat to cross-examine Sexton on covering up a felony had hit home. The tapes were a two-edged sword. When he had returned from the men's room after his run-in with Finnerty, d'Ortega and Finnerty were engaged in a deep discussion. Perhaps Finnerty had called Sexton and they had decided not to use the tapes. But Sheridan knew he still had Samuels to contend with. Samuels would try to ace him every chance he got.

As he left the counsel table, he looked over at Mayan d'Ortega. Their eyes held momentarily, and he thought a slight smile flickered on her lips. Maybe it was a "you won this one, gringo" kind of smile.

●

Sheridan pulled up in the parking area of the federal correctional facility in Danbury, Connecticut. From there, he would shoot up Route 5 to visit Donna at Greenbriar. He had told Buckley to make sure Anna and Dante DiTullio came into the office first thing the next morning so they could prepare for d'Ortega's depositions. Sheridan knew these might be tricky. Although the tapes were now inadmissible per se, d'Ortega could depose both as to Dante's possible criminal involvement, including giving his daughter performance-enhancing drugs. Sheridan would object to that line of questioning, but legally Dante DiTullio could be forced to answer. And Sheridan knew that Dante could easily fall apart, and so could Anna DiTullio. He would have to steel both for a hard-line interrogation.

When he entered the gray fieldstone building, he was

checked carefully, a photo name tag was pinned to his lapel, and he was ushered into a sparse room separated into two sections by bulletproof glass. Two guards brought in Carmine Perez, dressed in prison orange, who sat down on a plain wooden chair. Sheridan did likewise, then bent close to a small circular grille inlaid in the glass, through which they would communicate. Sheridan had been assured that no conversations between himself and his client would be taped. He didn't totally trust the assurance, but right now, he'd have to risk it.

"Carmine. ¿Cómo está usted?"

"So-so, Meestah Sheridan." He wiggled his hand.

"When we have trial?" he asked in broken English.

"The U.S. attorney for the Boston area isn't quite sure."

"¡No bueno!"

"I agree. Our Constitution guarantees everyone the right to a speedy trial. I've filed a motion that your trial be held within thirty days.

"The U.S. attorney wants you to make a deal."

"No hay acuerdo." Perez narrowed his flinty eyes.

"I pay you good money, amigo. Want out of here."

"Carmine." Sheridan leaned closer to the speaker grille. "Did you have me set up a day or two ago?"

"¿Cómo dice usted?" Perez was indignant.

"Someone tried to ambush me a few nights ago, tried to take me out with a rifle. I was jogging in the woods. . ."

"Meestah Sheridan, I no killer. My people are —what you say? Trabajando legalmente."

"Okay," Sheridan said, "I'll take you at your word. Hasta luego. I'll be in touch."

⬤

Raimondi asked around a bit. He knew a few small-time hoods, wiseguy wanna-bes, mainly, trying to earn their spurs with roving crap games, numbers, occasionally providing muscle for bill collectors. Through a friend of a friend, he was touted to Vinnie Coogan, who had an undertaking establishment in Charlestown. Vinnie was also in the travel business, taking care of all arrangements if you wanted to bury your dear grandmother or aunt or uncle or whomever, in their native Ireland. In fact, for almost a decade, Vinnie had done a thriving business. You'd get the full treatment, embalming, a plot in the native county—even in Armagh, Tyrone, or Belfast—a casket, flowers, a priest, and mourners, all for under five hundred dollars. Sometimes he'd have five or six caskets headed toward Eglinton Airport in Derry.

People wondered, what with transportation costs, how Coogan was able to do it. What they didn't know was that each casket was oversized and in a compartment underneath Uncle Ned or poor Aunt Mary were grenades, bazookas, rocket launchers, or SKS assault rifles, all neatly packed and ready for assembly when "the lads" came out to meet the special charter plane and unload the mournful "cargo." Vinnie could also supply a gun and ammo for "domestic use" or get rid of a hot piece, no questions asked, and the same for dead bodies. Vinnie Coogan was by reputation a man who could be trusted.

By prearrangement, Raimondi waited for Vinnie Coogan in the last pew, just inside the vestibule of St. Rocco's Church. Exactly on schedule, Vinnie blessed himself, genuflected toward the altar, and eased into the seat next to Raimondi. Both knelt and folded their hands in silent prayer as they waited for an elderly lady making the Stations of the Cross to shuffle past. Save for this sole worshiper, the church at two in the afternoon was empty and deathly still.

"Sal said you needed some info," Coogan whispered, keeping his eyes focused straight ahead.

"I do." Raimondi leaned toward Coogan.

"First," Raimondi said, pulling an envelope out of his pocket, "here's ten Ben Franklins—a contribution to the cause, so to speak."

The exchange was quick and deft.

"The lads will be pleased, believe me. You're very charitable." Coogan's voice assumed a confessional quietness.

"Now, what information would ye be wantin' to know?"

"Can you check these out?" Raimondi passed the plastic bag to Coogan. "There's a seven-millimeter slug and three shell casings. The imprint *VZ* stands for Van Zandt, a special-type bullet manufactured in the Netherlands."

Coogan extracted each item and studied it clinically, as a surgeon would examine a wound.

"I'm fairly familiar with this stuff," he said. "Pretty lethal artillery."

"Understand it's illegal." Raimondi paused for several seconds. "But where would I go to purchase several rounds?"

"Plan to do some hunting?" Coogan, a cautious IRA man, answered a question with a question.

"No. Keep it to yourself, Vinnie"—he leaned even closer to Coogan—"but a client of mine was shot at with this stuff a few days ago."

"Is he still around?"

"Yeah, *she's* still around."

A sly leprechaunish smile etched the corners of Coogan's mouth. He understood the dodge.

He cleared his throat. "Well, there's a guy down in Providence—can't give you his name, y'understand, but I could put you two in touch."

Raimondi nodded.

"Runs a legit rod and gun shop for anglers, hunters, NRA guys, and weekend warrior groups—you know, lawyers who dress up in OD fatigues and play soldier with rubber bullets. Well, he can get hold of any kind of stuff—stuff even the National Guard can't requisition."

"Vinnie, if I go down there myself, even if you vouch for me, I'm liable to spook him. I really don't want duplicate rounds. What I need is to try to trace these bullets. I've got to find out who in the Boston area purchases this kind of stuff."

Coogan thought for a few moments.

"Not easy, Manny. You want my supplier to rat on his customers." He paused and let it sink in. "Not easy."

"I've got another grand for your trouble." Raimondi patted his jacket pocket.

"I'll have to cook up a good story," Coogan said. "My source isn't stupid, and it's risky. Might be steppin' on some unfriendly toes."

"Here." Raimondi extracted the other envelope. "Again for the cause. And if you're successful, my client will see to it that another grand comes your way."

"Can't make any promises, mind you," Coogan said as he slid the envelope into his inside pocket. "I'll see what I can do."

"Hey, Vinnie, that's all my client asks."

Coogan blessed himself, then moved out into the aisle. He genuflected and bowed toward the altar.

"Vinnie," Raimondi said, "I think I'll stay and say a few prayers."

Coogan was about to move off toward the exit. He leaned back toward the pew, his cheeks bunched into a sly smile.

"That client of yours, Manny. T'wouldn't be a certain Boston barrister, would it now?"

"Sure'n what makes ye think that?" Raimondi imitated Coogan's brogue. Their eyes held momentarily. Each understood the other perfectly. No one was "BS-ing" anyone.

●

"I see some improvement in Donna's neurological status," Dr. Sagall said as he snapped the MRI onto the X-ray viewer. "We haven't the new stereoscopic viewers that they have at St. Anne's, but the clarity of these studies is most remarkable."

Sagall dimmed the overhead lights.

"Here." He clicked on a tiny arrow-tipped pointer light and zeroed in on the radiolucent images. "The hemorrhagic areas noticed at the base of the ventricles have been completely absorbed. That doesn't mean that brain tissue hasn't been destroyed, but the lesions noted previously have been circumscribed, and no further deterioration is detected." The arrow light traced the outlines of the brain's ventricles.

Sheridan listened intently.

"Once brain tissue dies, it's gone forever," Sagall said. "It doesn't regenerate like skin, or even broken bones. But as Jensen said before, other parts of the brain can take over.

"We still haven't been able to get her to communicate, but she does react to painful stimuli, tickling, and even touch.

"Separate pathways run up the spinal cord and transmit their own particular sensations to the brain. Proprioception, the ability to orient the body in space, is mediated by the posterior columns of the spinal cord, pain by what we call the spinothalamic tract, thermal sensation by the— I don't want to get too technical, but the mere fact that Donna can appreciate certain sensations means that the part of the brain that can integrate and discern is viable."

"Doctor, may I make a suggestion?"

Sheridan could follow the doctor's explanation, due to his own study of neuroanatomy, but he wanted to try to bridge the communication gap.

"Certainly," the doctor said. "We need all the help and input we can get."

"Donna communicates with me and not with medical personnel. Why?"

At that precise moment, a light sent a signal from somewhere in the recesses of Sheridan's mind. He puzzled over it briefly, then dismissed it.

"I think," he continued, "that Donna perceives people dressed in white—and that goes for doctors and nurses both— as inimical to her best interests. She equates white with her catastrophe, thinks that's what led to her condition. Again, Doctor, I'm no neurologist, but I've studied Lord Russell Quigley's book *Principles of Neuroanatomy. . . ."*

" 'A little learning is a dangerous thing.' " Sagall smiled patiently.

"I know—Alexander Pope," Sheridan said. "But a lawyer's got to bone up on the subject matter at hand, so that's what I'm doing.

"But why not come up with me? Get rid of your white jacket and the stethoscope—and have the nurses dress in pink when they attend her."

"Pink?"

"I saw the candy stripers in pink tunics; the receptionist has a pink jacket. I think Donna will respond."

"I think you're trying to make the *New England Journal of Medicine*, Mr. Sheridan." Dr. Sagall permitted himself a tolerant smile.

—

Dr. Sagall, arms folded, stood in the back of the room as Sheridan approached Donna. There was an immediate fluttering of her eyelids; Donna's brown eyes pooled with tears. There was a slight quivering of her mouth.

"Donna, it's me, Dan Sheridan." He picked out a yellow rose from the bouquet he had brought with him. He stood to one side and held the rose up slightly. Her eyes sought him out.

"I'm going to put these on your night table." He adjusted the flowers. "I have my friend with me, Mr. Sagall." Sheridan's eyes trained on Donna's, just a foot away.

"We're going to bring you back, Donna. Do you hear me? If you do—" She blinked her eyes. Sheridan held his breath and glanced over his shoulder at Sagall. The doctor nodded.

The communication continued for several minutes.

"Can you see the sunlight on the walls? . . . Do you like the peach pastels? . . ." Trivial stuff—but each question elicited an answer.

Sheridan kissed Donna on the forehead. Tears streamed down her cheeks. Again her mouth quivered as though she was trying to say something.

"I'll be back," he said. "Donna, you're going to be all right."

—

"I'm not sure I can replace the Dan Sheridan figure," Sagall said as he walked Sheridan to the hospital foyer, "but we'll adopt your suggestions. See what develops neurologically."

"I've got Donna's trial coming up soon." Sheridan paused at the electronic doors. "Do you think she could be transported down to Boston to testify—I mean in her limited way—at her own trial? I'll need your permission, of course."

Sagall shook his head.

"You'd be putting her at a grave risk, Counselor. I know you want her for the dramatic impact in front of the jury.

"I'm not a lawyer, mind you, but isn't there some sort of procedure where you can videotape the patient, show what she has to go through? We've done that here before. And don't you think the jury would feel that your wheeling her in with all the emergency trappings and attendants would be . . . er, a little un-dignified?"

Sheridan reluctantly agreed. "I guess you're right."

"If it's any consolation, Mr. Sheridan, your observation about changing the colors worn by the medical personnel while attending Donna will be put into practice immediately. Color is important to the human mind. Psychologically, black and white project opposite images. But here I think Donna connotes white with evil. Not that black would be a hell of an improvement. Pink, apricot—not exactly pigments Raphael would use—but we'll give it a shot."

Sheridan felt good as he sped along the Daniel Webster Highway, headed for the Massachusetts border. With every visit, he saw an improvement. And he had to agree with Sagall—it would appear tacky to wheel Donna DiTullio into the courtroom and place her in front of the jury. They could easily be turned off. Sagall's suggestion was more tasteful and would be more effective. He'd get Raimondi up in a week's time to film a day in the life of Donna DiTullio. Graphically and dramatically, this could melt any jury.

The beeper signaled a call on the car phone.

"Yeah?" Sheridan picked up the phone, keeping his eye on the stream of red taillights in front of him.

"Dan, it's Judy. Where are you?"

"Just outside Nashua, maybe ten miles from the border."

"Can you pull over to the side of the road?"

"What? I'm in four-lane traffic—the height of the rush hour. . . . What is it, Judy?"

"Keep your eyes on the road, Dan. What I've got to tell you isn't—"

"Come on, Judy, for chrissakes!"

A few seconds went by.

"I just got a call from Anna DiTullio."

"Yeah?"

"Dante DiTullio slammed into a tree on the VFW Parkway this afternoon."

"*What?*"

"He's dead."

30

S heridan addressed Judge Samuels. "Your Honor, I'm in no
shape to impanel a jury and start trial. All I'm asking is a
sixty-day continuance. It's bad enough that my client Mrs.
DiTullio has to cope with her daughter's tragedy and the trauma
of a full-fledged trial—but she's just buried her husband."

Samuels went through a predictable ritual. He measured a
glass of water from a silver decanter, pretended to take a few sips,
rocked back and forth in his chair, took off his glasses so he
could use them as a pointer, furrowed his brow, then looked down
from his perch as if he were some divine lawgiver.

"Mr. Sheridan, you and your clients commenced suit. They
were the ones who chose to be here, not the defendants. Sure,
any trial, criminal or civil, is not a high school play. The events
are often tragic, loaded with psychological pitfalls, involving roles
played out by real people. When you were last before me, you
gave me your assurance that on this current date you would be
prepared to go forward."

"Your Honor, unusual circumstances intervened. I'm sure
if you addressed defendant's counsel, she would pose no objection." He glanced over his shoulder and met Mayan d'Ortega's

implacable gaze. Not a nod, nothing. No help there. But Sheridan knew Samuels was making him sweat a little. And if worse came to worst, he would buttress Anna DiTullio as best he could and start impaneling a jury; then he'd put all the defendants on the witness stand and cross-examine them for several days. And then he'd lead with Dr. Shirley Wray, his economist, put on Dr. White to explain the medical misconduct, run the videotape of Donna DiTullio, have Dr. Sagall chronicle her injuries, the care she would require, and what the future held. Before they got around to Anna, a good ten trial days would be consumed, the battle would be joined, and Anna would have had the opportunity of watching the give-and-take of the courtroom infighting, and she'd know what was expected of her.

"All right," Judge Samuels said as he checked his calendar. "I won't give you sixty days. The trial will commence on Monday, January thirteenth. And, Mr. Sheridan, there will be no further continuances. Do I make myself clear?"

Sheridan rose. "Perfectly, Your Honor."

"And let me see both counsel at sidebar," the judge said, interrupting his clerk, who was about to read the closing statement.

Sheridan waited and extended his hand courteously so that Mayan d'Ortega would be first at the bench. She nodded a thank-you.

"Are there any preliminary matters pending, depositions, motions in limine, things like that?" Samuels stood and looked down at both of them.

"We had scheduled depositions of Mr. and Mrs. DiTullio, Your Honor," Mayan d'Ortega said. "In view of the circumstances, we'll reschedule Mrs. DiTullio. Say, in twenty days?"

"I'll check with my client, Judge," said Sheridan. "I'm sure that will pose no problem."

"Now that I have both of you together," the judge said, "and knowing what a case like this can cost—both economically and psychologically—as you both know, a settled case is the best case." His voice was soft, paternalistic.

"Have you two tried to get together, reach some sort of agreement?" Samuels leaned down from the bench, again tilting his head and peering at them over his glasses.

"There have been some discussions, Your Honor," Mayan d'Ortega said. "We made what we deem a reasonable offer, but—"

"How far apart are you?" Samuels would now assume the role of headbanger.

"Miles, Judge," Sheridan said, glancing over at d'Ortega. Her perfect black eyebrows arched slightly, but her look offered no openings.

"C'mon now, there's no case that can't be settled. It'll take a little give-and-take. Numbers"—he snapped his fingers noiselessly—"give me the numbers. Maybe I can prod you two—and then this case can be settled right here and now."

Sheridan placed both hands on the judge's bench as he looked up at Samuels.

"Judge," he said, "my young lady will be bedridden and institutionalized for the next forty years. . . ."

"C'mon, c'mon, Mr. Sheridan, you're not in front of a jury. Cut the histrionics. Let's lay the cards on the table—what's the offer and what's the demand? Ms. d'Ortega?"

"Three hundred thousand dollars, Your Honor."

Samuels rocked back in his chair and his mouth flattened into a "that's not too bad" position.

Sheridan was about to speak, but Samuels cut him off.

"Now, don't give me that 'she's going to live the next forty years entombed in her own body' stuff. If your client dies, the case dies. You're not naïve, Mr. Sheridan. Boston juries are conservative. No one's giving them a handout, and some jurors will be as hard up as your client, trying to feed a family, not knowing where the next buck is coming from. That's why they don't object to jury duty—collect thirty dollars a day from the county.

"Let me see what I can do. You got any leeway on that three hundred, Ms. d'Ortega?"

"Certainly, Your Honor. But I have no indication that Mr. Sheridan will be reasonable."

"Yes, I see." Samuels nodded in agreement. "No sense bidding against yourself. Look, I don't like to intervene like this, but this case should be settled, believe me, for everyone's sake. Suppose I recommend, Ms. d'Ortega, that you go back to Charlie Finnerty and tell him I told you to double the offer. I know, Charlie will kick and scream, but tell him I want him to put six hundred thousand on this case." The judge's blackberry eyes glittered as if he'd finally found the secret formula for judicial resolutions.

D'Ortega gave Sheridan an inquiring sideways look.

"I'm not interested, Judge," Sheridan said emphatically.

"*What*?" Samuels seemed to recoil.

"My price is twenty million."

Samuels shook his head. "You know, Sheridan, you're not thinking of your client. A law case isn't a lottery or a crapshoot. . . .

"Let me tell you something. Last big case tried before me, guy was a quadriplegic, an automobile rollover case. Sued a target defendant, big Japanese manufacturer. Guy was even a veteran. It was about a year ago.

"Jury came back on Pearl Harbor day, December seventh. There was a million bucks on the table. Like you, Sheridan, the attorney turned it down. Jury came back with a big fat goose egg!" Samuels formed a circle with his thumb and forefinger.

Sheridan remembered the case. He had caught segments of the trial, trying to gauge Samuels's judicial demeanor. And he remembered that Samuels, in his charge to the jury, had practically railroaded the plaintiff out of the courtroom. Trying to curb his indignation, he counted to five.

"Judge," he said, "these things happen. All my little girl asks in this case, all I ask, is an even playing field, a fair shake."

It took a few moments, but the barb stung.

"All right," Samuels said. His voice was mild, but with a frosty undertone. "I'll not try to intercede again." He sat down and gave Sheridan a dismissive wave.

"January thirteenth. I expect both sides to be ready for trial!"

—

Raimondi again met with Coogan, the undertaker, in the last pew of St. Rocco's Church. Coogan knelt for a while, holding his battered gray fedora in his hands over the seatback. He looked around cautiously; the church was vacant. Only the flickering votive candles disturbed the tomblike stillness.

Coogan mouthed a few more prayers, blessed himself, then settled back in the pew, resting his fedora on his lap.

"I ran into a bit of a snag," he whispered, cupping his hand over his lips.

Raimondi could almost guess what was coming.

"I couldn't get the actual list, and that's understandable, what with the feds always snooping around, but I did get some dope that might be of value to your client. . . ." Coogan paused several seconds. "Cost me the money you advanced. Had to give it to my source."

"That happens," Raimondi whispered back.

"It'll cost you another two G's."

"How reliable is the information?" Raimondi reached into his pocket and extracted a folded envelope.

"Most reliable," Coogan said, his voice ratcheted up into a stage whisper.

"Okay," Raimondi said, taking a peek into the envelope. He then gave it a little shake in Coogan's direction.

"I got the names of five buyers who are into this kind of stuff." Coogan removed the plastic packet containing the spent ammo from his coat pocket and shook it, imitating Raimondi. "All named Smith and Jones, mind you."

"What the hell!" Raimondi shoved his envelope back into his pocket.

"Wait, wait a minute." Coogan grabbed Raimondi's sleeve. "One guy's name *is* John T. Smith."

"This some kinda joke, Vinnie?"

"The envelope. You actually got twenty big ones in there?"

"What if I do?"

"Well, my source told me something else. John T. Smith isn't his real name."

"Really? Not his real name?" Raimondi rolled his eyes. "What is this, Twenty Questions?"

"Look," Coogan said, "nobody buys illegal stuff in their own name. You buy a bazooka and the feds will be banging at your door before sunset. The John T. Smith you're looking for is named McGinley Browne." Coogan spelled it: "B-r-o-w-n-e with an *e*."

"That's a complete dead end, Vinnie, and you know it. How about the other Smiths and Joneses?"

"Look, I'm not playing games with you. I think ya gotta concentrate on Browne. First name's McGinley."

"What's the Browne guy's address?"

"That's what's so interesting." Coogan grinned. "Monsieur Browne lives in Cambridge, not far from Harvard University. He's the caretaker of a manse owned by a prominent Boston doctor. Seems this doctor is quite a marksman, big outdoors kind of guy, infantry bird colonel in the National Guard."

Nothing else was needed, no notations, no slips of paper. The two exchanged a knowing look. The contract, if there was a contract, was sealed. Raimondi passed over the envelope and Coogan gave him the plastic packet.

"Tell me, Vinnie," Raimondi said, "how did you narrow down the Smiths and Joneses? I'm sure your source's clientele must have included some local mobsters, maybe some international sportsmen with Irish lineage."

"Same way you came up with the twenty Ben Franklins. How did you know? It was right on the button. Don't even have to count it." Coogan patted his pocket.

"Maybe we're both telepathic."

"Maybe," Coogan said, getting up and straightening the brim of his fedora.

"Good doing business with you, Manny." He slid out of the pew, genuflected, blessed himself twice, then moved off toward the church exit.

McGinley Browne. Not a name Raimondi would forget.

Maybe he'd tell Sheridan, maybe not. First thing to do is run down this Browne guy.

⬤

"I must tell you, Anna," Sheridan said to Anna DiTullio in his office, "that the offer in your case officially stands at *three hundred thousand dollars*, and it's our considered opinion that this should be rejected. It's ludicrous, really."

Anna DiTullio was wearing a black dress, but, unlike her appearance on previous visits, she now wore pearl earrings, a touch of apricot lipstick, and soft mauve eye shadow. The deep crescents under her eyes were still there, but their purple color had been disguised by creamy makeup. Sheridan realized that with Dante's death, a heavy anvil had been lifted from her drooping shoulders.

"Whatever you say, Mr. Sheridan," she said meekly.

"We're probating Mr. DiTullio's estate." Sheridan glanced at papers laid out on his desk. "Seems he had no life insurance. You have a heavy mortgage and no tangible assets."

"I know. Only this law case."

"Unfortunately, Anna, a lawsuit isn't a tangible asset. You can't borrow against it. Might be best to put your home on the market, move to an apartment. Then, if we get this case resolved, we'll be in a better position to advise you economically, and, more particularly, discuss what's best for Donna. Right now, she's getting the best medical care possible."

"I'm afraid Donna's care is going to be very expensive," Anna DiTullio said timidly.

"Let's not worry about that now. The medical examiner ruled Dante's death accidental. Apparently, he fell asleep, went off the road, and crashed into a tree."

"Yes, but he left a note. I have it right here." Anna reached into her purse and passed the folded piece of paper to Sheridan. "I found it the day after Dante was killed. He left it in Donna's bedroom." Anna started to sob.

Sheridan read it, one line on scratch paper.

"Donna, Anna, I love you. Dad."

Sheridan ripped the note into shreds and threw it into his wastebasket.

"The medical examiner ruled the death accidental. Let's keep it that way.

"Now, let's spend a few hours going over the questions you'll be asked at your deposition. I know Mayan d'Ortega. She's the young lady lawyer who will be asking the questions. She's thorough, a tigress, really. It could get kind of messy. I know some things you were unaware of."

"Oh?"

"What was your maiden name, Anna? You look kinda Irish to me."

"Mother was a Steinmetz. Came from Lancaster, Pennsylvania. You know, Pennsylvania Dutch." A wistful smile played upon her lips.

"Father was a Casey. Yes"—she nodded—"Irish. Worked for a brewing company in Hershey, not far from Lancaster."

"Pretty good combination. Mother Amish?"

Again the slight smile. She nodded.

"This lawyer, d'Ortega, she's a Mexican Indian. Had a white father. She's going to get into some pretty sordid stuff between Donna and Dante. She'll interrogate you on this . . . er, unpleasantness."

"I know all about it," Anna said quietly.

Sheridan was taken aback for a few moments, but, like the airline pilot warning his passengers about bumpy weather, he put his positive spin on it.

"I discussed the situation with Dante. This Sexton guy had Donna on tape—so-called therapy sessions. I got the tape suppressed as evidence and Dante said the allegations were completely untrue."

Anna DiTullio's voice was as far away as her gaze.

"They were true," she said.

●

"Irv, Charlie Finnerty here. Understand that Sheridan guy is impossible." Finnerty flicked some ashes from his cigar onto his desk ashtray.

Samuels didn't exactly relish Finnerty's call. He prided himself on being a legalistic prick—but an independent legalistic prick. Nobody told him what to do, how to rule—not even Governor Stevenson. But he knew that Charlie Finnerty had even more clout than the governor, and Charlie had gotten him his job. Chits and favors, that's what it was all about. And Irv Samuels never pretended to be St. Thomas More, nor did Charlie Finnerty, even though Charlie had been given the Thomas More Award from Boston College—bestowed by the cardinal, no less.

"I tried to talk some sense into him," Samuels said, "but he's a loose cannon—a real maverick. I recommended to Mayan d'Ortega that you double the offer. He still wants twenty million."

Finnerty took another puff on his cigar.

"He's goddamned ridiculous. We've got the best experts in the world to say Sexton, Puzon, and Lafollette did nothing wrong."

Samuels thought for a moment.

"You withdrew your opposition to Sheridan's motion to suppress the Sexton tapes. Why? In front of a jury, evidence like that is dynamite, like the Fuhrman tapes in the O.J. case. You have to consider the makeup of Boston juries. What do we have here? Eight hospitals, six teaching, four medical schools. Every juror has a connection or a relative working at a hospital, be it a nurse, a volunteer, or a laundry worker. Believe me, in the medical confraternity at every level, there's a sense of family, belonging. A doctor can cut the wrong leg off and juries will give him the 'to err is human' benediction. Juries want to acquit, want to find for the doctor, the healer, the hospital—just give them something to hang their hats on. It's a question of trial strategy."

"Mayan was against using the tapes, Irv, thought it might show that Sexton was countenancing a felony—running up his bill. You know how Sheridan could put a spin on it."

"Not with me ruling and charging the jury. Look," Samuels said, trying to even the score in the favors department, "if you want to reopen the motion on the Sexton tapes, I can make a favorable ruling. . . ."

"Let me think about it, Irv. That could be our fallback position."

"What will it *really* take to settle this case? Maybe I can again lend my judicial assistance."

"This case should be settled," Finnerty began.

"I know. What'll it take?"

"If we offer a million dollars, Sheridan won't take it. And he'll recommend that the DiTullio broad turn it down. She'll go along."

Charlie took a few more puffs on his Primera Macanudo and ground it into the ashtray.

"I've talked to Monsignor Devlin and Sister Agnes Loretta. She heads up St. Anne's. The magic price is two point one million dollars. We don't want to throw that out right now, Irv. No sense bidding against ourselves."

"You think Sheridan will go for that?"

"Of course not. But he's got to take it up with his client. Mayan d'Ortega's going to put her through the meat grinder. She'll get into the incest stuff—and we've talked to the medical examiner on Dante DiTullio's death. It's ruled accidental, but we gave him Sexton's tapes. Now the examiner believes it could have been suicide. I'll let you know after Mayan deposes Mrs. DiTullio. As I said, she's going into the incest stuff—and whether Dante left a suicide note. Mrs. DiTullio told the authorities that there was nothing."

"Two point one million, Charlie." Samuels chuckled. "Aren't you being a bit overgenerous? Wasn't it Pope Leo XIII who said, 'You must be just before you are generous'?"

"You always were a legal scholar, Irv. . . . And speaking of legal scholars, I was talking to Governor Stevenson the other day. There's going to be an opening on our supreme court when Damian Cabot reaches retirement age. That's in a short ten months. . . ."

31

Manny Raimondi didn't cue in Sheridan, not even Buckley, on his contact with Coogan. He checked the voter registration list at Cambridge City Hall—sure enough, McGinley Browne, age fifty-seven, listed his occupation as caretaker, 1340 Charles River Parkway. Another record check disclosed 1340 was owned by Robert M. Sexton, M.D.

The next morning promptly at six, Raimondi drove his '83 black Toyota along Storrow Drive, took a right turn at Harvard Stadium, and drove slowly past Sexton's residence. It was a chill morning, as the gray waters of the Charles caught the first glint of sun rising over the granite and glass prisms of downtown Boston.

Sexton's manse, a white Georgian colonial with chocolate brown shutters, was surrounded by a six-foot redbrick wall. A wrought-iron entrance gate looked formidable; an electronic call box was embedded in one of the brick pillars. Security seemed to be extensive. A crushed peastone driveway arched up to a porticoed front entrance. The lawn was well manicured, trees and bushes carefully clipped and groomed. There was a rustic charm about the place, typically wealthy New England, typically Harvard professional.

Raimondi made a turn at the Fellsway Circle and eased into a parking space some hundred yards from Sexton's estate. A few joggers loped past, and the Harvard crew made their way down the nearby boathouse ramp, carrying an eight-oar scull over their shoulders. Through his binoculars, Raimondi watched them launch their boat and glide downriver, their oars skimming the leaden surface of the Charles, a young woman coxswain bending forward, counting off the strokes.

His focus returned to the Sexton residence as he trained his high-resolution binocs on the front gate. He surveyed the wall again from front to back. Over the years, Raimondi had gained entrance to various secluded and protected places—motel rooms, homes, office buildings—legally, illegally, sometimes by charm, sometimes by chicanery. This one wasn't going to be easy. He knew Sexton was a bachelor, and McGinley Browne was the caretaker, but beyond those meager facts, he knew little else. Sexton appeared the type who would have a houseguest, maybe two or three. There had to be live-in help, besides Browne. Place was probably wired—might even be attack dogs.

At 7:15, the gate swung open and an ivory Cadillac emerged, driven by a middle-aged black driver wearing a green jacket and a visored chauffeur's cap. Raimondi figured it was McGinley Browne. The passenger in the back was obscured, engrossed in a newspaper. Had to be Sexton.

Raimondi knew this would have to be a one-shot deal. The odds were long, but would never be shorter. It was now or never.

Breaking and entering could get him twenty years. And he'd have a lame explanation. But the possible advantages outweighed the risk. He knew effective alarm systems were tapped into the nearest police precinct. But he had checked that out. Even if he set off an alarm, he had ten minutes' getaway time. The nearest cops were fifteen minutes away. And he had clocked this foray for rush-hour traffic. He again surveyed the grounds. If the place was triggered, he could beat a fast retreat, slip into the early-morning traffic, head toward Harvard Square, and disappear.

He laced up his Adidas sneakers, donned a gray sweatshirt, pulled a black knit watch cap down just above his ears, took the bag that contained his "tool kit" from the dashboard compartment, and walked briskly toward the wall. He waited a moment until two coeds with Harvard logos on their sweatshirts ambled past; then he followed the fence toward the rear of the grounds. Fortunately, there were no homes or other buildings to his left, just a parklike setting. He tossed his tool kit over the wall, then scaled it, landing in a clump of rhododendron bushes. He remained motionless for almost a minute. No alarms, no barking dogs. He picked up his bag and ran to the side of the house. Again, except for the drone of traffic along the Riverway, there wasn't a sound. So far so good.

He felt his way to the back of the building, again hugging the clapboards, as though he were breaking out of Stalag 17. The backyard was a replica of an English garden, and for a moment Raimondi took in the general design of the place: the rose beds, newly covered with salt marsh; the birches, their stark white branches fingering the sky; rows of azaleas bedding down for the winter; a small frog pond spanned by an arched stone bridge. Sexton had old-world taste or an exceptional gardener, Raimondi had to admit.

Raimondi snapped on a pair of latex gloves, examined the back door's lock, then fingered the glass panel for signs of wiring. Nothing visible. He checked the door—plain red frame. No storm doors were yet in place. He looked at his watch—7:40. He'd consumed two minutes.

He pulled out a thin wire from his bag. The spring lock was conventional; should be easy to pick. But he knew this could trigger an alarm. He selected a sharp rotor and proceeded to cut out a panel of glass, lifting it out carefully. Only took half a minute. He reached in and turned the inner doorknob. The door opened. No alarms, no shrieking maids, no barking dogs. He took out a tube of glazier glue—fine stuff—quickly applied it, and replaced the glass panel. It would take an expert to discover the mending.

He made his way through the kitchen—fine. There were dishes in the sink. No cook—maybe she had gone back to bed

He tiptoed through the living room and stopped a moment

to get a sense of the floor plan. As he made his way to the front door, he could hear a radio or a television coming from upstairs. It was playing music, a definite Latin beat. That had to be the maid.

Raimondi looked around. The house was old, perhaps a hundred years. The hallway had pegged flooring, cypress ceiling beams, and white stucco walls. He checked the dining room beyond and the oak-paneled library. Then he spotted a closed door—locked. Had to be Sexton's den. Again, he fingered the wall next to the door frame. Seemed okay. He got out his thin wire file and edged it into the brass aperture. A few clicks. To Raimondi, it was a piece of cake. He listened for a moment. The tango was still playing upstairs.

The den was typical rod and gun. Mahogany wainscoted walls displaying photos of Sexton with his National Guard unit, others in Africa, one of Sexton, complete with Jungle Jim outfit and safari hat, with several grinning Masai tribesmen, kneeling over a dead buffalo.

Then he spotted the gun rack. The weapons were neatly stacked, stocks highly polished, fine wood grain, dark blue metal shafts. He checked each quickly. The Bauer was a 7-mm, had fittings for laser and infrared sights. Others—a Beretta, Mausers, Brownings—were of different calibers. Raimondi wanted to lift the Bauer, but the rack had a cylindrical combination lock. It looked complicated, and he was running out of time.

Next, he checked the drawers. In one was a series of gun sights—telescopic, infrared. The other drawers contained ammunition boxes—Remingtons, Magnums, Smith & Wessons, and—*bingo!*—a box of Van Zandts, all carefully tiered. He counted the Van Zandts—eighteen. Six were missing. He extracted one and slipped it into his pocket. Another check of his watch. He had consumed eleven minutes. Time to get the hell out.

He relatched the den lock, closing the door gently, and turned toward the kitchen. He could hear mariachi music blaring away, lots of guitars, pretty loud. He opened the back door and again hugged the side of the house. He scampered toward the wall, first tossing his tool kit over, then bounding up, gripping the top, hoisting himself over, and landing feet first on the other side. He snapped off the gloves and the black knit cap and shoved them into his pocket, picked up his tool kit, and walked briskly toward his car. He avoided eye contact with several joggers. The entire operation had taken fourteen minutes. No sirens. With relief, he eased the Toyota into the early morning traffic.

—

"Danny me boy." Charlie Finnerty greeted Sheridan as he sat with Anna DiTullio in the sumptuous waiting room outside Charlie's office. Like an undertaker, Charlie quickly revised his waxy smile into a proper look of bereavement when Sheridan introduced him to Mrs. DiTullio. He shook her gloved hand.

"I'm sorry for your troubles, Mrs. DiTullio," he said. "You've had your share of tragedy. I wish things were different."

Anna DiTullio nodded lamely.

"The steno is setting up her equipment now, and Mayan is with her in the conference room. We'll try to make this as short and as easy as possible," Finnerty said.

"Er, Dan," Finnerty added, "let me see you a moment. Would you mind stepping into my office?"

"Okay. Anna, would you excuse me for a minute? I'll be with you shortly."

"Dan," Finnerty said, "let's cut the playacting. Mayan filled me in on all the gibberish before Judge Samuels. A judge gives me some advice, Dan, I usually take it. I've been around a lot longer than you; tried a lot more cases."

"I'm sure you have, Charlie. Way I heard it, you didn't win too many."

Finnerty's creamy smile turned into a smirk. He shook his head.

"Dan, I don't appreciate your insults. After all, we're all members of the bar. There's a certain code of civility, of collegiality; we should comport ourselves as professionals."

"What are you trying to say, Charlie?"

"Okay, Dan. I talked with Monsignor Devlin, Sister Agnes

Loretta, and claims manager Crimmins. We think we can win the case."

"That figures, Charlie. There are no ties in a lawsuit. Someone's going to win; someone's going to lose. And we're playing for a lot of marbles."

"Dan, let's cut the bullshit. What will it take to have Mrs. DiTullio sign releases right here and now, before Mayan puts her through the shredder?"

"Oh? I thought it was going to be short and easy."

"Look, Sheridan, right now I'm in a position to wind this thing up for a pretty substantial settlement. If we have to go to the mat, all bets are off. You know the score."

"How substantial?"

"Supposin', Dan, just supposin'—and this is all confidential—I make a recommendation, contingent of course on your making the same recommendation to your client. This is not an offer, mind you, but just supposin' I tell Crimmins to come up with a million dollars! We could structure the settlement so it could total out to three million over a twenty-year period, completely nontaxable. Keep Anna DiTullio in pretty good shape."

"I won't bullshit you, Charlie. One million is completely unacceptable. Make it nineteen million, nine hundred thousand and you got a deal."

Finnerty pressed his lips together and gave Sheridan a dismissive wave.

"It's your funeral," he said.

"Hey, Charlie, that's all I've been doing lately—going to funerals."

"You'd better take up the possible one million with Mrs. DiTullio. From what I hear, she's destitute. You want a few minutes with her before I let Mayan loose? I think you owe her that."

Sheridan didn't appreciate Finnerty telling him how to handle his own client or how to negotiate his trial strategy. He wanted to say something curt, but resisted the temptation.

"Thank you, Charlie," he said mildly. "You're truly magnanimous."

—

Sheridan ushered Mrs. DiTullio into the conference room, empty for the moment.

"Anna, please sit down for a few minutes before we get into the deposition." Sheridan pulled a leather swivel chair aside for her, then shut the door. Anna looked around nervously. The surroundings, compared with Sheridan's Spartan office, were intimidating.

"I just had a discussion with defense attorney Charlie Finnerty. In effect, he's offered a million dollars to settle the case. It's not actually on the table, but I know if you agree to take it, it will be paid."

"What do you say, Dan? I really don't know what to do. A million dollars is a lot of money."

"No question, Anna. The easy thing for me is to say take it. We can avoid a lot of messiness. This trial will be like guerrilla warfare." Sheridan looked deep into Anna DiTullio's weary eyes.

"But, Anna, one million's not enough to help Donna for long."

"What are our chances, Dan?"

"I'd say pretty good, better than fifty percent."

"Well, whatever you advise, Dan. You've guided me this far, and you say Donna's improving?"

"She's actually communicating with Dr. Sagall. She still blinks responses, but she's able to get through to the medical personnel. That's a big step.

"Sometimes in life, Anna, you have to make a stand. I think this is the time—for you, for Donna, and," he added quietly, "probably for myself.

"Now you just sit there and we'll go ahead with the deposition. You give the responses as truthfully as you can. Okay?"

"Okay." But somehow Anna's voice was frail, unsure.

—

Just as Mayan d'Ortega, Mary Devaney, and the court stenographer entered the conference room, Sheridan spotted Charlie Finnerty standing at the polished oak staircase. He pretended to be looking at a lawbook, but Sheridan knew he was biding his time, waiting for a reply.

Finnerty smiled guardedly. "Well, háve we got a deal?"

"We're closing the gap, Charlie," Sheridan said crisply.

"Now, you're not holding me up for more money. I'm going to bat for you for the one mil."

"I know, I know, Charlie. But you're offering an apple for an orchard. You've got a twenty-million-dollar liability policy. You add another nineteen million to your offer and we've got a deal."

"Nineteen?" Finnerty scoffed. "You're nuts, Sheridan, absolutely insane!"

"I know, I've been told that before."

Charlie closed his lawbook with an emphatic thud. He shook his head and stomped off toward his office.

———

Mayan d'Ortega's interrogation of Mrs. DiTullio was a work of art. She was soft at first, nodding in quiet understanding when Anna DiTullio was hesitant, quick to offer her a glass of water or to call a short recess when the witness began to break emotionally.

But Anna had been well schooled by Sheridan. She admitted that Dante DiTullio had sexually and physically abused her daughter. She held her own in gray areas. There were no surprise questions, *until* the last.

Mayan d'Ortega fixed Anna DiTullio with her intent dark eyes. "Mrs. DiTullio, did the medical examiner who ruled that Mr. DiTullio's death was accidental speak with you?"

"Yes," Anna DiTullio answered tentatively, "he did."

"Did he ask you if Mr. DiTullio left a note or anything that might indicate that he intended to take his own life?"

For a moment, Anna DiTullio looked uncertain, bereft. She stole a quick glance at Sheridan. D'Ortega noticed the subtle exchange.

Sheridan intervened. "I object to this line of questioning.

What you're asking her is completely irrelevant. What difference does it make to this case how Mr. DiTullio died?"

Sheridan was ready to meet a verbal onslaught from his adversary, but d'Ortega merely shrugged—it was a shrug that contained ancient origins. D'Ortega knew she was about to catch Anna DiTullio in a lie. And Sheridan knew it.

"I'll reserve on that question until time of trial," d'Ortega said almost too gently. "Thank you, Mrs. DiTullio, you've been most cooperative. And I'm awfully sorry for what you've had to go through."

—

After dropping Anna off at her home—and noticing a FOR SALE sign on the front lawn—Sheridan arrived back at the office a few minutes before six. Buckley and Judy had left, but Raimondi was there to greet him.

"How did the depo go?" Raimondi asked.

"It went as well as could be expected." Sheridan tried to dismiss d'Ortega's last question, but he knew he had booted it.

"C'mon in, Manny," Sheridan said. "I think we could both use a drink." He poured out straight bourbon in two Styrofoam cups, passing one to Raimondi.

"*Slainte agut!* as we say in Irish."

"*A sua saude!*" Raimondi raised the cup in a toast.

Sheridan drained his cup and poured another.

"I got something to show you, Dan." Raimondi nursed his drink as though it were a fine wine.

He removed two plastic bags from his jacket pocket.

"Here." He emptied the contents of one on Sheridan's desk.

"These are the cartridges and slug you dug up after the shooting. And . . . *here* is an identical Van Zandt bullet."

"Where did you get this?" Sheridan asked as he picked up the live round and examined it carefully.

"It cost me four grand." Raimondi nodded slightly. "But that bullet you're holding came from Dr. Robert Sexton's gun and ammo supply."

"How did you trace it to Sexton?"

"Let's just say I did."

"Okay. He gave it to you?"

"Again, let's just say I know it came from Sexton's armory."

Sheridan knew that Raimondi was very good at anything undercover, from tracing missing witnesses and deadbeat dads to finding lost pieces of evidence. And Sheridan seldom questioned Manny's methods.

"Hm." Sheridan picked up one of the spent cartridges and compared it to the live bullet. "No question, these are similar bullets," he said. "But without ballistic comparison, that doesn't prove that this bullet"—he shook the spent cartridge—"came from a gun owned by Sexton."

"No, it doesn't," Raimondi said, "but I happen to know Sexton owns ten rifles, and only one is a seven-millimeter—a German make—a Bauer."

"What are you suggesting?" As he eyed Raimondi, Sheridan expressed a mix of amusement and disbelief.

"Suppose we purchase Sexton's Bauer—in fact, his entire arsenal—for, say, thirty grand. I know a source that can set up a connection. Runs guns to the IRA."

"We're passing out money like penny candy." Sheridan shook his head. "No, Sexton would be suspicious. And what makes you think he'd want to sell? Why would someone, even in the IRA, want his entire arsenal? And those guns are registered. They could easily be traced. Sexton knows this."

"My source could assure him all markings and serial numbers would be effaced."

"No. Leave this stuff with me. I gotta figure this out. You run along, Manny. There are a few documents I've got to review."

"Here." Raimondi unzipped his jacket and reached into an inside holster and handed Sheridan a .32 Walther semiautomatic. "I think you're going to need this."

"I haven't got a permit."

"I'll take care of it," Raimondi said. "Here's the safety. Push it down to unlock." Raimondi demonstrated. "There're eight rounds in there ready to go."

Sheridan took the gun and ran his fingers along the blue-black grip. He hadn't held a gun in years. He had vowed he would never pick one up again. He passed the gun from hand to hand, feeling the heft of it. Time to break the vow.

He held the grip, checked that the safety was on, and his finger tugged gently at the trigger.

"Thank you, Manny," he said. "Guess maybe you're right."

Raimondi loosened his holster. "Put this on. The gun's really compact—hardly produces a bulge."

Raimondi was about to leave. "You sure you won't allow my source to see if he can't get ahold of Sexton's Bauer?"

Sheridan thought for a few moments.

"No, I really don't know if it was Sexton who tried to take me out."

"But the bullets—Van Zandts—aren't exactly BBs," Raimondi said. "And you got to sell your soul to get these babies, believe me. Circumstances add up to one person."

"I know," Sheridan said. "I'm sure that's what Marcia Clark told the O.J. jury.

"Something bothers me, Manny." Sheridan picked up the Walther and examined it again. "I've really got to figure this out myself."

"One other thing," Manny said as he reached into a paper bag on the floor at his feet. He pulled out a gadget that looked like a cross between a tuning fork and a charcoal-briquette lighter.

"When you get into your car tonight, open the hood, run this little gizmo around underneath, then bend down and run it underneath your car on both sides. This is spooky stuff—detects booby traps, mainly, but it can detect any wires that don't belong in the assemblage."

Sheridan again thanked Raimondi.

"You take off, Manny. I'll finish up here."

—

Sheridan had prepared questions for each defendant, and now he sat down to read over Dr. White's list of proposed interrogation topics. He worked them into his own legal hieroglyphics, his private symbols, and reduced them to a single yellow scratch-pad page. By the day of trial, he'd have these committed to memory so that he could call upon them instantly, discard some, improvise others, depending on answers elicited from witnesses on cross-examination.

He finished up at about nine and was going to put the gun and holster apparatus in his bottom drawer, but he thought the better of it. Whoever was after him wouldn't miss the next time around. He strapped on the holster, lifted the Walther, and slid it into place. He picked up Raimondi's gizmo, placed it in the paper bag, and headed out toward the elevators.

—

Raimondi waited in his Toyota until he saw Sheridan's TR6 emerge from the Beacon Street underground parking garage. He checked the late-night traffic. Nothing seemed unusual. He tailed along several car lengths behind Sheridan, again checking right and left and in the rearview mirror. His Rossi .357 Magnum was on the front seat beside him, the safety unlocked. He knew something was going to happen. Sheridan, like the night he was on patrol at Gia Dinh in Vietnam, was a sitting duck. But, unlike Vietnam, Raimondi could cover Dan. Maybe he could prevent a tragedy.

32

For the next several weeks, Sheridan and Buckley scrambled to get their evidentiary ducks lined up. They summarized and indexed the depositions and hospital records; had photo blowups made of St. Anne's interior, pinpointing where the group therapy session was held, the hallway leading to the Atrium, and shots of the exact location where Donna DiTullio jumped, from the ground floor up and vice versa. They contemplated using a three-dimensional model of the premises but then agreed that it might be overkill. The forty-thousand-dollar architectural fee also dictated budgetary caution.

Sheridan went up to Greenbriar for a day, taking Raimondi and a camcorder with him. Assisted by Greenbriar's medical staff, they made a series of shots, later edited down to a six-minute film, showing Donna DiTullio's present condition and her need for constant therapeutic and medical care, interspersed with clips of one of her championship tennis matches. The result was viscerally affecting and legally persuasive.

Sheridan knew that in the trial of a case, particularly a malpractice case, for every hour spent in the courtroom, ten hours of preparation were a necessity. And for an injured plaintiff to prevail, nothing could be left to chance; evidence had to be pluper-fect. Although the burden of proof in a malpractice case was the same as in any civil case, Sheridan knew that as a practical matter, his evidence had to be so strong that the scales in Donna DiTullio's favor would have to hit bottom. Juries, particularly Boston juries, were not going to castigate a healer. There almost always had to be a smoking gun or the defendant had to be caught in a gross lie, something even the most biased jury could not ignore.

While Buckley and Sheridan assembled documents and prepared a lengthy trial brief, Raimondi made a trip each morn-ing to Sexton's Riverway manse, waited at a safe distance in his Toyota, then tailed Sexton. During these weeks, the doctor seemed to follow a prescribed routine. His driver would drop him off at St. Anne's at approximately 7:30 A.M. and pick him up at 5:00 P.M. Except for four visits to Finnerty's Boylston Street of-fice, nothing seemed out of the ordinary.

Sheridan had let Buckley in on Raimondi's tracing the Van Zandts to Sexton. Buckley still thought they should go to the police, but Sheridan suspected that Raimondi had broken into Sexton's home; it would be tough to explain how he had obtained Sexton's ammunition. However, during the ensuing weeks, Sher-idan kept Raimondi's .32 Walther strapped to the hollow in his back. Also, each evening at the underground garage, he went through the Geiger routine with Raimondi's gizmo.

Sheridan became consumed with the case. Understandably, he hadn't gone jogging with Sheila again, and he made lame excuses for not seeing her. Luckily, she seemed to understand. This was the life of any trial lawyer; there were no second-place prizes in the courtroom. You won or you didn't eat. Occasionally, justice prevailed, and your client thought you were the greatest gladiator of the century, and your colleagues at the bar slapped you on the back and you picked up the tab. Some, feigning friend-ship and collegiality, secretly hated you for making a score. Judge Samuels made no pretense; he didn't like Sheridan or Buckley—period. And there was going to be no runaway verdict in his court.

He had given Finnerty his assurance. Although he rationalized otherwise, his thumb would be on the scales of justice.

—

The case was preempted by several criminal matters until Friday, and Sheridan, accompanied by young Buckley, met Charlie Finnerty and Mayan d'Ortega in courtroom 1206. Judge Samuels had requested a conference to iron out any differences and agree on items of evidence. That was the veneer. Finnerty, disturbed at Sheridan's cavalier and intransigent attitude on the subject of settlement, had called Samuels to set up the meeting. Samuels called it "conciliation," a soft legalistic euphemism for further judicial head banging. Finnerty wondered if Sheridan was holding an ace that he and d'Ortega didn't know about. Any other lawyer in Boston, even the best trial lawyer, would bend, negotiate, give a little, take a little.

And Finnerty had the odds stacked—Samuels was in his back pocket. Four of the most skilled psychiatrists on the Eastern Seaboard were ready to testify that the conduct of all defendants comported with good medical practice. Sheridan was suing the cardinal, Sister Agnes Loretta, three defendants with impeccable credentials. D'Ortega would tear Sheridan's expert apart in her courtly Mexican way. They had the transcript of every case in which Dr. White had testified—twenty-eight in the last five years. He had made over $200,000 for testifying in court. Not a bad supplement to seeing oddball patients. D'Ortega would work White like a matador works *el toro*, a skewer here, a pass there, until Sheridan's case finally toppled. In racetrack parlance, Finnerty felt it was a boat race. But something continued to nag at him. What was Sheridan's game?

The clerk, Kate McDonald, called the case.

"Judge Samuels will see all counsel in chambers," she said.

Charlie Finnerty left his bag at the counsel table. He'd let Mayan sift out the technicalities. But he was still disturbed. What in hell did Sheridan have up his sleeve?

—

"Well," Samuels said as he handed Kate McDonald his black robe, "nice to see all you combatants ready for trial.

"Kate," he said to his clerk, "would you go out and tell Bailiff Coyne to bring down a panel of sixty jurors. We'll give them their instructions and listen to their lamebrained excuses for opting off this case."

She nodded resignedly and left.

"Sit down, Ms. d'Ortega," Samuels offered. "Grab a seat, gentlemen, and let's go over some ground rules."

Mayan d'Ortega's black hair was now cut short, her smooth sepia skin shone, and, to Sheridan, her slanted Indian eyes seemed to have a Bengal gleam. For a moment, he was mesmerized by her beauty. "Tyger! Tyger! burning bright / In the forests of the night . . ." It was from a poem by William Blake that he had memorized in high school. He wondered, not for the first time, how d'Ortega would be in bed.

He was snapped out of his momentary reverie by Charlie Finnerty's cloying clichés.

"I think I can speak for both sides to this litigation, Judge. We feel honored to have a great lawman like yourself presiding as the trial judge."

Sheridan was tempted to leap to his feet and pull up his trouser cuffs and say, Boy, the crap's really starting to flow, but he merely nodded in quiet approbation. No sense in pissing off the judge before the trial even started.

Samuels acknowledged the elaborate accolade with a benedictive smile. "Well, I try, gentlemen, Ms. d'Ortega." He was careful to show no chauvinistic partisanship.

Buckley cupped his hand and whispered in Sheridan's ear, "You going along with this horseshit?" Sheridan said nothing. He knew there would be one last pitch by Samuels to settle the case. There was.

"You know, all of you are officers of the court," Samuels began. His voice had a familiar paternalistic ring. Sheridan had heard it many times from judges trying to force him to accept a plea bargain in a criminal case. He could almost lip-synch Samuels: "We owe a duty to these jurors," et cetera, et cetera.

"And before we start impaneling, I'm going to try, just one last time, to get you two together." He looked at d'Ortega, then at Sheridan. "I understand you've been offered a million dollars to settle this case. . . ."

"With all due respect, Your Honor," Sheridan said, "that's not quite accurate. Charlie said if I told him I'd accept a million, he'd see what he could do to get it." He glanced at Finnerty.

"Look, let's not quibble over rhetorical niceties. Mr. Sheridan, if I tell Mr. Finnerty to put a million on the table *right now*"—Samuels steepled his fingers into a pyramid and rocked back and forth in his chair—"will you accept it?"

"Judge, let me make myself perfectly clear. I'm all set for trial. We've worked our posteriors off on this case for the past several months. One million is a pittance. My girl—"

Samuels cut him short.

"Look, Sheridan, you've given me this bleeding-heart pitch every time I've tried to help you out. This trial's going to take at least three to four weeks. Not exactly the O.J. case, but these jurors are ordinary people who have to leave their homes and jobs for a lousy thirty dollars a day. As officers of the court, we owe a duty to these people."

Sheridan recognized the turning of the judicial screw. He was even amused by it.

"Judge," he said, "again with all due respect, the plaintiffs' case shouldn't be sacrificed to the economy of the Court's time or anyone else's."

"All right!" Samuels barked. "You're telling me that you're turning down a million dollars?"

"That's right, Your Honor."

"Okay." Samuels shook his head. "Let's go to work. We'll impanel a jury today! I'm sure it'll take us all day. Opening arguments begin at nine A.M. sharp Monday morning. We'll go straight through each day until four o'clock." He buzzed his clerk, Kate McDonald, on the intercom.

"Have the bailiff bring down the first panel of jurors."

Picking a jury is an art composed of hunches, instant recognition, sometimes luck, sometimes fool's play. Some trial lawyers were good at it. Most conceded it was a dice roll. A sheet listing the names, addresses, marital statuses, employment histories, and criminal records was issued to each counsel. In Massachusetts, there was no voir dire for a civil case, as there was in most states, where the attorney could probe into the background of jurors, pick up subtle indicia of bias or conformation that could help or hurt a client's cause. Although someone might profess total impartiality, bias—whether ethnic, economic, or cultural—is deeply ingrained. Each side tries to exploit or to guard against it. About half the panel of sixty jurors had been dismissed. Samuels listened to excuses, most legitimate hardship cases. One woman had three small children; two nurses said they couldn't be impartial, stating they felt there were too many malpractice cases. Others had sick aunts or mothers who required full-time care. Still others couldn't understand English well, were hearing-impaired, had been involved in unsuccessful lawsuits against hospitals or doctors, or disliked lawyers and admitted they couldn't be fair-minded.

Next came those with no excuse, who avowed that they could weigh the evidence with complete impartiality and saw no difficulty in sitting on the jury for three, maybe four, weeks. Each juror was called by a designated number.

Elizabeth Dolan, city of Revere, single, age forty-five, schoolteacher. As she took her place at seat number one, Sheridan assessed her quickly. Came from a tough neighborhood in Revere, he thought, Irish, not particularly attractive, could cut either way.

"What do you think?" he asked Buckley.

"The more women we have on this jury, the better for us," Buckley said. "No sense wasting a challenge. Keep Dolan."

"James Caprell Windsor the Third," the bailiff barked, "take seat number two." Windsor was nattily dressed in a dark blue tailored suit, Gucci Loafers, bright red tie. Mid-fifties, bank manager, divorced, lived on Beacon Hill.

"Scratch this guy," Buckley whispered. "He'd call in a note on his grandmother."

Sheridan agreed and put an X in the seat number two space on his diagram chart.

Twelve jurors and two alternates were finally seated. Among them were Alberto Vincenti, a longshoreman from East Boston; Dolores Andrews, who owned a boutique on fashionable Newbury Street; Rhea Dawkins, black, unemployed, single, with three children; Roberto Gonzalez, twenty-three, bicycle messenger.

"Keep Vincenti, Dawkins, and Gonzalez," Buckley whispered. Sheridan nodded agreement. They didn't want bankers, WASP Republicans, Newt Gingrich types; they wanted as many blacks, Hispanics, and poor people as possible people who had stood in lines, shopped with food stamps, who had been denied insurance coverage, who had generally been kicked around by the Establishment. These were the jurors Sheridan needed, but, of course, Charlie Finnerty and Mayan d'Ortega wanted just the opposite.

Seated in the back of the courtroom, handpicked by Charlie Finnerty, were two women psychologists from the state medical school, who specialized in assessing potential jurors who would favor the medical confraternity. These two women studied the jurors' rap sheets—noted each juror's demeanor as he or she raised a hand and took the oath of impartiality, then watched carefully as each walked toward the jury enclosure. They noted whether they slouched, walked briskly, whether there was any subtle recognition of either Sheridan or Buckley, or Mayan d'Ortega. And they knew what Sheridan wanted: Democrats, people on welfare, ordinary working stiffs, blacks, Hispanics, the unemployed.

Kate McDonald looked down at Sheridan and Buckley as they studied the information sheets once again and quickly assessed each juror. Without a voir dire, you had to trust your basic instincts.

"I challenge juror number two," Sheridan said to the clerk.

"James Caprell Windsor the Third, you have been challenged by the plaintiff," the clerk said. "Please step down." She then scrambled the slips in the jury-selection box and picked out another name.

"Pamela Watson," the clerk intoned, "please take seat number two, vacated by Mr. Windsor."

Watson was young, single, mid-twenties, attractive, a graduate of Dartmouth College.

"I'd get rid of the Ivy Leaguer," Buckley whispered. Sheridan glanced at his information sheet and noted that Watson had once been arrested for disturbing the peace at an abortion clinic. She was Waspish, all right, tall, springy blond hair. But to Sheridan, she looked feisty, probably a pro-choicer.

"No, we'll keep Watson," he said.

"The plaintiff is content with the jury as selected," Sheridan said, looking up at Judge Samuels.

Next, Charlie Finnerty, Mary Devaney, and Mayan d'Ortega huddled as they scoured the information sheets. Mayan quickly glanced through the front and back rows of jurors, making eye contact.

"May I take a moment, Your Honor?" Mayan d'Ortega requested.

"Certainly." Samuels nodded.

D'Ortega had twelve peremptory challenges—which meant she could reject a juror simply because he or she had red hair or she wasn't comfortable with the eye contact—again because of a hunch. One way or the other, this juror or that juror was pro- or anti-Establishment. And into this mix, she factored age, education, and ethnic background. She had already made her mind up to challenge Rhea Dawkins, the single black mother. She would retain Gonzalez. He was Hispanic; so was she.

"What do you think about the schoolteacher from Revere?" Mayan asked her two consultants. "Irish—I don't know."

"I think she'll be okay," one of the psychologists said. "She looks intelligent. I don't think she'll be swayed by emotion. She has a tough job teaching the eighth grade over in Revere."

"I agree," said the other psychologist.

"How about that Dartmouth grad?" d'Ortega said. "Mary and Charlie want to challenge her."

"No question about it," said the first psychologist. "She may be Ivy League, but there's something about her—she could take over the jury, and she has an arrest record. I wouldn't chance it."

But Mayan d'Ortega thought otherwise. She had a notion that she could win over Pamela Watson to her cause.

The give-and-take of challenging and reseating went on until midafternoon. Finally, both sides told the judge they were content.

Sheridan surveyed the final panel.

Not bad, he thought. Three blacks, two Hispanics, the Irish schoolteacher, an unemployed bartender from South Boston—a mug of an Irish face, looked as though he'd been kicked around a bit, wore the cauliflower ears of life—a tweedy professor type from Boston University, three working mothers, the boutique owner, the unemployed longshoreman, and Pamela Watson: twelve, plus two alternates. The judge would select the foreperson after he had charged the jury and just before they received the case for deliberation.

"All right." The judge turned and addressed the jury. "This is a very important case, and you have been selected to perform the highest civic duty anyone can be asked to perform in our free society. In most places in the world, there is no jury system. Even in England, civil cases like this are not heard by juries. You have been selected because you have no connection with any of the parties or their attorneys, and you have taken an oath to decide this case strictly on the evidence.

"This is Friday," he continued. "I want you to go home, and I admonish you, do not discuss this case with anyone, not with your spouse, not with any relative, not even with your best friend. We will commence each morning at nine A.M. and go through to one P.M. Lunch is on the Commonwealth. Bailiff Coyne will take you back and forth each day. We'll resume at two P.M., adjourn each day at four." Samuels nodded toward the bailiff, who was catching a few quick z's, but he snapped to attention when he heard his name. "Monday morning, we'll hear opening arguments from both counsel. Mr. Sheridan, plaintiffs' counsel, will address you first, and he will be followed by Ms. d'Ortega. Any questions?"

Sheridan studied each juror as Samuels went through his spiel. They were overly attentive, but he knew that could change. Jurors were only human—they could get bored easily, especially as the late-afternoon sessions droned on. He'd follow the trial lawyer's stratagem. Lead with your best evidence, even on cross-examination. Make it crackle; have it hit home early. And the jurors, having been inundated by the O. J. Simpson case, expected electricity. Sheridan would provide it. He looked back over his shoulder and glanced at d'Ortega. No slight smile flickered on her lips. Her tiger eyes now had a predatory focus.

33

Charlie Finnerty met Phil Reston, feature writer of the *Boston Tribune*, for drinks and dinner at the Bay Tower Room, one of Boston's more upscale dining establishments. On the thirty-third floor of the Sheraton Building, its bright mustard decor and polished brass pillars complemented the impressive sweep of Boston Harbor. Below, the historic Quincy Market district was alive with tourists, its acreage more visited than Disney World. The Old North Church, of Paul Revere fame, its white Bulfinch spire thrusting skyward, was a familiar landmark. And across the way on the Charlestown shore, *Old Ironsides*, the USS *Constitution*, its spars and bars illumined with tiny white lights, rode at quiet anchor.

Here Boston's shakers and makers came to dine. It was a place to be seen, to blow kisses, and, despite the white-gloved service, the view was more spectacular than the food.

Between the chilled Chardonnay and the lobster Savannah, Reston laid out the details for an article to run in the Sunday magazine section of the weekend edition.

"Want to thank you for the interview with Monsignor Devlin," Reston said as he dabbed his lips with the white linen napkin.

"I was happy to help," Charlie Finnerty said as he signaled the waiter for another bottle of wine.

"The editors feel it's the best thing we've done on the current malpractice crisis," Reston said. "We've interviewed the heads of the top hospitals in the state, and, of course, Governor Stevenson. We explained how an unfortunate judicial ruling prevented the St. Anne's case from coming under the aegis of the new charitable immunity cap on damages. And we're running an editorial Monday morning backing the governor's stance. We included a piece from Professor Saul Katz, who teaches at Harvard Law, backing Stevenson on the statute's constitutionality."

The waiter, in a white commodore's jacket with gold epaulets, poured the wine reverently. Charlie tasted it and nodded approval. Charlie knew it was a good French wine. At $125 a bottle, it had to be a vintage year.

"Phil, you're one of the best feature writers in the city," Finnerty said as they toasted each other. "You should be moving over to the *Globe* or the *Herald*."

"That's my ultimate goal," Reston said.

"I know quite a few people at both papers," Finnerty said as he unwrapped an after-dinner cigar and offered another one to his guest.

"No thanks, it hurts my drinking." Reston made a stab at being witty.

Finnerty pulled out his silver lighter, then fondled the fat Macanudo for a moment before lighting up.

No one, not even the tuxedoed maître d', was petty enough to disturb Finnerty by pointing out that he was seated next to a window in an area designated as *nonsmoking*. Finnerty was a good customer and known as a generous tipper. Thirty percent was his rule, especially when the expense could be passed on to a client.

●

"Son of a bitch!" Raimondi said as he read the *Tribune* article. "What a time for this to come out. Every juror will digest this nonsense."

He called Sheridan at home.

"Yeah, Sheila just left here," Sheridan said. "Dropped off the paper. She thinks I should ask for another continuance and impanel a new jury."

"This piece sure takes a negative stand against lawyers who handle malpractice cases," Raimondi said. "Calls them 'money-grubbing,' take any kind of case, trying to squeeze out settlements. . . . And Dan, I notice you were mentioned three times. Not libelous, mind you, but came goddamned close! And the members of the medical profession came off as icons. What a crock! When they kill and maim, everyone's supposed to look the other way."

"Well, I'll file a motion first thing tomorrow morning to question the jurors. The *Tribune*'s a tabloid, goes for the dirt, but unfortunately, everybody reads it."

"You think Samuels will grant a continuance?"

"Of course not. But we'll file anyway; take an immediate appeal to an adverse ruling."

"How about asking Samuels to quiz Finnerty, d'Ortega, and Devaney, find out whether any of them planted the story?"

Sheridan kicked off his slippers and put his feet up on the breakfast table.

"I'll file every motion in the book, but even in criminal cases, we have difficulty getting a change of venue based on pretrial publicity. And Samuels will suddenly turn into a First Amendment advocate. I know that bastard."

"Well, can I do anything? Talk to Reston, maybe the editor of the *Tribune*? See what leads he had for the story?"

"No, just pick up Anna DiTullio and have her in court at eight-thirty tomorrow morning. I'm headed for the office, meeting Buck and Judy to get our motions finalized."

—

"Dan, I wish you luck tomorrow." Sheila's voice over the phone seemed hesitant.

"I'm going to need it. I'm sure Finnerty planted that stuff. You okay, Sheila?"

"Not exactly. My brother Pat just called. Dad had a stroke; he's in intensive care at St. Elizabeth's Hospital in Chicago. He may not make it. . . ." She started to sob.

Sheridan let her grief run its course before he spoke.

"Sheila, I'm really sorry. I met him only once. But he was a great guy . . . and I'll always remember his baseball stories, how he took you to Wrigley Field. Phoned in sick to his office, penned a little note to Sister that you were sick, too. You both played hooky." But Sheridan knew it wasn't working. It was too soon for humorous memories. The grief was too immediate.

"Sheila, if by some miracle I can get out of this case tomorrow, I'll go with you. When are you leaving?"

"Got a flight out tonight, United at eleven-ten."

"Okay, Sheila, it's times like this that pull us all together. St. Elizabeth's Hospital, Chicago, you say." He paused as if jotting it down. "If I don't get caught in Samuels's compactor, I'll take the first flight out. If I can't get away, I'll give you a call at the hospital during morning recess."

"You're a good guy, Sheridan," she said, but her voice sounded far away, as if he were hearing it for the last time.

"Sheila," he said, trying a different tack, "these things happen. My father was a no-good son of a bitch. Ran off with some floozy and left us without a penny. My mother died two months later. He didn't even show up for her funeral."

"Sheridan," she said, her voice a little more steady, "I'm sorry. I'm really not myself.

"And Dan . . ."

Funny, Sheridan thought, she never calls me Dan, always Sheridan, even in the most intimate moments.

"You and I, we're good for each other. Whatever happens, happens. I love you, Dan. If Dad goes, he goes. But you and I are the future."

Sheridan tried to speak, but he choked up. There was a long pause.

"Go get 'em, you crazy Irish stud!" she finally said.

Sheridan and young Buckley took a cab to the courthouse.

"You see the morning *Trib*?" Buckley took the paper from his briefcase.

"I saw it," Sheridan said.

"The editorial was bad enough. Lawyers getting rich on nurses and doctors who try to help people, but what about that cartoon? A lawyer handing his card to a patient on the operating table. . . . And Dan, I've got to hand it to the cartoonist. The lawyer looks just like you—lantern jaw. . . ."

"Yeah, I noticed. I think the eyes were a little too big."

"Sure, you were passing out your card when the patient was undergoing a triple bypass. Doctors screw up, you're in clover. Who wouldn't have big bulging eyes?"

Buckley was about to laugh, but he sensed an unusual reticence in Sheridan.

"Look," he said, "we attack the editorial and the cartoon in our motion for a continuance."

Sheridan looked at Buckley. "There's no way in hell Samuels is going to allow a continuance or impanel a new jury. He revels in this sort of stuff. I'm amazed that Court TV hasn't contacted him. . . . Maybe they have."

The cab pulled up in front of the courthouse steps.

"Raimondi's bringing in Mrs. DiTullio," Sheridan said, "and Judy's got a van coming up with the props."

"You ready, Dan?" Buckley wasn't quite sure.

"We'll knock their socks off!" Sheridan said with exaggerated bravado.

—

"Kate, have Bailiff Coyne hold the jury," Samuels said. "We have a preliminary matter to attend to.

"Sit down, Ms. d'Ortega, Ms. Devaney, gentlemen."

The judge sat at his gray metal desk and shuffled some papers.

"I've read your motion, Mr. Sheridan. These things happen. Look at the O.J. case, the Menendez brothers' trial. Just because a reporter puts a spin on a topic, that's no reason to continue the case."

"But, Judge," Sheridan's voice was taut, "you saw the cartoon in this morning's *Tribune*."

Samuels chuckled. "Pretty good likeness, I'd say—at least you're getting a lot of free ink."

Finnerty, with an ingratiating smile, tried to echo Samuels's humor. "Dan, you'll probably get fifteen or twenty new cases from that cartoon alone."

Sheridan sidestepped Finnerty's remark. "Judge, do I take it that you're not going to allow a continuance?"

"That's correct, Mr. Sheridan. Anything else?"

"Your Honor, would you allow me to poll the jury as to whether they read the articles and saw the cartoon, and if so, let me inquire as to whether either or both would influence their impartiality? And, Your Honor, if you are not going to allow this limited voir dire, I want my request and your denial placed on the record so that I can take an immediate appeal to our state supreme court."

Sheridan shelved his other motion to inquire whether Finnerty planted the articles. There was no judicial gag order—and he knew he'd be spinning his wheels on that one.

Samuels realized that if he denied Sheridan's request on polling the jury, more than likely the state's highest appellate court would deem it to be prejudicial error. He didn't appreciate Sheridan's having worked him into a judicial corner. He had been reversed more times than any other trial judge in the Commonwealth. With yet another reversal, his shot at the supreme court might be in jeopardy. He removed his glasses and proceeded to polish them with great ceremony, holding them up to the overhead light and studying them for several moments before sliding them back on.

"Not everyone reads tabloid journalism like the *Trib*," he said finally. "If any juror out of the panel has not read Reston's article and the editorial, or seen today's cartoon—with you calling attention to them, they surer'n hell are going to read them, regardless of my admonition."

"I'll take that chance, Judge," Sheridan said tersely.

"Okay." Samuels smiled to cover his annoyance. "But I'll handle the voir dire, Mr. Sheridan. You write the questions for the jurors, but I'll do the asking. Got that?"

—

Behind the counsel rail, wooden benches tiered six rows deep held lawyers, witnesses, consultants, and the usual courtroom spectators. Anna DiTullio sat in a corner next to Judy Corwin. Judy surveyed each juror as they filed in and took their positions. Somehow, she liked the jury's composition. A little on the old side, but there didn't appear to be any hard-liners. In the other corner in the front row sat the coterie of defendants, Drs. Robert Sexton, Consuela Puron, Pierre Lafollotte, Nurse Adamson, the psych nurse, was dressed in a white uniform with a navy blue cape pinned at her neckline, a nurse's cap with navy piping sitting decorously on her auburn hair. Joe Sousa, the social worker, wore a black suit. Sister Agnes Loretta wore a gray dress suit with a white cross embroidered into the left lapel. Nothing in his apparel designated Monsignor Devlin's status, no red biretta or scarlet sash. He wore conservative priest's attire, Roman collar, a plain black suit, and sat beside Sister Agnes.

"The jurors are all present, Your Honor." Bailiff Coyne beamed up at the judge. The clerk, Kate McDonald, turned and handed Samuels the handwritten questionnaire prepared by Sheridan.

Samuels stood at the bench and leaned toward the jurors. "Ladies and gentlemen, it's been brought to my attention that an article ran in Sunday's *Tribune* highlighting our current malpractice crisis. . . ."

"Wait a minute, Judge." Sheridan snapped to his feet. "Please, there's no crisis—that article was a one-sided attack on lawyers who attempt to get justice for injured victims. . . ."

"Mr. Sheridan," Samuels barked, slamming his gavel. "You're entirely out of order! I'll see all counsel at sidebar." He motioned with his head.

Samuels was visibly steamed, and so was Sheridan, as they met at the far side of the judge's bench, well out of earshot of the jury. Mayan d'Ortega and Charlie Finnerty stood to the rear.

"Sheridan, I'm running this Court, not you," Samuels flared. "You pull a stunt like that again in front of the jury and I'll hold you in contempt. . . . And get all of this down, Miss Wong!" He beckoned the court reporter, who hustled over with her recording machine.

Sheridan looked up at Samuels. "Judge, you used the word *our*—'our current malpractice crisis.' That language only reinforces the *Tribune* article. There is no such thing as a malpractice crisis—period. Some doctors misread mammograms, leave forceps inside surgical patients, fail to monitor fetal distress, sometimes amputate the wrong leg. Why don't you preface your remarks with a few of these examples?"

Samuels slid his glasses to the end of his nose and glared over them at Sheridan.

"Are you trying to get me into some kind of pissing contest so you can get a mistrial? Because if that's your tack, it's just not going to work. I'll instruct the jury. You don't like my instructions, you file your objection. You don't interrupt me. You got that straight, Counselor?"

Sheridan sucked in his breath and looked up at Samuels. Their eyes collided.

"All I want is a fair shake, Judge. I want you to apologize to the jury for the use of the term 'our malpractice crisis.' " Sheridan wasn't backing down. The court reporter's fingers caught every exchange.

Samuels thought for a moment, realizing that Sheridan was cagey.

"All right," he said, "how would you have me characterize the *Tribune*'s article?"

"Just ask the jurors, Judge, if any of them saw Sunday's article in the *Tribune*, or this morning's editorial and cartoon. Don't even mention malpractice. I'm not alleging malpractice. I'm alleging professional negligence. If no hands are raised, fine. If some do raise their hands, call each one to a sidebar and ask them if, after reading these articles, they could still be fair, still weigh the evidence with strict impartiality—and fulfill their oaths as jurors."

Samuels didn't appreciate Sheridan's lecture.

"Miss d'Ortega, Mr. Finnerty," he said, "you have any problem with that?"

Finnerty caught the judge's subtle exchange. It wasn't exactly a wink, more an expression, a "let me handle this" kind of expression.

"We have no problem with that instruction, Your Honor," Finnerty said. He looked at d'Ortega.

"No problem," she said.

—

"Ladies and gentlemen," Samuels addressed the jury. "It's been brought to my attention that in Sunday's *Tribune* there was a lengthy article about the type of case before us today. Also, in today's issue, there was an editorial and a cartoon on the same subject. Anybody see these?"

All fourteen jurors raised their hands.

"I see," Samuels said. "Now, that's not going to influence you in deciding this case strictly on the evidence and the testimony of witnesses, am I correct? . . . If any of you feel that you can't be fair-minded, please raise your hand."

No one stirred.

"Let the record reflect," Samuels said, "that all jurors are mute." He turned to Sheridan. "All right, Counselor, let's proceed. . . ."

The butterflies were winging in the pit of Sheridan's stomach. Veteran that he was, he never got used to the starter's gun, that brief moment before his opening statement.

"Go get 'em, boss!" young Buckley whispered.

Sheridan rose slowly. He glanced back at the spectators, the lawyers, Finnerty's paralegals with laptop computers, the defendants, who sat in stoic anticipation. Then his eyes fell on Sister Agnes Loretta seated next to the monsignor. A faint flicker of a smile etched her lips. Her hands were folded in her lap, but just before he was about to turn toward the jury, ever so slightly, almost imperceptibly, he thought she gave him a thumbs-up! He shook his head in disbelief. It had to be her thumb, he thought. She certainly wouldn't be giving me the finger.

34

Sheridan rose from the counsel table, nodded up at the bench, walked toward the jury, paused for several seconds, then caressed the jury rail as if he were touching the hand of an old friend. He backed off a few feet, standing just to the left of the center juror. He paused again, surveyed the panel, making eye contact front to back.

"Ladies and gentlemen of the jury," his voice quavered with a splinter of nervousness. "Please forgive me if I choke up. I've been trying cases for twenty years, but I never quite get used to this particular moment. Right now, I have an awesome responsibility. It is presenting the case of my client Donna DiTullio. But you have an even greater responsibility. I am not on trial. I come here to represent a young woman and her mother. I am doing what I have been asked to do as a member of my profession.

"You are the ones who bear a tremendous burden. A few days ago, you were complete strangers to each other. Now you've been brought together to determine the outcome of this controversy between my client, Donna Rebecca DiTullio, and the defendants.

"You know, the jury system was born in England some eight

hundred years ago at a place called Runnymede. Before that time, the king, the sovereign, could do no wrong. People like you and me had no individual rights.

"But since that time, we have had the right of trial by jury. If we have disputes, arguments, or have experienced tragedy for which there is legal redress, we have the right to have the issue decided—not by the sovereign, or the state, not by these defendants, or their counsel"—he looked back at Finnerty, d'Ortega, and Devaney—"but by you, twelve strangers, twelve citizens who were selected for your impartiality, integrity, and courage. I don't know what fates combined to bring all of us here today, but we are here, and you are the collective conscience of this community. Your combined backgrounds, educations, intellects, and fairness will ensure that the administration of justice in our community, in our section of the country, will be preserved.

"On behalf of this Court, all parties to this litigation, and all counsel, I want to thank you, here at the outset. We are privileged and proud that you will sit in judgment of this important case."

The jurors sat in rapt attention. Sheridan knew what all effective trial lawyers know. He had center stage and he intended to keep it. He didn't stalk up and down like a caged lion, didn't slap a handful of notes into his palm—in fact, he had no notes. He stood in one place and focused on the audience; the audience, the jurors, homed in on him. And he also had the advantage of first impression. At this instant, he had to bond with the jury; he had to establish his own integrity, make sure that they knew he believed in his client's cause. It wasn't easy. Few trial lawyers mastered it. He wasn't quite sure that he ever had. After the opening nervous quiver, his voice became steady, modulated, just tinged with suppressed emotion. The crescendo, the fiery conviction, would come later, in final summation.

Finnerty leaned over and whispered to d'Ortega. "For chrissakes, Mayan, he's arguing his case right here in the opening statement. Object to this crap! He's getting away with murder!"

"He hasn't said anything I wouldn't say," d'Ortega responded in a stage whisper. "I'll interrupt if and when I think it's necessary."

For the next forty minutes, Sheridan outlined his case. He explained the events carefully, again in modulated tones, making certain his narrative was accurate. He articulated the horrendous injuries to Donna DiTullio, and at times his voice faltered.

Finnerty noted that several jurors were misty-eyed: a few, including the Irish bartender from Southie, were actually crying. Charlie Finnerty didn't like the way things were going. He felt he might have underestimated Sheridan.

"Ladies and gentlemen." Sheridan approached the rail, again fingering it lightly. Again the lengthy pause. "I want to thank you for giving me the courtesy of your undivided attention." Again he made eye contact with the jurors. "I have had the privilege and advantage of speaking first, but let me tell you this. There are two sides to every story. I've given you my version, what I think my evidence will prove. But fairness is the hallmark of our system of justice. Listen to both sides and keep an open mind. Don't make a decision until all the evidence is in, one way or another, the pro and the con, and above all, be fair to both sides and be true to yourselves and to each other. If she could speak, Donna DiTullio, my client, would ask for nothing more.

"Now, the defense attorney, Mayan d'Ortega, will address you. I am sure that you will extend to her the same courtesy, the same consideration, the same attention"—he glanced in d'Ortega's direction—"that you have shown to me. Thank you."

No one spoke. There was no shuffling of feet, no coughing. Finnerty noticed that now even juror Pamela Watson was teary-eyed. It was a persuasive opening. Everything was there: drama, a hint of intrigue, self-deprecating charm, an appeal to provincialism. Finnerty knew it. So did d'Ortega, even Samuels. And Sheridan knew it, too. Right now, he had the jurors in the palm of his hand.

There was an interminable silence.

"Ms. d'Ortega"—Samuels looked down at the defense table—"your opening statement."

D'Ortega rose slowly. She knew she could put a few dents

into Sheridan's narrative, but she also knew she couldn't completely defuse it. It was the best opening statement she had ever heard. She thought for a few moments, then glanced at Charlie Finnerty.

"Attack every point Sheridan made, step by step," Finnerty whispered. "Thank the jury—puff them up. Seize upon the fairness issue, Mayan. Seize the upper hand!"

"Your Honor," d'Ortega addressed Samuels, "with the Court's permission, I would like to reserve my opening statement until after completion of the plaintiffs' case."

"A mistake, Mayan." Finnerty tugged at her sleeve. "We finally got the ball. You don't punt on first down!"

Even the judge was surprised. He had presided over numerous cases where d'Ortega had been the prosecuting attorney. She was as good as Marcia Clark, and he knew that the defense had to neutralize Sheridan right at the outset.

D'Ortega shot an aside in her colleague's direction. "Charlie, I know what I'm doing. I couldn't top that opening if I were Johnnie Cochran's publicist. . . . We'll have our inning."

●

Sheridan glanced at his witness list, then at the group of defendants surrounded by aides, consultants, and paralegals. He looked at Sister Agnes Loretta. No hand signal, but the slight smile was there. Then he looked at Dr. Puzon, Dr. Lafollette, and finally at Robert Sexton, whose gaze was fixed somewhere near the ceiling.

"I call to the witness stand Dr. Robert Sexton, the defendant." Sheridan returned his attention to Judge Samuels.

"Dr. Robert Sexton," Bailiff Coyne intoned.

The jury knew from Sheridan's opening that Dr. Sexton was the key witness. Donna DiTullio had been Sexton's patient for nearly a year. And Sexton was chief of Psychiatry. The jurors studied him carefully as he made his way to the witness stand. He walked with an erect and dignified posture. From his appearance, they knew he was not some way-out mind-bender. He wore a charcoal gray suit, white button-down shirt, and a light blue tie. No cuff links adorned his wrists. The gold Piaget had given way to a modest timepiece with a black leather strap. No handkerchief fluffed from his breast pocket. With his trim build, he looked like a doctor, a caregiver. Sheridan knew his direct examination of Sexton had to be crisp and carefully crafted, somewhat like examining a state trooper in a drunk-driving case—eliciting only yes or no responses, allowing little room for lengthy articulation or explanations, and not asking any question he didn't already know the answer to.

All eyes in the courtroom focused on Sexton as he raised his right hand and took the oath to tell the truth, the whole truth, calling on the Deity as witness.

Sheridan stood slightly to the rear of the last juror in the front row. Although there was a lectern for his notes, he considered papers to be an encumbrance. His inquiries and Sexton's answers had to have a telling effect, had to be the cornerstone upon which Dr. White would build his testimony. And Sheridan knew that, unlike Perry Mason and more up-to-date TV practitioners, he wasn't going to destroy Sexton. This witness was an erudite speaker, had a Phi Beta Kappa intellect. He would be difficult to confuse or fluster. Sheridan would not browbeat this witness—no sarcasm. He would treat Sexton with utmost professionalism, but it would not be a soft examination. Jurors, indoctrinated by the O.J. case, expected a joust of adversaries, some legal infighting; sparks had to fly.

The preliminary interrogation went quickly. Sheridan touched upon Sexton's scholastic and medical background, omitting the many honors that Sexton had garnered over the years. No sense in letting the jury hear this twice; he knew d'Ortega would embroider them in her cross-examination of the witness, probably adding a few of which he was unaware.

Sheridan had deliberately selected his position at the far end of the jury box so that Sexton would have little eye or voice contact with the jurors. To reply directly to Sheridan, his voice had to carry past the jurors. He knew d'Ortega had instructed Dr. Sexton, when answering yes or no, to direct his attention to Sheridan. However, if Sexton saw an opening in which he could explain his testimony, then he should address the jurors, looking directly and intently at each of them.

"Lean toward the jurors, lecture them as you would your residents and interns; cite homey examples," she had advised, "no arcane rhetoric—just plain Anglo-Saxon. Break everything down so that the baker, the housewife, and the gas station attendant can understand it."

Sheridan's cadence was deliberate and Sexton soon fell into it. The jurors seemed to appreciate the rhythm of Sheridan's interrogation. Now for the hard stuff.

But to the surprise of Sexton and d'Ortega, Sheridan didn't start with day one of Sexton's treatment of Donna DiTullio, nor did he proceed in logical sequence, eliciting diagnosis or details of treatment during the months that Donna had been under his care. In effect, Sheridan defied the rule of trial logic. He started at the end.

"Dr. Sexton, when this tragedy occurred, and you met with Mr. and Mrs. DiTullio, what did you say to them as to how the accident occurred?"

"What did I say to them? I believe Sister Agnes Loretta and Monsignor Devlin were present when we spoke."

"Yes," Sheridan added politely, although tempted to say, "I didn't ask you who was present." "Now, please tell this Court and jury what you said to Mr. and Mrs. DiTullio when you first met them in your office after this tragedy, and what they said to you."

Sexton glanced briefly at d'Ortega. Mayan looked down at her notes. She didn't want the jury to see them exchanging nods or signals.

"Well." Sexton cleared his throat. "I told Donna's parents what happened and how sorry we all were, because Donna had been coming along so well."

"When you said what had happened, just what did you say? Give it to the jury just as you gave it to Mr. and Mrs. DiTullio."

"The exact language?" Sexton appeared a little exasperated.

"Yes, the exact language."

Sexton thought for several seconds. "Well, I told them that

Donna was going to be discharged and was attending a group therapy session in the Atrium wing with two other patients, Ted Marden and Janet Phillips, that the session had gone on for fifty minutes or so, that Donna responded well, appeared calm, showed no signs of anxiety—in fact, I told them that she was in the best mental condition I had observed during the time that she was under treatment. . . .".

"Yes, go on."

"I said that we all broke for a ten-minute period and that Donna remained with Mr. Marden and Ms. Phillips. We do this so the patients have a chance to rehash the therapy on their own."

"Now, you didn't tell that to Mr. and Mrs. DiTullio, Doctor, did you . . . your explanation of why you left her alone?"

"Er, no, but I thought the jury would want our rationale."

"Please, Doctor, all I want and all I asked you was the *exact* conversation you had with Mr. and Mrs. DiTullio."

"Well, I told them that shortly after we left, Donna proceeded to walk into the Atrium corridor. . . ."

Sexton now was teary-eyed. He shook his head.

"I . . . I—" He choked up.

"Would you like a drink of water?" Judge Samuels leaned over from the bench toward the witness, his brow furrowed with concern.

"No, I'm all right," Sexton said courteously. "It's just—just that she was such a promising patient and such a lovely person."

Jesus, Sheridan thought, I don't know who's up for the Academy Award—Sexton or Samuels. He advanced a few feet toward the witness.

"Please continue, Doctor," he said.

"I told them that I spotted Donna as she climbed up on the rail. I yelled at her not to jump, but . . . but . . ." He lowered his head and rubbed his eyes with the back of his wrist.

"Your Honor," he sighed, "I think I'll have that drink of water." Sheridan realized Sexton was putting the sympathy spin on the moment, but it was nothing he could prevent.

"Now, was that *everything* you said to Mr. and Mrs. DiTullio as to *how* the accident happened?"

"Yes, that's about the substance of it. I did say how terribly sorry we all were, that we loved Donna, not only as a patient but as a person. Also, we've never had an accident at St. Anne's since I became chief of Psychiatry."

Sheridan now stepped up his direct examination, still focusing on the end of the event, not on its beginning.

"Now, Doctor, I understand you met the next day with the cardinal, Sister Agnes Loretta, and Monsignor Devlin."

"Yes."

"Who else was present at that meeting?"

"Mr. Charles Finnerty"—Dr. Sexton looked toward the defense table—"a Mr. Walter Crimmins, and the group therapy team Dr. Puzon, Dr. Lafollette, Nurse Adamson, and the social worker, Joseph Sousa."

"Is that Charles Finnerty, your attorney, who is seated at the counsel table?"

Sexton nodded. "It is."

"What did the ten of you discuss?"

"Objection!" D'Ortega snapped to her feet.

"Sustained." Samuels peered over his glasses at Sheridan.

"Did you tell the cardinal and Monsignor Devlin what you told Mr. and Mrs. DiTullio as to how the accident had occurred?"

"Objection!" D'Ortega's voice was crisp and incisive.

"Sustained."

"Well, just tell the jury what you said at that meeting—not what the monsignor said or what anyone else said, since that would be hearsay—just tell us what *you* said."

"Your Honor," d'Ortega injected tersely, her tone edged with the proper degree of frustration. "Any conversation that Dr. Sexton had at the meeting was privileged communication between client and attorney . . . and I object most strongly to Mr. Sheridan's persistence on this line of inquiry."

"Your Honor," Sheridan responded quickly, "if someone kills another human being due to recklessness—say, by running a red light—and then hustles out and gets an attorney, that doesn't mean that I can't inquire about what he told the police, other investigating authorities, or anyone else, for that matter."

"Hold it, hold it, Mr. Sheridan," the judge barked. "You object for the record—don't argue the objection."

Sheridan shot a helpless "this-guy's-killing-us" look at Buckley. They both knew that Samuels should have given the same judicial chastisement to d'Ortega.

"Attorney d'Ortega's objection is sustained," the judge said.

Sheridan nodded acquiescence.

"Please note my objection to Your Honor's ruling," he said, just a hint of sarcasm in his voice.

"Now, Doctor Sexton," Sheridan continued, "that day—and I'm sticking to the day after the accident—you met with the cardinal, Sister Agnes Loretta, Monsignor Devlin, your lawyer, Mr. Finnerty, and I believe a few others, and it was decided to glass in the Atrium and move your psychiatric offices to the first floor. Have I stated that fairly?"

"You have."

"And you say that Ted Marden and Janet Phillips were with Donna DiTullio in the group therapy session on that near-fatal morning. . . . Is that correct?"

"That's correct."

"Okay, let's back up a bit. Did you always hold these group therapy sessions on the fifth floor of the Atrium during your tenure as chief of Psychiatry?"

Sexton glanced down at Charlie Finnerty, then looked at Sheridan.

"Yes, we did."

"How long had this been going on?"

"Throughout my tenure as chief of Psychiatry at St. Anne's."

"For five years?"

"Yes. And we had never lost a patient," Sexton added gratuitously.

"Well, you lost Donna DiTullio," Sheridan said with subtle sarcasm.

"That was unfortunate."

"And that's why we're here, Doctor," Sheridan countered.

"Now—and just answer 'yes' or 'no,' Doctor—when you were holding that group therapy session with mental patients up on the fifth floor of the open Atrium, did you ever say to anyone, including yourself, or did anyone ever say to you, 'Hey, some of these patients have tried to commit suicide'?"

"Well, you have to realize . . ." Sexton interrupted.

"Please, Doctor," Sheridan left his position at the rear of the jury rail and advanced toward Sexton, "later your attorney will allow you to explain—if not this bridge, there's another bridge—your theory. Right now, for the Court and for this jury," his hand shifted toward the panel, "please answer my question. . . . Did you or anyone ever say, 'Maybe for the safety of the patients we shouldn't be holding these sessions up here'?"

There were several moments of silence. Sheridan advanced a few more steps toward the witness stand.

"No, that never happened," Sexton said quietly.

"You want to leave it with this Court and jury that you never had any qualms whatsoever—nor did Sister Agnes Loretta, Dr. Puzon, Dr. Lafollette, the nurses, social workers, interns, or residents—and that no one ever said, 'Gee, we're holding therapy sessions on the fifth floor of a wide-open Atrium with mental patients who recently tried to kill themselves and, gee, maybe we shouldn't be doing this sort of stuff, maybe someone's going to jump.' No one, in the five years of your stewardship, ever mentioned that to you?"

It was a speech packed with all the damaging innuendo Sheridan could muster. In fact, Sheridan really didn't care how Sexton answered it.

Sexton waited for d'Ortega's objection. None was forthcoming.

"That's right," he said quietly.

Sheridan's jaw tightened. Buckley turned slightly toward the jury and rolled his eyes toward the ceiling.

"I think it's time for the morning recess." Samuels smiled at the jury. "We'll resume here at eleven-thirty."

—

Sheridan hustled out to the corridor telephones. He hadn't had a chance to get a critique from Buckley or Judy, but he thought his direct examination of Sexton was going reasonably well.

Raimondi was still pressing his plan to get a hold of Sexton's Bauer, but Sheridan nixed it. The attempt on his life, while not forgotten, had given way to the immediate combat—the trial, with its voraciousness and all-consuming demands. And he knew there would be no ties—at the end only one side would be standing.

He succeeded in getting a call through to the waiting room at St. Elizabeth's Hospital in Chicago. The nurse-receptionist said that Mr. O'Brien's condition was guarded. After a long delay, Sheila got on the line. Her voice was heavy, laden with grief.

"Dad's not going to make it," she said slowly. "He's in a coma. Had a major stroke. We're already making arrangements."

"I'm sorry, Sheila," Sheridan said softly.

"How is your case going?" She tried to sound interested.

"It seems to be going pretty well. I've got Sexton on the witness stand now.

"Sheila, I'll give you a call tonight at your father's house. I'll be thinking of you."

●

Mayan d'Ortega, Charlie Finnerty, and Mary Devaney huddled with claims manager Walter Crimmins in the attorney's consultation room.

"Charlie," Mayan d'Ortega said, "Sister Agnes Loretta told me that she was uneasy about holding group therapy sessions in the Atrium and that she had talked to Dr. Sexton about it. How are we going to square that? And there was a young resident, Dr. Broderick, who told one of our investigators that he questioned the practice. . . . I have his statement right here." D'Ortega leafed through her indexed trial documents.

"Look, Mayan, the resident never told anyone in authority about his concerns. And any statements he gave to our claims investigators are our work products and, as privileged documents, can't be discoverable."

"Suppose Sheridan calls Dr. Broderick to the witness stand?"

"Again, he's merely a psychiatric resident, a minor role player. And we've taken care of his being called as a witness."

"Oh?" Mayan eyed Finnerty curiously.

"Sheridan didn't put him under summons, so we gave him a month's sabbatical with full pay. Seems he comes from Oakland, California. We even picked up his round-trip fare."

"Okay, how about Sister Agnes Loretta?"

"I'll take care of that, Mayan. There was nothing in writing. She questioned Sexton when he first set up the psychiatric ward. That was five years ago."

Mayan thought for a moment. She sensed that Sister Loretta was about to change her story.

"I don't know, Charlie." She looked at Mary Devaney, then at claims manager Crimmins. "Sheridan will put Sister on the witness stand, probably right after Dr. Sexton."

"Not to worry, Mayan, you just rehab Sexton with your cross-examination."

●

"Now, Doctor," Sheridan addressed Sexton, "during your morning testimony, I think we left it that no one in five years ever questioned the practice of holding group therapy sessions five floors up in the open Atrium, is that correct?"

"That's correct. We never had any mishap whatsoever."

"Except Donna DiTullio."

"Yes, and that was unfortunate."

"Now, when you met with Sister Agnes Loretta, Monsignor Devlin, and the cardinal after this . . . unfortunate accident, as you put it . . . who first broached the subject of glassing in the Atrium?"

"It was a mutual decision."

"Then you all agreed. Is that what you're telling us?"

"That's correct."

"Okay, but who first said, 'Let's see, holding group therapy on a wide-open fifth floor. No' "—Sheridan shook his head—" 'from now on, that's not going to happen'?"

"I believe it was Sister Agnes Loretta who suggested we move to the first floor and glass in the Atrium."

"And did you say, 'I believe for the safety of all patients, not only psychiatric patients, we should glass in the Atrium'?"

"Objection, Your Honor." D'Ortega half-rose from her counsel table.

"Sustained."

"Mr. Sheridan," Samuels formed a pyramid with his fingers and drummed them together to show his impatience, "you must ask questions that have a factual basis. You can't say to the witness, 'Now, you know you were drunk that day.'"

"Your Honor, with all due respect," Sheridan interjected, "the Atrium was wide open when my client fell. The next day, a decision was made to glass it in. I have a right to inquire who said what and at what time."

Mayan d'Ortega jumped to her feet. "Your Honor, Mr. Sheridan hasn't the right to inquire into after-the-fact repairs—that's black-letter law. If he did have that right and if he could get this information into evidence, no one would repair anything."

"That's correct," the judge said. "I want you to leave this line of inquiry, Mr. Sheridan. Pose your next question."

"But, Judge—"

"Next question!" Samuels snapped.

"Please note my objection, Your Honor. I'll move on."

But Sheridan persisted. He knew d'Ortega would be shouting objections and Samuels rapping his gavel, but the question, objectionable or not, contained the answer he wanted the jury to hear.

"The reason the Atrium was glassed in and the psychiatric offices were moved to the first floor was for the protection of the patients, more particularly, the psychiatric patients, isn't that correct, Doctor?"

D'Ortega bolted from her seat. Samuels banged his gavel.

"Mr. Sheridan. You've been over this ground! I'm giving you fair warning. . . ."

Sheridan gripped the jury rail in front of the center juror.

"But, Your Honor—"

"Mr. Sheridan, you will pose a different question!" The judge was seething.

Sheridan shook his head, then refocused on the witness.

"Now, Dr. Sexton, let's return to your doctor-patient relationship with Donna DiTullio."

Sheridan reassumed his position to the immediate rear of the last juror. This time, he spread out Sexton's medical notes on the dais. Sexton did the same on the small shelf on the witness stand. But again, Sheridan didn't start from day one of treatment. His line of interrogation surprised even Buckley.

"Did you ever see Donna DiTullio play tennis, Doctor?"

"I believe I did."

"Where was that?"

"At the U.S. Open in Flushing Meadows, New York."

"She was pretty good, wasn't she, Doctor? She beat the seventh seed, Irene Athanas from Greece, in the first round."

"Yes, I watched the game."

"Personally? By that I mean, were you in the stands?"

"Yes. I thought I could give her some psychological and moral support."

"Where did you stay when you were at the Open?"

"At the Plaza, in Manhattan."

Something tugged at the red zones of Sheridan's mind.

"When I first questioned you, Doctor, as to whether you had seen Donna play tennis, you said, 'I believe I did.' Now you seem certain that you did see her play."

Finnerty bent toward d'Ortega. "Mayan, object to this crazy line of questioning."

D'Ortega's eyes remained on Sexton, and she flicked her pencil in Finnerty's direction.

"Sexton can handle this strategy," she said in a muffled voice. "He may even score a few points."

"Now, when you saw Donna play at Flushing Meadows," Sheridan continued, "she had been under your professional care for . . . how many months?"

"About twelve months."

"She was a manic-depressive—wasn't that your clinical impression and working diagnosis?"

"That's correct."

"And you knew her quite well, did you not, Doctor? Not only did you admire her athletic ability but you also knew her most intimate thoughts, her secrets. You were her psychiatrist, isn't that correct?"

Sexton glanced toward d'Ortega. Her stoic Indian eyes disclosed no cue, no direction. Sexton was on his own.

"I was her psychiatrist," he said quietly.

"She trusted you, did she not, Doctor?"

Samuels looked down at d'Ortega. There was not a semblance of an objection.

"I'm sure she did."

"Now, a manic-depressive disorder means that a patient sometimes has abnormal highs—translating that to Donna DiTullio, she could beat Steffi Graf—or at least at times she thought she could—and then something happens, is triggered, and the patient plunges to rock bottom." Sheridan lifted his hand and slapped it down on the jury rail.

"Well, that's an oversimplification," Sexton said. "All of us have good days and bad days." He followed d'Ortega's advice and looked at the jury.

"That's the human condition," he continued. "If you and I were always upbeat, that would be abnormal. We get the blues sometimes. But we're not going to take on the world one day, announce it from the rooftops, and then plunge into total darkness some twenty-four hours later, then rebound again to newer heights. If a patient does that, then psychiatrically we can safely diagnose that he or she is a manic-depressive."

"And that was your diagnosis of Donna DiTullio?"

"That was my working diagnosis."

"Did it ever change?"

"No, it never changed."

"What medication did you put Donna on during that twelve-month period of treatment?"

"Zoloft and Xanax."

"And what was that designed to accomplish?"

Sexton again looked at the jury.

"Donna had a deep-rooted disorder. Psychiatric science can't eradicate that; we try to help the patient to live with the condition. It can be like having a chronic bad back. You teach the patient how to lift with his or her knees, not to bend over, to use the natural fulcrum of the body—to cope—to live with the disorder."

D'Ortega noted that several jurors, including the Irish bartender, nodded agreement. Sexton's message was hitting home.

"Doctor, I asked you, did I not, what the administration of Zoloft and Xanax was designed to accomplish?"

Sexton paused before answering. Again he made eye contact with the jury.

"There are many drugs in our medical pharmacopeia—Prozac, Xanax, Lithium, Librium. I'm familiar with all of them. Zoloft was designed to keep Donna on an even keel mentally. I prescribed Xanax for when she had anxious moments—before a big match or when she was scheduled to fly on an airplane. It's an antianxiety medication, short-lasting but quite effective. Those were the two medications I had Donna on, and they seemed to be working well."

Again the speech to the jury. Sheridan knew he had to tighten the interrogation.

"Now, for some reason, Doctor, despite the Zoloft and the Xanax, Donna slashed her wrists and had to be admitted involuntarily to St. Anne's, isn't that correct? And please, Doctor, may I have a yes or no to that question?"

"Yes. But the cutting of her wrists—"

"Doctor, please, you're represented by competent counsel." Sheridan gestured toward the defense table. "When your attorney interrogates you, there will be ample opportunity for you to explain. In the interest of time, please just answer my question, all right, Doctor?" Irritation crept into Sheridan's voice.

Sexton nodded, but he knew he was parrying the questions quite well. And d'Ortega knew it, and so did Charlie Finnerty.

"Now, during Donna's hospitalization, you changed her prescription to Capricet, correct?"

"Correct."

"And Capricet is not approved by the FDA for general prescription."

"Yes, but—"

"Doctor, can you please answer this question yes or no?"

"That's not quite fair," Sexton replied. "May I explain?" He glanced up at Judge Samuels.

"Yes," Samuels said, "if you think you need to explain it, go right ahead."

"Your Honor"—Sheridan advanced a few steps toward the bench—"Dr. Sexton is a defendant here. He's an adverse witness. I have the right—not only the right but also the duty—to interrogate him in accordance with established rules of civil procedure."

Samuels gave an exaggerated sigh. He knew Sheridan was right, and d'Ortega hadn't rushed in with some recent case citation.

"All right, Mr. Sheridan, I'm just trying to speed things up a bit. . . ."

I'm sure you are, you black-robed son of a bitch! Sheridan felt like saying.

Instead, he murmured, "I appreciate that, Your Honor," and nodded to Samuels in apparent approbation.

"Now, to be fair to you, Doctor, I know that the FDA approved Capricet for limited clinical trials, and you received consent from Donna's parents to try her on a regimen of this particular drug. But when you prescribed Capricet, neither you nor any member of your staff knew anything about the long-term effects of the drug, or whether there could be deleterious side effects, isn't that medically true?"

"We were unaware of long-term side effects; the drug was new. It worked in the short term."

It was nearing the one o'clock lunch hour. Sheridan had to close on a strong note.

"Well, Doctor, Donna DiTullio and others on this drug were in fact guinea pigs, isn't that the case?"

"The drug was authorized for clinical studies."

"Yet this drug Capricet *still* has not been medically approved for general prescription, isn't that correct, Doctor?"

"It's been approved in the United Kingdom, and in many European nations—France, Italy, the Scandinavian countries. . . ."

"But, Doctor, Donna DiTullio was being treated in the United States, in Boston, Massachusetts, and the drug still has not received FDA approval here in this country for general prescription. Isn't that factually correct?"

"That's correct."

Sheridan was tempted to say something sarcastic, like "Thank you for this piece of candor, Doctor," but he let it go.

—

"Ladies and gentlemen, it's now one o'clock." The judge glanced at his watch. "Ordinarily, Bailiff Coyne would take you for sandwiches, tea, soda pop, whatever, courtesy of the Commonwealth of Massachusetts. But I've been advised that there is an old-fashioned nor'easter going to hit here about four o'clock. Eighteen inches of snow is predicted. So I'm going to let you go for the afternoon. You'll be on telephone call, so don't plan to go tobogganing with the kids. Unless there are blizzard conditions, we'll resume at nine o'clock tomorrow morning."

It was exactly the respite that Sheridan needed. There was something he had to check out with Donna DiTullio—and it didn't involve her father. If the storm hit, driving up to Greenbriar and back would be impossible.

"Judy," he said after the jury had filed out, "call Hanscom Field, get me Joe Gaynor's Flying School. I want to speak to Joe personally. He's an old client. I need an immediate hitch up to Vermont in one of his Cessnas."

Judy picked up her cellular phone and did the necessary.

Finnerty and Walter Crimmins were huddled with Sexton.

All seemed to be in a jubilant mood. D'Ortega was gathering up her notes. Sexton had held up remarkably well, she thought, but a trial's momentum, like an athletic contest, could swing the other way quickly. And she still wondered about Sister Agnes Loretta.

35

"You going to be long up at White River?" Joe Gaynor leaned from the pilot's seat and shouted at Sheridan over the roar of the engine.

"Not if I can help it," Sheridan shouted back as he noted thick cloud cover moving toward them off the port wing.

"We get socked in up here, might be two, three days before we get out," Gaynor said loudly.

"You're IFR-rated, aren't you, Joe?"

"Yeah, *I follow roads*—but all the instruments in the world won't get us through that white muck coming our way."

Sheridan glanced down. He recognized a gray ribbon cutting through the green scrub of the New Hampshire countryside: I-89. It seemed that Gaynor's flimsy Cessna was not even keeping pace with the automobiles.

"We're doing a hundred and twenty knots—bucking a forty-mile headwind," Gaynor said, again leaning toward Sheridan. "That boils down to an air speed of about eighty-five miles per hour. Should be in White River in another twenty minutes."

Shortly, Gaynor checked in with White River Airport and was cleared to land.

"This approaching storm," he asked the controller, "when's it due to hit? I plan to be on the ground for two hours, then head back to Boston. Over."

The controller's voice crackled over the receiver. "Seven-zero-five Zulu. If you get out within an hour, I'd say you have a fifty-fifty chance of getting back to Boston. Otherwise, you'll love the White River no-tell motel. It's Monday night—great bingo game in the Maple Syrup Lounge. Over."

"Roger." Gaynor sighed and throttled back the engine as he eased the yoke forward and began his descent.

"You know, Sheridan, fifty-fifty odds in this business ain't that enticing."

Sheridan grinned. "Hey, Joe, you're an old pilot from way back. . . ."

"Yeah," Gaynor said, his eyes riveted on the approaching runway, "there are *old* pilots and *bold* pilots, but there are no *old, bold* pilots. You better be back within fifty minutes."

—

Sheridan took a cab from the airport to Greenbriar, a short five miles. He had told Judy to call Dr. Sagall and alert him that he was en route.

He was ushered by the receptionist to Dr. Sagall's office—no cooling his heels. They knew who he was, and he was a paying customer.

"We've made tremendous gains," Dr. Sagall said as they walked toward Donna's floor. "She still can't emit any intelligible sounds, but she's making cooing noises. Everyone here is quite pleased with her progress. The bedsores have almost disappeared."

"I haven't much time, Doctor. I took a light plane up here from Boston. Pilot's waiting at the airport, and I told the cabdriver to keep the motor running."

"How's your case going?" the doctor asked before checking into the nurses' station.

"Just started, really. The main defendant is under direct examination. It's . . . you know." Sheridan wiggled his hand.

"Like the weather—fifty-fifty," Sagall said with a slight smile.

The nurse put on a pink jacket and escorted them to Donna's room.

Fifty-fifty—Sheridan thought about it. Somehow, he didn't like the odds.

The nurse fluffed Donna's pillow and smoothed her bed-sheet. Donna's eyes were wide open. Her face was less haggard, and the purple crescents beneath her eyes had disappeared. Her hair had been washed and combed.

"You have a visitor, sweetie." The nurse smiled and gently brushed a strand of hair back from Donna's forehead.

"Can you two leave us alone for a couple of moments?" Sheridan glanced at Dr. Sagall. "I want to go over a few simple questions. It might be kind of stressful."

"Sure." The doctor nodded toward the nurse. "You just push the call button when you're through."

—

"Donna." Sheridan leaned forward and reached for her hands, which were cupped together. He looked into her eyes. They were no longer vacant. A slight film of mist heightened the dark brown glow.

"You're going to be all right." Sheridan's own eyes misted.

"You know who I am!" This time, the wink was quick; then came the cooing sounds, and her lips began to quiver.

"Donna, I'm trying to help you." Sheridan hesitated for several seconds. This was going to be tricky. He knew the next few moments were crucial. He might plunge her back into the abyss. It was a grave risk, but he'd have to chance it. He bent closer.

"I want you to answer me. This is for your benefit. I'm *your* lawyer. Do you know what a lawyer is?"

Again the quick wink.

"Okay." He knew he had to frame this in stark simplicity. He took a deep breath.

"Do you recall walking to the Atrium at St. Anne's Hospital in Boston?"

Again the quick wink, but the cooing stopped abruptly. The dark eyes, now wide, stared back at him like laser beams. Sheridan wasn't sure how to read this. Was it terror? Hard to tell.

He again patted her hands. "Donna, were you pregnant? I mean, were you going to have a baby?"

Again the wink.

Sheridan almost decided to terminate the painful interview, but he had two more questions. He'd come this far, so had Donna. She had to trust him.

"Was Dr. Robert Sexton the father of your baby?"

For a long moment, Donna just stared back at Sheridan. There was no cooing, but he heard a slight sigh. She closed her eyes, then opened them.

He didn't hesitate.

"Donna, did Dr. Robert Sexton *push* you over the railing that morning at St. Anne's?"

She closed and opened her eyes. Her head nodded ever so slightly, and tears streamed down her cheeks.

"I see," Sheridan said quietly. Again, he reached for Donna's hand and he gave it a light squeeze. She squeezed back.

—

Joe Gaynor kept up a bellyaching banter on the flight back to Boston.

"Glad you took only forty minutes," he yelled over to Sheridan. "Control upgraded our odds to sixty-forty. I called Hanscom Field; they're still open. Snow's whipping the Cape, Nantucket, and the Vineyard. Visibility in Boston is less than half a mile. Still within regulation, but barely. We'll be scud-running."

Somehow, Sheridan wasn't too concerned with the weather. He knew Joe Gaynor, knew he had been a fighter pilot in Korea—probably had ten thousand hours. Joe was of the old barnstorming school; could plunk the Cessna down in somebody's backyard if he had to. Sheridan had handled Joe's divorce and a slight misunderstanding with the FAA free of charge.

Although he tried to follow Gaynor's foreboding chatter, he was more troubled about his client's revelation of what he had always suspected. How truthful was Donna? Could she be making all this up? He doubted that. She had nothing to gain, and the thing that bothered him most was that she had everything to lose by being truthful, and right now, he was the only one in the world to realize it.

Gaynor called ahead to Hanscom Field. "This is Skyhawk seven-zero-five Zulu. I'm five miles north of the field. It's starting to spit up here pretty good. You still open? Over."

"Positive," the controller said. "Report downwind for runway one eighty."

Sheridan leaned his head against the flimsy backrest. The sleet was now lashing the windshield. Gaynor ran through his landing checklist, lowered his wing flaps a notch, and switched on his landing lights.

"We won't have to worry about a midair collision ruining our day," he groused good-naturedly. "We're the only goddamned fools up here. Even Logan's rerouting traffic to Portland."

Sheridan's mind was far from the imminent landing, however hazardous. For a moment, he harbored the crazy thought that it might be just as well if they did crash—not fatal—just enough to land him in the hospital for a few weeks—even St. Anne's—long enough to get a mistrial.

No, that's ridiculous. He shook his head. But he knew he had a terrible problem.

As Gaynor called in downwind, then turned for his final approach, Sheridan should have had white knuckles and been studying the terrain as intensely as Gaynor, but his mind was elsewhere. If Sexton's malpractice policy was written with the same exclusion contained in a lawyer's professional liability policy or most other policies, he knew that deliberate acts were not covered. If someone intentionally ran over a person with his automobile, no matter how horrendous the victim's injuries, Sheridan knew that the insurance company would snap their bag shut and the defense attorneys would walk away—disclaim. "*No coverage.*" He recalled a case Buckley had once on a home owner's policy. Seems a young girl was on a neighbor's property. A bully of a boy, the home owner's son, some five years the little girl's senior, started pelting her with rocks, trying to chase her away. One stone was too accurate—it put out the girl's eye. An injury on the premises, even due to negligent conduct on the part of the home owner's family members, was covered under the $300,000 policy—*except for deliberate acts*. Buckley had represented the injured girl and her family. Fortunately, he got to the home owner before the insurance company did. The company paid the $300,000.

A few bumps jolted Sheridan from his dark reverie. He looked out at the runway. Big wind-driven flakes swirled over the tarmac.

"Good landing, Joe." He quickly returned to the present.

"Yeah, all six of them." Gaynor laughed slightly and adjusted the throttle as they taxied toward the turnout.

"You're still an *old, bold* pilot, Joe, in my book."

"At least we didn't buy the six-foot farm," Gaynor said loudly, "but this is one flight that's not going down in my log." He popped his door open and stuck his head out, trying to get a better look. "Any landing you walk away from is a good landing," he shouted with good-natured sarcasm.

Sheridan was glad they hadn't crashed after all, but knew that he now faced his real problem. Gaynor maneuvered into a spot on the line. They tied the plane down and made their way against the blinding sleet up to the hangar clubhouse.

"Want to buy me a drink, Dan? The suicide run is on the house."

"Sure," Sheridan said. "I'd say we need a bourbon or two—maybe three or four."

●

True to the forecast, Boston was hit with a full-blown blizzard. Sheridan braved the elements and walked to the office. He was surprised to see Judy Corwin and young Buckley sipping coffee in the conference room and poring over a list of documents on the DiTullio case.

"Jesus," Buckley said as he looked at Sheridan caked with snow. "You look like Nanook of the North."

Sheridan stamped the snow off his feet, removed his parka and knit cap, and shook them, showering ice and snow all over the reception area.

"Just got a call from Samuels's law clerk," Judy said. "Trial won't resume for at least two or three days. We're supposed to get hit with twenty inches."

Sheridan hung his wet parka on the reception area coatrack, slipped off his boots, then tossed them out into the hallway.

"Want a cup of coffee, Dan?" Judy had an innate sense that Dan was troubled, even though his face failed to disclose it.

"That would be nice, Judy. Make it strong black. Seems I did a little too much celebrating with Joe Gaynor."

Judy merely nodded and went off toward the coffee room.

"How'd things go up at Greenbriar?" Buckley asked.

"Fine," Sheridan said as he thumbed through the file documents, looking for St. Anne's insurance policy. "Donna's coming along very well. We had quite a give-and-take."

Sheridan wanted to tell Buckley exactly what had happened, but he wasn't about to brush a dear friend, let alone his law partner, with complicity in an act that he was contemplating, something that for a member of the bar and an officer of the court would be quite unethical if not unthinkable. Nor was he quite sure where this new knowledge would all lead. Right now, it was his personal demon and only he could live with it . . . or die with it. Sheridan forced a grin.

"Do you remember when you got the three hundred thou for the little Twomey girl who lost her eye; next-door neighbor's kid hit her with a rock?" Sheridan looked at Buckley almost nonchalantly.

"Sure do. It was a helluva settlement. We could've wound up with zip. I beat the insurance company's investigator by a couple of hours."

"How'd you pull it off? You never did fill me in on the details."

"Well," Buckley said with a sheepish grin, "the way the little Twomey girl had it—the kid pelted her with rocks. Of course, a deliberate act isn't covered under the home owner's liability policy. I hustled to the neighbor's house, talked to the kid's father. I'm looking out the window at a backyard birdhouse. I see some squirrels climbing up a pole and stealing the goodies meant for the cardinals and finches.

" 'Look,' I says to the father, 'if your boy was throwing rocks at those squirrels out there and accidentally hit the Twomey girl, then your home owner's coverage would apply. On the other hand, if he intentionally aimed at Mary Jane Twomey and hit her with a rock, then there's no coverage, your insurance company disclaims, and you wind up paying the tab yourself, including my legal fee.'

" 'Let me talk to my boy,' the father says. Comes back five minutes later. 'Yep,' he said, 'the boy was chasing the squirrels— goddamn bandits! You can see them out there now.' He points to the birdhouse. And that's the way it went down. I just gave the father the law—he supplied the facts. . . . Why do you ask?" He looked curiously at Sheridan.

"Just thinking of some other case," Sheridan said, "insurance coverage can be tricky—the companies rig the exclusions in their favor."

But young Buckley had known Sheridan for ten years. They shared the good times and the bad. In a law partnership, there were no secrets. Somehow, he knew that Sheridan didn't risk a two-hundred-mile jaunt in a flying shoe box, braving a nor'easter, just to chat with Donna DiTullio. Something was up, but he was smart enough to let the matter drop.

Judy returned with the coffee.

"Snow's really coming down, Dan," she said, handing the cup to Sheridan. "Lucky the case is off for a few days. Want me to get Dr. White in here tomorrow? That's if he can make it. . . ."

Suddenly, the phone rang. Judy answered with professional dexterity. "Sheridan and Buckley," she said crisply.

"Probably Finnerty checking up to see if we're working," Buckley chipped in.

Judy's face and voice turned grim. "Yes," she said into the receiver. "I'm sorry. Dan"—she held the phone out to Sheridan— "it's Sheila. Her dad passed away last night."

Dan took Sheila's call in his office.

"I'm awfully sorry, Sheila. . . . Then again, with a stroke . . . brain damage . . . might be a blessing. . . ."

"The wake's tomorrow night," she said, "Casey Brothers Funeral Home, LaSalle Street, Chicago. Mass is at ten, Blessed Sacrament Church, a few doors down."

He logged it into his memory. "I'll be there," he said.

"No, the case is on hold. We're in the throes of a blizzard.

"Look, I'll be there. I know Logan's closed. I'll get there!"

Sheridan made one other call—to Dun & Bradstreet in New York. He wanted a credit check on Dr. Robert Sexton.

"Yes, as immediate as you can make it," he said. "Charge my account."

He rejoined Judy and Buckley.

"Got to catch a train for New York," he said. "Understand Manhattan's not getting hit too bad. I'll grab a plane for Chicago out of La Guardia."

Judy shook her head. "Dan, you're likely to get stranded. I'm not even sure you can get a cab . . . and you have to go home and change."

"I'll take the MBTA to South Station," Sheridan said as he put on his still-damp parka. "Buy some clothes en route. I'll fly back after the funeral." And quickly Sheridan was gone.

Judy shook her head and her lips flattened as she looked at Buckley quizzically.

But Buckley knew this was a trip Sheridan had to make. He knew Sheridan had to mend some fences, pay his respects, and he also knew something else. Sheridan was in a terrible dilemma. And there was only one person in the world he would confide in—Sheila O'Brien. He hoped for all their sakes that Sheridan would make the right choice.

36

Sheridan lucked out. He caught the Northwest red-eye and
landed in Chicago at 2:30 A.M. He checked into the O'Hare
Hilton, tumbled into bed, and slept until noon. Later, at
the airport arcade, he purchased a ready-made suit, tie, shirt,
and shoes, and he sent a funeral piece from the flower shop. He
returned to his room, was tempted to call Sheila, then decided
against it. Nursing a bourbon from the room minibar, he skimmed
through the *Chicago Tribune*. After a light dinner at the coffee
shop, he took a cab to the Casey Brothers Funeral Home on
LaSalle Street, arriving there a little after seven. He signed the
register and joined a line of mourners moving slowly toward the
casket. He could see Sheila in a black dress, standing with a
priest and two young men he assumed were her brothers, receiving the mourners. The room was filled with plainly dressed people
chatting in subdued tones. Although Declan O'Brien was old Chicago Irish, there was no keening among the women. Some were
saying the beads; others huddled in small groups, exchanging
snatches of gossip. But as he moved toward the casket, he suspected that more than a few of the male contingent were in the
back room hoisting a few in Declan's memory.

He stopped at the open bier. The Irish tricolor was draped over the foot of the casket.

"Declan never looked better," one old-timer remarked as the mourners blessed themselves, standing for a few moments, then moving on.

Sheridan was not religious. An altar boy in grade school, in his teens he had participated in CYO, mainly baseball and basketball. He had even won a Miraculous Medal for some youthful achievement. But through the years, he struggled with the church's arcane rites and symbols, the implausible doctrines. Then came Vietnam, and somehow his tottering faith deserted him. He witnessed too much brutality and senseless bloodshed on both sides to continue to believe in a divine and just Deity. But if he was an agnostic, he struggled with that, too. He reasoned that all this stuff—the world, the universe, the poetic symmetry of an oak leaf—could not have come about by pure chance. At best, he was a marginal disbeliever.

He gazed down at the benign unwrinkled face of the elder O'Brien. Declan's hands clutched rosary beads, and in the lapel of his sedate gray suit was a St. Christopher medal. Sheridan wasn't sure, but he thought St. Christopher bit the ecclesiastical dust some years ago, along with Jude, Michael, and scores of other saints. Sheridan blessed himself. The gesture was awkward. He hadn't done that for years, not even in Vietnam. But the Hail Marys came easily, as if he were back with the Notre Dame nuns at Holy Redeemer Grammar School.

"Sheridan!" Sheila cried, bursting into tears. After a steadying arm and a handkerchief from her brother, she groped for composure.

"How in the world . . . I understand Boston's completely buried."

Sheridan grasped both her hands and kissed her lightly on the cheek.

"I caught a flight out of New York," he said. "I'm awfully sorry. He was such a great guy."

"I know." She smiled briefly. "Dad struggled all his life—

worked two jobs. Told us kids whatever came in life—adversity, temptation—always do the right thing.

"Hey, I'm getting pretty maudlin." She clung to his arm. "I don't think you've met my family. This is my brother Dennis; he's in his last year at Loyola." Sheridan shook hands with Dennis. He was tall, the spitting image of Declan O'Brien.

"And my brother Pat. Finishing up at Northwestern Law." Again Sheridan shook hands and murmured condolences.

"And my cousin, Father Paul Killiane. He's a Holy Cross father, teaches English lit at Notre Dame. Father, this is my fiancé, Dan Sheridan." Sheila's voice had a sudden exuberance. The two men exchanged handshakes, and Sheridan could see the subtle surprise in the cleric's eyes. Sheridan seemed to have a good twenty years on Cousin Sheila, and right now it showed.

●

Father Paul led the group in the rosary and the mourners began to splinter, filing slowly past the casket, blessing themselves, some touching Declan's hand for the last time. Sheridan hung back. Finally, he and Sheila were alone except for one of the attendants, who arranged the floral pieces and folded the spindly chairs. Even Father Paul and Sheila's two brothers had departed, tactfully leaving them alone.

"Can we go somewhere for a drink, Sheila?" Sheridan asked guardedly. "I'm sure this isn't the time or the place, but I want to run something by you. Something I can't mention to anyone else—not even to Buckley or Judy."

●

They sat in a corner booth in Shanahan's Pub, a few short blocks from the funeral home.

"I'll take a cab back to the Hilton," Sheridan said. "I'll be at the church tomorrow at ten."

"Sheridan," Sheila exclaimed, "you're going to stay with us. We've plenty of room. You're family; you'll ride with us in the limo."

"No, I think just the immediate family should be together.

I'll join you at the church. I can get a ride to the cemetery with one of the Caseys."

They sat quietly for several moments, each sipping a Duquesne beer. Sheila talked about her dad—little memories, nothing earthshaking; like the day he took her to Wrigley Field to see Hank Aaron break the Babe's record and his pride at her graduation from Fordham Law School. She rambled on, blocking out a tidal wave of grief that threatened to engulf her. Sheridan finished his beer and ordered another. Perhaps he shouldn't intrude with his own problems, he thought. But then he thought again. This was the young woman he intended to marry. There would be little secrets they would each keep to themselves. But this wasn't going to be one of them.

"Sheila." He reached for both her hands and clasped them lightly. "I really need your opinion. I'm convinced now that it was Dr. Sexton who tried to shoot me that day on the Wampanoag trail, and I'm sure that he'll try again."

Sheila broke through her flood of memories and looked at him carefully. She recognized the shadow of doubt, the troubled look on Sheridan's face.

"You want me to call a few of my contacts at the bureau?"

"No. I don't want any authorities in on this one. I'll handle Sexton in my own way. You know about Sexton's live-in girlfriend?"

Sheila nodded.

"I think that Sexton got rid of her. That he was the one who ambushed her in Central Park.

"Well, it's a long story, Sheila, but I've learned that Sexton knocked up Donna DiTullio and Donna didn't jump—Sexton planned the whole thing, just waited for the opportune time."

"You don't mean . . ."

"That's exactly what I mean. I asked Donna if Sexton pushed her over the rail. She answered that he did. I suspected it all along. Sexton probably gave her some drug that induced nausea. When everyone else left, the doctors and attendants, he had the ideal cover. All anyone heard was Sexton calling to her, begging her not to jump."

"I don't know." Sheila looked puzzled. "It's going to be a girl with brain damage and a psychiatric history against a respected doctor. You plan to bring Donna in to testify in her limited capacity?"

"Let's say I do." Sheridan released her hands and took a good swallow of beer. "Say the jury believes her, hits Sexton with—hell, if they're pissed off enough, they could bring in a verdict of twenty, forty, maybe fifty million dollars."

Sheila thought for a few moments. As a law clerk, she had worked on insurance-disclaimer cases. She knew that in this situation, the insurance company would walk, leaving Sexton dangling in the wind.

"I'd say you had a *big* problem, Counselor," Sheila said unenthusiastically. "How do you plan to deal with it?"

"Right now, Sheila, I haven't got the foggiest idea. I want St. Anne's to pay the full policy—twenty million. Somehow, I've got to arrange it. It's not going to be easy."

Sheila studied Sheridan for several seconds.

"You're not going to do something crazy?" she said.

Sheridan returned her gaze. "Perhaps," he said. "Some might think it's not exactly kosher. But it'll take twenty million to rehab Donna. She's got a chance, Sheila, a real chance." He reached for her hands again and cupped them in his.

"I might just be able to get Sexton to dictate to his defense counsel that he wants the case settled for the policy limits. The cardinal, after all, is Sexton's uncle."

"But . . ." Sheila couldn't believe what she was hearing. "But you'd be covering up an attempted murder!"

Sheridan could read the censure. "Look, Sheila, I'm not going to take a fee, not a nickel—*zero!* It's a life for a life. You know sometimes you have to do things they don't teach in law school."

There was a troubled glint in her eyes.

"It's getting late, Dan." She gathered up her purse. "Call a cab, drop me off at the house. I'll see you at the Mass."

Sheridan knew he'd made a terrible mistake. This was one demon he should have wrestled by himself.

—

Sheridan watched as the short procession, Sheila and her two brothers, walked slowly toward the first pew in the cavernous old nave. It was the kind of church Sheridan remembered—vaulted ceilings, ornate pulpit, plaster statues of St. Joseph, St. Teresa clutching her roses, others.

Father Paul said the Mass. He ascended the steps to the pulpit and delivered a brief eulogy, recalling the good times, the good deeds done by Declan in his lifetime, how devoted he had been to his wife, Kathleen Killiane, who had died in childbirth with the delivery of their younger son. He mentioned that Kathleen was his aunt.

"If a man has any greatness about him," Father Paul concluded, "it comes to light, not in one flamboyant moment, but in the ledger of daily work. And Declan O'Brien, humble, yet a man of stature, was true to his family, and to his friends, a man of integrity, a man of God."

"Good-bye, old friend." Father Paul's voice quavered. He cleared his throat. "You taught us, you taught *me*, always to do the right thing." He paused, looking first at the O'Brien family, then at the draped casket. *"Ar Dheis lamb de go raibh se."* He spoke the Gaelic blessing softly. "May you be at the right hand of God."

Sheila glanced over her shoulder and looked at Sheridan. Their eyes held for a moment, then moved away as if by agreement. There was something in her look that went beyond sadness—it was a hint of disappointment.

—

Sheridan's flight was rerouted to Philadelphia and he was able to catch the Amtrak Senator to New York, then to Boston. During the seven-hour ride, his mind wandered back to the funeral. It had begun to snow at the cemetery. Only a small group huddled under the canopy as Father Paul read the last prayers and poured the vial of earth on Declan O'Brien's casket.

Sheridan kept in the rear, bareheaded, the chill sleet stinging his eyes and matting his hair. Sheila had invited him back to the house, but he declined, giving the excuse that he had to be back in Boston to meet with Dr. White. Sheila was assisted into the limo by her brothers, and he watched as it pulled away. She gave him no wave or sign of recognition. He could hear the ghostly echo of Declan saying, "Always do the right thing" to his daughter. Well, this time he and Sheila might not agree on what was right.

Aboard the Amtrak train from New York, he had a few bourbons in the club car, then made his way back to his seat. At New Haven, he helped an attractive blonde place some luggage and a luxurious sable coat in the overhead bin. She smiled invitingly and sat down beside him, trying to drum up a conversation.

"I'm a television commentator on KBCT in New Haven," she introduced herself, adding, "What do you do?"

Sheridan looked at her. She was about the same age as Sheila, a little taller, very attractive, a Janet Phillips type.

"I was just released from Attica," Sheridan said, his eyes half-lidded.

"Attica? The New York prison facility?"

Sheridan nodded. "Served six years. It was a bum rap."

It wasn't long before she excused herself, taking the sable with her. Sheridan again made his way to the club car. Another bourbon, a pretty good nap, and he was back in Boston.

—

Sheridan met Raimondi early the next morning at a coffee shop in Harvard Square.

"Do you think you can get hold of Sexton's Bauer, run some ballistics tests, and get it back before Sexton knows it's gone? And here, if you're successful, run the ballistics on the slug and casings that I pried out of the Wampanoag trail." Sheridan passed him the plastic envelope containing the bullets.

Raimondi sipped his coffee slowly, but his mind was already in gear.

"Sexton going to be on the witness stand all day?" Raimondi asked quietly.

"I'll keep him on all day," Sheridan replied.

"I know a ballistics expert at the New Bedford crime lab—Portugee like me. Owes me a few favors."

Raimondi knew this assignment was even more risky than the last. If Sexton had discovered that the glass in the rear door of his house had been tampered with, or noted the missing Van Zandt, the place would not only be wired; it would be teeming with camcorders covering every means of entry.

"Let me see what I can do."

●

"Ladies and gentlemen of the jury." Judge Samuels gave the panel his usual morning platitudes, noting that all jurors plus two alternates were present. "I see you have braved the storm. You are to be commended. You have taken your assignment most seriously. I congratulate you on your commitment.

"Now, Counselor." He looked down at Sheridan. "I believe you have Dr. Sexton, the defendant, under direct examination. Are you ready to proceed?"

"Yes," Sheridan said crisply. "And Your Honor, would you kindly remind Dr. Sexton that he is still under oath."

Samuels's lips tightened in obvious disapproval. He didn't appreciate Sheridan's reminders of his judicial prerogatives.

"Yes, Mr. . . . Mr. . . . "

"Sheridan, Your Honor. Daniel Sheridan."

"Mr. Coyne"—Samuels motioned to the bailiff—"will you please call Dr. Robert Sexton."

The doctor wore a gray suit, white button-down shirt, dark maroon tie. A thin black beeper peeped out of his breast pocket. This was an added prop, not present previously. Sheridan thought it was probably one of Charlie Finnerty's inventions, possibly rigged to go off when Sexton needed a time-out.

As Dr. Sexton took his seat on the witness stand, Sheridan eyed him carefully. He knew that he was facing a diabolical killer. Before, it had been just a strong suspicion. Now he was virtually certain. This man had destroyed two lives—and Sheridan knew that whatever way the case turned out, either he or Sexton alone would remain standing. Both could not survive.

37

Raimondi made a call on José Viveiros, another cousin of sorts, whose locksmith shop was located on lower Washington Street, a sleazy enclave honeycombed with strip joints, seedy gin mills, and peep-show arcades where hookers, hustlers, and transvestites separated sailors, suburban johns, and Harvard undergrads from their greenbacks. The area had earned its reputation as the "Combat Zone." But to Viveiros, whose hole-in-the-wall enterprise was sandwiched between an X-rated bookstore and an all-night porno theater, the security-lock business was brisk and the rent was cheap.

Manny showed Viveiros the photos he had taken of the cylindrical combination lock to Sexton's gun rack. Viveiros was smart enough not to ask questions as he examined each print.

"Seen that type of lock before, Joe?"

Viveiros scratched his chin. "It's a Seth Williamson, manufactured right here in Watertown. Pretty good security, as locks go."

"Joe, I have an unusual request. If I bring this lock in, can you decipher the combination?"

"You don't know the numbers?"

"I don't. But I need to get hold of an extra lock—same type—Seth Williamson, you say. If you can give me the original combo, I want you to reset it in the new lock. . . ."

"Same combination?"

"Same."

"I should be able to get a lock from my supplier. Trying to decipher the original combination from the click of the tumblers is going to be well nigh impossible."

Raimondi reached for his wallet and pulled out ten Ben Franklins.

Cousin José's eyes suddenly brightened. "I'm not saying it can't be done, Manny."

"Here, Joe, for your trouble—a thousand dollars."

There was a no-nonsense exchange. Viveiros knew that no receipt was needed or intended.

"Let me see if I'm reading you," Viveiros said as he slid the bills into his pocket. "You're going to bring me the original Seth Williamson and you want me to get the combo and reset it in the new lock?"

Raimondi nodded.

"When do you need this?"

"Like yesterday, Joe. I gotta get this all done by this afternoon."

Viveiros puffed out his cheeks and let out a soft whistle.

"I'll have to get the new lock now. It'll be an imposition. . . ."

"I know your skill, Joe."

Viveiros somehow didn't appear impressed with the blandishments.

"You do this job for me, Joe, and there'll be an extra grand in it."

"Okay. Say I get the Seth, when do you give me the old lock? Picking the exact combination will take some doing, believe me. These locks are guaranteed burglarproof. . . ."

"I should have it by noon, twelve-thirty at the latest."

Viveiros shook his head. "These tumblers are tricky. How many days do I have to figure it out?"

"About an hour, Joe, two at the most. Gotta get out of your shop by two."

"Okay," Viveiros said, "I'm on my way. No guarantees, mind you."

"Hey, Joe, nothing's certain in life, *Assim e' a vida*, as old Grandmother Ferreira used to say."

"Yeah, see ya, Manny. *Va com Deus!*"

●

Sheridan again positioned himself just to the rear of the last juror in the front row.

"Dr. Sexton, I think when you were last on the stand we were discussing why the Atrium was glassed in and why your psychiatric offices were moved to the first floor. I think your response was that it was Sister Agnes Loretta's idea. Do you recall that?"

"I do."

"Let me ask you this, Doctor. Donna DiTullio was in pretty bad shape when she was admitted under your care to St. Anne's Hospital, was she not?"

"She was distressed."

"Distressed?" Sheridan furrowed his brow and looked at Sexton quizzically. "She was more than distressed, Doctor. She had slashed her wrists, and you as her physician-psychiatrist signed a document committing her involuntarily to St. Anne's— isn't that the truth of the matter?"

"I had her committed after discussing it with her parents."

"And when you have a patient *involuntarily* committed, you know that this can be done only upon your assessment that the patient is a danger to herself and a danger to others, isn't that medically correct?"

Sheridan plucked the pink commitment form from among the documents on the dais and gave it a little shake.

"In fact, you signed this commitment form, and those exact words are on the form over your signature, isn't that so, Doctor?"

"Yes." The reply was almost inaudible.

"So, from a psychiatric standpoint, Donna DiTullio was then in dire straits?"

"She was having a breakdown."

"And she had no say as to whether or not she required confinement, isn't that correct?"

Sexton nodded.

"Doctor, so that the court reporter can record your reply—you just answered yes, isn't that correct?"

"Yes." The doctor cleared his throat. "That's correct."

"In your assessment, the danger to herself in Donna Di-Tullio's case was that she might commit suicide; that is why she was confined to a controlled hospital setting—isn't that true?"

"Yes, we didn't want further harm to come to Donna."

"And in this controlled hospital setting, the ultimate harm did in fact come to Donna; isn't that a fair statement, Dr. Sexton?"

"For chrissakes, Mayan," Finnerty whispered to d'Ortega, "he's chewing our guy up out there. Start objecting. If you don't, I will."

She leaned toward her associate. "Charlie, I'm trying the case. I'll object if I have a legal basis."

"Legal basis my ass! Object!" Finnerty hissed. "You've got to get Sheridan out of his rhythm."

Sheridan paused a few moments and looked at the defense table, taking in the muffled exchange. So did the jury.

"When all of you broke for your coffee on that fateful morning," Sheridan continued, "what time was it?"

"About eight-fifty."

"Who left first?"

"What do you mean?"

"I mean, among the psychiatric personnel present—Joe Sousa, the social worker; Elaine Adamson, the nurse; Dr. Puzon; Dr. Lafollette; and you—who left the group therapy session first?"

"We all left at about the same time."

"That's not completely accurate, Doctor, is it?"

"I don't know what you mean."

"As a matter of fact, Doctor, you were the last person to

382 \ BARRY REED

leave. I talked with the other two patients who were in the group therapy session, Ted Marden and Janet Phillips. . . ."

"I understand you have," Sexton interjected coldly.

"They both stated that everyone left and you left about a minute later. Then Donna DiTullio walked out."

"If you say so."

"No, Doctor, it's not what I say. I'm asking *you*."

"I was the last of the team to leave the group."

"Did you see Donna leave?"

"Yes. We left together. I was headed back to my office and had forgotten some notes, so I was returning to the group therapy room."

"And as I understand it, Doctor, and correct me if I'm wrong, on your way back, you happened to glance to your left, through the glass doors leading to the Atrium, and you spotted Donna at the rail."

"She was up on the rail."

"Do you recall Donna telling you prior to your leaving the therapy room that she felt nauseous and was going out into the Atrium for a little fresh air?"

"I seem to recall that."

"Now, how much time elapsed between the moment you left the group therapy session and the time you spotted Donna at the rail?"

"I didn't time it."

"I know you didn't, Doctor. No one did." Irritation crept into Sheridan's voice. "But just enlighten us a little—what's your best estimate?"

Sexton issued a sigh.

"Was it more than a minute, Doctor?" Sheridan pressed.

"No."

"Thirty seconds?"

"Maybe twenty to thirty seconds," Sexton replied.

"Where were Dr. Lafollette, Dr. Puzon, Nurse Adamson, and Joe Sousa at that time?"

"I don't know."

"As a matter of fact, at that moment, they were nowhere in sight, isn't that right, Doctor?"

"That's right."

Sheridan now was ready to hatch his plan. It might work, might not. He abruptly changed the pace and the subject matter of his direct examination.

"You are a lieutenant colonel in the National Guard, are you not, Dr. Sexton?"

Sexton looked at Sheridan curiously, as did Finnerty and d'Ortega. Why parade someone's war record or military service, especially that of your adversary?

"I am," Dr. Sexton replied firmly.

"You are not in the medical branch of the National Guard, Doctor, but serve in the infantry." Sheridan again picked up a document from the dais. "Battalion Corps commander, I believe?"

"Battalion commander," Sexton corrected as he looked at the jury.

"You served in Desert Storm?"

"I did."

"It says here"—Sheridan glanced at the note—"that your specialty is weaponry—automatic-rifle fire. In fact, you hold the Expert Rifleman Award?"

"I do," Sexton answered diffidently.

The defense team, and even Buckley, thought that Sheridan was losing it. Buckley looked at Sheridan, and with a hand concealed from the jury with a yellow scratch pad, he gave the slash sign across his throat. The signal was not lost on Finnerty or d'Ortega.

Sheridan changed his line of inquiry.

"Now, I understand that you gave a statement that you rushed toward Donna and yelled, *'Don't jump!'*—something to that effect—but it was too late; she had already jumped. Is that correct?"

Sexton lowered his head and shielded his eyes with his hand.

"Christ," Buckley swore under his breath, "here comes the onion-in-the-handkerchief act."

He was absolutely correct. Sexton broke into a sob, his shoulders heaving.

The jury remained transfixed. Buckley knew their empathy now went out to Sexton. He couldn't believe Sheridan had taken this tack. He glanced back at Judy. Her lips were tight and she gave a slight disapproving shake of her head.

Judge Samuels offered Sexton some water. Sexton filled a glass from the chrome carafe, took several sips, and wiped his eyes with his handkerchief.

"I think this would be a good time to take our morning recess, don't you agree, Mr. Sheridan?" Samuels stood and flexed his shoulders in an effort to relieve tension.

"I agree, Your Honor," Sheridan said deferentially.

Samuels addressed the jury. "We'll be back here in twenty minutes, and let me see all counsel in my chambers."

Buckley took Sheridan aside after the jury left. "Jesus, you had this guy on the goddamned ropes," he steamed. "All you had to do was finish him off. What the fuck was all that crap about him being a lieutenant colonel—and Desert Storm, no less!"

Sheridan looked a little amused. "Buck, I know what I'm doing."

"Yeah?" Buckley retorted. "Well, if you do, you're the only goddamned person here who's in on it, including the jury—especially the jury."

●

In tailing Sexton for the last few weeks, Raimondi had established a certain routine in the Sexton household. Sexton's driver would drop him off at St. Anne's, usually about 7:30 A.M., then pick him up at 5:00 P.M., drop him off at times at some of the smart shops on Newbury Street—and occasionally wait for him when Sexton dropped in for a cocktail at the Ritz lounge.

Sometimes after the chauffeur's morning run, he'd double back to Sexton's manse, pick up the maid, and they'd go off for the day. This morning, the Cadillac left at 9:00 A.M. Raimondi thought they would be headed for court. Because of the storm, the session didn't start until ten today. Raimondi pulled his Toyota into the parking area along Charles River Drive, some hundred yards from Sexton's residence. He was hoping this was one of the days the chauffeur and the maid would go out on the town. The snowbanks obstructed his view, so he waited outside the car, occasionally craning his neck for a better view. Sheridan had promised to keep Sexton on the witness stand all day, which would be until four o'clock. But time was running against him; he now had only a slight window, maybe twenty minutes. Of course, he could try tomorrow—but from what Sheridan had told him, he'd conclude with Sexton at the close of this trial day.

Raimondi was about to abort his enterprise when, close to 12:30, the chauffeur drove up, tooted the horn. The maid came out the front door, got into the front seat of the Cadillac, and they drove off.

Raimondi didn't have a second to waste. Fortunately, in near-freezing temperatures, there were no Harvard students jogging along the Charles River footpaths. But he knew the snow would pose a problem. The drifts in some places were three feet high. He wore oversized boots, size thirteen, and trudged toward the brick wall, threw a sawed-off rake, then a duffel bag, over the top, and scaled it easily, plunging into the snow-covered rhododendrons. He secured his gear, slipped off his black knit cap, and put on a ski mask. If the place had been secured with camcorders, best to have a complete disguise. Snapping on latex gloves, he made his way to the back porch, fortunately cleared of snow, and tested the door latch. He fingered the lower pane of glass and could see the striations of the previous cut. Using his cutting tool, he traced along the same seam, quickly removed the panel of glass, reached in, and opened the door. He left the rake near the rear stairs, took off his boots inside the vestibule, and then threw them back out onto the porch. In double-stockinged feet, he made his way directly to Sexton's den. He produced a thin file, a few probes, and he pushed the door open. He glanced quickly around the room. No camcorders, at least none visible. But he knew that any alarm wouldn't sound like a fire truck clanging to a fire; rather, it would subtly inform the nearest Cambridge police precinct. He had no time to spare.

He quickly examined the cylindrical lock. Only one way—he had to break it open, hopefully without disturbing the sensitive combination. With a hammer and chisel, he cracked the clasp ring quite easily, shook it loose from the rack, and slid it into his pocket. He grabbed the Bauer rifle, stuffed it into the duffel bag, left the den door unlocked, and moved quickly to the back door. He slipped on his boots, put the glazier's glue on the pane of glass, and patted it into place. No time to check. This would have to do. He made his way to the wall, scaled it, and landed again in the deep snow. He'd pack some snow up on the wall the second time around, also use the rake to try to cover his tracks. Putting the new lock back within his limited time frame was going to be marginal at best. He thought about it—like mountain climbing, coming down could be worse than climbing up.

As he drove off, he checked the time: 1:15. He would have to race to Viveiros's shop and hope that he could work in the new combination, then race back before the chauffeur and the maid, and maybe even Sexton, arrived home.

—

"Can I perform a little experiment?" Raimondi said to Viveiros as he carted in his duffel bag.

"Sure," Viveiros said as he scrutinized the Seth Williamson lock. "Go down in the basement, shut the doors, flush the toilet, and have all the taps running." Viveiros adjusted his jeweler's specs and fingered the cylindrical lock, then put on some acoustical earphones attached to a rubber cord resembling a doctor's stethoscope. Somehow, Viveiros knew what Raimondi was up to.

Raimondi did as instructed, took out the Bauer, inserted a Van Zandt. It was risky—the bullet might explode like a hand grenade. He held his breath as he fired into a pillow stuffed with rags and steel wool. Fortunately, no fireball. He retrieved the spent bullet and cartridge, slipped them into his pocket, and again slid the Bauer back into his bag.

When he returned upstairs, Viveiros was still slowly turning the barrels of the cylinders and listening intently. *Click, click, click*. Nothing. He shook his head.

"I don't think I'm going to be able to crack this, Manny. These Seth Williamsons are built to foil exactly what we're doing."

"Okay," Manny said calmly, telling himself not to panic. "Give me the new lock; that'll have to do."

"Right now, three zeros opens the lock," Viveiros said. "If you can leave it for another few days . . ."

Raimondi shook his head. "I appreciate your efforts, Joe. Here." He pulled out his wallet and handed Viveiros five one-hundred-dollar bills.

Viveiros didn't hesitate or refuse. "As I say, a few more days . . ."

"No, this'll have to do. Appreciate your efforts, Joe. *A Deus!*"

"Anytime. *A Deus, amigo.*"

●

Samuels invited all counsel to sit down. He was curious as to where Sheridan was going with his queries on Sexton's military service. If Mayan d'Ortega tried to elicit that information on cross-examination, it would seem crass, almost egregious puffery. Samuels didn't know whether Sheridan was stupid or had made a classic mistake.

"How long are you going to be with this witness?" Samuels asked Sheridan. "Seems you could be done around one P.M., then put on your next witness and go until four."

"I'll be all day with Dr. Sexton, Your Honor. He is the main witness."

"All day?" Samuels shook his head.

"Okay. . . . You people made any progress to resolve this case?"

"No progress, Judge." Sheridan answered for all.

"All right, we'll resume in fifteen minutes."

●

Raimondi again scaled the side wall to Sexton's residence, toting along his duffel bag. The reentry was made without difficulty and he quickly returned the Bauer to the gun rack and clicked the new lock into place. Sexton wouldn't be able to open the lock, but maybe he would think something had gone awry with the combination. The new lock looked exactly like the original. He locked the den and back doors from the inside and covered his tracks as best he could, this time smoothing the snow with the rake as if he were leaving a sand trap on a golf course. He then sped along the Charles River Drive, crossing the Prison Point Bridge into Boston. From there, he caught the Mass Turnpike and switched over to the Fall River Expressway. Knowing that any calls on his car phone could be easily traced, he stopped at a Burger King and dialed Domingo Silva—a longtime friend who was chief ballistics expert on the New Bedford Police Department.

It was about 3:15 when he pulled into the lot behind a line of police cruisers. Silva was waiting, and let Raimondi in the back door, avoiding the ID routine at the front desk.

Silva led Raimondi down to the cinder-block basement, unlocked the door, and they stepped into the ballistics lab.

"We just got an electronic scope—came from the FBI lab in Washington."

On the phone, Raimondi had told Silva that he wanted a comparison of bullets.

"Here, Dom." Raimondi produced two clear plastic bags and emptied the contents out on the white ceramic table.

"These are Van Zandts. Two slugs and four spent cartridges. You know about Van Zandts."

"Pretty deadly." Silva picked up one slug and examined it carefully. Like Viveiros, Silva didn't want to appear too inquisitive. Because of his association with the police department, he didn't want to be burdened with any specific knowledge. He slipped on some magnifying specs and examined both slugs side by side.

"These bullets were fired from what type of gun?"

"The one on the right was fired by a seven-millimeter Bauer.

I've reason to believe the one on the left came from the same gun."

"One slug is pretty well mashed," Silva said, "but the lands and grooves should be delineated under our new scope. If they came from the same gun, we'll soon know."

He first placed the slugs side by side on a glass slide. The microscope resembled a giant Mixmaster. Silva peered, adjusted the dials, peered again, made more adjustments, then proceeded to take several shots with the scope's built-in camera.

"Here, take a look," Silva said to Manny. "See those lands and grooves—they mesh almost perfectly. No question that both slugs were shot from the same gun."

Next, the cartridges were put to the same test.

"See those markings and striations?" Silva again allowed Raimondi to take a look. "These cartridges, same as the slugs, came from the same gun."

Silva clicked several shots of both cartridges, developed the prints in the lab's darkroom, and gave them to Raimondi.

It was now close to 4:00 P.M. Raimondi gathered up the bullets and cartridges and replaced them in the plastic envelopes.

"Want to thank you, Dom," he said as he took out his wallet.

"This is on the house, Manny," Silva said. "Hope everything works out okay."

"I'm not sure where I'm going, Dom. Want to thank you again. But seriously." He was about to replace his wallet in his pocket.

"Tell you what," Silva said, "send what you were going to give me to St. Rosa's Church, care of Father Damian Santiago Sort of an anonymous donation—those are the best kind."

Raimondi sped back toward Boston along the Southeast Expressway. St. Rosa's would be the beneficiary of a thousand, and maybe he'd add a few more of the new Ben Franklins.

—

Sheridan had aimed a steady stream of questions at Sexton about the care and treatment of Donna DiTullio during the period she was under his care. He went over the St. Anne's medical record, questioning the doctor on every entry, every consult, every nursing note, and the medication chart. Sexton seemed to hold up well. This was his field; he ran with his answers, looking at the jury when he saw the opportunity. When Sheridan tried to cut him off, explaining that the questions called for simple yes or no answers, Samuels chided him in front of the jury, stating that the witness should be allowed an explanation.

It was nearing four o'clock. Sheridan paused to compose himself.

"You have much more with the doctor?" Samuels glanced at his watch.

"Only a few more questions, if Your Honor pleases."

"Go ahead."

Sheridan left his position behind the last juror and took several steps toward the witness stand. He waited for several seconds.

"Dr. Sexton, when was the last time you saw Donna Di-Tullio?"

"You mean as a patient?"

"No. I mean, when was the last time you saw Donna DiTullio in any capacity, as a physician or simply as a concerned visitor?"

"I dropped in on her while she was on St. Anne's neuro-surgical service."

"That was only on one occasion, correct, Doctor?"

"Yes, there was nothing I could do for her."

"Do you know where she is now?"

"I believe at Hampton Rehabilitation Clinic in Boxford."

"Would it surprise you to know, Doctor, that Donna is recovering from her injuries at Greenbriar Lodge in White River Junction, Vermont? Did you know that?"

"I was unaware—"

"You've heard of Greenbriar, have you not, Doctor?"

"Yes, it's a fine hospital. Connected with Dartmouth College, I believe."

Sheridan moved a few steps closer to Sexton and looked directly into his eyes. "Doctor, would it also surprise you to know that Donna DiTullio has regained mental and communicative capacities so that she can actually relate the events that occurred that fateful morning?"

Suddenly, Sexton seemed to fold within himself. Surprise registered on his face as if he'd been struck by some unseen force. The calm veneer, the military posture, suddenly deserted him.

"Yes," he blurted, visibly shocked, "it would surprise me."

To Buckley and Judy, the jury seemed unaffected. If anything, their empathy was still with the doctor. Only Sheridan knew that he now had the great Dr. Sexton, seducer and killer, finally at bay. But Sheridan well knew that an animal at bay could be unpredictable and extremely dangerous.

38

Sexton sat in his office, contemplating the turn of events. No time to panic. He sipped his second cup of coffee and downed two Valiums. It was after 8:00 P.M. The secretaries and receptionist had left around six and Dr. Puzon and Dr. La-follette were making evening rounds over in the Kennedy Wing. He had called and told McGinley Browne that he'd be back close to midnight—that he'd take a cab home.

He thought about using the pay phone in the Atrium lobby, but he decided to be up-front when he checked on Donna Di-Tullio. He picked up his desk phone and had the operator connect him to Greenbriar Lodge at White River Junction.

Fortunately, instead of the usual sterile directions telling him to select from a menu of numbers, a pleasant woman's voice answered immediately.

"Hello," he said, "I'm Dr. Robert Sexton, calling from Boston. I'd like to check on a former patient's condition.

"Name's DiTullio, Donna DiTullio. She's presently a patient at your facility."

"You want Patient Information, Doctor. Let me connect you." There was a short delay. Sexton took another sip of coffee and his fingers drummed on his notepad.

"Patient Information," came another cheerful voice. "How can I help you?"

"I'm Dr. Robert Sexton, calling from Boston." His voice was steady, controlled. "I'd like to check on a former patient's condition. . . . Name's DiTullio, Donna DiTullio."

"Oh, yes, Doctor. Donna's condition is described as fair. She's out of intensive care. I know the case. Terrible injuries, but I'm happy to report she seems to be coming along."

"Well, that's certainly encouraging," Sexton said. "It was a most unfortunate case. Can you tell me what prompted her admission? I treated her when she was at St. Anne's in Boston, and she was convalescing at a state hospital here in Massachusetts. A wonderful girl. I thought I'd take a ride up and stop in to see her tomorrow. Can she receive visitors?"

"Oh, yes. She's made remarkable progress. Not out of the woods, mind you. She had a thrombosis in her femoral vein— now on a full heparin drip."

"That's what I understand," Sexton said as he scratched down the word *heparin* on his desk pad and began to formulate his plan. Heparin was an anticoagulant administered to prevent blood clots.

Yes, he thought to himself, this should work out perfectly.

—

"There's no question that the Van Zandt bullets, the one you dug out of Wampanoag and the sample here"—Raimondi dangled both plastic bags in front of Sheridan—"came from Sexton's Bauer. Here are the ballistics tests I had run. Lands and grooves of both slugs are a match." Raimondi spread the magnified prints out on the conference table. "Also, the markings on the cartridges coincide."

Sheridan studied each shot.

"I knew we should have gone to the police at the outset." Buckley shook his head. "Now we're in a goddamned bind. What do we do? Explain that there was an attempted murder weeks ago—and here's the proof? . . . All we got now is two bullets that came from the same gun." He looked at Raimondi curiously.

"Sexton, of course, let you borrow his gun? . . . And we're losing sight of the DiTullio case. . . ."

"I've got to have time to think this out," Sheridan said. He still hadn't let young Buckley or Raimondi in on his communication with Donna—although Buckley had a pretty good idea what was involved.

"You plan to bring Donna down to testify, the blinking of the eyes stuff?" He addressed Sheridan but glanced inquiringly at Raimondi.

"No, I thought of it. We'll play your video of Donna for the jury, Manny, and then go with Dr. White. D'Ortega and Finnerty think I'll lead with Sister Agnes Loretta. Maybe I should."

"I think you gotta start with the nun," Buckley said. "She may break the case wide open. Remember, it was the good sister who glassed in the Atrium, relocated the psychiatric service to the first floor. If you press, she might concede that she had requested this procedure many times in the past. That would toss the lie back into Sexton's face. Give us the smokin' gun we need."

"No, we'll open with White. I'm not sure what Sister Agnes Loretta is going to say. But right now, we've got to put our best spin on the case."

Buckley wondered why Sheridan had discontinued Sister Agnes Loretta's deposition. Only by deposition can you bolt a witness down to an absolute set of facts. "I dunno." He shook his head. "White's our sole expert. If the Mex cuts him up, and I think she will, we'll have to scramble for the one million—if, in fact, it's still on the table."

"That's just what I hope d'Ortega will do, try to stomp him. White can handle the infighting. He's testified in hundreds of cases."

"That's what bothers me," Buckley said without much enthusiasm. "Miss Brass Tits will spend three days going through all these cases, point by point, try to paint him as a money-hungry charlatan."

"I'm well aware of that possibility," Sheridan said. "Maybe in direct examination, I'll take the wind out of her sails." He gathered up the prints and tucked them into the plastic bags. "Hold on to these, Manny; we may need them."

"Unless White scores a complete KO," Buckley persisted, "we gotta think of bailing out, taking the million and getting the hell over the county line as fast as we can."

"If that remains our sole option, sure." Sheridan didn't seem as concerned as the moment dictated. "We'll burn that bridge when we get to it."

Buckley glanced at his watch. "Dan, say we bring Donna in before the jury—with the nurses dressed in white, her attendants—the whole life-support regalia. Forget the videotapes. Let the jurors see the flesh and blood, what's really involved. It would have a hell of an impact."

Then he added, "Now, Dan, maybe you can fill me in. . . . Just what is Donna going to communicate? Anything different from what we already know?"

"I don't plan to bring her down from Greenbriar." Sheridan, too, glanced at his watch. It was late, a few minutes past midnight.

"Too much theater for the jury. I think they'd be turned off."

Buckley let it drop, but he was smart enough to know that Sheridan hadn't answered his question.

—

Raimondi parked at the rest area as usual, not far from Sexton's home. It was about 7:00 A.M., and every so often he studied the residence and grounds with his high-powered binoculars. He waited patiently, at intervals turning off and restarting the engine, trying to keep warm in the freezing temperature. He knew that Sheridan had planned to lead with Dr. White and he surmised that Sexton and the other defendants would be listening intently to every word of testimony. He passed the time by reading the morning paper, working the crossword, and catching a few quick winks, waking abruptly if he heard a car door slam or an engine start. More than three hours elapsed, with no activity at the Sexton household. Raimondi checked his watch.

Strange, he thought, court started at nine, and in the past, the chauffeur has left with Sexton around eight.

At 10:30, Raimondi was jolted from his catnap by the sound of garage doors opening. They were Sexton's, and as Raimondi watched, out came the ivory Cadillac, with Sexton at the wheel.

Raimondi trailed him several car lengths back, but as soon as Sexton got on I-95, heading north, away from Boston, Raimondi decided at least for the time being that Sexton posed no problem and apparently hadn't discovered the break-in or the replaced lock on his gun rack. Pulling into the up ramp of a traffic circle, Raimondi headed back to Boston. He'd check into the courtroom to see how Sheridan was doing.

—

Sheridan had completed his direct examination of Dr. White. As always, White's delivery was smooth and erudite, yet couched in homey analogies readily understood by the jury. He left no doubt in their minds that in the treatment of Donna DiTullio that fateful day, the proper standards of psychiatric and medical care had been breached by all defendants.

"You watch these vulnerable patients as you would watch your three-year-old child or grandchild," White concluded as he addressed the jurors. "If you have a swimming pool in your backyard, you don't let them out of your sight, even for an instant."

The jurors leaned forward and seemed to hang on every word. Sheridan knew White was hitting home. And none of it was lost on Finnerty and d'Ortega.

The judge nodded toward the defense table. "Miss d'Ortega, your cross-examination."

"Just a few moments, if Your Honor pleases," she said as she gathered up her notes.

"White did a masterful job," Buckley whispered to Sheridan. "Really came across. I watched the jurors, especially the back row—that's where you win or lose it, the last row. Jurors can really hide back there, goof off, fall asleep. But Dan, they were on the edge of their seats."

"I hope so, Buck, but I don't underestimate d'Ortega. Too early to bet the farm." Sheridan glanced back over his shoulder, past Finnerty, d'Ortega, and Devaney, who at the moment were in a huddled conference. He looked at Judy, whose thumb and forefinger formed an affirmative circle, and she gave it a little shake in his direction. His gaze took in Anna DiTullio, who sat rigid, her lips tight and expectant.

He then tried to get a glimmer of recognition from the defendants—Drs. Puzon and Lafollette, Nurse Adamson, and Joe Sousa. They sat expressionless, as did Monsignor Devlin and Sister Agnes Loretta. No read there. But he knew White had done a good job. Unless d'Ortega blew him out of the courtroom, Samuels would be forced to let the case go to the jury. And under the civil judicial system, just as Sheridan had had the advantage of giving his opening statement first, he would have the double advantage of the last word. In final summation, he could rebut d'Ortega, but there would be no surrebuttal, no chance for d'Ortega to attack his final argument.

Suddenly, something pinged in the red zones of Sheridan's mind. *Sexton—where was Sexton?* The courtroom was jammed— the defense consultants, maybe ten strong, lawyers, and several newspaper reporters he recognized. Many spectators were standing against the back wall. He surveyed the crowd quickly. Sexton was nowhere in sight. He rechecked the row of defendants. Where the hell was Sexton? He should be here—White's testimony was crucial. Sheridan thought for several moments.

D'Ortega had picked up her yellow scratch pad, together with her notes.

"With Your Honor's permission . . ." She nodded.

The judge smiled in paternal approbation, then turned to the jury.

"Ladies and gentlemen, you have just heard what we call the direct examination of Dr. White—the plaintiff's professional witness."

"Son of a bitch!" Buckley groaned. "Guy is killing us. Imagine emphasizing the word *professional*! Didn't exactly use the term *hired gun* or *trained seal*, but I'm sure the jury got the message."

But as d'Ortega, smartly dressed in a light gray suit, walked toward the dais, Sheridan's mind was elsewhere. Something was wrong. He glanced back at Judy. Nothing. Where in hell was Sexton?

———

Mayan d'Ortega assembled her notes on the dais and paused for several seconds, her eyes taking the measure of her adversary.

"Dr. White," she began slowly, calmly, "so that the jury will understand your exact position in this case . . . and as Mr. Sheridan repeatedly requested during his direct examination of Dr. Sexton, please answer in the affirmative or the negative, yes or no.

"You never treated Donna DiTullio, isn't that true?"

"Yes, that's true."

"You merely reviewed deposition transcripts and medical records, isn't that correct?"

"That's correct."

"And based on the study of those records, you gave your opinion here today, isn't that true?"

"I based my opinion on those documents, and of course I heard Dr. Sexton's testimony. I formulated my opinion on these factors and my lengthy experience in handling psychiatric cases."

"Let's get into that for a few moments." D'Ortega left the dais and advanced a few steps toward the witness stand. "You've testified in the courtroom how many times?"

"I don't know the exact number."

"As a matter of fact, Doctor, over the past five years, you have testified in the courtroom"—she glanced down at a paper she held in her hand—"on twenty-eight cases, isn't that a fair statement?"

Mayan stood near the center juror and cupped her ear, pretending to listen for White's reply.

"I would say that's about the number," he said calmly.

"Twenty-eight cases where you actually testified . . ."

"Is that a question?" White said, his voice steady, respectful.

Mayan ignored the slight dig.

"And, Doctor, you got paid for your testimony on those cases, isn't that correct?"

"No, that's not correct. I got paid for my time, just as you are being paid for your time."

The judge gave a sharp rap of his gavel. "Doctor, please just answer yes or no—don't embellish your answers."

"I'm sorry, Your Honor. I thought I was responding fairly to an unfair question."

"Please, Doctor. You just answer the question and don't argue with the Court." The judge's lips tightened and he shook his head in displeasure.

"Please continue, Miss d'Ortega."

"In addition to actually testifying in the courtroom," she said, "you reviewed cases for lawyers and rendered opinions in their cases, isn't that a fact?"

"Yes. I've reviewed cases on both sides of the ledger, for both defense and plaintiff attorneys, some for the prosecutor's office. . . ."

D'Ortega cut him off. "And sometimes you reviewed cases for criminal defense attorneys trying to advance a theory of temporary insanity in homicide cases, isn't that true?"

"Yes." White's voice had a touch of frustration. Sheridan recognized it, but he knew any objections to d'Ortega's collateral attack wouldn't be sustained by the judge; in fact, Samuels might land on him hard in front of the jury. In this type of examination, White was on his own.

"In addition to testifying in twenty-eight courtroom cases, how many cases did you review for lawyers?"

"What time frame are you referring to?"

"Let's stick to the last five years."

White thought for a few moments. "I'd say about twenty to thirty, give or take a few cases."

"Let's compromise, Doctor. Let's call it twenty-five.

"Now, with regard to this total of fifty-three cases, you got paid, as you say, for your time, did you not, Doctor?"

White was tempted again to say something flip, but he didn't want to endanger the favorable impression he knew he had built up in the jury's collective mind.

"Yes," he said quietly. "I was paid on most of the cases."

"Well, you make a pretty good living doing this sort of stuff, isn't that a fair statement?"

"Doing what sort of stuff?"

"Testifying and reviewing cases for lawyers."

"Please, Ms. d'Ortega." White saw a slight opening. He looked at the jury. "I testify and review cases based on merit. I've reviewed many cases where I've had to tell the litigants and their attorneys that they have no case or no defense. My expertise is not for sale; I am not a partisan. I testify only if I feel there is a meritorious claim or defense. As a matter of fact, I testified for the district attorney's office when you were assistant prosecutor. The truth is that not enough physicians are willing to get involved in these cases, especially when they are Massachusetts physicians asked to testify against local doctors, and as in this case, psychiatrists. In fact, there is a wall of silence prevailing in Massachusetts, dictated by the medical societies. Hopefully, I'm knocking a few bricks off that wall."

"Are you finished, Doctor?" D'Ortega's voice was etched with sarcasm.

"Yes," he said. "I merely wanted to answer your question."

D'Ortega had introduced and pursued the line of inquiry, and she knew she couldn't move on without having the last word.

She moved a few feet closer to him, her eyes now hungry, predatory. "Doctor White, in this case, you formulated an opinion before you had Dr. Sexton's medical notes, before you heard Dr. Sexton's testimony, and even before you had St. Anne's hospital record for Ms. DiTullio's admission to the Psychiatric Ward, did you not? And please answer that yes or no."

"Well . . ."

Judge Samuels decided to help. He leaned toward White. "Doctor, that calls for a yes or no answer. Either you did have these documents or you didn't have them. Don't give any speeches. Just yes or no!"

"No, I didn't have the further data, but that didn't diminish or detract from my medical opinion. When I did review these documents, it reinforced my opinion."

"Please, Dr. White." Samuels rapped his gavel. "From now on, you answer the questions as posed, no evasion or augmentation, do I make myself clear?"

"Certainly, Your Honor," White replied courteously, nodding toward the judge.

"Son of a bitch!" Sheridan swore softly to himself. D'Ortega doesn't even object, and there's Samuels leaping in to help her.

"Now, you agreed for a fee to testify in this case, did you not, Doctor?" D'Ortega again advanced a few steps toward White.

"It was not a fee. As I said before, I am being paid for my time."

"How much are you charging to be here today?"

"I charge three hundred dollars an hour."

"And all told, including the time you spend testifying today, how much time will you have logged on this case?"

"Just an estimate—perhaps twenty hours."

"So that will be about six thousand dollars."

"That's approximately correct."

"Will you receive anything extra if your side prevails?"

"With all due respect, Ms. d'Ortega, I am not on a side, and to answer your question—certainly not!"

The collateral attack on White's credibility gave way to a withering cross-examination on White's proffered opinion that the defendants had provided substandard care and treatment to Donna DiTullio. D'Ortega had done her homework. Gifted with a photoretentive memory, she engaged White in a battle of statistics, psychiatric precepts, and medical probabilities. But on these, White held the high ground, and despite the judge's repeated admonishments to curtail his testimony, White waited patiently for an opening, and when it came, which was not often, he buttressed his position with persuasive articulation.

●

Sheridan felt satisfied with the way White was holding up. He felt no redirect testimony would be needed, and unless d'Ortega elicited some telling concessions, he would have no further questions.

Suddenly, Buckley passed him a note. "Call for a recess. Judy." He glanced back. Judy was seated with Raimondi, and she gave the T signal with her hands. He waited another ten minutes, until d'Ortega had completed her cross-examination.

"Mr. Sheridan, any redirect?" Samuels peered down from the bench.

"No, Your Honor." Sheridan stood.

"Call your next witness."

Sheridan looked up at the bench. "Your Honor, may we have a short recess? You know . . ." He hopped on one leg and then the other. Samuels almost smiled.

"Well, it's twelve-thirty. We'll take an extended lunch hour. Be back here at two."

Sheridan watched the jury file out. Despite his years of trial experience, he never was able to read a jury. Maybe Judy or Buckley could. He couldn't afford the luxury of trying to study a jury. He had to remain focused on the witness, opposing counsel, and the trial judge.

Raimondi pulled Sheridan aside as the spectators and others filed out of the courtroom.

"I didn't tell you," Raimondi said, "but in addition to getting the Van Zandts, I got to learn something about Sexton's routine."

"For some reason, he's not here today," Sheridan offered. "I think it's kind of strange—especially with White on the witness stand."

"Well, I checked at his residence this morning. Usually, his chauffeur drives him to the courthouse, but Sexton left driving his Caddy, and I tailed him until he got onto I-Ninety-five heading north."

"*What?*" Sheridan seemed startled. "Heading north? You sure?"

"I left him at the Fellsway overpass and came back here."

"*Jesus!*" Sheridan swore. "What time was this?"

"Ten-forty. I checked my watch."

"Buck!" Sheridan yelled over to his associate, who was

stacking documents on the counsel table. "I've got to get out of here fast, and I won't be back this afternoon."

"What? Dan, you can't just up and leave. Samuels will croak us—slap us with sanctions."

"Tell Samuels I've had an emergency, that I'll explain later. "Manny, meet me out front as fast as you can!"

—

"Jesus, Judy," Buckley said as they stood at the bank of elevators. "Sheridan takes off like a big-ass bird"—he skidded one palm off the other—"and now I've got to ask Samuels to continue the case and what do I use as an excuse?"

"Somehow, I think it has something to do with Sexton," Judy said. "Manny told me he tailed Sexton this morning to the Fellsway overpass and when he left him, Sexton was headed north on I-Ninety-five."

"North?" Buckley thought back to the tail end of Sheridan's direct examination of Sexton. He now pieced it together.

"Judy," he said as the doors slid open, "you go ahead and get a bite to eat. I've got to see the judge and give some cockeyed excuse why Sheridan won't be available. I'll plead for a continuance, but Samuels won't allow it, I know. He'll make me finish up—but hell, I know the case as well as Sheridan. I'll put Lafollette on the stand. Sheridan always suspected there was some friction between him and Sexton. We'll soon find out."

39

D r. Sexton checked his watch, and pressed down on the gas pedal. The needle edged eighty-five.

He stopped in at a gas station at the Vermont border and asked directions to Greenbriar.

Fine, he thought as he sped off. Should be there in fifteen minutes.

—

Judge Samuels remained tight-lipped as Buckley tried to explain Sheridan's absence.

"Must have something to do with his kidney problem, Judge. It's an emergency, whatever it is."

D'Ortega, Devaney, and Finnerty were not pleased at Buckley's request to suspend until Monday morning.

"Well, he'd better have a pretty good excuse—sudden death in the family—or he's going to be in a peck of judicial trouble. Imagine disappearing in the middle of a trial, not even taking it up with me.

"What do you want me to do, Charlie?" Samuels turned to

Finnerty. "We've already lost a couple of trial days due to the storm."

"Judge," Finnerty said, "Mr. Buckley is here; his appearance is on file. Let him finish up the rest of the day in Sheridan's absence."

"Your Honor," Buckley protested, "I'm merely assisting Mr. Sheridan. My forte is criminal law. With all due respect—"

"Look," Samuels snapped, "once an attorney files an appearance for a client, he assures the Court that he is ready, willing, and able to take whatever steps are necessary to protect his client's rights. . . ."

"But Judge, I don't know the case, and I've never tried a malpractice case."

"There's always a first time." The judge smirked. "You be ready with your witness at two, understand, Mr. Buckley? And you get hold of Mr. Sheridan. I want to see him in my chambers after today's adjournment."

"But Judge . . ." Buckley sighed, his eyes mawkishly imploring, like Emma Gallagher's Saint Bernard asking for food.

"Two o'clock, Mr. Buckley!"

●

Buckley joined Judy at the Beacon Hill Deli.

"Are we excused for the rest of the day?" she asked.

"No way. I gave Samuels the excuse that Sheridan has a kidney condition that must have flared up. But I've got to try the case for the rest of the afternoon."

"So he really knuckled you!"

"Yeah, Judy, he kicked me right into that big ole brier patch!" Buckley grinned. "And boy, am I hungry! Think I'll have a double scotch."

●

Sexton wasn't going to duck around corners. He had freely use
his car phone, calling his office and residence from several N

Hampshire locations. While en route, he had charged a full tank of gas on his credit card.

He signed the hospital register and engaged the receptionist in light banter.

"Hi," he said, "I'm Dr. Robert Sexton, from Boston. Here's my card. Came to visit a former patient of mine, Donna DiTullio."

The receptionist smiled as she checked his card.

"Oh, yes, Doctor. Donna is Dr. Sagall's patient. Coming along quite nicely. She's in the Mary Hitchcock Wing, fourth floor. Take those elevators right behind me."

"And where is Dr. Sagall's office? I'd like to have a chat with him."

"He's in the doctors' wing, Rockefeller Three. Would you like me to page him?"

"No. I'll just visit with Donna and drop in on him afterward."

"And do you have a flower shop in the hospital?" Sexton asked.

"Yes, right next to the pharmacy, down that hall to your right. You can't miss it." The receptionist pointed with her pen.

Sexton purchased half a dozen red roses, had them wrapped, and then rode the elevator to the fourth floor.

"I'm Dr. Robert Sexton, from Boston," he said politely to several nurses gathered at the nurses' station. "I was Donna DiTullio's doctor when she had her unfortunate accident."

"I'm Anne Reddington, the head nurse." A matronly woman in her late forties smiled pleasantly and extended her hand to Sexton. "Donna's in one twelve, just down the hall. Would you like me to put those roses in a vase, Doctor? They're very pretty. Donna loves flowers, especially roses."

"No." Sexton hesitated. "I'll just leave them in her room, thank you. One twelve, you say?"

"Fifth room on the right, Doctor. I'm sure Donna will be ──sed to see you. . . . And Doctor . . ."

"──?"

──don't stay too long—maybe fifteen minutes. Donna
──vertebral arteriograms done this morning. She's

pretty well sedated. I'm sure Dr. Sagall can fill you in on her progress."

"I understand Donna is doing well," Sexton said. "Can she speak or make any sounds yet?"

"No, just soft cooing when she's happy. She can smile—a faint smile. Her improvement is really miraculous."

"That's wonderful," Sexton said. "I won't be long."

It was almost too easy, Sexton thought as he opened the door to 412, slipped into the room quietly, closed the door and locked it.

Donna was asleep, or at least her eyes were closed. He walked carefully, making no noise, and quickly extracted a hypodermic syringe and vial from his suit pocket, ripped open the sterile wrapper, uncapped the syringe, and secured it to the vial with the needle. He held the vial and syringe up to the light and drew the contents of the vial into the syringe, then detached the syringe from the vial, putting the empty vial back in his pocket. The syringe contained Koaki frog venom, a lethal toxin used by the Urangi Indians in the Amazon as a dart poison. A full unrefined dose would kill within seconds, sending the heart into a wild arrhythmia, causing immediate cardiac and respiratory arrest. But over the years, he had experimented with the drug, and from his knowledge of pharmacology, a diluted dosage, such as was now in his syringe, would take twenty-four to thirty-six hours before causing cardiac standstill, especially when further diluted with heparin. The heparin drip was a slow, measured process. The plastic heparin IV was three quarters filled. Fine. It would last another five hours before needing replacement. By then, he would be far from the scene of the terminal event.

He smiled a bit as he thought about it. When Donna died, Sheridan's case would die with her. And when the end came, Dr. Sagall would insist on an immediate autopsy. Koaki, like a few other rare venoms, killed without a trace. No pathologist in th world would come up with anything but cardiac arrest as cause of death. Given Donna's debilitating injuries, she was ceptible to heart failure at any time. He could almost re pathologist's report which would attempt to get Greenbriar off the hook.

He held the syringe at eye level and gave the plunger a slight push. The venom squirted.

As he unhooked the heparin IV from the needle catheter, he shook his head sadly.

"It's for the best, Donna," he said softly. "You don't want to go through life like this."

He lowered the IV bag onto the floor and aimed the syringe into the tubing.

"Hold it right there, Doc! Drop the syringe on the floor and don't do anything foolish or I'll blow your head off!" Sheridan's voice was like ice.

Sexton felt the cold steel of Sheridan's gun against the back of his neck. One jab into Sheridan, he thought.

"I mean it!" Sheridan snapped. "Now!"

Sexton dropped the syringe. Being plastic, it bounced but didn't shatter. Sheridan slid his gun down Sexton's back, poking it into his midsection.

"Sheridan," Sexton said, his back still turned and his hands in a half surrender, "let's be reasonable . . . I was really trying to put Donna out of her misery. A mercy killing."

"Sure," Sheridan said as he reached down and retrieved the syringe, dropping it into his coat pocket. "Like when you shoved Donna over the rail. And when you beat Emanuela Rivera to death in New York."

"Dan, look." Sexton sighed and shook his head. "You want to help Donna? I'll make a deal with you."

Sheridan's plan was falling into place, and sooner than expected. Thank God for Joe Gaynor, a twin-engine Saratoga, and a strong tailwind. He beat Sexton to Greenbriar by ten minutes, took the back stairs, slipped into Donna's room without being ~~noti~~ced, and hid in the bathroom. He had figured it right.

"~~G~~o on, you haven't much time." Sheridan stuck the gun ~~in~~ Sexton's neck.

"~~I haven't g~~ot a dime, believe me. I'm mortgaged to the hilt. ~~You~~ ran a Dun and Brad on me, so you know."

"So you haven't got a dime."

"Look, don't you think I died a thousand deaths over Donna? You don't know what it's like."

"No, I don't know what it's like. I killed in Nam just to survive. I hadn't a goddamned thing against those Cong soldiers. It was me or them."

"Maybe it's the same, Sheridan."

"Boy, you sure have a warped sense of priorities." Sheridan bristled.

"Sheridan, what can I do for Donna? I mean it, I'm at the end of my rope."

"Okay," Sheridan said, "a life for a life."

"What are the terms?" Sexton saw an opening.

"You fly back to Boston with me. We take our leave, all nice and jovial-like. We even drop in on Dr. Sagall and thank him for his excellent care of Donna. But remember, I'll have my gun trained on your gut at all times. Leaves a pretty big hole."

"What else?"

"You're going to tell the cardinal and d'Ortega and Finnerty that you lied in your courtroom testimony, that you were at fault. You rushed to Donna, thinking she might fall, since she was feeling nauseous. You accidentally bumped into her, and over she went. Got that?"

"I think so."

"You get the cardinal to make the insurance company settle Donna's case for the policy limit, twenty million."

"You'll be making a pretty good fee."

"Cut the shit!" Sheridan pressed the barrel of the gun deeper into Sexton's spine. "Once this is done, you get the fuck out of the country. Have the cardinal arrange for you to go to some mission in Rwanda or South America—or join the French Foreign Legion."

"But my home, my practice."

"You leave right after the releases are signed. Who knows, maybe you'll do some good for once in your goddamned miserable life—maybe become an Albert Schweitzer.

"All right, let's go. We march out all smiles."

Sexton lowered his hands. He turned around and faced his adversary, his mind working overtime.

"And don't think you can make a run for it or take me out later." Sheridan kept the gun trained on Sexton, this time at chest level. "I have the syringe. I'm sure it contains some real lethal stuff. And this entire conversation is on tape." He tapped his breast pocket.

"The only way you'll get out of this alive is with me—understand!

"Let's move!"

—

Sheridan and Sexton were ushered into Dr. Sagall's office.

"Well, this is a surprise." The doctor pumped both of his visitors' hands. "May I take your coats?"

"No, we have only a few minutes, Doctor," Sheridan said, his left hand, with the gun, buried deep in his raincoat pocket.

"Weren't you two at loggerheads?" Sagall gave a slight smile, trying not to look too well informed.

"We recently reached an accord," Sheridan said. "Just have to work out some minor details."

"Well, that's wonderful. . . . And Donna—were you surprised to see her coming along so well, Doctor?" He looked at Sexton.

"Yes," Sexton said with feigned enthusiasm. "I was most pleased. She's come a long way."

The leave-taking seemed cordial, at least to Sagall.

"Keep up the good work, Doctor, for Donna," Sheridan said. "I'll be in touch.

"You drive," Sheridan directed. "We'll leave your car at the airport. I'll send my man up for it tomorrow."

"You know, Sheridan, you're breaking a lot of laws—kidnapping, for one, extortion, and, this deal you want me to make, you're aiding and abetting a felony. Things could get very messy for all of us."

"Shut up!" Sheridan snapped. "From here on in, you just carry out your assignment."

Before they turned into the airport road, Sheridan called the office on his pocket phone, luckily catching Buckley.

"Where in the hell . . ." Buckley began.

"Buck, I'll explain later. I'm with Sexton."

"Sexton? Dan, I always thought you took too many to the head in Nam. What in Christ's name . . ."

"We're going to set up a meeting at the cardinal's residence for nine tonight. Sexton wants the case settled for the policy limit."

"Settled? Dan, whaddya been smokin'?"

"I may need your help. We'll be in touch."

Sexton pulled the car into a parking space behind the main hangar.

"Give me the cardinal's private number," Sheridan barked at Sexton.

"Area code six-one-seven-five-five-five-nine-two-oh-oh."

Sheridan punched in the numbers.

"Cardinal's residence. Mrs. Foley speaking."

"Here," Sheridan said, handing Sexton the phone. "I want your uncle to round up Monsignor Devlin, Sister Agnes Loretta, Charlie Finnerty, and that claims man, Walter Crimmins."

"Sheridan," Sexton said wearily, "this isn't going to work. I'll need time."

"You have no time. It works or you're a goner. And this weekend, you're going to be on a plane for Cairo or someplace else far away."

Sexton shook his head. If only I could get hold of Sheridan's tape, he thought.

As they waited for Mrs. Foley to get the cardinal, Sheridan could read Sexton's thoughts.

"Besides killing the Rivera girl, and trying to snuff Donna, you also tried to scratch me."

"How do you know that?"

"The bullets were Van Zandts, fired from your Bauer. Don't

ask me how I know—I just do. And again, don't try anything crazy. I'd just as soon put a bullet into you right now. Save me a lot of trouble."

●

They met in the cardinal's parlor a little after ten. Finnerty didn't like it, but he knew he couldn't cross the cardinal, and from the cardinal's grim look, he knew they weren't invited for tea.

Sheridan stood in the background.

"I've had a talk with Bob," the cardinal said crisply, "and with Sister Agnes Loretta." He addressed Finnerty and Crimmins.

"Bob wants the case settled for the twenty-million policy; so does Sister. Mr. Sheridan here said he'd have the necessary releases and court documents signed."

"But Your Eminence." Finnerty's syrupy voice changed to a nauseating whine.

"Sister warned Bob about using the Atrium for group therapy."

The cardinal's tone had the ring of finality. "I also had my doubts."

"But it runs counter to what Dr. Sexton said on the stand," Finnerty said.

"I'm well aware. That's one reason why the case has to be settled. We have a question of perjury here, and Bob admits he lied under oath—says he was upset."

"Lied about what?" Walter Crimmins asked.

"The real truth is that he accidentally bumped into the DiTullio girl, causing her to fall.

"Either you pay the twenty million dollars"—the cardinal leaned down into Crimmins's face—"or the church will pay it, then sue your company for indemnification and exoneration. Tell Mr. Crimmins, Charlie, that this is not an idle threat."

●

"Well, I assume you want a structured settlement, Mr. Sheridan," Crimmins said, perspiring uncomfortably as he loosened his tie.

"And your fee, how would you like that handled? It will have to be approved by Judge Samuels."

"I'll take care of the annuity structure. We'll sign the necessary documents, even agree to a dismissal against all defendants. Make sure you have a certified check—*twenty million dollars*—payable to Anna DiTullio, conservator of the estate and person of Donna DiTullio. I'm taking no fee."

"What?" Finnerty almost scoffed. "Sure, I know . . ." His face had a knowing smirk.

"No, you don't know, Charlie. I'm charging no fee. Prepare the necessary documents. We'll sign everything tomorrow morning. Tell Samuels that the case is settled."

—

Sheila called Sheridan from Chicago. It was after midnight. He sat in his bathrobe, downing his third bourbon.

It started off well. Sheila felt she hadn't treated Dan too well. She had been close to her father, maybe too close. She wanted to make amends.

"I'll be back Monday," she said.

Sheridan thought he'd be up-front. He detailed the day's events carefully. His explanation took a good half hour.

There was a long silence.

"I don't know what to think, Sheridan," she said finally. "You're committing a gross fraud. Sure, the end result is good. Even Al Capone distributed bread baskets to the needy here in Chicago during the Depression.

"But you're a lawyer, Dan, same as me. Stealing is stealing, and that's what you're doing. I don't care how you look at it."

Sheridan listened and said nothing.

"Dan, you've got to go to the police. You can't make a deal with a killer, even for a hundred million. Dan, if I mean anything to you—*anything*—you'll do as I ask."

"Look, Sheila, we can live with this."

"You can, Dan, but I can't.

"You go back into court immediately and rectify this situation or I'm staying here in Chicago. . . . I mean it, Dan!"

"Sheila, I can't go back on my word!" Sheridan pleaded.

"Dan, we had a good run. Take care of yourself. . . ." Her voice trailed off like a regret.

He heard an unmistakable click.

40

Buckley picked up Judy and they took a cab to the courthouse. In a way, despite the success of yesterday's direct examination of Dr. Lafollette (everyone said he did a great job), Buckley was glad it was over. It was a great settlement, no question, and he had a rough idea how Sheridan had pulled it off. But the victory didn't come without a price. He winced when he spotted a notice in the social page of the *Globe* that Karen Assad was engaged to a doctor at Mass General Hospital. Young Buckley's feelings for her were not in his usual "love 'em and leave 'em" mode.

"You know how much time and money we sank into this case, Judy? Maybe seventy-five, a hundred grand?"

Judy knew Buckley wasn't pleased with Sheridan's waiving the fee and costs.

"I've done work for free before," he said, "relatives, mainly. And then they get a big case—does it come my way? No. Some nephew grabs it. You do work for zip, Judy, and the client thinks less of you, not more, believe me, I know."

"Buck, cheer up." Judy gave him a bemused look. "There'll be other cases."

"What bothers me is that Dan agreed to have the court papers impounded and is going to sign a confidentiality agreement. The *Globe* and the *Herald* will be completely in the dark. We can't even toot our own horn. No one's going to know what noble paladins we are."

"These secrecy agreements, are they constitutional? Seems to be an abridgement of freedom of speech, a restraint of something."

"They've been upheld. We leak stuff out and the insurance company will be over us like a pack of wolves. They'd go after the proceeds.

"I'll tell you, Judy, I'm not exactly ecstatic."

"Look at it this way, Tommy. You guys finally brought all defendants to heel. I'll bet Charlie Finnerty isn't doing cartwheels over the outcome. And think of the good you did. There's more to life, even to a lawyer's life, than making a buck."

Buckley looked over at Judy as the cab stopped.

"Listen, Judy," he said curtly, "I'm getting goddamned tired of your Yiddish platitudes. What we need is cash. As far as cash flow is concerned, we're looking up at the bottom. Want to waive your salary for the next three months? You got a good saying about that one?"

●

The jury was kept on hold, and Bailiff Coyne escorted the lawyers and the court stenographer into Judge Samuels's chambers.

Samuels was wearing his black robe and looked a little baffled as they all filed in.

"Charlie, I just got word from the clerk that the case is settled. Am I hearing correctly?"

"That's right, Your Honor." Finnerty tried to appear gracious. "We reached an eleventh-hour agreement. Mrs. DiTullio has signed the proper documents, and we've drawn up an order for Your Honor's signature that all documents are to be impounded. Mr. Sheridan has also agreed to a confidentiality agreement and, for the official court record, he's signed a stipulation of dismissal as to all defendants."

"Okay," Samuels said, "you want me to approve the settlement?"

"Yes, Your Honor," Finnerty said quickly.

"We have a conservatorship involved." Samuels looked at Sheridan. "How much is the settlement?"

"Twenty million dollars, Judge," Sheridan replied.

"Twenty million?" Samuels's mouth opened in disbelief, he blinked, and his head shot back quickly, as though he'd been hit by a wet rag.

"That's right, Judge," Finnerty interjected. "We think it's fair for all parties."

"I'll say it is!" Samuels scratched his head and rocked back in his chair. He thought for a few moments.

"You absented yourself yesterday, Mr. Sheridan, without leave of the Court. . . ."

"My kidney condition, Your Honor."

"So I've been told.

"Okay, let me see all the papers." Samuels seemed placated. "And what's your fee? You're regulated by statute, you know. It can't exceed twenty-five percent." Samuels made some quick mental calculations; one-fourth of $20 million was $5 million. He hated to see a lawyer make a good payday, especially a windfall, and more especially a score by Dan Sheridan.

"No fee, Your Honor."

"No fee?" Again, Samuels had a baffled expression.

"That's right, Judge. I want all payments to Donna and her mother to be regulated by the Court. I'll see to the necessary documentation."

"Mr. Buckley, you heard Mr. Sheridan. Your firm is charging no fee. You in agreement with that proposal?"

"Absolutely, Judge," Buckley said as soberly as he could. "Sometimes there's more to a lawyer's life than making a buck."

—

The courtroom was deserted. The spectators and lawyers had filed out. Judge Samuels thanked and discharged the jury. Buckley, Judy, and Raimondi had taken most of the documents and evidentiary props back to the office. Finnerty had left, a little puzzled at the outcome but satisfied that he was able to accommodate the cardinal. Time sheets would be filled out generously and his fee would be substantial.

Sheridan lingered for a while and took in the gloomy confines of the old courtroom. He walked to the jury enclosure, paused, leaned forward—hands clasped, elbows resting on the rail—and looked at the empty chairs.

"May I see you for a moment, Counselor?" Mayan d'Ortega's voice came from the back of the courtroom.

"Sure." Sheridan turned slightly. "I always stay behind after winding up a case." He forced a grin as she approached.

They stood together in silence for a few moments at the jury rail. She had the faintest hint of a smile as she shook her head.

"You won again, gringo." She extended her hand.

"It wasn't a win, Mayan," he said, reluctance creeping into his voice. "More a business transaction, a transfer of assets from someone who didn't need it to someone who really did."

"One thing bothers me," she said.

"Only one thing?" Sheridan tried to look amused.

"You charged no fee. Why?"

"You a Catholic, Mayan?"

"At times."

"Well, let's just say it beats a good act of contrition."

She nodded in quiet understanding. "Good-bye," she said. Again they shook hands.

"I suppose you'll take some time off," he said.

"I think not; I'm leaving Finnerty. Defending multimillion-dollar corporations, even the church, is not my idea of practicing law."

"What'll you do?" he said.

"I don't really know. Go out on my own, I guess. Maybe I can still make a difference."

She paused.

"I met Sheila O'Brien," she said. "We had a nice chat."

"Oh?"

"Of all places, we met accidentally in the steam room at the health club. She's lovely, and I think you should be quite happy together."

Sheridan gripped the jury rail and stared vacantly at the jurors' chairs.

"Sheila's back in Chicago," he said. "Her father died and she's kind of winding things up for the family."

But Mayan recognized the rueful catch in Sheridan's voice, and she had some vague intuition that all was not well with the relationship.

She turned to leave. "Until next time, amigo," she said.

"Yeah." Sheridan simply nodded. "There's always a next time."

41

Sheridan popped open a can of Bud Light and sat in his easy chair, watching the late news. It was six months after the DiTullio case settled; Donna was progressing well up at Greenbriar, had even started to talk, and would soon be able to get around in a wheelchair. Sheridan got up there to see her every couple of weeks. But he still ruminated about the real price that he had paid. The case had taken its toll. He could see it in his mirror when he shaved each morning, the deepening crow's-feet about the eyes, the pinched expression, the weariness in his face. Buckley had lost Karen Assad, and his own world had collapsed when Sheila walked. Like Buckley, he learned from a newspaper notice that Sheila had become engaged to a communications specialist in Chicago. He had called Sheila's cousin, Father Paul.

"You'll like him, Dan, a strapping lad," the priest said, "used to play linebacker for the Chicago Bears. . . ."

Somehow, Sheridan knew he wouldn't like him.

He took a good pull on the Budweiser and smiled as Janet Phillips came on the screen, plugging some local restaurant. She had tried to contact him on several occasions, but he had declined the calls.

And Sexton hadn't gone into good works overseas after all. He was still around. But he was six feet under at Mt. Auburn Cemetery. Sheridan thought about it. After Sexton gave the concocted story to his uncle, his conscience started gnawing away at his soul. He was scheduled to go to some foreign mission, and before leaving went to confession, to none other than the cardinal, admitting that he had murdered Emanuela Rivera, and relating the true facts about his involvement with Donna DiTullio. The cardinal refused to grant absolution unless he gave himself up to the police.

Sheridan finished the beer. He remembered the night Sexton had called him, just days after the case had settled, telling him of the cardinal's insistence.

"I'm leaving a note," Sexton said. There was a loud clap, then silence. Sexton had put a pistol into his mouth and had blown his brains out. A life for a life. The suicide was front-page news for a while. But Sexton's note didn't mention Emanuela Rivera. It reaffirmed that Donna DiTullio's fall was accidental. As a dying declaration, it was the highest probative evidence in the law. A person about to meet his Maker speaks the truth. It wasn't exactly what he had told his uncle, but the cardinal's lips were sealed.

Sheridan thought about it. Sexton not only gave up his life; he was willing to lose his soul. But maybe in that dark final moment, he did the right thing. And maybe whoever was up there might take that into consideration.

He had almost dozed off when the phone jangled the stillness. He sprang to his feet and shut off the television.

"Dan." Buckley's voice was slurred. "Got a couple of live ones down here at Sam Adams's pub." His voice faded and Sheridan could hear a muffled conversation. "Where you lovely ladies from?

"Dan, real beauties, just came in from Pittsburgh. Our type, believe me."

"No, not tonight, Buck. We've got the Perez trial coming up in ten days, and I have to catch for the Giants Monday night."

"Dan, for chrissakes," Buckley stammered, "you're getting

too goddamned old for baseball. That's a kids' game. What are you, forty-six?"

"Forty-seven," Sheridan corrected.

"Well, you'll soon be out of the only game in this life that counts. . . . There's first place and also-rans. . . . Excuse me, young ladies"—again the muffled voice—"I'll be right with you."

Sheridan snapped open another can of beer. Now wide-awake, he knew he was too wired to try to sleep. He thought back on his earlier life: the struggle of growing up, his abusive father, and a mother who suffered in silence; Vietnam, the young nurse, Vi Quoc Tuan, who had brought him back from the dead when he was shot up at Gia Dinh; his wife and only son killed by a drunk driver. They were all gone from his life now—Jean, his wife; his son, Tommy; the Vietnamese nurse; Sheila O'Brien.

"Goddamn it, *no!*"

He slammed the beer can down on the coffee table and dialed United Airlines. After an interminable wait, an operator came on, saying all connections were busy. He stayed on the line as instructed, and finally someone introduced herself as Sylvia.

"What's your earliest flight tomorrow morning out of Logan for Chicago?" he asked.

"The Executive Special, flight Five-five-seven, leaves at six forty-five, arrives O'Hare at nine twenty-nine, central time. Would you like a reservation?"

"Yes, the name is Sheridan, Dan Sheridan." He reached for the beer and took a final swig.

Time to get packed, he said to himself. Former linebacker for the Bears—hell, he'd played left end for St. Ignatius High, and linebackers weren't exactly his favorite kind of people. And he knew Buckley was right—in this game, there were no silver medals. If he was going to go down, he wasn't going to go easily.